JUDGMENT DAY

a Mike Daley Mystery by

SHELDON SIEGEL

Also by Sheldon Siegel

Special Circumstances
Incriminating Evidence
Criminal Intent
Final Verdict
The Confession

JUDGMENT DAY

a Mike Daley Mystery by

SHELDON SIEGEL

MACADAM CAGE

MacAdam/Cage
155 Sansome Street, Suite 550
San Francisco, CA 94104
www.MacAdamCage.com

Library of Congress Cataloging-in-Publication Data

Siegel, Sheldon (Sheldon M.)
Judgment day / by Sheldon Siegel.
p. cm.
ISBN 978-1-59692-290-7
1. Daley, Mike (Fictitious character)—Fiction. 2. Fernandez, Rosie
(Fictitious character)—Fiction. 3. Lawyers—Fiction. 4. San Francisco
(Calif.)—Fiction. I. Title.
PS3569.I3823J83 2008
813'.54—dc22
2007050795

Manufactured in the United States of America

10 9 8 7 6 5 4 3 2 1

Book design by Dorothy Carico Smith.

For David Poindexter

Friday, July 10. 11:03 a.m.
8 days, 12 hours, and 58 minutes until execution.

The oldest man on death row is eyeing me from his wheelchair. Despite his frail appearance, his grip is firm and his baritone is still forceful. "Welcome to the Row, Mr. Daley," he says to me. "We need your help. We're running out of time."

More than 650 inmates are awaiting lethal injections on California's death row. Every one of them is running out of time.

"Thank you for coming on such short notice," he continues. "Did you have any trouble getting inside?"

"Nothing out of the ordinary," I say. Sometimes it seems harder for lawyers to get into San Quentin than it is for our clients to get out. It took me an hour to fill out the stack of forms, sign the multiple releases, and pass through the two metal detectors, before I was locked inside one of a dozen windowless six-by-six-foot cells separated by interlaced steel bars covered by scuffed Plexiglas. The death row visitors' area is just a stone's throw from the little green chamber where the State of California conducts its executions. It's a dark reminder of the burdens borne by the denim-clad prisoners, who pass their time going about the mundane business of being incarcerated while their lawyers try to prolong their lives. "Mr. Fineman—" I say.

"It's Nate," my host insists in a genial manner.

Fine. "I'm Mike." Nate Fineman may be confined to a wheelchair, but I've learned the hard way never to let my guard down. The first client I ever visited on the Row was a remorseless psychopath who had stabbed his ex-girlfriend twenty-seven times with an ice pick. Instead of shaking my hand, he introduced himself by slamming me against the wall. His hands were clasped around my throat when the guards finally wrestled him to the floor. He never got around to thanking me for getting his death sentence commuted. Every lawyer who handles death-penalty appeals has a similar story. "I'm flattered that you'd like us to help with your defense," I say, "but practically speaking, it's really too late to replace your lawyer."

He strokes his trim gray goatee. "I have no intention of replacing my lawyer," he assures me. "That would be crazy."

Crazy as a fox, perhaps. At seventy-seven, Nate Fineman has been on the Row for ten years. This bootlegger's son doesn't fit the usual demographics of his neighbors, most of whom are poor, uneducated, and African American. He's the last of a long line of flamboyant San Francisco legal legends whose ranks included Joseph Alioto, Melvin Belli, Jake Ehrlich, and Nate Cohn. Known as a street-smart hustler with a glib manner and a photographic memory, Nate "the Great" finished first in his class at Hastings Law School, married the daughter of a superior-court judge, then went to work at the public defender's office, where he developed a reputation for courtroom histrionics and self-promotion. He also won a lot of cases. He earned a spot in the San Francisco Legal Hall of Fame when the DA took a swing at him on the steps of the Hall of Justice after he manipulated the California Rules of Evidence to convince an overmatched judge to dismiss a murder charge against a man who had shot a police officer four times at point-blank range in front of two witnesses. That incident cost the DA his job and made Nate a household name.

An inveterate publicity hound and savvy opportunist, Nate parlayed the notoriety to open his own shop in the graceful Russ Building on Montgomery Street. He used his father-in-law's connections to become the head of the Jewish Community Federation. He became a regular contributor to Herb Caen's legendary gossip column, which ran for years next to the Macy's ad in the middle section of the *Chronicle*. He was also one of the ringleaders of the fabled Calamari Club, a group of businessmen, politicians, labor leaders, lawyers, and influence peddlers who have been meeting for lunch in the back room of Scoma's at the Wharf every Friday afternoon for a half century.

Over the years, Nate represented many of San Francisco's most notorious mobsters and drug dealers. He was never apologetic in expressing his view that it was his job to do whatever it took to keep them out of jail. He proudly boasted that his most famous client, Danny "the Meat Hook" Cortese—a dapper man-about-town who also happened to be the longtime boss of the San Francisco mob—never spent a day in prison over the course of a criminal career that spanned five decades. Never one to shy away from controversy, Nate defended three thugs who ran the Griffith Housing Projects and were accused of distributing bad heroin to local high school kids—three of whom died. Through a series of creative (some would say questionable) legal maneuvers, Nate persuaded a judge that a cache of drugs found in the apartment of the ringleader of the "Bayview Posse" had been obtained through an illegal search and seizure. This led to the dismissal of the charges—much to the chagrin of the DA and the SFPD. Paradoxically, Nate also garnered numerous community-service awards for setting up San Francisco's first legal-aid clinic and donating millions to charity. Depending on who was telling the story, he was either a principled crusader who stood up for the underprivileged and the unpopular, or a highly paid mercenary who was as much a part of the drug and underworld culture as the criminals he represented.

Nate was at the top of his game when he was charged, ten years ago, with killing three people in a back room of the Golden Dragon

Restaurant in Chinatown during a summit conference of drug dealers on a rainy night. One of the victims was Nate's own client. The second was a competitor, and the third was the competitor's lawyer. Nate was found unconscious in the alley behind the restaurant with a semiautomatic pistol under his arm. Ballistic tests proved the slugs had been fired from that gun. Nate steadfastly claimed the weapon had been planted. He had fallen off a fire escape while leaving the building following the shootings, and sustained the injury that cost him the use of his legs. The prosecutors argued he was attempting to flee. Nate insisted he was only trying to dodge the bullets.

He hired an all-star lineup of San Francisco's best-known criminal-defense attorneys to represent him. His legal team was led by his law school classmate and card-playing buddy, Mort "the Sport" Goldberg, a theatrical showman who presided over a carnival-like trial that drew almost as much national media attention as the Laci Peterson case. The prosecutors portrayed Nate as a man who had spent his career helping mobsters and crack dealers stay out of jail—a charge that Nate never denied and Goldberg couldn't refute. Goldberg trotted out a dozen character witnesses to testify that Nate was a doting husband and father who had raised millions for charity and never turned away a potential client just because he couldn't afford to pay. Nate even took the stand in his own defense. Throughout intense questioning that lasted for days, he insisted the shootings were part of a coup by disloyal members of his client's organization. Without a witness to corroborate Nate's claim that he was ambushed by a masked assailant, it took the jury less than three hours to convict him of first-degree murder—much to the delight of the SFPD. The legal system has played its course, and Judgment Day is fast approaching.

Unlike most death row inmates, who view attorney visits as an opportunity to vent their frustrations and plead their innocence, Nate's tone is professional. "I want to hire you as special co-counsel," he explains. "I think you can provide some additional perspective on my case."

He needs more than perspective. He's scheduled for a lethal injection a week from Sunday at 12:01 a.m. By law, a death warrant must be carried out on a specified date. California conducts its executions at one minute after midnight at the very beginning of the twenty-four-hour window, to provide the maximum amount of wiggle room if there are any glitches and to reduce the number of protesters who gather at the gates of San Quentin. By my watch, that gives us eight days, twelve hours, and fifty-two minutes to do what his dream defense team couldn't do in ten years. Am I nuts to be in this room?

The third person in the cramped cell clears his throat. Louis Cohen is an eloquent former public defender who looks like Joseph Lieberman. One of California's top appellate specialists, he grew up a few doors from Nate in the Richmond District. He's been fighting the good fight on behalf of his childhood friend for the past decade. "We've filed new habeas petitions with the California Supreme Court, the Federal District Court, and the Ninth Circuit," he explains. "If they turn us down, we'll take it up to the U.S. Supreme Court. We've also asked the governor for clemency."

Despite countless well-intentioned attempts by our legislators to speed up the system, the Byzantine appellate process in death-penalty cases remains excruciatingly slow. You start with a mandatory direct appeal to the California Supreme Court—a fine idea with limited practical value. The California Supremes have time to hear just a handful of these cases, and you may only assert claims that arise from the trial record itself. It took them four years to turn down Nate's appeal—which had no chance from the start. It took the Feds three more years to come to the same conclusion.

After you've exhausted your direct appeals, you file a petition for a writ of habeas corpus in state and then in federal court. Cutting through the legalistic mumbo jumbo, it means you claim your client

has been imprisoned in violation of his constitutional rights. The good
news is, it's the first time you can introduce evidence that wasn't pre-
sented at trial. The bad news is, you have to prove "freestanding
innocence," which means the new evidence must be so clearly and convincingly exculpatory that no reasonable jury could have convicted
your client in the first place—a standard that's almost impossible to
prove. It's customary to file successive habeas petitions right up until
the very end, but your chances of prevailing become slimmer as the
execution date gets closer. The final judicial recourse is to the U.S.
Supreme Court, which rarely soils its hands with death-penalty cases.
There's also a possibility that the governor will grant clemency. Given
the current political climate in Sacramento, your chances are about the
same as those of winning the California lottery.

If your client manages to live long enough to exhaust all of his
appeals, he will be executed in accordance with a tightly scripted procedure. First, he'll get an injection of Sodium Pentothal, which causes a
loss of consciousness. Next, they'll administer a dose of pancuronium
bromide, which leads to paralysis of the voluntary muscles. Finally, he'll
get a shot of potassium chloride, which induces cardiac arrest and finishes the job. Theoretically, it shouldn't be nearly as dramatic as an
execution carried out by hanging, the guillotine, the firing squad, the
electric chair, poisonous gas, or the other methods of killing that
humankind has developed over the centuries. The process should be
concluded in about fifteen minutes, but it frequently takes much longer.
Sometimes it takes the technicians several tries before they can get the
needles in the right spots to allow the chemicals to flow properly.

"What's the likelihood of a stay?" I ask.

"Slim," Cohen replies.

"And clemency?"

"About the same."

I was a priest for three years before I went to law school. I still believe in miracles, but the Row is a place for cold-eyed pragmatism. "What do you expect me to do in eight days?"

Nate responds for him. "Prove the police withheld evidence and covered up the identity of the real killer."

"You couldn't do it," I remind him. "You've had ten years to try."

"That's why we need you."

"What makes you think I'll be able to find any new information?"

"Roosevelt Johnson headed the investigation."

The legendary homicide inspector is a meticulous man of unquestionable moral authority who began his career walking the beat with my father fifty years ago. They were the first integrated team in the SFPD, and their partnership turned into a lifelong friendship. Pop was thrilled when Roosevelt moved up the ranks and became the first African American in the homicide division. My dad was at heart a beat cop who turned down several promotions to stay on the street. He died of lung cancer a few months after Nate was convicted.

"I know Inspector Johnson well enough to get a meeting," I say, "but he isn't going to reopen the investigation just because he used to work with my father."

"There was a police conspiracy."

Every convicted murderer thinks he's Oliver Stone. "What about the pistol they found under your arm with a perfect set of your fingerprints?"

"It was planted."

"By whom?"

"The cops. It was payback for getting the charges dropped in the Posse case."

"The jury didn't buy it."

"They were wrong. The cops covered up and closed ranks."

"What were you doing at the Golden Dragon in the first place?"

"I was representing a Bayview heroin distributor who was at war with a Chinatown drug ring. I was negotiating a truce."

Nate's trial was the top story on the news for weeks. From what I recall reading in the papers, that part of his story hasn't changed.

"We had everything worked out," he says. "Then a man came in and started shooting. I jumped out a window and ran down the fire escape, but I slipped. That's the last thing I remember."

He fell two stories and landed on his back. "Do you have any idea who the shooter was?"

"He was wearing a mask."

"Did you bring a gun into the restaurant?"

"Of course not. Everybody was searched when they entered the building. It was a stolen gun. The serial number had been removed."

"You're still saying somebody else brought in the gun and killed three people?"

"I was lucky they didn't kill me, too."

And all I have to do is prove it in the next eight days. "You didn't pick my name out of the Yellow Pages," I say. "There are other lawyers who have contacts with Inspector Johnson and the SFPD."

"We want you and we're prepared to make it worth your while." Nate nods to Cohen, who reaches into the breast pocket of his jacket, pulls out a white envelope, and places it on the table. "That's a fifty-thousand-dollar retainer," Nate says. "It should cover your fees and costs for the next eight days."

It should cover us for the next six months. There might be something left over for Christmas presents. I can feel my eyes opening wide, but I don't take the envelope. Our firm has only two lawyers. We spend most of our time representing small-time drug dealers and petty criminals who frequently have to choose between paying us or making bail. Most opt for the latter. It's a big day when some poor soul charged with driving under the influence gives us a fifteen-hundred-dollar retainer.

"It might make more sense to spend your money on a private investigator," I say.

"We'd also like to hire your brother."

He's done his homework. My younger brother, Pete, was a beat cop at Mission Station before he and some of his colleagues broke up a street fight in the plaza adjacent to the Sixteenth Street BART station with a little too much enthusiasm. When one of the participants filed the inevitable police-brutality claim, the city caved. Pete and two of his buddies were summarily dismissed. He's been justifiably bitter about it ever since. Now he works as a PI.

"His rate is a thousand dollars a day plus expenses," I say. It's a slight exaggeration.

"We'll pay him two thousand."

He's serious about hiring us or he's desperate—or both. Pete recently became a father for the first time. This may be an opportunity to make amends for the times I've strong-armed him into helping me for free. "I'll call him as soon as we're finished," I say, "but I still need to talk to my partner."

"What's there to discuss?"

How much time do you have? Rosita Fernandez and I have been working together for almost two decades, first in the PD's office, then for the last seven years in private practice. Rosie is the managing partner of Fernandez and Daley. I defer all financial decisions to her. It's an important reason why our law partnership has lasted longer than our marriage, which began after a highly enthusiastic romance while we were at the PD's office, and was called a few years later on account of irreconcilable living habits. Our daughter, Grace, just turned fourteen. Our son, Tommy, is two. Tommy's arrival was a pleasant and unplanned surprise long after Rosie and I had split up. Old habits—we can't live with each other, yet we can't seem to get enough of each other. We wouldn't have it any other way.

"We never take on new matters without discussing them first," I tell him.

Grace and Tommy live with Rosie in a rented bungalow a couple of miles from here. I have my own apartment three blocks from them. Life with a teenager and a toddler presents logistical and financial challenges. Recently we decided to cut back on our workload to give parenthood more focus.

The wily old trial lawyer flashes a confident smile. "We're willing to bet fifty grand that you'll give it your best shot."

"I still have to talk to Rosie."

He shifts to flattery. "We're cut from the same cloth, Mike. We became lawyers to help people. You have a reputation as somebody who is more interested in finding the truth and doing what's right than making a bundle of dough."

My bank account attests to the fact that he's right. Rosie and I also agreed to avoid capital cases until Tommy is out of diapers. A fifty-thousand-dollar retainer causes me, at least, to revisit that policy. Rosie may be somewhat more flexible, too. She recently persuaded her landlord to remodel her fifties-era kitchen, which will undoubtedly lead to a commensurate increase in her rent. There is also the reality of Grace heading to college in four years.

Nate is still talking. "We both cut our teeth at the PD's office. We've represented unpopular clients. We've handled more than our share of pro bono matters. That makes us kindred spirits—even colleagues."

Except I've never been convicted of murder.

His tone turns somber. "I believe everybody is entitled to die with self-respect. Being strapped to a gurney and injected with poison for a crime I didn't commit isn't the way I want my wife, children, and grandchildren to remember me. That's not the legacy I had in mind. Besides, you have a personal interest in the case."

What? "How's that?"

"Your father was part of the police cover-up."

Friday, July 10. 1:05 p.m.
8 days, 10 hours, and 56 minutes until execution.

M y ex-wife's dark brown eyes stare intently into mine as she taps her fingers on her IKEA desk that's piled high with file folders. Rosie rarely raises her voice and never pulls any punches. "So," she says, "Nate Fineman and his lawyer think your father was part of a police cover-up?"

"So they say."

"That's preposterous. Who are they insinuating he was trying to protect?"

I pause to gather my thoughts as I look up at the bare walls of the cramped space that doubles as Rosie's office and the conference room of Fernandez and Daley. We work in a thirties-era walk-up at 84 First Street. It's above the El Faro Mexican restaurant and down the block from the Transbay bus terminal in what might charitably be described as the pregentrified portion of San Francisco's South of Market area. It's one of the last downtown structures where the windows still open—a concept that's more charming in theory than in reality. Our building is in one of the few pockets of San Francisco with warm summer weather, and we don't have an air conditioner. We spend July and August trying to decide whether it's preferable to wilt from the heat or asphyxiate from the fumes emitted from the El Faro's exhaust fan.

"That's what they want us to find out," I finally say.

Rosie's shoulder-length, jet-black hair is pulled back into a tight ponytail. A cream-colored blouse and a pair of faded Levi's complement a toned figure that reflects a torturous daily regimen at the gym. Her full lips, chiseled cheekbones, and glowing olive skin belie forty-seven years and the birth of two children. A native of the Mission District and a graduate of San Francisco State and Hastings Law School, she's fought countless wars with prosecutors, judges, cops, and me. Her toughest struggle came four years ago, when she was diagnosed with breast cancer. She battled through a mastectomy and radiation treatments with stoic determination. We don't talk about it much, but I can tell you that she's been cancer-free for three years, nine months, and four days.

"Come on, Mike," she says. "For all of his faults, your father was probably the most honest cop in the SFPD."

It's only a slight exaggeration. We rarely agreed on political or social issues, and he had a multitude of shortcomings as a father. Still, he never gave me a reason to question the direction of his moral compass.

She isn't finished. "I trust you'd agree that Fineman's allegations are untrue?"

"Yes, I would."

Arguing with Rosie is like undergoing an intense cross-exam. She frames her questions in a manner that elicits the response she wants.

"Then why are we having this discussion?" she asks.

"I can think of fifty thousand reasons."

The corner of her mouth turns up slightly. "I have nothing against being paid, but it's too late for Fineman to change lawyers."

"This isn't some nutcase who walked in off the street."

"He made a career out of representing scumbags like Danny Cortese and the Bayview Posse. Not to mention the fact that he was convicted of murdering three people at the Golden Dragon."

"Maybe the jury was wrong."

She looks up at the ceiling. "Why did I decide to practice law with the patron saint of hopeless causes?"

"It's just one of the many ways that I bring excitement to your life."

I get the smile I was hoping for. "Hopeless causes aren't exciting," she says. She plants her tongue in her cheek. "Did you ever consider the possibility that I like boredom?"

"Not a chance."

Her lips turn down. "I don't like it, Mike."

I'm not crazy about it either, and I'm *really* not in the mood for a catfight on a Friday afternoon when I have tickets for the Giants game tonight. Though we've had our share of high-profile cases over the years, ours is still a nickel-and-dime operation. Our only employee is a former heavyweight boxer and small-time hoodlum named Terrence "the Terminator" Love, who works as our receptionist, secretary, process server, photocopier, and bodyguard. He had also been one of my most reliable customers at the PD's office. Standing seven feet tall and weighing 320 pounds, the soft-spoken giant retired after four unsuccessful professional bouts to pursue a more lucrative career in theft. He became quite adept at breaking and entering, but he was less accomplished at escaping. His rap sheet ran well into its third printing.

The proceeds from Terrence's criminal activities went to buy enough booze to keep a three-hundred-pound man in a drunken stupor for the better part of two decades. There was little left over for necessities such as food, housing, and clothing. Things came to a head a couple of years ago, when he was facing a life sentence under California's so-called three-strikes laws. Rosie and I persuaded the judge to reduce the charges, subject to the condition that we would find him gainful employment and treatment for his alcohol addiction. There wasn't a huge market for the services of a third-rate prizefighter and second-rate shoplifter, so we hired him with the understanding that we would fire him immediately if he showed up late or started drinking again. He hasn't missed a day of work and he's made enough money to ditch his room in the flophouse on Sixth Street for a tiny apartment in the Bayview. In our line of work, we measure progress in baby steps.

I try an appeal to Rosie's practical side. "You're always on my case for not bringing in enough paying clients," I say.

"Obviously, that isn't a problem here. I can't even get a countertop for my kitchen in eight days and you want to try to free a man on death row?"

"It will enhance the visibility and reputation of our firm."

She shakes her head with authority. "I'd rather not get a high pro-file for a lost cause. We'll have to go around the clock. There isn't a realistic chance we'll be able to do anything for him. It's a waste of our time and his money."

"He wants to die with dignity."

"It smells."

"We've handled smellier stuff. He was one of the best lawyers who ever worked at the PD's office. He started the Legal Aid Society. His rep-utation was stellar until that night at the Golden Dragon."

"He's no saint, Mike. He played fast and loose when he represented Cortese. They said he was paying people to intimidate witnesses during the Posse case."

"Those charges were never proven."

"Get real, Mike."

"We'd be out of business if we start ducking cases because we think our clients are scum."

She responds in the sanctimonious tone that I've found profoundly irritating for two decades. "I'm well aware that it's our job to represent scumbags," she says. "On the other hand, they found his prints on the murder weapon. He admitted that he organized a meeting of a couple of drug bosses. Nobody bought his story about a phantom masked shooter who disappeared into the night. What makes you think the jury was wrong?"

"I'm prepared to work through the process to try to find out."

"Don't be naïve, Mike."

"Don't give up so easily, Rosie."

"It's a case we can't win."

"That's never stopped us." I think of the faded citation hanging on the wall of my office. The Nathan Fineman Award used to be given by the San Francisco Bar Association to an attorney who demonstrated exemplary commitment to community service. Though the commendation is no longer named after Nate, it's still one of my most prized possessions. "I used to admire him," I say.

"So did I." Rosie glances down at the engraved gavel that her colleagues gave her as a going-away present when she left the PD's office—another tradition that Nate started. "This couldn't come at a worse time. I'm buried with other work. There will be contractors at my house for the next two weeks. My life is a zoo right now."

Every home-improvement project takes on a life of its own. Her weeklong kitchen-remodel job is already well into its second month. She declined her landlord's offer to put her up in a hotel for a couple of weeks because she didn't want to uproot Grace and Tommy—a decision she says she now regrets.

I offer a morsel. "I'll help with your case load. We'll eat out. We could use the extra money. You know your rent will go up as soon as the new appliances are in."

"If my landlord doesn't sell it to the highest bidder," she says, "which isn't going to be us unless we win the lottery or we get a substantial infusion of cash from another source."

"All the more reason to do it. There's an unwritten rule that new clients only call when it's hopelessly inconvenient. It isn't as if we have a lot of prospective cases to choose from right now."

"A last-minute death-penalty appeal isn't exactly what I had in mind, Mr. Rainmaker."

"Do you have anything more interesting in the pipeline?"

"At the moment, no."

"Then I think we should go for it."

Her scowl becomes more pronounced. "Lou Cohen is bringing us in for a reason," she observes. "Maybe he's trying to set us up to take the fall in a last-minute IAC claim."

Asserting an Ineffective Assistance of Counsel claim is a standard legal tactic in death-penalty cases. If you have nothing more convincing, you argue that the attorneys screwed up. It's one of the reasons trial lawyers rarely handle appeals for their clients—it puts them in the awkward position of having to assert IAC claims against themselves.

"There isn't enough time," I tell her. "It won't fly in a habeas petition."

"Lou is a smart lawyer."

"He also admitted that we aren't going to stop the execution with esoteric legal theories."

"Which means our only hope is to prove freestanding innocence in the next eight days. As a practical matter, that also means we'll have to find the real killer—assuming it isn't our potential new client. That isn't going to happen unless we find some guilt-ridden soul who pops out of the woodwork and confesses."

"Not necessarily," I say. "We just need to find enough new evidence to persuade the California Supremes or the Ninth Circuit to order an evidentiary hearing." Easier said than done. "If we can delay the execution, we might be able to come up with something more substantial." Or Nate could die of natural causes before they can get around to rescheduling his execution.

This elicits the all-too-familiar eye roll that I've always found so infuriating—and infatuating—since our days at the PD's office. "Come on, Mike," she says.

"I know it's a long shot. You have to admit, though, that if we pull off a miracle, we'll be heroes. If we don't, Fineman is no worse off than he is today. Either way, we're fifty grand to the happy side. Plus, we might be able to save a dying man's life."

She acknowledges that I have a point, then treads into murkier water. "Did you ever talk to your father about the case?"

"Not much. Fineman was arrested during one of our noncommunicative periods."

We had many of them. Thomas James Charles Daley Sr. was born seventy-four years ago at St. Mary's Hospital. He grew up on Garfield Square in the Mission District. Pop married his high school sweetheart the week after they graduated. The newlyweds moved into a furnished one-bedroom apartment two doors from her parents. My dad joined the SFPD on his twenty-first birthday. My mom stayed home to take care of us.

When I was ten, we moved to a small house in the Sunset, where our family dynamics were closer to the Osbournes' than the Brady Bunch's. My older brother, Tom Jr., was a star quarterback at St. Ignatius and Cal before he volunteered to go to Vietnam and never returned. I was the rebellious second son who protested the war, in Berkeley. When the antiwar movement didn't provide enough answers after Tommy died, I ended up in the seminary. My father didn't talk to me for a year after I left the priesthood to attend law school. We made an uneasy peace when I graduated. We took another hiatus from communication when I joined the PD's office. My mom spent years conducting shuttle diplomacy between the two of us. Pete was the diligent third son, whose greatest transgression was that he wasn't a jock like Tommy or an excellent student like me. He became a cop to show our old man that he was just as tough as he was.

"My father was one of the first officers at the scene," I say, "but he didn't testify at the trial. Evidently, they had more than enough evidence without him."

"What did your father think of Fineman?"

"Every cop in San Francisco hated his guts—especially after the Posse case."

"Didn't Fineman's lawyers make some allegations of police misconduct during his trial?"

"They claimed the cops had planted the murder weapon. The charges were never substantiated. Internal Affairs did an investigation after the trial was over. Everybody was cleared—including my father."

She isn't satisfied. "Would he have lied to protect another cop?"

"Absolutely not." I try not to sound too defensive. "He wasn't that kind of a cop. He was old-school, but he was his own man. He did what he thought was right. It's one of the reasons he was never one of the more popular guys on the force."

She gives me a skeptical look. "If we take this case," she says, "we'll have to revisit his involvement."

"There's no legal conflict of interest. It's part of our job."

"How do we figure out if he was telling the truth?"

"We'll talk to Roosevelt."

"He has a vested interest in protecting the conviction—and himself."

And maybe my father, too. Loyalty runs deep at the SFPD. "Roosevelt wouldn't cover up evidence if somebody was about to be executed for a crime he didn't commit."

"Are you prepared to attack your father's reputation to defend our client?" She always goes straight to the heart of it.

"I'll deal with it," I tell her.

"Sure you will." She glances at the framed photo of our daughter that sits on the corner of her desk. "What about our promise to Grace that we wouldn't take on another death-penalty case for the foreseeable future?"

"The circumstances are unusual."

There's an interminable hesitation. "You're absolutely sure about this, Mike?"

"Yes."

My pragmatic ex-wife starts reciting her conditions. "You and your brother will not play cops and robbers."

"Agreed." It's a long-standing bone of contention. I like to tag along with Pete when he's working. Rosie thinks we take unnecessary chances.

"You will also let the police handle any matters involving illegal activities."

"Understood."

Her eyes turn to cold steel—it's the sign that she's ready to go to war. "Okay," she says. "I'm in."

When push comes to shove, she'll never back down. That's why I will always love her—no matter what.

There's a knock on the door. My brother saunters in with his thumbs tucked inside his pockets. Pete is five years younger than I am. He's a stockier version of the standard Daley family model, but there isn't an ounce of fat in the two hundred pounds he carries on his five-eight frame. His slicked-back hair was once a darker brown than mine. It's still thick, yet now almost completely gray. A two-day stubble covers his pockmarked face. His silver mustache is neatly trimmed. Ever a slave to fashion, he's wearing black jeans and a faded orange Giants T-shirt with Dusty Baker's picture on the front. He's never forgiven the team for letting his favorite manager go to the Cubs.

He's spent the last week doing round-the-clock surveillance on an unfaithful husband. He's in no mood for pleasantries. "What's the big emergency?" he rasps.

"We have to talk to you about a new case," I say.

"Are we still going to the Giants game tonight?" First things first.

"That may be a bit of a problem."

Not the answer he wanted. He turns to Rosie. "What's going on?"

"We've been asked to work on Nate Fineman's appeal," she says.

Pete's expression indicates that he thinks we've lost our minds. "Isn't his execution a week from Sunday?" he asks.

"Yes," she says.

"Next you'll say we have a week to find the real killer."

"Essentially."

"That isn't going to happen."

"We know the odds."

My brother takes a seat on the windowsill. "Why are you doing this?" he asks.

It's my turn to respond. "It's what we do."

"The guy is pure slime."

"He's entitled to a defense."

"He defended the guys who sold bad heroin to a bunch of kids."

"Allegedly sold."

"Gimme a break, Mick."

"They were entitled to a defense."

"It doesn't bother you that three kids died from that crap?"

"Yes, it does."

"Then why do you want to represent the scum bucket who defended them?"

"Somebody has to."

He shakes his head with disdain. "How much is he paying you?"

"Fifty grand up front."

"So you're willing to sell your soul for fifty grand?"

"We're willing to represent a client who is prepared to pay us."

He turns to Rosie and says, "You're okay with this?"

"For now."

His annoyed expression gives way to an inquisitive look as he turns back to me. "Where do I fit into this picture?"

"They've asked for your help."

"Does that mean I'm getting paid, too?"

"Two thousand dollars a day, plus expenses—in advance."

"They're serious."

"Yes, they are."

He stares out the window.

I wait a long beat. "Are you in?" I ask.

My brother's response is equal parts surprising and troubling. "I wouldn't touch it," he says.

3/ MURDERERS COME IN ALL SHAPES AND SIZES

Pete and I have had our share of brotherly issues over the years, though we get along reasonably well nowadays. Nonetheless, Rosie correctly surmises that we may get more out of him if she initiates this discussion.

"How much did your father tell you about the Fineman case?" she asks him.

"A little." My brother inherited our dad's proclivity for short answers. "He said he was guilty."

"Did you believe him?"

"Pop was genetically hardwired to tell the truth."

So is Pete. His expression indicates he's prepared to leave it there, but I'm not. "I met with Fineman earlier today," I say. "He didn't strike me as your garden-variety murderer."

"Maybe he's your garden-variety sociopath."

"Gimme a break, Pete. He was a defense lawyer."

"Same thing. He spent his life hanging out with drug dealers and mobsters. Murderers come in all shapes and sizes."

"Pop could have been wrong."

"He was never wrong."

"Sure he was."

He jabs his finger in my direction. "About parenthood, yes. About murder, no."

Pete was always more protective of our parents than I was. He also spent more time with them. After our father died, he moved back home to take care of our mother when her Alzheimer's got worse. Pete lives with his wife and daughter in the little house at Twenty-third and Kirkham that my parents bought over forty years ago—back in the days when cops could afford them. I've suggested that it might be healthier if he moved somewhere with fewer memories. He insists he's staying put.

"Pop was losing interest in police work toward the end," I observe. "Remember that stakeout in the Tenderloin?"

Pete chased a couple of crack dealers into a roadblock set up by our father and his partner, but they weren't able to stop them. Pop insisted it was bad luck. Pete said our dad lost his nerve.

His tone turns testy. "What does that have to do with the Fineman case?"

"Pop told me he wasn't going to get his ass kicked before he collected his pension." Ironically, he died within months after he retired. "Maybe he wasn't at the top of his game when the Fineman case came down."

"Easy for you to say. You never worked on the street." My brother divides people into two categories: those who have experience in law enforcement and those who don't. Pete was always the first to come to Pop's defense in police matters. "He wouldn't have let Fineman rot in prison if he knew he was innocent. Neither would Roosevelt."

"Pop was near the end of the line," I say. "Roosevelt was interested in getting a conviction."

"Are you saying they covered for each other?"

"I don't know."

"I don't like to mix business with family," Pete says.

Neither do I. "Pop's gone," I say. "He didn't testify."

"He was one of the first officers at the scene. There were allegations that the cops planted the murder weapon. Lou Cohen is no dummy. He's bringing you in for a reason."

"You think he's using us?"

"Call me a cynic."

Or a realist.

"Besides," he adds, "Fineman is a first-rate asshole."

"Says who?"

"Says Pop. He spent years working on the task force that finally pieced together enough evidence to bring charges against the Bayview Posse. It was dangerous work. They were *really* bad guys. They had a rock-solid case, and then Fineman found a way to weasel them out of jail."

"Just because he represented gang bosses and drug dealers doesn't mean he committed murder. He started the San Francisco Legal Aid Society. He raised a ton of money for charity."

"Spoken like a defense attorney. He was a mob lawyer who made a mint manipulating the legal system to keep drug dealers out of jail."

Spoken like an ex-cop. "Drug dealers are entitled to representation, too."

"They aren't entitled to sleazebags who will do anything to get their clients off. He was paying people down in the Bayview to intimidate witnesses in the Posse case. There's a fine line between defending criminals and becoming one yourself. Fineman crossed it. He wasn't just a lawyer—he was part of the problem. It wasn't just dirty clients or shady courtroom tactics. The word on the street was that he wasn't just representing the drug dealers—he was helping them run their operations. There were also allegations that he was getting things fixed at the Hall of Justice."

"Who?"

"You name it: cops, judges, bailiffs. Maybe even some of the ADAs. The head brass wanted him so badly that we had him under surveillance. We knew there were payoffs, but the money was always laundered through an intermediary. We never had enough to nail him until he killed those guys at the Golden Dragon."

"Can any of this be corroborated?"

"Not a chance, Mick."

"Is there a chance the cops nailed Fineman as payback?"

"Pop wasn't that kind of a cop."

"He wasn't the only one involved in this case."

"I know."

I ask him straight up. "Do you think Fineman killed three people?"

"Pop thought so."

"What do *you* think?"

"I don't know. I wasn't there."

"Is there a chance he may be innocent?"

"There's a chance he didn't kill the guys at the restaurant, but he's far from innocent."

I need to lower the volume. "What did Pop do that night?"

"He and Joey D. helped secure the scene."

Our father's last partner was a punk from the Excelsior District with anger-management issues, a gambling problem, and a Napoleon complex who also happened to wear a uniform. "Little Joey" D'Amato placed a higher priority on making arrests than on observing legal niceties. There were rumors that he extracted protection money from the businesses on his beat. Later, he was "asked" to take early retirement after he was accused of shaking down some pimps in the Mission District to cover his gambling debts. The allegations were dropped when he agreed to retire.

"What's Joey up to nowadays?" I ask.

"He's running a currency exchange in the Tenderloin."

"Is it legit?"

"As legit as any business that gouges people to cash their welfare checks. Some people whose opinions I respect think it's a front to launder drug money."

"Is he still playing the ponies?"

"I don't know."

"Why don't the cops nail him?"

"Joey is still one of the smartest assholes you'll ever meet—especially when it comes to looking out for himself."

He also hated my dad's guts—a sentiment that was reciprocated in kind. They came at police work from opposite ends of the spectrum. Pop did things by the book. Joey believed in expedience—even if it meant stretching the rules and taking a few bucks on the side.

"What do you know about the three victims?" I ask.

"Christ, Mick. The damn trial was on the front page of the *Chronicle* for weeks. Fineman's client was a guy named Terrell Robinson. He operated out of the Sunnydale projects. He was a construction contractor who controlled the heroin trade down to South City. He came from the Saddam Hussein school of management—he killed anybody who disagreed with him."

"Not a consensus builder."

"Nope. Robinson was at war with a Chinatown gang run by a man named Alan Chin, who was every bit as ruthless. He controlled everything north of Market Street. The third victim was Chin's attorney. His name was Lester Fong."

I recognize the name. Fong was Chinatown's most flamboyant contribution to the San Francisco criminal-defense bar. The cagey lawyer was a regular at the Hall of Justice, where he had a reputation as a zealous advocate for his clients. He was also a well-known spokesman for political interests in Chinatown at City Hall.

"Why would Fineman have killed the lawyer?" I ask.

"Maybe he was the only witness. Maybe he was in the wrong place at the wrong time."

"Maybe."

Pete quickly adds, "They all died of gunshot wounds from bullets fired from the pistol found on Fineman."

You need a scorecard to keep track of all the drug dealers. "What made them think Fineman was involved?"

His voice fills with sarcasm. "It may have had something to do with the fact that they found his fingerprints on the murder weapon."

"Look at it this way," I tell him. "It's two weeks of work for a fat paycheck. You may get some good publicity. You may even help save a man's life. What's the downside?"

"For one," he says, "I was still on the force when this case came down. Fineman and his lawyers took a bunch of potshots at the cops. Nobody down at the Hall of Justice was heartbroken when he was convicted —including me. Some people are going to be unhappy if the execution is delayed."

"Since when did you start worrying about hurt feelings at the Hall?"

"I still have friends down there."

Pete won't duck a case just because a few people might get their noses out of joint.

"For two," he continues, "Mort Goldberg made a big stink that the murder weapon was planted. Pop said it was a bunch of crap, but they still brought in IA to investigate. All things being equal, I'd rather not work on a case where we may have to smear Pop's reputation to help a client."

His point is well taken—even though neither of us had an especially warm and fuzzy relationship with our father. "Aren't you remotely interested in trying to find out what really happened?" I ask.

"I'm willing to give Pop the benefit of the doubt. So should you."

"If he was telling the truth, we have nothing to worry about."

He looks intently at Rosie for an interminable moment, then he turns back to me. "You really want to do this, don't you, Mick?"

"Yes."

"Are you prepared to pay for backup for me?"

"Yes."

"Are you going to second-guess everything I do?"

He knows me too well. "Probably," I say.

His mouth turns up slightly. "It's just a couple of weeks of my life that I'll never get back. I'm in if you are."

Swell.

"Where do you want me to start?" he asks.

"With the victims. We need everything you can get about Robinson, Chin, and Fong. Then I want you to track down Joey D'Amato."

"Okay."

Rosie stands up. "I'll start looking at the trial transcripts and the appellate briefs," she says. "Where are you going first?"

"To talk to Roosevelt."

Friday, July 10. 9:05 p.m.
8 days, 2 hours, and 56 minutes until execution.

Original Joe's is a mecca of California cuisine—of sixty years ago. It was opened in 1937 by a Croatian immigrant named Ante "Tony" Rodin as a fourteen-stool diner with a narrow counter and sawdust on the floor. Nowadays, the muscular grill seats 140 patrons in a groaning building smack-dab in the middle of the teeming Tenderloin District, just west of Union Square. Tony's place should have gone belly up when the neighborhood went from dicey to outright dangerous in the sixties, but it didn't. The trend toward lighter fare should have killed it in the eighties, but it couldn't. Generations of locals still make the pilgrimage to Taylor and Turk to consume twenty-ounce porterhouse steaks, panfried local sole, and huge portions of chicken parmigiana. If you want artisan cheese, baby greens, and arugula, you're in the wrong spot.

The mist of grease from the frying calamari hangs heavily in the air. Massive burgers and chops broil over the white-hot coals. Many people erroneously believe the open restaurant kitchen was invented by the designers of stylish eateries such as Boulevard and Chez Panisse. The concept was actually pioneered by Tony Rodin. He didn't have room for a full kitchen, so he set up a small assembly line behind his cramped counter and let his patrons enjoy the show. He opted to use mesquite charcoal because it was cheaper, hotter, and longer lasting than regular briquettes. Thus, an entire genre of cuisine—such as it is—was born.

Tony presided at Original Joe's until he was well into his nineties. Declining health finally forced him to grudgingly turn over the reins to his daughter, Marie Duggan, who still bucks the trends with a similarly capable iron hand. Tuxedoed waiters who have worked here for decades continue the tradition of serving slightly uptown steaks and chops to loyal customers who squeeze into the burgundy booths. Legend has it that when a snooty food critic had the audacity to point out that the menu hadn't been updated in decades, Marie responded with a single-digit salute. My dad used to order the mile-high filet, a twenty-ounce slab of tenderloin that's hand-cut in the basement. I've always been partial to the often imitated Joe's Special, a concoction of ground beef, scrambled eggs, spinach, Parmesan cheese, olive oil, and whatever other leftovers happen to be available in the kitchen. Trendy it isn't, but the smart money says they'll be serving oversize burgers and Joe's Specials on skid row a hundred years from now.

I take a deep breath of the aroma of mesquite-grilled steak as I look across the starched white tablecloth at the imposing figure of my father's first partner. Roosevelt Johnson is a dignified African American with a noble presence and a lyrical baritone. Fifty years ago, he and my dad used to eat burgers and drink Budweisers here after their shifts had ended. Times have changed. Roosevelt and this restaurant haven't. We arrived at nine o'clock on Friday night without a reservation. We were immediately escorted to his favorite booth in the back, away from the raucous counter area. As always, Roosevelt's every whim is catered to by Angelo Viducic, who has been sweating it out in his ill-fitting tux day in and day out since the sixties. Angelo isn't the kind of guy to recite a canned introduction or a memorized list of daily specials. He was Joe DiMaggio's favorite waiter. Without being asked, he brought Roosevelt a gargantuan plate of liver cooked medium and smothered with onions and crispy bacon.

The homicide inspector takes a sip of scalding coffee from a plain white mug. Roosevelt doesn't drink decaf. He's tried to retire three times, but he keeps getting drawn back to work on unsolved cold cases as only he can. He insists he's going to retire for good at the end of the year. I have doubts. His commanding voice is tempered slightly by seventy-five years of experience as he talks about his children and grandchildren—an exercise that takes him a good half hour. He operates at his own pace and he's doing me a favor, so I try not to push too soon. Eventually, he finishes his liver and turns to business. His tone is purposefully indignant when he asks, "What is possessing you to represent a convicted murderer like Nathan Fineman?"

"He hired me," I say. "He's entitled to a lawyer."

He adjusts the cuffs of his blinding white shirt. He still wears a dark suit and a subdued tie to work every day. He dresses conservatively in deference to the victims whose cases he investigates. Pop used to say that he also does it to set an example for his younger subordinates who have the audacity to wear business casual. He believes their clothing choices reflect a lack of respect for the sanctity of their jobs. "Why are you *really* doing this?" he asks.

"He was one of the most respected defense attorneys in the Bay Area."

"Not anymore."

"I'm more forgiving than you are."

"That's why you're a defense lawyer and I'm a cop. He defended Danny Cortese and the Bayview Posse. He wrote the book on keeping mobsters and drug dealers out of jail. Doesn't it bother you that you're being paid with drug money?"

It's my turn for a little indignation. "You don't know that for sure. Besides, I never ask my clients where they get the money to pay me."

"Perhaps this would be a good time for you to start."

He's a little testier than usual tonight. "Nate had a thriving law practice," I say. "He made a lot of money legitimately."

"He also made a fortune representing drug traffickers and pimps."

"That isn't illegal."

"Some people think he was doing more than providing legal services."

"Then you should have arrested him."

He wipes his wire-rimmed glasses. "You're as obstinate as your father," he says.

I wink. "I got my independent streak from my mom."

This elicits an amiable smile as he tugs at the perfect Windsor knot in his tie. I'm willing to duck the few live shells that he'll lob in my direction in exchange for information. He gestures to Angelo, who freshens his coffee. "Have you looked at the files?" he asks me.

"Briefly." It's the opening I've been waiting for. I start with sugar. "As far as I can tell, it was a clean conviction."

He's pleased. "So why are we having this conversation?"

"Because you're the only person who might be willing to talk to me." I wait a beat and add, "And because I'm family."

He knows I'm saying it for effect. It also happens to line up with the truth. His family lived a few blocks from us. They used to come over for dinner every Sunday night. He taught my older brother how to throw a spiral. He showed me how to grip a changeup. Out of respect for my father, he's helped me on several cases over the years.

His mouth turns down. "Lou Cohen had ten years to appeal," he says. "You aren't going to change the outcome in eight days."

"Doesn't it bother you that they're going to execute a seventy-seven-year-old man who can't walk?"

"You know I'm more interested in finding the truth than executing people in wheelchairs." He shoots another glance at Angelo, who returns with a traditional zabaglione, served as always in a sixteen-ounce beer schooner. Roosevelt looks at the frothy concoction that the waiters call "honeymoon sauce" for its alleged restorative properties. "It was a legitimate conviction," he tells me. "If you're as smart as I think you are, you'll drop it. I'm trying to save you some time and aggravation."

"I have plenty of time, and I like aggravation."

This gets another smile. "Just like your father," he says. "We're off the record."

"Fair enough." I want to see if he'll tell me who was there and what led to the allegations that the murder weapon was planted. Realistically, he'll tell me exactly what he wants me to know—and nothing more. I ease into the discussion slowly. "I understand my father and his partner helped secure the scene at the Golden Dragon."

"They did. Dave Low got there first."

Low was an undercover cop who earned a Medal of Valor for busting a Chinatown drug ring. He was killed in the line of duty about five years ago while making an arrest a few blocks from the Golden Dragon. He left a wife and three young kids. A thousand cops showed up at his funeral.

"Any chance he was involved?"

"He didn't get a Medal of Valor for writing parking tickets. He had a stellar reputation."

"Was anybody with him?" I ask.

"He worked alone."

"Were there other undercover cops in the area that night?"

"We always had undercovers in Chinatown. If you're asking if anybody else was watching the Golden Dragon that night, the answer is no."

"I understand there were claims that the murder weapon was planted."

He responds with a well-practiced look of disdain. "Every defense lawyer tries that one to see if it will stick," he says. "There wasn't a shred of evidence."

"Then why was Internal Affairs called in?"

"Standard procedure." He places his coffee mug in its saucer and measures his words. "IA conducted a full investigation. Everybody was cleared."

That's all he intends to tell me. "Who handled the IA investigation?"

"Kevin Fitzgerald."

"Do you know him?"

"Yeah. Solid cop."

"Would he have covered for his friends?"

"Absolutely not."

"What about Joey D'Amato?"

"What about him?"

"It's no big secret that my father didn't like him."

"He and your father didn't see eye to eye, but Joey was a good cop, too."

"Why did they make him take early retirement?"

"He liked to spend time at the track."

"I heard he liked to shake people down."

"I don't know anything about that."

Roosevelt is old-school. He isn't going to rip another cop unless he has the goods. "What do you know about the victims?" I ask. I'm looking for anything that wasn't revealed at the trial.

"Read the record," he says.

"I will. I was hoping you might give me the highlights."

He plays with the handle of his coffee cup as he tries to decide how much he wants to tell me. "There were four people in the room," he says. "Fineman, his client, another drug dealer and his lawyer. Fineman was the only one who came out alive."

"What about bodyguards?" I ask.

"We think there were some other people in the building, but it should come as no surprise that we couldn't place anybody else there.

Security people for mob bosses are reluctant to testify at murder trials."

"Who took over the drug-distribution channels after Terrell Robinson and Alan Chin were killed?" I ask.

"It never takes long to fill a void in the drug-distribution business."

He's being uncharacteristically coy. It suggests to me that he may be holding something back. "You got any names?"

"I'm afraid not, Mike." He finishes his coffee and abruptly reaches for the bill, signaling that this conversation is coming to an end. "My treat tonight," he says.

"Hand it over," I tell him. "You're doing me a favor."

"Forget it." He places his credit card on top of the check.

"Thanks, Roosevelt." I shoot up a final flare. "If you were in my shoes, where would you go first?"

"Mort Goldberg."

I've worked with Fineman's trial attorney a couple of times. The experiences weren't always pleasant, but they were never dull. "Do you know where I can find him?"

"The Jewish Home." His expression turns somber. "He may not be of much help. He had a stroke that's affected his memory."

# # #

"Fitz was a lazy ass-kisser," Pete says.

Suffice it to say, Pete's take on Lieutenant Kevin Fitzgerald is slightly different from Roosevelt's. Then again, his experience with the Internal Affairs division wasn't especially positive. I'm standing in the doorway of Original Joe's with my cell phone pressed against my ear at eleven-thirty on Friday night. "Was he a good cop?" I ask.

"His record was clean. He worked as hard in IA as he did on the street."

"Meaning?"

"He knew how to play the system. He did his job—and nothing more. Let's just say that nobody ever sweated too much when Fitz was handling their case."

"Was he the kind of guy who would have protected other cops?"

"He would have given them the benefit of the doubt."

Got it.

"There's one more thing you should know," he says. "Fitz went to the academy with Little Joey D'Amato. They were friends."

"Good enough friends that he may have been willing to cover for Joey?"

"I wouldn't rule out the possibility." He pauses for a beat. "You realize that if he was covering for Joey, he may have been doing the same for Pop."

# # #

The call comes in to my cell phone at ten minutes after midnight. "Where are you?" Rosie asks.

"The bridge," I reply. I'm midspan on the Golden Gate in a light fog. I can make out the Alcatraz beacon, but the Berkeley Hills are covered by the mist. The sun-hardened windshield wipers on my ancient Corolla provide little assistance.

"Can you stop at my place on your way home?" she says.

"Sure. What's wrong?"

"I just got an emergency call from Lou Cohen's office. Our co-counsel is dead."

Saturday, July 11. 1:04 a.m.
7 days, 22 hours, and 57 minutes until execution.

My ex-mother-in-law puts a finger to her lips. She motions me into Rosie's living room, which is cramped with the kitchen table and chairs. It's been this way since the remodeling project started. Except for her gray hair and the tiny crow's-feet at the corners of her eyes, Sylvia Fernandez could pass for Rosie's older sister. She celebrated her seventy-seventh birthday earlier this year, and she moves at a speed that would put people half her age to shame. Sylvia still lives in the tidy white bungalow in the Mission District that's served as Fernandez family headquarters for almost sixty years. Luckily for us, she spends much of her time here in Larkspur with her grandchildren. She's wearing her customary beige velour jogging suit and Reebok running shoes. She gets up every morning at four-thirty and starts her day with a brisk two-mile walk. The unpredictable logistics of our criminal-defense practice would be impossible to navigate without her help.

"Rosita is on the phone," she whispers.

Telephone conversations in the wee hours are in the job description when you handle death-penalty appeals. The aroma of freshly brewed coffee is mixed with tile and sawdust from the remodeling work. The ten-by-twelve room with a brick fireplace serves triple duty as Rosie's living room, home office, and breakfast room. The area is unlikely to be used in a *Sunset* magazine spread. The eclectic chaos reflects the lifestyle of a working mother in the new millennium. The furnishings include a small color TV, an overworked mahogany desk, two mismatched steel file cabinets, a tired green sofa, and a soon-to-be-retired playpen. The DVDs in the rack range from Barney the Dinosaur to Britney Spears to *Schindler's List*. The gutted kitchen is stripped to the bare two-by-fours and the plywood underfloor. A new refrigerator, dishwasher, stove, and sink are in crates on the back porch.

Rosie is sitting on a card chair behind her desk. She's pressing a cordless phone against her right ear. Her hair is pulled back. Wire-framed reading glasses have replaced her contacts. Her navy blue sweatshirt bears the logo of Hastings Law School. She holds her left thumb a half inch from her index finger—the signal that she won't be long.

I turn back to Sylvia. "Is Tommy asleep?" I whisper.

"Yes, Michael."

"Did Grace go out with Jake?"

"They went to a movie."

Our daughter has a budding romance with an older man who lives around the corner. He's a good-looking honor student who is the ripe old age of sixteen. They met five years ago in the traditional way—she was the star pitcher on their Little League team and he was a weak-hitting outfielder. Since then, he's grown a foot and his fastball tops eighty miles per hour. He pitches for the Redwood High School varsity. Grace is the starting shortstop on the softball team. As far as we can tell, their relationship—such as it is—has been pretty tame. I'm hopeful they'll continue spending most of their time talking about sports. I get nightmares, though, worrying about the various meanings of getting to second base. Our ability to control matters is likely to become increasingly difficult after Jake obtains his driver's license. At that point, he and I will have the long talk that I've been rehearsing in front of the mirror every night for the last fourteen years. I plan to do most of the talking. If he knows what's good for him, he'll agree with everything I say.

"What time did they get home?" I ask.

"Around eleven."

Too late. "Did they spend any time on the porch?"

"A little."

Too much. I'm going to be a wreck by the time she leaves for college. I gesture toward Rosie. "Who's she talking to?" I ask.

"Carolyn."

Carolyn O'Malley used to be our law partner. She was appointed to the superior-court bench a few years ago, leaving a gaping hole in our firm. She provides a unique resource on state- and federal-jurisdiction issues at all hours of the night. The fact that she's a judge lends credibility to her views, but we must obtain her advice off the record. We try to seek it judiciously.

Rosie thanks her profusely and presses the Off button. "Looks like we're flying solo," she says.

"There must be some grounds for delay if the lead attorney dies seven days before an execution," I say.

"Not necessarily. It isn't as if he's without representation. We can argue it to the California Supremes and the Ninth Circuit. Carolyn says there's no authority on point."

"There's no way we'll be able to get up to speed in time."

"We're going to have to try. Cohen's associate is going to walk me through the record. I've already spoken to the CAP attorney who is working on the case."

The California Appellate Project, or CAP, is a nonprofit organization that's been providing counseling on capital cases for two decades. It was organized to provide a "buddy" for court-appointed appellate lawyers, who frequently had limited experience handling death-penalty appeals. The lawyers at CAP help brainstorm strategies and prepare briefs. I derive a modest level of comfort from knowing they're available.

"What happened to Cohen?" I ask.

"His associate called and said he had a heart attack. One minute he was there, the next he was gone."

Sylvia puts it into perspective. "All things considered, if your time is up, it isn't a bad way to go."

I ask Rosie if anybody has informed our client about his lawyer's untimely demise.

"He's probably heard about it by now," she says. "Cohen's associate is going to see him in the morning."

"We should go with her," I say.

Grace makes her entrance from the hall that leads to the small bedroom she shares with her grandmother when Sylvia stays here. The resemblance to her mother is striking. The braces on her teeth are gone, her figure is filling out, and her long black hair cascades down her back. She's wearing a T-shirt for a hip-hop band whose music could sterilize small animals.

"How's Jake?" I ask.

Her tone is guarded. "Fine." She quickly changes the subject. "Are you here about the Fineman case?"

Rosie answers for me. "Yes, honey."

"I thought you weren't going to do any more death-penalty cases."

She's inherited her mother's propensity for directness.

"Mr. Fineman's attorney had a heart attack," Rosie says. "He's dead."

Grace correctly points out that we started working on the case yesterday afternoon. "He was still alive then."

"We're all that he has left."

Our daughter folds her arms in the same manner as Rosie always does. Except for the difference in their ages, it's like watching someone standing in front of a mirror. "You're going to work round the clock, aren't you?"

Grace could open her own law practice right now.

"It won't be long," Rosie says.

"How long?"

"Eight days."

Grace tugs at her ear. "So much for our agreement."

"I'm sorry, Grace. It's a special situation."

"It's *always* a special situation." She scowls. "They said on the news that Nate Fineman represented the Bayview Posse."

"He did. Where did you hear about that case?"

"At school. They warned us about buying bad drugs."

High school has changed since I was fourteen.

Grace's eyes narrow. "Doesn't it bother you that you want to represent a guy who defended those people?"

Yes. "It's part of being a lawyer, Grace."

She pushes out a melodramatic sigh. "You aren't public defenders anymore. You're choosing to take this case."

She's right. "We might be able to help him."

"As if there aren't a zillion other lawyers out there." She looks over my shoulder for an instant, then her eyes lock back onto mine. "They said on the news that Grandpa was the arresting officer."

"Actually, he was the first officer at the scene," I say.

"Does this mean you're going to try to prove that he screwed up?"

Rosie and I exchange a quick glance. "He didn't do anything wrong," I say.

"But you have to look into it, don't you?"

"Yes."

"And if you find that he did, you have to report it, don't you?"

"If it would help our client."

"Am I the only one who has a problem with this?"

It will serve no useful purpose to offer a platitude or be disingenuous. "You aren't," I say.

"Then why are you doing this?"

"Good lawyers take on tough cases," I say.

She waits a long beat, then decides it isn't worth a fight. "I can deal with it," she says. "Can I still go to the Giants game with Jake next Saturday?"

"Of course."

As she's moved into her teens, she's spending more time with Jake and her other friends. Intellectually, I knew this transition was inevitable. Emotionally, I miss my baby daughter.

Grace turns to Sylvia. "Looks like we're going to be spending a lot of time together, Grandma. Maybe we can take Tommy to the mall tomorrow."

She never invites *me* to the mall. I try not to be jealous. There is something special about the relationship between a grandmother and a granddaughter.

Sylvia smiles. "Sounds fine," she says.

Grace is starting to make her way toward her room when she turns around. "Was Grandpa a good cop?" she asks.

"One of the best," I say.

"Did he ever get into trouble?"

"Only with Grandma," I tell her.

She isn't amused. "Is Nate Fineman guilty?"

The question catches me off guard. I exchange silent glances with my ex-wife and ex-mother-in-law. It's Rosie who answers her. "We'll know more after we look through the files," she says.

Grace takes my nonresponse in stride. "Just wondering," she says, walking away.

# # #

Rosie and I are sitting at opposite ends of her sofa at 4:00 a.m. We've spent the last three hours poring over appellate records, trial transcripts, and police reports. It's a tedious slog that will continue all weekend. Time is not on our side, but we can't afford to miss something important. My capacity for all-nighters dropped substantially when I turned forty, twelve years ago.

I hear a familiar high-pitched voice behind me. "Hi, Daddy."

"Hi, Tommy," I say. This elicits a gleeful smile as our energetic son bounces into the living room and onto my lap. Except for the fact that Rosie and I are divorced and we have less than eight days to save a condemned man's life, we could be reenacting a scene right out of *Ozzie and Harriet*. "Why are you up?"

"There's a monster in my room."

This is his stock explanation for his frequent appearances in the wee hours. When I used to have nightmares as a kid, my dad always came into my room to chase the bad guys away. It was reassuring to have a father who was a cop. It was also some of the only quality time that we spent together. After he cleared the room of imaginary creatures, we would retreat to the kitchen for a bowl of cereal. Pop wasn't much of a talker, but he always seemed to enjoy eating Cheerios with me in the middle of the night.

"What kind of monster?" I ask.

He holds his arms out wide. "A *big* one," he says.

It's *always* a big one. "I saw him a little while ago," I say. "He went outside to play with the owls."

Tommy's big blue Daley eyes open wider. He still buys everything I say. This certainly isn't the case with his sister. He gives me the grin that always gets him what he wants. It won't work nearly as well when he's sixteen. "Did you go to work today, Daddy?"

Now I'm sure he's filibustering. "Yes, Tom. I worked very hard."

"I played very hard."

"So, we're even."

The smile transforms into a thoughtful look. "Do *you* ever get to play, Daddy?"

Not in the middle of a death-penalty appeal. "Sometimes," I tell him. For the next eight days, I'll settle for a few minutes of sleep. "It's more fun to be a kid, when you can play all the time. Why don't you get back in bed and I'll come in and check on you in a minute?"

"Okay, Daddy. I love you."

"I love you, too."

Tommy hops off my lap and practically sprints to the bedroom he'll be sharing with Rosie until the remodel is finished. Two-year-olds move at only one speed—fast.

"I wish it were that easy with Grace," Rosie says.

"At least she's out of diapers. Wait until Tommy turns fourteen."

"There's always military school."

"It isn't a bad option." I close a heavy black binder that's filled with appellate briefs. "Did you find anything that might be grounds for a stay?"

"Lou Cohen found the stronger appealable issues." Her eyelids flutter as she yawns. "We'll come up with a few creative arguments for another habeas petition. You know what it's like with last-minute death-penalty appeals. We'll just keep throwing stuff at the courts."

It's true. In the final days before an execution, you argue anything and everything that you can think of and hope a sympathetic judge will bite. The odds are always stacked against you.

"In the meantime," she adds, "it would make our lives a lot easier if Pete can find something—even if it's just some credible evidence of police misconduct."

"He's already looking." The pedal is about to hit the floor.

Rosie leans over and kisses me softly.

"What's that for?" I ask.

"For getting us into this mess."

"I'll make it up to you."

"Yes, you will."

I pull her toward me and kiss her back. "How's that?" I ask.

"Not nearly good enough." I lean forward and try again, but she pulls away. "I don't think so," she says. "We have to stay focused."

I wink at her and say, "I am."

"We have to think about our client's best interests. You're a better lawyer when you're desperate for a little action."

"I'm plenty motivated, Rosie."

She squeezes my hand. "We'll continue this discussion after the case is over. By then you'll have even greater motivation to think about *my* best interests, too. There may be something extra in it for you."

I may be having a second birthday this year.

Her smile disappears as she turns back to domestic matters. "Grace is handling this pretty well," she says.

"So far."

"She's more interested in hanging out with Jake than with us."

"Don't count us out just yet."

She gets a faraway look in her eyes. "Do you think she'll ever become more communicative with me?"

"Maybe after she gets out of college. I'm told that parents tend to get a lot smarter when their kid turns twenty-five."

I get another smile. "Where are you going to start later this morning?" she asks.

"With Mort the Sport."

"How the hell have you been?" Mort "the Sport" Goldberg rasps. His customary greeting hasn't changed in sixty years, though his once authoritative voice is now a hoarse whisper.

"Fine, Mort," I say.

His tired gray eyes are hidden behind huge aviator-style glasses as his attendant wheels him into a sun-drenched atrium in the sprawling Jewish Home for the Aged. The inveterate glad-hander was once among the most dynamic defense attorneys in the Bay Area. His face is now drawn, his complexion pasty. At seventy-six, he's one of the younger residents in a facility where the average age is eighty-eight. His right hand convulses uncontrollably. His left arm doesn't move. The legs of the onetime expert skier are limp appendages that must be delicately hand-lifted onto his wheelchair. They're covered by a red and gold 49ers blanket.

His tone turns melancholy. "It's been a long time."

"Yes, it has." It's also been a long morning. Rosie and I started the day at San Quentin, where Nate took the news of Lou Cohen's death with grim resignation. Rosie went to the office to meet with Cohen's associate. I came here to see Mort.

"I expected to see you last night," he tells me point-blank.

"We weren't hired until yesterday afternoon."

"That was almost twenty-four hours ago. You don't have time to screw around."

He hasn't lost his edge. "I just saw your old client," I tell him. "He's holding up pretty well under the circumstances."

"This isn't the Ritz," he says, "but it still beats the hell out of the Row."

The Jewish Home's bright hallways lack the pungent odor typical of similar facilities. Located in four reasonably cheerful buildings at the corner of Mission Street and Silver Avenue, just south of the 280 freeway, it was founded in 1871 as a residential care center for a dozen seniors in a neighborhood that once had a significant Jewish population. The Jews fled to the suburbs decades ago. The Jewish Home didn't.

Mort cuts to the chase. "How are you going to stop the execution?"

"We're already looking for new information," I say. "At the moment, we're focusing on claims that the cops may have planted the murder weapon."

"I couldn't prove it," he says.

"We're going to try. If that fails, we'll need to find another way to prove freestanding innocence."

"That isn't going to happen unless somebody steps forward and confesses."

The years and the ailments haven't dulled his lawyerly instincts. "We'll throw everything into the next round of habeas petitions," I say.

"Maybe." His right eyebrow darts up over the top of his thick glasses. "You'll come up with something. As I recall, you used to be a pretty good lawyer."

Ever the schmoozer. His ancestors came to San Francisco during the gold rush. They started a successful men's clothing business that was bought by the prominent Magnin family. He grew up in the Richmond District and became the president of Temple Beth Sholom at Fourteenth and Clement, where he and Nate served together on the board. The childhood friends became genial rivals and occasional collaborators who ran competing law practices at opposite ends of the sixteenth floor of the Russ Building. They could be seen lunching together on petrale sole in a booth at Sam's a couple of times a week.

Mort mellowed considerably with age. Eventually, he developed a reputation as a "pleader"—a defense attorney who was more interested in cutting deals than trying cases. Ultimately, he became a full-time TV commentator on Channel 4. "Mort's Torts," as his daily segment was known, was a freewheeling cross between Court TV and David Letterman. It gave him a platform to expound upon everything from political issues to the Niners' quarterback. He pretended to have an ongoing flirtation with the attractive young traffic reporter, even though it was common knowledge that he'd been married to his childhood sweetheart for more than fifty years. He worked at Channel 4 until he suffered the stroke that paralyzed his left side. His wife died a short time later. The longtime benefactor of the Jewish Home took a room in the wing that bears his name.

I move in closer. "We had some sad news last night," I say. "Lou Cohen passed away."

His pained expression indicates that he hasn't heard the news. He struggles to clasp the unlit Cuban cigar that's attached to his wrist by an elastic cord. He isn't allowed to light up, but they can't deprive him of his favorite prop. "That's bad," he says quietly. "Too many of my friends are dying. When's the service?"

"Monday."

He glances at his attendant. "Let's see if we can make arrangements to go."

The young man nods.

Mort jabs the cigar in my direction. "I spend a lot of time going to funerals," he says. "I'm going to fool my doctors. I'm going to outlive them all."

He just might. Mort stormed the corridors of the Hall of Justice for more than five decades. After hours, he held court at the legendary Cookie's Star Café, a dive on Kearny Street where prosecutors, defense lawyers, cops, judges, politicians, criminals, and reporters used to gossip, make book, and dole out informal justice over beers, dice, and cigars. Its colorful and profane proprietor, Lawrence "Cookie" Picetti, provided a needed demilitarized zone for the warring factions in San Francisco's criminal-justice system. Defense lawyers conducted informal discovery there. A dwindling group of Cookie's old regulars still gather on his birthday every year to hoist a few beers in his memory. Like Cookie's place, Mort the Sport is a part of San Francisco that's fading into history. There are good lawyers who will pick up the gauntlet. But there are few bigger-than-life characters left in our profession.

I've been warned that his memory fades in and out, so I have to get what I can during his lucid moments. I start by easing him into a discussion of his favorite topic—himself. "How are you feeling?" I ask.

The frustration in his voice is palpable. "I can't hold my cigar without a spotter." He shoots an appreciative smile toward his attendant. "If I light up, he's supposed to light me up. You'd think the doctors would understand that I'm not going to die young."

The young man touches his arm gently. "You know the rules, boss," he says. "Do you want some tea?"

Mort playfully pretends to burn his finger with the unlit cigar. "I'd like some scotch."

"It's a little early."

"I suppose. Let me have a moment with Mr. Daley."

The attendant gestures toward a woman whose wheelchair is parked down the hall. "I'm going to check on your girlfriend," he says.

"I'll be right here."

"Thanks." Mort turns back to me. "He's a sophomore at City College. I'm trying to convince him to go to law school. I promised to teach him everything I can remember. Hell, if I can find my Rolodex, I can get him some clients."

I take a seat on the bench next to him. "How are you really feeling?" I ask.

He looks down at his useless legs. "I have a few good days and a lot of bad ones. First it's cataracts, then it's a stroke, then your kidneys quit."

I offer a weak platitude. "You have to keep plugging."

"You're still a kid. I'm in worse shape than they're telling me. It's always a bad sign when your doctors whisper to each other."

"It's probably nothing."

He forces a chuckle. "It's always something, Mike. If you're living here, you aren't going to get better. You just hope you don't get worse too quickly, and you pray for a painless end. I try not to dwell on it. Sometimes I think Nate has a better deal. We're getting to the finish line—at least he knows when the race is going to end. The only saving grace is that half the time I can't remember what it was like to be healthy. You caught me on one of my good days. If you come back tomorrow, I might not recognize you."

"My mom used to say that getting old isn't for sissies."

"She was very wise." His eyes light up. "You want some free advice?"

I'd like some free information, but I can't possibly stop him. "Sure."

"You'll want to write these down."

I prepare to take notes. "I'm listening."

"Mort the Sport's three rules to live by. Number one, don't get old. Number two, don't get sick. Number three, don't get old *and* sick at the same time. It's bad for your health."

I'm glad I caught him on one of his good days.

"So," he says, "I presume you're here to talk about Nate's appeal."

"I am."

The affable expression disappears. "His case didn't make my personal highlight reel."

It was the only murder trial that he ever lost. "The execution is a week from tomorrow. I was hoping I might persuade you to help us."

His scowl becomes more pronounced. "I haven't talked to Nate in years. I didn't appreciate it when Lou Cohen filed that IAC claim against me."

He can remember every slight from fifty years ago. "It was a legal strategy," I say. "It wasn't personal."

"It was a losing argument and a gratuitous swipe. If I'd been running the case, Nate would have gotten a new trial by now."

"You can help us remove the only blemish from your otherwise perfect record." I give him a sly grin. "It would also give us a chance to work together again."

"I'm no longer licensed to practice law."

"We'll hire you as a consultant."

His tired eyes twinkle. "Are you really willing to pay me for my time?"

"Sure." I can be magnanimous with a fifty-thousand-dollar retainer. Besides, he doesn't need the money.

"You can't expect me to remember the details of Nate's case."

"I think you can remember the details of every case you ever tried."

He gives me a knowing look. "Lou brought you in to take the blame if the last appeal fails," he says.

"I prefer to think he hired me because I have a long-standing relationship with Roosevelt Johnson—and with you."

"He should have done it sooner."

I put a gentle hand on his shoulder. "Better late than never," I say.

The wheels start turning. "Can you persuade a judge to delay the execution because of Lou's death?"

"We're going to file papers on Monday morning."

"On what grounds?"

"Among other things, ineffective assistance of counsel."

"Against Lou?"

"Against ourselves."

His quivering lips transform into a smile. "Is there any legal authority?"

"Not really."

"You're still going to have to prove freestanding innocence."

I give him an admiring nod. Mort didn't get to be one of the best hired guns in town on his good looks and family connections. "I'm in a tough spot," I tell him. "You know this case better than anybody. I could really use your help."

He pretends to sniff his cigar—which is still wrapped in cellophane. "Why the hell not?" he finally says. "What do you want to know?"

"Did Nate kill those people at the Golden Dragon?"

He shakes his head. "We had our differences," he says, "but he isn't a murderer."

"Was he trying to take over Terrell Robinson's heroin-distribution business?"

"No."

"Then how did he end up in an alley with the murder weapon?"

"It was a setup."

"By whom?"

"The cops."

"Which ones?"

"If I knew the answer, I wouldn't have lost the case in the first place."

Perhaps. "Maybe we can start with what happened that night."

He uses the cigar to gesture as he lays out a story that jibes with Roosevelt's.

"How did Nate get a gun inside the restaurant?" I ask.

"The cops said he'd planted it in the bathroom down the hall. That was bullshit."

"Nate admitted that he used the bathroom just before the shooting started."

"It doesn't mean he planted a gun. He was searched when he entered the building and when he returned to the meeting. Roosevelt claimed they didn't frisk him carefully enough or the bodyguards were paid off. That was another load of crap."

"Where was Nate when the shooting started?" I already got this information from Nate. I want to see if Mort can fill in any additional details.

"He was sitting at a table in the middle of the room. He pushed it over when the shooting started. It was riddled with bullet holes and probably saved his life. He ran to the window and jumped onto one of those old-fashioned iron fire escapes that you see in Chinatown. It was slick from the rain. He fell two stories into the alley. It's a miracle that he wasn't killed on the spot."

This is consistent with Nate's version. "They found a gun under his arm."

"I know. Somebody put it there."

"Who?"

"I don't know."

"What happened to Alan Chin's operations after he was killed?"

"I don't know. Chin's family got out of the drug business. His son runs a bank in Chinatown."

"What about Terrell Robinson's business?"

"A guy named Marshawn Bryant took over Robinson's construction firm."

"Did he also take over Robinson's drug business?"

"You'll never be able to prove it. Bryant is a big success story. He grew up in the projects in the Bayview. He worked his way up to vice president in Robinson's operation. Now he's the head of one of the largest minority-owned contracting firms in the Bay Area. He's given a lot back to the community."

"Did you talk to him?"

"Of course. We talked to everybody who worked for Robinson."

"Where was he on the night of the shootings?"

"With his girlfriend. She backed up his story."

"She could have been protecting him."

"We couldn't refute her alibi. She isn't going to change her story. They got married a few years ago. It was all over the papers. She runs a hotshot design firm." He grabs his cigar and twirls it. "For what it's worth," he says, "the cops found a witness who saw a black man in the alley behind the Golden Dragon around the time of the shootings. The description loosely fit Bryant. Then again, it also fit about a million other men in the Bay Area."

"Does the witness have a name?"

"Eugene Tsai. He worked nights at the Chinese Hospital. He was on his way home from work."

"Did he testify at the trial?"

"He never had a chance. He was stabbed to death in an armed robbery a couple of days after the shootings at the Golden Dragon. The cops never figured out who killed him."

"Did you talk to him?"

"No. He was killed before we had a chance."

It has to be more than a coincidence. "Did you get this information from the cops?"

"No, we got it from Tsai's brother, Wendell."

"Is the brother still alive?"

"As far as I know. He used to work at Brandy Ho's."

It's a well-known Hunan restaurant on Columbus Avenue. "Did

Wendell testify at the trial?"

"Nope."

"Why not?"

"He refused to get involved after his brother was killed." He shrugs. "He wouldn't have been a strong witness. His English was poor and he was scared to death. Besides, his testimony would have been inadmissible hearsay."

"Did you consider the possibility that Eugene's death was more than a coincidence?"

"Of course. We had no proof."

I press him, but he has no additional details. "What can you tell me about the claims that the cops planted evidence?"

"The crime scene looked like it was staged by somebody who knew what they were doing."

"What makes you think so?"

His eyes open wider. "They found a pristine set of Nate's prints on the gun—too clean, if you ask me. It was pouring rain. At best, they would have been smeared."

"Anything else?"

"There was no gunpowder residue on Nate's hands."

"It was raining."

"The cops said it washed away. They were full of crap. They should have found traces—even in a rainstorm."

"You really think the cops planted the gun?"

"It was no secret that they were out to get Nate after the disaster in the Posse case."

"You got any proof?"

"Nope."

"Was anybody else involved?"

"An undercover cop named David Low was the first officer at the scene. I went after him at the trial, but I couldn't nail him. He had a clean record and a Medal of Valor. The rest of the cops closed ranks."

"Did you hire a PI to look into it?"

"Yep. We used Nick Hanson."

The entertainment value of this case just went up exponentially. Nick "the Dick" Hanson is an octogenarian PI who is a throwback to simpler days. His agency in North Beach employs four generations of Hansons. In his spare time, he writes mysteries that are slightly exaggerated recountings of his most colorful cases. "Have you seen him lately?" I ask.

"He stops in every couple of weeks. He had arthroscopic surgery on his knee after he ran the Bay to Breakers."

Every May, seventy-five thousand costumed runners trudge seven and a half miles from downtown to Ocean Beach in a bacchanalia that's one part race and ten parts street party. Nick has finished it sixty-nine times.

"We'll talk to him," I say.

Saturday, July 11. 12:02 p.m.
7 days, 11 hours, and 59 minutes until execution.

"Let me see if I have this straight," Rosie says to me. "Mort the Sport hired Nick the Dick to work on Nate the Great's case?"

"More or less," I say.

"Priceless."

It would have greater practical value if the guys with the colorful nicknames could help us find the real killer—assuming it isn't our client.

I'm pressing my cell phone tightly against my ear as I stand in the entrance alcove of the Jewish Home. A warm breeze is whipping down Mission Street. Rosie takes in the description of my conversation with Mort without comment. Good lawyers are good talkers. Great lawyers are excellent listeners.

"I just got off the phone with Roosevelt," I tell her. "He confirmed that a man named Eugene Tsai told him that he saw a young African American male in the alley behind the Golden Dragon around the time of the shootings. He also confirmed that Tsai was killed in an armed robbery a few days later. That case was never solved."

"Why didn't Roosevelt mention it sooner?"

"Tsai didn't make a positive ID."

I can hear the skepticism in her voice when she asks, "Did Roosevelt pursue the lead on the African American man?"

"Yes. He said they turned up empty."

"Tsai's death had to be more than a coincidence," Rosie says.

"Maybe. He promised to send over a copy of the case file. He said there wasn't much in it. I've asked Pete to try to track down Tsai's brother—if he's still alive. Did you subpoena the IA file?"

"Yes. I prepared a subpoena for Fitz, too."

She's always a step ahead. "Did you get anything useful from Lou Cohen's associate?"

"She started walking me through the police reports, trial transcripts, and appellate briefs, but we still have a long way to go. I contacted the clerks at the California Supremes and the Ninth Circuit. We'll start by filing papers on Monday to request a stay based upon Cohen's death. Don't hold your breath."

I ponder our options for a moment. "I think our best bet is pursuing the possibility that the cops planted the gun."

"Nobody in the SFPD is going to talk to us about it. It might also implicate your father."

"I know."

"What's Plan B?"

"We need to find Tsai's brother. Maybe there was somebody else in the alley. Maybe we can persuade a judge to let him testify about what his brother told him."

"That would be inadmissible hearsay," she says.

"Then we'll have to persuade a judge that it's better to bend the rules of evidence than to execute an innocent man."

# # #

My brother greets me with a terse "What took you so long to get here?"

"I was meeting with Mort Goldberg," I tell him.

His tone softens. "The Jewish Home isn't so bad—as nursing homes go."

"No, it isn't."

Pete and I had what we called The Nursing Home Conversation when our mother's Alzheimer's got worse, but she lived at home until she died.

Pete's eyes move constantly as we stand on the sidewalk at the busy intersection of Market, Jones, and McAllister, where the epicenter of the Tenderloin pulses with an edgy energy at twelve-thirty on Saturday afternoon. The area around United Nations Plaza is a crowded melting pot of the disenfranchised and the destitute. Working-class immigrants are walking to the nearby farmers' market. Ill-smelling homeless people are panhandling the few misguided tourists who took a wrong turn when they left their posh hotels at Union Square.

The sticky sidewalks reek of urine and garbage. Drug dealers are conducting business openly, despite a significant police presence. A fourplex cinema on the south side of Market shows X-rated movies. A crumbling old bank across the street was converted into a makeshift police station a few years ago after the drug wars became especially ugly. The city has put up colorful banners in an unconvincing effort to persuade the uninitiated that we're standing in an area known only to civic propagandists as Little Saigon. It feels like a third-world country.

Joey D'Amato's currency exchange occupies the ground floor of a Depression-era three-story structure that needs a sandblaster. The upper floors house a residential hotel that will never be mistaken for the gold-trimmed jukebox Marriott two blocks down Market. It appears that Joey and his neighbors have developed certain economic synergies among their respective businesses. Some of the residents cash their welfare checks at Joey's place, then quickly turn over the proceeds to the huge, tattooed man selling crack in the doorway.

I ask Pete if he got anything useful from his sources at the Hall of Justice.

"I felt like an insurance salesman," he says. "The room cleared out as soon as I started asking questions about the Fineman case. I'm going to check with a couple of other people."

"May I ask who?"

"You may not." Working with Pete is always a need-to-know deal. "Joey got here a little while ago. He's a little hotheaded, so you might want to let me do the talking."

# # #

Little Joey D'Amato doesn't look the part of your typical financial mogul. Then again, managing a currency exchange in the Tenderloin isn't quite the same as running Bank of America. The diminutive, hyperactive former street cop is dressed in generic khakis and a navy polo shirt. His mustache is a dignified shade of silver. His slick hair, on the other hand, is the victim of an atrocious dye job. It looks as if he stuck his head in a bottle of black ink. It's hard not to stare.

Our father's last partner is sitting at a beat-up desk in the corner of his fine establishment. He's clutching a stained copy of the *Daily Racing Form* and glaring at us through the scuffed Plexiglas that separates Joey and his two employees from the unwashed masses who pay his exorbitant fees to get their welfare checks cashed. "Why the hell are you here?" he barks.

The low-overhead operation with the barred windows isn't much larger than Rosie's living room. Plywood counters and chipped walls are painted mismatched shades of prison gray. The furniture is bolted to the floor. Hand-lettered signs in a dozen languages instruct his customers to present two photo IDs to initiate any transaction. Two muscle-bound armed guards stand adjacent to the iron front door.

When your business involves the exchange of significant amounts of cash, the best defense is the conspicuous display of firepower.

Pete attempts to soften Joey up with small talk. He has to raise his voice to be heard through the Plexiglas. "How've you been, Joe?"

He makes no attempt to hide his contempt. "Terrific."

Pete tries again. "How's business?"

"Terrific."

So much for chatting him up. Joey's elocution is just a cut above grunting. His voice sounds as if he massages his vocal cords with sandpaper every night before he goes to bed. My dad grudgingly agreed to work with him when nobody else was willing. Pop always got the short straw on partners after Roosevelt moved up the ranks.

Joey's ratlike eyes form narrow slits. "Let's cut the bullshit," he says. "What do you want?"

Pete plays it straight. "Information about the Fineman case."

"I don't talk about old cases."

"Come on, Joey."

"Your client was guilty. End of story."

My brother feigns exasperation. "Look," he says, "we can do this the easy way or the hard way. If you answer our questions, we'll get out of your hair. Otherwise, we'll come back with a subpoena and the same conversation will become significantly more unpleasant."

"I don't know anything," Joey says.

"You haven't even heard our questions," I say.

"Doesn't matter."

Asshole. "What happened that night?" I ask.

"Read the record."

"We have. I want to hear your side of the story."

He flashes irritation. "Your father and I went to the Golden Dragon as soon as we got the call. Fineman was unconscious in the alley, with a loaded piece. We helped Dave Low secure the scene. Reinforcements got there right away. Roosevelt took over when he arrived. That's it."

"There were allegations that the murder weapon was planted."

"That was crap. Nothing was proven. We did everything by the book."

"Why did they call in IA?"

"It was a high-profile case. Every defense lawyer tries to prove the cops screwed up. Mort Goldberg tried to pin it on us years ago. He was wrong then. He's wrong now. If you believe him, you're wrong, too."

Helpful. "We understand an eyewitness saw an African American man in the alley around the time of the shootings."

"You'll have to talk to Roosevelt about it."

"I already did. What about bodyguards?"

"You'll have to talk to Roosevelt about that, too."

I feel like pounding my fists on the stained Plexiglas. "There's something about this case that I don't understand. Fineman had a thriving law practice. He was rich. There was nothing in it for him."

"Money."

"He didn't need it."

"You think Fineman was the only lawyer on the face of the earth who got greedy? He wanted a bigger piece of Robinson's action. Robinson told him to go fuck himself. Fineman got pissed off. End of story."

I lean forward and place my hands on the window. "I heard Fitz did the IA investigation."

"He did."

"I heard you guys were buddies."

"We went to the academy together."

I raise the stakes. "Your pal was in a position to smooth things over."

"There was nothing to smooth over. Besides, Fitz wasn't that kind of cop."

"Maybe he was that kind of friend."

"You're full of shit. It was a clean arrest and conviction."

"Prove it."

"We did—a long time ago."

"Maybe we'll lean on Fitz. Maybe we'll look at the IA report."

"Be my guest." He runs his stubby fingers through his greasy, badly dyed hair. "Just remember this: if you try to drag me through the mud, I'll drag your father with me."

Saturday, July 11. 1:05 p.m.
7 days, 10 hours, and 56 minutes until execution.

"That was bullshit," Pete says.

My ever-so-judgmental brother. "What makes you think so?" I ask.

"His lips were moving."

We're walking up Grove Street past the new library toward Civic Center Plaza. His irritation is exacerbated by a lack of sleep and the gale-force winds hammering us as the city hall rotunda comes into view.

He's still expounding. "What a crock," he says. "The cops couldn't come up with a real motive, so they played the greedy lawyer card. It might have made sense if Fineman was a small-time schmuck like you."

I ignore the dig. I trust his instincts and I want him to keep talking.

"Fineman was a prominent attorney with great connections," he says. "He had a house in St. Francis Wood, a couple of Jags in the garage, and a condo in Maui. Do you really think he would have been stupid enough to pop a couple of drug bosses?"

"The jury bought it."

"Juries are made up of idiots."

I let it go. "Does that mean you think he's innocent?"

"It means I think Joey wasn't giving us the whole story. Did you see the weasel look in his eyes when you asked him about a planted gun?

He was covering his ass."

"Or Pop's," I say.

"Pop said Joey was the biggest asshole he ever worked with."

Our dad expressed similar feelings about all of his partners after Roosevelt. His animosity toward Joey turned into outright hostility when Joey failed to watch his back after Pop tackled a gunman who had knocked over a convenience store in the Mission.

"We need to find something besides the possibility of some crooked cops," I say. "It's going to be damn near impossible to find anybody in SFPD who will break ranks—especially for Nate."

"Where does that leave us?" he asks.

"We have to find Tsai's brother," I say.

"I'll see what I can do. We should also try to track down the guy who took over Robinson's heroin-distribution business," he says. "Maybe he had a grudge."

"Or maybe he was the black guy in the alley," I say.

"Maybe."

We turn into the alley behind the Bill Graham Civic Auditorium, where Pete illegally parked his old police-issue Chrysler. He comes to an abrupt stop and glares at the smashed windows of the gray car. "Goddamn it," he mutters.

I survey the wreckage. "Did they take anything?" I ask.

"Nope."

"You didn't check."

"There was nothing to steal. I never keep anything in the car except water bottles and energy bars."

The diet of a PI. "It was probably some punk trying to steal your car," I say.

"You lawyers don't have a clue about life on the street, do you? It takes an experienced thief about ten seconds to hot-wire an ignition. A rookie would have smashed just one window. It's tough to drive without windows—even criminals don't like to get cold and wet."

"What are you saying?"

"Somebody is trying to tell us to mind our own business."

# # #

"So," Rosie says with her tongue planted firmly in her cheek, "did you have a nice day, dear?"

"A great day to be a lawyer," I say.

Pete is in no mood for banter. "Are you guys done?" he snaps.

It's four-fifteen on Saturday afternoon. Rosie's cramped office smells of a combination of coffee and Friday's lunch special downstairs at the El Faro. My head feels like somebody hit me with a two-by-four. My gray polo shirt is sticking to my back and I'm in desperate need of a shower. The extra shirts that I keep at the office are at the cleaner's. Still, I'm in better shape than Pete, whose mood turned outright foul after we had his car towed to his favorite repair shop in the Mission. He's very possessive about that old Chrysler. His disposition got worse after we spent the afternoon talking to some of his old friends at Mission Station, all of whom gave us a decidedly cold shoulder.

Rosie is sitting behind her desk. Her arms are folded as she looks at us over piles of manila file folders and black binders. She listens intently as Pete and I describe our less than enlightening conversations with Mort the Sport and Little Joey. She spent the day in a marathon session with Cohen's associate. Her prognosis is as depressing as it is succinct. "Realistically," she says, "unless we can show the SFPD planted the murder weapon, our only prayer is to find new evidence that would prove freestanding innocence."

I'd put our odds at a thousand to one.

Rosie holds up a palm in frustration. "What about Little Joey's claim that Nate wanted to take over Robinson's business?"

"I asked Nate about it," I say. "He denied it."

"You didn't expect him to admit it, did you?"

"Of course not."

"Did you get anything that might be remotely useful?" she asks.

"We're trying to locate Eugene Tsai's brother," I say. "I also put in a call to Nick Hanson. He promised to meet with me Monday night."

"That's all you have?"

"We were hired yesterday afternoon."

"We only have a week. We need to make every second count."

I'm all too aware of that. "Did you get the subpoena served for the IA file?" I ask.

"Yes."

"When do you expect to get a copy?"

Rosie's lips form a tight line across her face. "I don't."

"What do you mean?"

"I mean the file is missing."

"What are you talking about?"

"Just what I said. It was in a box at an off-site facility. They found the box, but the file was gone."

"How could that have happened?"

"The bureaucrat who runs the records division didn't know. He's only been working there for about six months. The box was sent to storage ten years ago. He had no idea if the file was stolen, misplaced, or purged."

My mind shifts into overdrive as I speculate about who had access to it. Fitz prepared it. Little Joey may have looked at it. "Somebody must have taken it."

"We shouldn't rule out the possibility." She clears her throat. "There's another problem."

"Which is?"

"If you're the subject of an investigation, you can review your file in the IA office. You can't take it with you or make photocopies."

"Did they keep a checkout log?"

"Yes. They found it. Roosevelt looked at the file. So did Joey D'Amato."

No big surprise. "So what's the problem?" I say.

"Your father was the last person who checked it out."

Saturday, July 11. 4:22 p.m.
7 days, 7 hours, and 39 minutes until execution.

"Did he check it back in?" I ask Rosie, desperately trying not to jump to conclusions.

"According to the log, yes."

"Then they can't point a finger at him. Somebody must have been watching him when he looked at it."

"Maybe, but we'll never know for sure. The guy who was running the records division at the time died a few years ago." She takes a moment to gather her thoughts. "This changes everything. We have seven days to try to exonerate Nate Fineman. Now we may have to clear your father, too."

Pete isn't buying it. "Just because Pop's name was on the log doesn't mean he took it."

"Then who did?" I ask.

"How the hell would I know, Mick? It doesn't mean it was stolen. Stuff gets lost all the time at the SFPD."

True enough. I've gotten acquittals in capital murder cases when key pieces of evidence have disappeared into the SFPD's black hole. "Have you come across any SFPD files at the house?" I ask.

"Of course not."

"Just checking. Did he ever say anything to you about looking at the IA file?"

"Nope."

Our job just got harder. "Who might know something about this?"
I ask.

"Big John," Pete replies.

"Big John" Dunleavy runs a saloon in the Sunset that's been our
family's second home for decades. He was married to our mother's sister for forty-seven years before she died, which makes him our uncle
and Pop's brother-in-law. They were more like brothers than in-laws.

"What makes you think Pop would have talked to Big John about
it?" I ask.

"Because he talked to Big John about everything."

Saturday, July 11. 5:25 p.m.
7 days, 6 hours, and 36 minutes until execution.

The genial bartender extends a massive hand across the bar. "What'll it be, lad?" he asks.

Big John Dunleavy was born at St. Francis Hospital seventy-five years ago. He's never set foot outside the United States, but he can turn on a lilting Irish brogue at will. He always says that if you run an Irish pub, you have to sound the part.

"The usual, Big John," I say.

My uncle was "Big John" even when he was little—which he never really was. He weighed in at almost thirteen pounds at birth. He was already six-two and a muscular two hundred pounds by the time he finished eighth grade at St. Peter's. He developed his strong hands by lugging beer kegs up from the basement of his father's saloon. He was an all-city tight end at St. Ignatius. He would have played at Cal if he hadn't blown out a shoulder catching the winning touchdown pass in the city championship game almost sixty years ago.

A wide smile crosses his ruddy face. His large jowls shake as he squeezes my hand. His full head of hair is now more gray than red, yet he retains an infectious youthful exuberance. I pull up a stool as he sets a pint of Guinness on the worn wooden bar that his father built when Big John was in grammar school.

Dunleavy's Pub hasn't changed much over the years. The original dark wood–paneled walls are covered with photos of County Galway. The aromas of Guinness, cod, burgers, and fries waft through the narrow room. You can make out the stench of cigarette smoke baked into the walls from the old days. Smoking is now permitted only on the small outdoor patio. The clientele hasn't changed much, either. The neighbors are eating fish-and-chips at their regular spots at the small tables as they watch ESPN on the TV above the bar. A couple of people are shooting pool in the back room. Later, a three-piece band will come in to lead the crowd in Irish standards and a few bawdy folk songs.

The old building on the Judah streetcar line would fetch well over a million bucks if Big John were inclined to sell it. He isn't—not now or in the future. It would be tantamount to selling his heritage. His youngest son, known as "Little John" even though he stands six-four and was a star defensive lineman at St. Ignatius, is beginning to take over the day-to-day operation of the neighborhood icon. The saloon is an extension of every home in the vicinity. Big John relishes his role as everybody's uncle.

He wipes the bar with a worn dish towel. "Haven't seen you around much lately," he says. It's his standard lament. I stop in to see him at least once a week. He longs for the days when Pete and I used to come by on our way home from school.

"Tommy and Grace are keeping us pretty busy," I tell him.

"I never should have let you move to the suburbs, Mikey."

He's the only person on the face of the earth who calls me by my childhood nickname. He's earned the right. He was in the waiting room with my father on the day I was born.

"I see a lot more of your brother," he says.

"He lives around the corner," I observe. Big John lives in an identical house two blocks from Pete.

"It's only a fifteen-minute drive for you," he says.

"Across the bridge."

"That's no excuse."

No, it isn't. He inquires about Rosie and Grace. I assure him that they're fine. "How's your son?" he asks. He still finds it difficult to mention Tommy by name. To Big John, there will always be only one Tommy Daley—my dad.

"Tommy's fine, too," I tell him.

"Glad to hear it."

He means it.

"So," he says, "to what do I owe the pleasure of a visit from one of my favorite nephews?"

"I'm working on a new case."

"I know." He nods toward the TV. "I saw you on the news earlier this afternoon. Why are you getting involved in a death-penalty appeal for a slimy lawyer who defended a bunch of lowlifes who were selling bad heroin to kids?"

"Because he asked. He's actually planning to pay us for our services."

He glances at the Dunleavy family crest, which hangs from the ceiling. My uncle has an endearing habit of trying to communicate with deceased relatives. "Tommy," he says to my father, "I don't know where you went wrong with this one."

No reply.

Big John gives me a skeptical look. "What do you think you're going to do in a week?" he asks.

"Stop the execution."

"Sure, Mikey. What brings you here?"

Sometimes my lawyerly bravado gets a step ahead of my judgment. "Paying a visit to my favorite uncle."

"I'm your *only* uncle, Mikey."

"You're still my favorite."

His eyes dart toward the ceiling again. "I know I promised to look after him, Tommy, but there's only so much I can do."

Still no response from above.

He draws himself a Guinness and sets it on the bar between us. "I'm not a lawyer," he says, "but I might have started with the convicted man's attorney."

"I already talked to him."

"You think a tired old saloon keeper can get your client off?"

"You aren't tired and you aren't old," I say. "Pop used to stop here almost every night on his way home from work. He must have told you something about the case."

"Not much."

"He told you more than he told me."

He squeezes his dish towel. "Sorry, Mikey. Your dad used to come here to unwind. He didn't like to talk about work. We spent most of our time talking about our wives and our kids."

I start treading gently. "Fineman's lawyer suggested that the murder weapon may have been planted by the cops."

The genial bartender's tone quickly disappears. "That was crap, Mikey. You defense lawyers are always trying to point fingers at the cops. I never saw your father so angry, and I don't blame him. He was a good cop. Internal Affairs did a full investigation. The matter was dropped. You should do the same."

I've touched a nerve. "Sometimes good cops make mistakes."

"Not your dad." He leans forward and places his elbow on the bar. "Let it go, Mikey. He was family."

The police Code of Silence is nothing compared with our family's. "Family members make mistakes, too."

He moves a little closer to me. "Not your dad. He said your client was guilty. That was plenty good enough for me."

"The cops didn't like Fineman."

"With good reason. He has no conscience."

"Did they dislike him enough to set him up for murder?"

His massive right hand tightens around his pint of Guinness. "I can't speak for the entire SFPD," he says, "but I can speak for your father. He wasn't that kind of a cop." He snaps his dish towel. "There wasn't any funny business, Mikey. Drop it."

"Then there's no reason to drop it."

He bites his lower lip. "Your dad always said you were the smartest one."

He never mentioned it to me.

"He also said that sometimes you got a little too smart for your own good."

"What do you mean?"

"He said you never knew when to let things go."

He had a point. "I'm just trying to find out what really happened." And maybe save a man's life.

He holds up a huge hand. "I don't know anything that would help you."

"Would you tell me if you knew something but you couldn't say what it was?"

He doesn't answer.

"I'm going to take that as a no."

"You can take it any way you'd like. Are we done?"

Despite his outgoing nature, my uncle can also be a stubborn cuss. "The IA file is missing," I tell him. "Pop was the last one who checked it out."

He waits a beat before he responds. "Are you saying he stole it?"

"No, I'm just saying it's missing."

"Things get lost."

I place my mug on the bar. "Did Pop tell you that he was going to look at it?"

There's a slight hesitation. "Yes."

"Why?"

"It was the only time he was investigated by IA. He was getting close to retirement. He wanted to be sure that there wasn't anything in the report that he needed to worry about. It was no fun for him—I can tell ya that, lad."

"They couldn't have taken away his pension."

"He didn't care about his pension, Mikey. After all those years, he cared about his reputation." He points a finger toward me. "At the end of the day, that's all you really have."

So true. "How was he after he looked at the file?"

"Relieved. He said everybody was cleared. It was a big load off his mind."

That's good news for my father. It isn't good news for my client. "Did he mention anything else about the file?"

"Nope." He finishes his Guinness and taps the bar to signal that our conversation is coming to a close. "Unless you're better than I at talking with people who've passed on," he adds, "you're never going to find out."

# # #

My cell phone rings as I'm leaving Dunleavy's at six-thirty on Saturday night. I flip it open and hear Pete's raspy voice. "Where have you been, Mick?" he asks.

"With Big John."

"Did he know anything about the IA file?"

"He said Pop looked at it and was cleared."

"Anything else we can use?"

"Nope. What have you got, Pete?"

"Meet me at the corner at Thirty-fifth and Clement at nine o'clock tonight," he says.

"Did you find Eugene Tsai's brother?"

"No, but I found Fitz."

"What are we waiting for?" I ask Pete. I can see my breath as the summer fog begins its nightly creep over the Richmond District between the Golden Gate Bridge and Land's End.

"Let's give him another minute," he says.

His eyes are fixed on a carefully tended green Victorian that's wedged between two apartment buildings across Clement Street from the eighth tee of the picturesque Lincoln Park Golf Course. San Francisco's oldest public links were laid out a hundred years ago, when this area was covered by sand dunes. It's showing signs of age. The greens need sod. The rusted fence is too short, but the city lacks the funds to erect a net. As a result, Fitz and his neighbors occasionally find stray Titleists in their living rooms.

I tap the dashboard of my old Corolla and force myself to remain patient. I've learned to defer to Pete when it comes to finding witnesses. A moment later I say, "Why don't we just ring the doorbell?"

"I want to catch him as he's leaving. He's less likely to slam the door in our faces."

Perhaps. "What makes you think he'll be leaving anytime soon?"

"He walks his dog at this time every night."

"How do you know?"

"You're paying me to know things like that."

On cue, the door opens. A fit man with perfect military posture and a silver crew cut leads an energetic German shepherd across the street to the fence that separates the golfers from the neighborhood. Fitz is better dressed than your average retired cop. He's wearing an Eddie Bauer work shirt, an REI vest, and a pair of top-of-the-line Nike running shoes. He's also better preserved. His chiseled face has a healthy tan that he obtained on a vacation somewhere sunnier than the Richmond.

Pete and I get out of the car and approach him cautiously from behind. "Lieutenant Fitzgerald," I say, "can we have just a moment of your time?"

He turns around and flashes a half smile. "Tommy Daley's boys," he observes. "I heard you were working on the Fineman appeal. I figured you might show up on my doorstep sooner or later."

"I guess this means it's sooner," I say. "Mind if we ask you a few questions?"

"You'll have to walk with me."

"That's fine."

As he's leading us at a brisk clip through the weeds along the fence, he turns to Pete and says, "You still working as a PI?"

"Yes."

"For what it's worth, I think you got a bum deal. Let me know if you ever decide to apply for reinstatement. I'll make a few calls."

"Thanks," Pete says. He'll ask for his old job back a couple of days after they're ice fishing in hell.

We're still making our way along the fence when I say to Fitz, "We understand you handled the IA investigation for the Fineman case."

"I did." He slows his pace slightly. "In fact, I got a call from the records office about it earlier today. They said you subpoenaed the case file."

"We did. It's missing."

"So I understand." His tone turns accusatory. "I heard your father was the last person who checked it out."

"According to the log, he was."

He shifts to a patronizing voice. "It doesn't mean he took it, Mike."

"No, it doesn't."

He's a little too anxious to tell us what we want to hear when he adds, "It was a long time ago. It probably got lost."

"Probably."

"For what it's worth, there was nothing in it that would help your appeals. Mort Goldberg made the usual wild claims about mishandled evidence. At one point, he even suggested that our guys planted the murder weapon. Everybody knew he was just blowing smoke. The guys who secured the scene were some of our best people. Everybody was cleared—including your father."

"You knew him?"

"Of course. He was a good cop with a spotless record. It was the only time he ever was investigated by IA."

Pete has been taking this in while studying every nuance of Fitz's body language. "The same can't be said for his partner," he says, trying to elicit a reaction.

Fitz doesn't bite. "Joey was a good cop, too," he says in a measured tone.

Pete isn't backing down. "Then why was he forced out?"

Fitz shakes his head a little too forcefully. "He took early retirement. You know I'm not allowed to talk about personnel matters. Department policy."

Weasels always try to hide behind procedural subterfuge. "Roosevelt told us that you and Joey were pals," I say.

"We went to the academy together."

"Wasn't there a conflict of interest when you were asked to handle the investigation in the Fineman case?"

"Not really." Pete and I follow him as he leads his dog across the empty street. "Cops in IA are allowed to go out for a beer with their friends every once in a while."

"They aren't allowed to investigate them," I say.

He holds up a dismissive hand. "We weren't that close," he says without looking at me.

"Do you have any idea what happened to the file?" I ask.

"I'm afraid not."

"When was the last time you saw it?"

"When I closed the investigation and sent it to storage."

"You didn't keep a copy?"

"Nope."

"Are you willing to testify as to its contents?"

"If I have to." He waits a beat. "You'll have to pull a subpoena."

"We will."

"Fine." He comes to an abrupt halt and squints at me through the fog. "Look," he says, "every time a big case comes down, the lawyers try to foist the blame over to the cops. Ninety-nine times out of a hundred, they're cleared."

And in cases that you investigated, they were cleared *every* time.

He isn't finished. "There wasn't any dirt in that file."

"At the moment," I say, "they can't even find it."

The genial tone turns decidedly testy. "I can't help you there. All I can tell you is that everybody was cleared. I'm prepared to testify to that effect if you insist on sending me a subpoena, but I can assure you that my testimony won't help your client." He gives me another snarky glare before he adds, "Unless you have any other questions, I need to get home." Without waiting for a response, he and his dog make their way into the foggy night.

As soon as he's out of earshot, I turn to Pete and say, "It's about what I expected."

His take is slightly more cynical. "He's an asshole."

# # #

At eleven-thirty on Saturday night, I'm back in my office, going over a draft of the first of several habeas petitions that we'll be filing over the course of the next seven days. Rosie is down the hall. Pete is parked in front of his laptop outside my office. He's searching the internet for information about Eugene Tsai.

There's a knock, and the imposing figure of Terrence "the Terminator" Love fills my doorway. Our receptionist's gentle eyes have an uncharacteristically serious cast. "You have a call," he says to me.

"Who?" I ask.

"Jerry Edwards is on hold."

My day is now complete. Edwards is the *Chronicle*'s self-appointed watchdog on real and imagined issues relating to morals, ethics, graft, and corruption. He uses his daily segment on *Mornings on Two* as a bully pulpit to whine about depravity in local government and the justice system. Our rocky relationship dates back twenty years, when he accused Rosie and me of manufacturing evidence in a murder trial when we were PDs. The accusations were dropped only after Rosie and I were put on leave for three excruciating months. The last time we were in his crosshairs was a couple of years ago, when he raked us over the coals in his column until we grudgingly agreed to take on the pro bono representation of a dying man accused of killing a hotshot venture capitalist who was buying drugs on Sixth Street.

"What does he want?" I ask.

"To congratulate you on your new case."

For a man with no formal education who used to beat the daylights out of people for a living, Terrence has a fairly advanced sense of irony. I punch the blinking light on my speakerphone. "This is Michael Daley," I say.

I'm greeted by an emphatic smoker's hack. "Jerry Edwards," he wheezes. "*San Francisco Chronicle*."

"Nice to hear from you, Jerry," I lie.

"Long time since we last talked," he says.

Not long enough. "What can we do for you?"

"I understand you're taking over Nate Fineman's appeals."

"We are."

"You have no qualms about representing the guy who manipulated the system to get the charges dropped against the Bayview Posse?"

I know better than to engage. "No comment."

"Are you going to get a stay?"

"Yes."

"You seem pretty confident."

"I am."

His coughing cuts his guffaw short. "I sat through your client's trial," he says. "He was guilty as hell."

"You're wrong."

"You really think you're going to get an appellate court to overturn the jury?"

"Yes." Enough. "Why did you call, Jerry?"

"I got an interesting call from Lieutenant Kevin Fitzgerald. I understand you're looking for the IA file on the cops who were involved in the investigation of the Fineman case."

"We are." Fitz isn't wasting any time trying to control the spin.

"Lieutenant Fitzgerald also told me that the file is missing."

"That's true."

"Do you know where it is?"

"Sorry."

"Lieutenant Fitzgerald also informed me that your father was not only one of the subjects of the investigation, but he was also the last one to check out the file."

"Also true."

He clears his throat. "You have to admit that it's quite a coincidence. I was hoping you might care to provide a comment."

"That's all it is, Jerry—a coincidence. It's a matter of public record that my father was one of the first officers at the scene. He signed out the file legitimately."

"Does that mean you're denying the obvious implication that he took it?"

"That's correct." I can feel my throat starting to tighten. "He had no reason to keep it. There isn't a shred of evidence that he did."

"Then what happened to it?"

"I don't know. That's a question for Lieutenant Fitzgerald."

"He said he didn't know, either."

"Maybe he took it. Maybe he's trying to hide something."

"Like what?"

"Evidence that proves the cops planted the murder weapon in the Fineman case."

"That's a very serious accusation. Do you have any evidence to corroborate it?"

"We're still investigating."

"Are you suggesting your father may have been involved in a cover-up?"

"Absolutely not."

"Lieutenant Fitzgerald told me that he concluded there was no wrongdoing by the SFPD."

"So I understand."

"Do you believe him?"

"I am absolutely certain that there was no wrongdoing by my

father. Otherwise, I have no way of making any other determinations, because the file is missing. We're also looking into the conduct and scope of Lieutenant Fitzgerald's investigation."

"Can I quote you for the record on that?"

"You bet." I decide to stir the pot. "Incidentally, our sources in the SFPD have refused to talk to us about the case."

"Are you saying they've been instructed *not* to discuss it?"

Not exactly. "It appears that way."

"What do you want me to do about it?"

"Report it." I can feign moral indignation with the best of them. "The public has a right to know about corruption within the SFPD—especially when it may result in the execution of an innocent man."

"You're blowing smoke."

Yes, I am. "We're trying to find the truth, Jerry."

His voice fills with sarcasm. "How admirable."

"My investigator's car was also vandalized after he started asking questions."

"San Francisco is a big city. Random acts of vandalism happen all the time."

"We believe this one was a blatant attempt to intimidate us."

"Do you have any proof?"

"Not yet."

"That isn't news. It's speculation."

So is your daily column. "If you help us find the real killer, *that* would be news."

I can hear him wheezing as he ponders his next move. "If I agree to make a few calls," he says, "are you willing to give me exclusive access to your client?"

"Sure."

"Deal."

"Was there some other reason that you called me at this hour, Jerry?"

"As a matter of fact, there is. I finally figured out why your client killed those people at the Golden Dragon."

12/ HE'S MADE A FORTUNE IN GARBAGE

'm still staring at my speakerphone. "What's the motive?" I ask Edwards.

"Money."

Oh, please. "Couldn't you come up with something a little more original than the old saw about the greedy lawyer?"

"I have. Your client owed a developer a million bucks on a project in Vail."

My airless office is silent. It's pitch-black outside my small window. There is no traffic on First Street. The blinking fluorescent ceiling light is the only source of sporadic illumination. It's hard to read the notes that I've been scribbling on the legal pad in my lap. "A million dollars is pocket change for a guy like Nate," I say.

"He was fronting the costs for a couple of big cases. Cash got tight."

It isn't uncommon for defense attorneys to advance thousands of dollars in investigation costs. Still, it seems like a stretch. "His wife has family money," I say. "She lives in St. Francis Wood. They were loaded."

"Evidently, she was unhappy about the deal and didn't want to pony up. The developer was one of his clients. A default would have brought more than a nasty letter from a collection agency."

"You're saying his own client threatened him?"

"Maybe."

"What happened to the debt?"

"Fineman's wife paid it after he was arrested."

"Who was the client?"

"A man named Alexander Aronis. He's made a fortune in garbage."

"Excuse me?"

"Aronis's company has a monopoly on trash collection from Vallejo to San Jose. He's used his garbage money to fund real estate investments."

"Where did you get this information?"

"A source in the Alameda County DA's office. Aronis is under investigation for allegedly trying to bribe a member of the Oakland City Council. The DA's investigator found some old correspondence about the Fineman investment. He remembered that I had covered the trial for the *Chronicle* and he called me."

"Is your source willing to testify?"

"Probably. I can't imagine it will help your client's case."

Neither can I. "Am I to take it you're planning to publish this information?"

"It's news. I was hoping you'd be willing to comment."

"You had to ask me about it in the middle of the night?"

"I also wanted to ask you about the IA file. I was guessing you might still be at the office. That seems to be standard operating procedure for death-penalty specialists the week before an execution."

"You guessed right. We have no comment."

"Then I'll just have to run with it as is."

Something doesn't add up. "Are you saying Nate intended to take over his client's heroin-distribution business to cover a debt to the Garbage King of Oakland?"

"Not exactly," he replies. "According to a second source, it may have been a quid pro quo deal. Aronis was going to forgive the debt if

Fineman popped Terrell Robinson and Alan Chin."

"That makes no sense. Robinson was his client."

"My source tells me Aronis also controls several major heroin-distribution channels in the East Bay. He wanted to move into the San Francisco market. In lieu of paying the debt, Fineman agreed to kill two of the big players in the city."

I'm staring at the phone in disbelief. "He didn't need the money," I repeat.

"Yes, he did, and the other pieces fit. Fineman had access to Robinson and Chin. Aronis had a track record for this sort of thing. He was once investigated for allegedly offering a hit man a hundred grand to kill one of his competitors." His voice fills with smug satisfaction. "Guess who Aronis hired to represent him? Guess who got the charges dropped?"

"Nate?"

"Correct."

It seems Nate has represented every scumbag in the Bay Area at one time or another. "Do you have any hard evidence that Aronis talked to Nate about setting up the hit?"

"Just the word of my source."

"Was your source present when this alleged conversation took place?"

"No."

"Then how the hell would he know?"

"Let's just say my source was close to the situation."

"Nate never mentioned it," I say.

"Do you think he was going to admit somebody offered him a million bucks to pop his own client?"

Now he's starting to sound like Pete. "Who's your source?" I ask.

"I can't reveal it."

"You mean you *won't* reveal it. The execution is in a week. You have an obligation to come forward."

"I have an obligation to my source," he says.

"An innocent man is going to be put to death."

"You're the one who claims he's innocent—not me."

"You have to give us something, Jerry."

"No, I don't."

"I'll go to a judge and get a court order."

"Be my guest. My newspaper has an army of lawyers who are very good at First Amendment cases."

We'll be arguing those legal issues long after Nate is executed.

# # #

First Street is empty at one o'clock on Sunday morning. Rosie went home a half hour ago. Pete and I are walking through a shroud of cool fog. I can see my breath in the heavy air. The sound of our footsteps echoes off the dark buildings around us.

"Do you think Pop took the file?" he asks me.

"He wasn't the kind of guy to cover his tracks by stealing a file." He was, however, the kind of guy who would have done everything in his power to put away a lawyer who represented San Francisco's most notorious heroin dealers.

Pete nods. "What about Edwards's claim that Fineman was paid to kill Robinson and Chin?"

"I find it hard to believe. We'll need to ask our client about it. And his wife."

"Where are you starting in the morning?" he asks.

"The deputy attorney general who is handling the case has agreed to meet with us about the IA file."

"Is the missing file enough to get a stay?"

"I doubt it."

My car comes into view as we approach my usual parking space in a cheap pay lot around the corner from the bus terminal. "Look at that," Pete says.

My eyes struggle to focus through the thick, moist air. It takes me a moment to realize that the windows of my Corolla have been smashed.

"So," he says, "do you think this is just a coincidence, too?"

13/ THAT'S PREPOSTEROUS

Sunday, July 12. 9:03 a.m.
6 days, 14 hours, and 58 minutes until execution.

Deputy Attorney General Irwin Grim is a small, intense man in his late fifties who has represented the state in more death-penalty appeals than any other lawyer in California history. The aptly named capital-punishment zealot has been dubbed "Dr. Death" by his colleagues. He has the thankless job of responding to everything we throw at him for the next six days. Dr. Death seems to enjoy the battle.

"You are overreacting, Mike," he lectures me.

"You've lost a critical file in a capital murder case," I say.

He strokes his gray hair, which is combed straight back. "I didn't lose it," he snaps.

"Either way," I say, "a key piece of evidence is missing."

He exhales heavily. Grim has turned sighing into an art form. "You're blowing things out of proportion."

"No, we aren't."

We've attracted a crowd to the SFPD file center in the bowels of the Hall of Justice on Sunday morning. The current director of Internal Affairs, an assistant chief, and the head of the records division are here. So is Fitz. Despite his attempts to downplay the situation, the presence of the assembled masses suggests Grim may be more concerned than he's letting on.

After less than four hours of sleep, I'm running on empty. I'm also in no mood for diplomacy. "The execution is in a week," I snap. "You need to find that file."

"We will," Grim assures me.

"I sure as hell hope so." Then again, maybe I don't. The California Supremes or the Ninth Circuit may be more amenable if we can demonstrate that a critical piece of evidence has vanished. "This is a matter of life and death."

Grim responds with another sigh. It's frustrating to argue with him because he never raises his voice. "It isn't that critical," he says. "It will turn up sooner or later."

He's perfectly content to try to run out the clock. "It had better be sooner, or we're going to have a serious problem."

"We're doing everything we can. If all else fails, Lieutenant Fitzgerald is prepared to submit a sworn statement as to the file's contents."

Fitz can't contain a smug nod. "I'd be happy to do a full debriefing," he offers.

He'll solemnly swear that he prepared his report with utmost care and diligence and was able to clear the hardworking and dedicated members of the SFPD. I turn to Grim and try to play to his fears. "This creates a major appealable issue," I tell him.

"Be practical, Mike."

"I am, Irwin. You're going to look terrible if you can't produce that file."

"You know as well as I do that no appellate court is going to stop the execution because of a missing file."

"It reflects sloppy police work."

"No judge will buy it."

"We're going to file papers first thing tomorrow morning."

"That's your prerogative. We will respond as quickly as possible."

He knows that we're going to file a new appeal tomorrow and every day thereafter. That's the way death-penalty cases work. The corner of his mouth turns up slightly. "I understand your father was the last person who checked it out."

This was going to come up at some point. "According to the log, that's true."

"You understand that we will have to mention that in our papers."

"That's *your* prerogative."

"Do you have any information about its whereabouts?"

"Of course not. My father followed the procedure to look at the file. If you're suggesting he kept it, you're dead wrong."

Dr. Death responds with a sigh.

# # #

Rosie and I are back at the San Quentin visitors' area two hours later. During our drive over here, we agreed to take a more direct approach with Nate. There isn't enough time to be diplomatic.

Rosie leans forward on the heavy table and addresses our client. "At the moment, we're focusing on an argument that the cops planted the gun and then tried to cover it up. That's why Internal Affairs was called in."

The bags under Nate's eyes have grown visibly larger and his voice has become raspier since yesterday. "You got any proof that the fix was in with the cops?"

"We were hoping you could give us some ammunition."

"The IA report was a piece of crap," he says. "Fitz did a quick and dirty investigation. He went through the motions and papered the file."

"Which is now missing," Rosie says. "We're going to file papers in the morning to argue for a stay because a key piece of evidence is missing."

"Do you think it will fly?"

"Hard to say," Rosie says. "Fitz is prepared to testify that he did everything by the book and everybody was cleared."

"Which means we need more."

"It would help. Did you find any evidence that the cops covered for each other?"

"Nope. They closed ranks."

Rosie keeps pushing. "Did you find anything to suggest Fitz was protecting Little Joey?"

"Nope."

"How about Dave Low?"

Nate's jowls vibrate as he shakes his head. "That's going to be even harder. You won't find another cop who will say anything bad about him."

"He isn't around to defend himself."

"We'll need more than unsubstantiated accusations to get to free-standing innocence."

He's right. "Was anybody else out to get you?" I ask.

He makes no attempt to mask his frustration. "The entire SFPD."

Time for full disclosure. "My father was the last person who checked out the file," I tell him.

Nate temples his fingers in front of his face as he chooses his words. "He probably wanted to see what was written about him. It doesn't mean he took it."

I'm grateful for the show of support, but it doesn't help our case. "Nate," I say, "did you have an overdue debt of a million dollars on a development in Vail?"

He gives me a circumspect look. "What does that have to do with a missing IA file?"

"Nothing. We're looking into some other possibilities."

"Did my wife tell you about it?"

His defensiveness is cause for concern. "No. Jerry Edwards at the *Chronicle* did."

He holds up a hand. "I owed a million bucks to one of my clients.

I paid it off after I was arrested."

"Where did you get the money?"

"From my bank account." He quickly corrects himself. "More precisely, it came from my wife's trust fund. I'm using the same account to pay you."

A trust fund—it must be nice. "We understand she wasn't happy about the deal."

"That's true. I didn't mention it to her until after I'd signed the papers." He shrugs. "We worked it out."

She may have a different take. "Edwards said she didn't trust the promoter."

"She didn't. My client, Alex Aronis, let me invest in the project as a favor after I got the charges dropped when he was accused of offering to pay somebody to take out one of his business associates."

I already knew that much. "Was Aronis guilty?"

Nate's chin juts out and he points a stubby finger in my direction. "People are innocent until proven guilty. The charges were dropped."

Amazing. After all these years, he's still talking like a lawyer. "You didn't answer my question. Was Aronis guilty?"

He summons his remaining strength to find his best lawyer voice. "Guilt is determined by a jury. My opinion doesn't matter."

I get into his face. "You aren't his lawyer anymore, Nate. You don't have to defend him. Saving your life trumps the attorney-client privilege."

He sits back in his wheelchair. "Let's just say the accusations were not entirely without merit."

Rosie has been observing this exchange in silence. She lowers her voice to a notch just above a whisper. "Any truth to the rumor that Aronis was also distributing heroin in the East Bay?"

Nate shakes his head. "The cops were never able to nail him. You won't either."

I don't believe this. "We aren't trying to nail him," I say. "We're trying to save your life. Is he involved in the sale of drugs in the East Bay?"

"Let's just say that some people whose opinions I respect seem to think so."

"I'm going to take that as a yes. Has he ever been convicted?"

"Nope."

"Did he really threaten you?"

"We had a few pointed telephone conversations about payment."

"Why are you protecting him?"

"I'm not."

"Edwards said Aronis wanted to move into the San Francisco heroin market."

"There may be some truth to that statement."

"That would have given him a motive to set up a hit on Robinson and Chin."

"That would be a logical conclusion."

I'm getting frustrated. "We don't have time for games, Nate."

"I'm telling you everything I know."

"Edwards also claimed he has a source who is prepared to testify that Aronis approached you to do it."

"That's preposterous. I was a lawyer, not a hit man."

Some might argue that the two professions are, in many respects, quite complementary. "I take it that means you're denying it?" I say.

"Absolutely."

"Edwards also suggested that you were pissed off at Robinson because he wouldn't give you a piece of his action."

Nate is becoming more agitated. "That's insane. Who's feeding him this crap?"

"He wouldn't give us a name," Rosie says. "We were hoping you could tell us."

"How the hell would I know?"

"Because Aronis was *your* client."

Nate doesn't reply.

Rosie places her long fingers on the table in front of her and lays it on the line. "If you want us to help you," she says, "you need to help us. You've been living with this case for ten years. We've been living with it for two days. We don't have time for all of this shucking and jiving. You're in line for a needle in less than six days. That means you need to tell us the truth right now—straight and fast. I'm going to ask you once more and I want a straight answer. Who is Edwards's source?"

He thinks about it for a moment. "It might have been Patty Norman," he finally says.

"Who's she?" I ask.

"Aronis's ex-wife. Last I heard, she was running one of those new age bookstores in Petaluma."

"Why would she be making these accusations now?"

"To make her ex-husband look bad." He grimaces before he adds, "And because she hates my guts."

14/ MY HUSBAND IS NOT A MURDERER

"What did you do to her?" I ask Nate.

"Long story."

"We aren't going anywhere."

He leans forward in his wheelchair. "I got in the middle of the ugliest divorce I've ever seen."

"How bad could it have been?"

"As bad as it gets. Alex and Patty had known each other since they were kids in Piedmont. Both families were loaded. His father made a mint in trash collection. Her father made a bundle in cement."

"What happened?" I ask.

"Everything started out great," he says. "They bought a nice house. Their kids went to the best schools. He coached Little League. She ran the PTA. He was promoted to the chairman of the board of East Bay Scavenger when his father died. She became a vice president of Alameda County Cement."

"What went wrong?"

"Patty's father had mob connections. The Feds were after him for years. They finally nailed him for supplying crappy cement when a freeway overpass almost collapsed. He cut a deal to plead guilty to fraud charges. He didn't do any jail time, but it bankrupted the company. They took every penny. Patty wasn't charged, but she lost her job and a boatload of money."

"I take it there were adverse consequences at home?"

He nods. "Around the same time, Alex hired me when he was being investigated for trying to hire somebody to kill one of his business associates. The charges were dropped, but it created a lot of tension at home. Neither of them handled it very well. He started staying out late. She was drinking. He ignored their kids. She ignored him. It was a mess."

"It sounds like something out of *Desperate Housewives*," I observe.

"It got *much* worse. She hired a PI to watch him. He hired one of his own to watch her. Her PI caught him in bed with his secretary. His PI caught her in bed with her tennis instructor. Counseling didn't work. A trial separation didn't help. Things spiraled completely out of control."

"These situations generally don't end well."

"This one certainly didn't. They spent a year ripping each other to shreds. They spent another year fighting about custody. It got really nasty."

Rosie hasn't said a word. I'm sure she's doing a mental calculation of how much psychological damage we've already inflicted upon Grace and Tommy.

"I can understand why she's still angry at her ex-husband," I say, "but you didn't handle the divorce. Why is she mad at you?"

"I had to pick sides. I chose Alex."

Rosie finally breaks her silence. "There has to be more to this than taking sides in an acrimonious divorce," she says. "What did you really do to her?"

Nate takes a deep breath. "I became more involved in the divorce case than I ever intended—or wanted—to be. Alex's divorce lawyer lacked imagination. I offered a few creative suggestions during the custody hearings."

"Like what?"

He gives us a sheepish look. "I came up with the idea of hiring a couple of good-looking guys to pick her up at bars and get her drunk. We had a PI take a bunch of pictures of her in compromising positions. Then we filed papers to have her declared an unfit mother because of her drinking." His grimace reflects a hint of remorse. "It wasn't the proudest moment of my legal career."

Rosie's lips turn down. "The court bought it?"

"Patty didn't have the money to fight us. She couldn't pay her lawyers. She couldn't afford experts. We overwhelmed them with paper. We paid an army of shrinks to testify that she was a danger to herself and her kids. We were able to get her committed for a year of rehab." He gives me a thoughtful look and adds, "To her credit, she came out sober."

"And without her children."

"Alex got full custody."

"How did she find out that it was your idea to have her committed?"

"I brought it up during a settlement conference. I was playing the 'bad cop.' I tried to justify it at the time by telling myself that I was help-ing a client. In hindsight, I wish I'd never gotten involved. When Alex first asked me to help with the divorce negotiations, Patty was already in bad shape. By the time it was over, she was destroyed. So was her relationship with her kids. It took her years to get back a small degree of self-respect."

"Did any of this come up at your trial?" I ask.

"No. Patty was still in rehab. The prosecutors knew she would have made a lousy witness."

"Why would she bring this up now? She certainly has no reason to help us."

"Maybe she thinks it's a chance to finally nail Alex," he says.

The chickens always come home to roost at precisely the wrong time.

# # #

Ninety minutes later, Nate's wife is sipping coffee from a bone china cup in the understated living room of her home in St. Francis Wood. This enclave of custom-built houses in the area just west of Twin Peaks was constructed as part of the post-earthquake building frenzy beginning in 1908. The results were most distinguished. The gated entrance to the community is enhanced by fountains designed by John Galen Howard and Henry Gutterson. By edict of the local neighborhood organization, the homes on the tree-lined streets were required to be in the Mediterranean Revival style. Most have picturesque Spanish grillwork, tile roofs, and ornamental windows and brickwork.

In a tribute to Ilene Fineman's perseverance, her home has been painstakingly maintained. The colorful red tiles have been freshly scrubbed. The elaborate ironwork has been buffed and polished, and the textured stucco walls have a fresh coat of white paint. Sculpted bushes surround a lush green lawn highlighted by blooming red roses and climbing bougainvillea.

Ilene is wearing a light blue cashmere sweater, a gray skirt, and a touch of makeup. Now in her mid-seventies, Nate's wife is the former chair of the symphony, ballet, and library boards. She bears an uncanny resemblance to Barbara Bush. She has the former First Lady's outspoken streak, too. Her confident smile was once a regular feature on the *Chronicle*'s society page. Her public presence receded after Nate's arrest. Nevertheless, she's been her husband's most unwavering and outspoken supporter, despite the overwhelming public perception that Nate was guilty. Ilene has been a regular on local television and radio to plead for a reopening of Nate's case.

She struggles to keep her hands from shaking as she grasps her coffee cup. Rabbi Neil Friedman is sitting in one of the antique armchairs next to her. He reaches over and touches her hand. The charismatic community leader has been holding court at Temple Beth Sholom for three decades. "Everything is going to be fine," he whispers to her. "Mr. Daley and Ms. Fernandez are here to help."

Ilene sets the cup in a saucer on the antique end table. The walnut-paneled walls are covered with photos of her three grown children and eight grandchildren. Through the picture window I can see her seven-year-old grandson and her four-year-old granddaughter playing on a new swing set in the yard. Their gleeful voices are a stark contrast to the somber mood inside the house. A wedding photo of Ilene and Nate is on the mantel. Their youthful smiles seem forever frozen in time. There is no indication that Nate hasn't been home in almost a decade.

Rosie's touch is softer than mine. We agreed before we arrived that she would take the lead. "Thank you for seeing us," she says.

"I'm ever so grateful for your assistance," Ilene replies. Her diction has the clipped inflection of a woman educated at boarding schools. Her lips tighten and she wills herself to maintain her composure as she tells us that the retainer was intended to cover only our initial costs. She assures us that she's happy to provide additional resources. "Whatever it takes to save Nate," she says.

Rosie's voice fills with genuine compassion. "I can't begin to imagine what you've been going through," she says.

"Thank you, Ms. Fernandez."

Rosie folds her hands and places them in her lap. "We're sorry to trouble you, but we need to ask you some questions about Nate's case."

"Of course."

She's interrupted gently by the rabbi. "We appreciate your efforts on Mr. Fineman's behalf," he says. "He devoted countless hours to the Bay Area Jewish community. I am appalled that the legal system has treated a distinguished citizen with such callous disdain."

His views have been documented in several op-ed pieces that he's published in the *Bay Area Jewish Bulletin*. His opinions are unlikely to influence the course of the legal system.

"We're doing everything we can, Rabbi," I tell him.

"I hope that's going to be enough."

So do I.

"It's all right, Neil," Ilene says. "Nate spoke very highly of Mr. Daley and Ms. Fernandez."

I suspect that relatively few members of Rabbi Friedman's synagogue call him by his first name. More important, I hope we can justify her faith in us and somehow match her grace under the most trying of circumstances.

Rosie starts slowly, by asking about her family. Ilene paints a picture of a tightly knit group that's held together through difficult times. She tells us that two of her children are lawyers. The third is a teacher. All of them have been unfailingly supportive of Nate. Her grandchildren range in age from eight months to nineteen years. The eldest is a sophomore at Stanford; the youngest is a freshman at nursery school. Ilene looks out the window at the children on the swing set. "The younger children have never met their grandfather," she says. "It's a terrible loss for them—and for Nate."

I catch a glimpse of Rosie's eyes. Her father never got to spend time with Grace or Tommy.

Ilene's voice flattens as she provides a somber description of the night Nate was arrested. She's been through this exercise countless times, and it hasn't gotten any easier. Her tired eyes take a downward cast when Rosie shifts the discussion to her husband. "He's a lot sicker than he's letting on," Ilene says, trying to mask the cracks in her voice. "It's hard for me to watch. He's more worried about us than himself. He's putting up a good front."

So is she. In the Daley household, we handled our problems through a cathartic process of yelling, followed by days of recriminations leading to grudging apologies. I can't imagine how we would have handled the circumstances she's been facing.

Her anger and frustration finally bubble to the surface. "I don't know why they're so obsessed with killing my husband. His kidneys are failing. He needs round-the-clock medical care. The doctors have told us he won't live longer than a year. Even if by some miracle he's released from jail, he's going to spend the rest of his life in a nursing home. It isn't enough that they took away the last ten years. Now they want to take away his last shred of dignity."

The words of comfort I learned at the seminary are escaping me now.

The rabbi tries to soothe her frayed nerves with a gentle pat to her shoulder. Seeming irritated by the gesture, she pulls away. "What are his chances of a stay?" she asks bluntly.

Rosie answers her honestly. "Not so good, I'm afraid. We're trying to prove the police planted the murder weapon, but we haven't been able to find anybody who can corroborate that theory. We're also looking for new evidence that might lead to the identification of the real killer. We're in regular contact with the California Supreme Court, the Federal District Court, the Ninth Circuit Court of Appeals, and the U.S. Supreme Court. They understand our urgency."

Ilene leans forward in the high-backed blue velvet chair. "Is this just a rote exercise for them to paper the file?" she asks.

"The people who handle the final stages of death-penalty appeals are very conscientious," I say, in hopes of providing some comfort. It's a high-pressure, low-reward endeavor—not unlike being a public defender. People seek out the positions because they have strong feelings about the death penalty. The courts try to recruit qualified people because there is no margin for error. I suspect my message rings a bit hollow, though, when I add, "We can't give up hope."

Ilene's tone fills with frustration. "Why are they doing this to my husband?"

Rosie responds with a truthful, albeit highly unsatisfying, answer.

"It's the law."

"It says you should execute a dying man who has spent ten years in a wheelchair?"

"Yes."

"That's insane."

"That's the law."

We all sit in stark silence for a surreal moment in which the only sound is from the high-pitched voices of Ilene's two grandchildren as they play outside on the swings.

Rosie tries to refocus Ilene back to Nate. "Was he a good husband?" she asks.

The question elicits a bittersweet smile. "The best. He is a kind, thoughtful, and funny man who never missed any of our children's Little League games or birthdays. Nate was a fighter in court, but he has a gentle soul."

"Did it ever bother you that he chose to represent drug dealers?"

"All the time. It reflected his personality. He came from modest beginnings. He started as a public defender. He always fought for the underdog. It was his nature. In the end, it became his undoing."

Some of us might not consider drug dealers and mob bosses to be underdogs. I glance at Rosie, whose eyes are locked on Ilene's. "It's been suggested that Nate wanted to take over his client's operations," Rosie says.

This elicits an indignant look from Ilene. "That's nonsense."

"But you would acknowledge that he liked nice things?"

"So do I." She looks around at the tasteful furnishings. "Nate had a successful practice. I come from an affluent family. He never needed to solicit for the purpose of acquiring wealth. That was contrary to everything he stood for."

"Were you having any financial difficulties or personal problems?"

"No."

"Mike and I have two children," Rosie says. "We've represented some tough characters. We know about some of the issues that you faced. Did you ever fear for Nate's safety, or the safety of your children or grandchildren?"

"Sometimes. Things were very tense when he represented the Bayview Posse."

"Is there any chance Nate might have felt threatened by any of the people who were killed at the Golden Dragon?"

"Absolutely not," Ilene says indignantly.

To me, her responses are starting to sound a little forced.

Rosie shifts subjects. "We were contacted by a reporter named Jerry Edwards last night. He said Nate owed a million dollars to a man named Alex Aronis in connection with a real estate deal. Evidently, Aronis needed the money in a hurry."

We get another hint of impatience. "I paid the debt. What's your point?"

"Edwards claimed you were unhappy about it."

"I was, but it was a legitimate debt. If Edwards is suggesting Nate killed those people because he needed money, he's wrong."

"He also suggested that Aronis may have offered to forgive the debt if Nate agreed to kill Robinson and Chin."

Ilene shakes her head slowly from side to side. "That's beyond preposterous."

"Why didn't any of this come up at the trial?"

Ilene now has a stranglehold on the arms of her chair. "Because it had nothing to do with the case. Nate and I weren't trying to hide anything."

I wonder if there is anything else that she and Nate *have* tried to conceal.

Rabbi Friedman signals his irritation by holding his palms face out. "I think those are probably all the questions Mrs. Fineman has time to answer today."

Ilene overrules him. "I am not just going to sit here and play the role of the hand-wringing widow, Neil. We have to do something. As uncomfortable as it might be for me, I am prepared to answer any questions and to do whatever it takes to save Nate's life." She turns back to us and it all comes pouring out. "I tried to be supportive, but his career made my life a living hell. Nate is right where I told him he would be if he didn't stop representing those lowlifes. He couldn't stop himself. He never wanted to turn away a client—especially the high-profile mobsters and drug dealers. It wasn't about money. He lived for the adrenaline rush in court. He loved the attention from the press. He was like a kid in a candy store during the Bayview Posse case.

"I started thinking about divorcing him even before he was arrested. The stress was unbearable. Do you know how many nights I stayed up late with the children while he was attending a meeting with a mobster or a drug dealer? Do you know what it's like when you have no idea if your husband is going to come home alive? To have your children ask you when you're putting them to bed, 'Why can't Daddy be here now?'"

Kind of. My father was a cop.

"On the night Nate was arrested," she says, "I was certain they were calling to tell me that he had been killed. What sort of life was that?" Her eyes shift from Rosie to me. "I talked to a lawyer several times before Nate was arrested. I got so angry that I had him draw up divorce papers. Nate never knew about it. A few years after he was convicted, I went to San Quentin and told him that I wanted to start a new life. He said I should divorce him and that he would let me keep everything except a few stocks to cover his legal fees. That's Nate."

"You're still married," I whisper.

"After all these years, I've never filed the papers. I couldn't leave him. I still love him and I always will. Nobody could replace him—not for me."

Rosie notices the tears welling in Ilene's eyes and hands her a tissue. "We'll do everything we can to help you," she tells her.

"I know." The room fills with an awkward silence. Finally, Ilene Fineman wipes the tears from her eyes. "My husband is not a murderer," she says softly. "If you can stop this execution, you'll be getting two people out of prison: Nate and me."

15/ YOUR CLIENT MURDERED MY FATHER

Sunday, July 12. 2:17 p.m.
6 days, 9 hours, and 44 minutes until execution.

"Johnson," the familiar baritone says. I called his cell phone.

"Daley," I reply.

"Where are you?" Roosevelt asks.

"On our way downtown." Rosie is driving—her car still has windows. We left Ilene fifteen minutes ago. We're heading down Market past Castro. The fog has lifted. It's a spectacular summer afternoon. Holding the cell phone, I'm also trying to shave with an electric razor that's plugged into the cigarette lighter. Death-penalty cases require creative multitasking. I turn off the razor and ask, "Are you at work?"

"Why would I want to be anywhere else on a beautiful Sunday?"

I knew it. "Have you ever heard of a man named Alexander Aronis?"

"He runs a big trash-disposal business in the East Bay. He's also a reputed heroin distributor." His tone is businesslike.

"Did his name ever come up during the Fineman investigation?"

"Just once." He waits a beat. "His ex-wife claimed he wanted to hire somebody to take out Robinson and Chin."

"That would be Patty Norman?"

"That would be correct."

"I didn't see her name in the trial transcripts."

"She didn't testify."

"Why not?"

"Her story wasn't credible. She had an ax to grind against her ex-husband. She was spinning out of an ugly divorce and rehab."

"Why didn't you mention it to me when we talked?"

"It was irrelevant."

Bullshit. "Aronis had a huge motive to take out Robinson and Chin."

"So did every other drug dealer in the Bay Area. It doesn't mean that he did."

"Are you holding anything else back?"

He turns testy. "I'm a cop, Mike. It isn't my job to help you defend Nate Fineman."

"I'm going to take that as a yes."

"You can take it any way you want."

He knows more than he's telling me. "Did you happen to see Jerry Edwards's column in this morning's *Chronicle*?"

"I did."

"Why is Patty Norman making these accusations about her ex-husband now?"

"I don't know. Maybe she sees it as an opportunity to settle some old business."

"Is there any chance Aronis was involved in the events at the Golden Dragon?"

"Not that I could prove. I leave the rumors and innuendos to lawyers."

The only currency Roosevelt accepts is hard evidence that will stand up in court. "Why didn't you arrest Aronis for selling drugs?"

"That's up to the law enforcement authorities in the East Bay. He operates outside my jurisdiction."

I feel like throwing my razor through the windshield. "Let me ask you about something else," I say. "It seems the IA report on the Fineman case has disappeared."

"So I'm told."

"My father was the last person whose name appeared in the log."

"I've heard that, too. It doesn't mean that he took it, Mike."

We can agree on that. "Did you ever read it?"

"Yes."

"We're going to make a stink about it. Was there anything in it that will make my father look bad?"

"No. Everybody was cleared—including your father."

"And the allegations that the cops planted the murder weapon?"

"Completely unfounded."

"Did you have any reason to question the conclusions in the report?"

"It isn't my job to second-guess IA investigations."

That's all I'm going to get. "Did I mention that the windows on my car were broken?"

"You didn't."

"I think somebody involved in the Fineman case is trying to intimidate us."

"I wouldn't know."

"Your people aren't investigating it with a great deal of enthusiasm."

"We have limited resources. Perhaps you should ask the mayor to put a few more uniforms on the street."

"I'll see what I can do. Incidentally, we haven't gotten an especially warm reception from the cops we've interviewed."

His tone turns pointed. "Your client is guilty, Mike. You shouldn't expect any extra cooperation from the highly trained and hardworking professionals of the San Francisco Police Department."

I punch the Off button. My head throbs as I lean back and close my eyes.

Rosie senses my frustration. She reaches over and squeezes my hand. "Roosevelt isn't giving you the full story, is he?"

"He's still a cop, Rosie. Realistically, there's only so much that he can do for us. He doesn't want to blow a conviction or implicate any other cops after all these years."

"Even if it was a bad conviction?"

"That's up to us to prove."

"Where does that leave us?"

My mind races at a hundred miles an hour. "We can't expect to get a stay just based on the missing file. We need a backup."

"So what's the plan?"

"There is none. You know as well as I do that death-penalty cases are improvisational theater. We need to keep pounding until we find somebody who might give us something that would convince a judge to stop the execution."

"Snapping at me isn't going to make this exercise any easier."

I feel like a jerk. It's my turn to squeeze her hand. "Sorry, Rosita."

"Forget it. The next six days will be hard enough without us going at it with each other. I take it that means you want to talk to Patty Norman and Alex Aronis?"

"I do. And I want to talk to Marshawn Bryant and anybody else who might have known something about Robinson's operations. I want to see what we can find out about Alan Chin's business, too. Pete is down in Chinatown, looking for Eugene Tsai's brother." My cell phone vibrates. I flip it open and see Pete's name. "Did you find Tsai's brother?" I ask.

"Not yet. I've run his name through all of the usual databases. He has no phone—listed or unlisted. No driver's license. No listed address. I'm going to try to track him down at Brandy Ho's later today."

Wendell Tsai isn't the only person who lives in the shadows in Chinatown. "Why did you call?" I ask.

"I need you to meet me at Rincon Center," he says. "I found Alan Chin's son."

# # #

The best spot in San Francisco for dim sum isn't in Chinatown. The place to go for the traditional appetizers and tea cakes is in a cavernous space in the old post office on Rincon Hill, just north of the Bay Bridge, in what has become a trendy residential neighborhood. The mail-sorting room was remodeled in the eighties into a mixed-use property with office space surrounding a five-story atrium that houses a dozen restaurants. Rincon Center is especially lively during weekday lunch hours, when a pianist plays show tunes and contemporary standards on a baby grand adjacent to a man-made waterfall that flows down from the glass-covered ceiling. It's a little like eating your burritos at Nordstrom, but the overall effect is a significant upgrade from your typical shopping-mall food court.

Yank Sing is a neatly appointed, white-tablecloth, Hong Kong–style dim sum emporium, where weekend brunch is in full swing at two forty-five on Sunday afternoon. Extended families in their Sunday best come to sample handcrafted dumplings, barbecued pork buns, and crab delicacies. Waitresses clad in white uniforms are pushing double-deck carts loaded with exquisitely prepared dishes.

Rosie and I wait in the atrium. Pete has gone inside the restaurant to look for Chin's son, who had a two o'clock reservation.

My brother scowls as he walks out of the packed restaurant. "He's inside," he says, "with his wife and four kids and a couple of aunts and uncles."

Swell. "I take it this wouldn't be an opportune time to approach him?"

"Good thinking, Mick. His car is probably in the garage. There's no way he's going to make the kids and relatives traipse down there. He'll pick them up outside."

"So, all we have to do is find his car and wait for him?"

"Correct." He pulls out a piece of paper with a few handwritten notes. "He drives a black Mercedes." He recites the license number.

Pete's attention to detail is unmatched. "What makes you think he'll talk to us?" I ask.

"That's where we'll need your silver tongue."

# # #

"Excuse me, Mr. Chin?" My tone is respectful as Pete, Rosie, and I follow him into the Rincon Center garage.

A middle-aged man with black hair and a custom-tailored Hong Kong suit turns around to face me. At five-five and 130 pounds, Jeffrey Chin isn't an imposing physical specimen, although the intensity in his eyes transcends his slight build.

It will serve no useful purpose to be antagonistic or disingenuous. "My name is Michael Daley," I say to him. "We're representing Nathan Fineman. We would appreciate a moment of your time."

His wiry body tenses. "You'll have to call my office. My family is waiting for me."

"Is there a possibility that we might be able to meet in the next couple of days?"

He remains polite. "I'm afraid not. My schedule is completely filled."

It could be true. In addition to running the largest independent bank in Chinatown, he's the president of the Chinese Consolidated Benevolent Association, commonly known as the Six Companies, a legendary community group that dates back to the 1860s. Its membership includes representatives of each of the six traditional *huiguans*, or Chinese social organizations. Originally formed to protect Chinese immigrants from discrimination, it has evolved into one of the great social institutions in Chinatown.

"Please, Mr. Chin," I say. "This will take just a minute."

The politeness turns to pointed anger. "Your client murdered my father."

Instinctively, I hold up my hands in a defensive posture. "I'm terribly sorry," I say. "I know it must have been very difficult for you and your family."

There's more than a hint of sarcasm in his tone when he says, "Thank you, Mr. Daley."

I have to push forward. "Mr. Fineman's attorney died suddenly on Friday night. Our firm was just hired to assist with his final appeals. As you're probably aware, the execution is scheduled for a week from today."

"So you decided to shortcut the process by accosting the victims' survivors in parking lots?"

It's a fair point. "We tried to reach you at the office. We need just a few moments of your time."

"Your client shot three people—including my father—in cold blood."

I'm not going to be able to convince him otherwise. "Were you anywhere in the vicinity of the Golden Dragon that night?" I ask.

"Are you suggesting I was involved?"

"No, Mr. Chin. We're simply trying to figure out who was there."

"I wasn't."

"Do you know anybody who was working at the Golden Dragon that night?"

He ponders for an instant before he decides to throw us a bone. "Vince Hu is the manager. He's also my cousin."

Which means he'll tell us precisely what Chin tells him to say. Nevertheless, we'll talk to him. "Do you know why your father was meeting with Mr. Robinson?"

He measures his words. "It has been well documented that they were trying to resolve certain disputed matters relating to the distribution of illegal substances. My father was involved in some endeavors that brought great embarrassment to our family. I have never condoned what he did to provide for us."

This would not be an ideal time to point out that his hands may not be squeaky clean, either. It's possible that he used some of the money his father earned from drug sales as seed capital to start his bank. "I've been through the record in detail," I lie. "I haven't found any suggestion of your involvement in your father's business activities." We will, of course, continue to look.

"The reason you found no such evidence is because there is none." His eyes remain locked on mine. "My relationship with my father was strained. The media coverage about his death was very difficult for our family. The revelations about his illegal activities were also very hard on all of us."

And I thought it was tough living with a father who was a cop. "I can't begin to imagine how difficult it must have been for you," I say.

"No, you can't. In my mother's memory, and in an attempt to reha-bilitate our reputation, I started a community bank that focuses on providing funding for small businesses in Chinatown. I'm very proud of our work. It has taken our family almost ten years to try to put this terrible episode to rest. Now you show up unannounced and want to reopen all of the bad memories. Is this a new form of ambulance chas-ing? Are you so desperate for new clients or cheap publicity?"

I backpedal quickly. "You have an excellent reputation in the com-munity," I say, attempting to move the conversation in another direction. I try not to sound too defensive when I add, "I didn't mean to offend you."

"You must be able to appreciate why I am reluctant to talk to you about this subject."

"I'm sure it brings back difficult memories for you."

"It does."

"We simply want to be sure that our client gets a fair hearing."

He adjusts the sleeve of his blue oxford shirt. "We aren't interested in retribution, Mr. Daley, and we aren't planning to attend the execution. I believe it is better to have justice than revenge. I am absolutely certain of Mr. Fineman's guilt. I would also acknowledge that it would be highly unfortunate if the wrong man is put to death."

Yes, it would. "Do you know if anybody had a grudge against your father?"

"I wasn't involved in the business. However, I was told that my father and Mr. Robinson were having difficulties dividing the market for their products."

Even drug lords worry about market share. "What can you tell me about Lester Fong?"

"His death was almost as devastating to me as my father's. He was my father's lawyer and best friend. I regarded him as my uncle." There's a hint of a reserved smile. "Living in Chinatown, we adopted many aunts and uncles over the years."

"Is it possible that somebody may have been out to get him?"

"That isn't what happened, Mr. Daley." I've worn out his patience. He pulls his keys from his pocket and pushes the remote door opener.

"Have you ever heard of a man named Alexander Aronis?" I ask.

He turns to me and gives me a look as if to say, "Are you clueless?" He gets into his car and puts his key in the ignition. "He was one of my father's competitors."

I continue hurriedly before he slams the door. "We've heard that he was attempting to procure the services of a professional killer."

"I read that in the paper this morning. I don't know anything about it."

"Do you know if your father had any contact with Mr. Aronis?"

"Whether it's banking, law, or drug trafficking, the players tend to know each other—at least informally. Most likely, the answer to your question is affirmative."

I shoot a frustrated look at Rosie, then turn back to Chin. "Did Mr. Aronis want to take over your father's business?"

He closes the door and starts the Mercedes. The automatic window descends an inch. "Every drug dealer in the Bay Area wanted to take over his business," he says, as if he's stating the obvious. "Instead of bothering me, you should be talking to the man who took over my father's drug-distribution business."

"Was that Aronis?"

"No. It was the man who took over Robinson's construction business: Marshawn Bryant."

16/ ALL I KNOW IS WHAT I'VE READ IN THE PAPERS

Sunday, July 12. 4:37 p.m.
6 days, 7 hours, and 24 minutes until execution.

Marshawn Bryant stands at midcourt in the spacious gym of the recently completed Yvonne and Marshawn Bryant Community Center in the heart of the Bayview. The new facility boasts two full-size gyms, a pool, a weight room, five classrooms, a library, and several meeting rooms. The gleaming glass structure provides a hopeful contrast with the crumbling housing projects across the street.

"Thanks for seeing us on short notice," I say to him. Rosie is with me. Pete went back to Chinatown to try to find people who were in the vicinity of the Golden Dragon on a rainy night ten years ago.

"Not a problem," Bryant says. The owner of Bayview Construction is a tall, athletic man whose meticulously cropped black hair, chiseled shoulders, and unblemished skin make him appear younger than his forty-one years. Clad in a Nike sweatshirt and state-of-the-universe Air Jordans, he looks as if he could hold his own against the Warriors' starting backcourt. He flashes an engaging salesman's smile. "Give me just a minute," he says.

He blows his whistle and a dozen enthusiastic eight-year-old girls surround him. Their eyes open wide as the charismatic Bryant towers over them like the pied piper. He tells them to break up into small groups to practice free throws. He takes an extra moment to give the smallest girl a few pointers on how to grip the ball. She gives him a passionate high five and joins her teammates.

A glowing Bryant joins Rosie and me back on the sidelines. "That's my daughter," he says. "She isn't the tallest player, but she has the biggest heart."

As a veteran of six seasons managing Grace's baseball and softball teams, I give him credit for being involved. "Do you have any other kids?" I ask.

"Our son just turned three."

I gaze up at the electronic scoreboard. "Nice place you have here."

"Thanks. We've needed something like this in the community for a long time. Yvonne and I grew up across the street. We think it's important to give something back." He explains that the city donated the land for the facility. His firm donated time, labor, and materials. "We're very happy with the way it turned out. It gives the kids someplace to go after school."

"Do you still live here in the neighborhood?"

"We live over in Noe Valley."

It's a couple of miles north of here. It's also considerably more affluent. I keep my tone conversational. "We understand your wife runs an interior design firm," I say.

"Yes, she does." He flashes another proud smile. "Yvonne was written up in *San Francisco* magazine last month."

Quite the power couple. She obviously had something to do with the design of this building, too. "How long have you been married?"

"Nine years."

"Congratulations." Better than me by a long shot.

"Thank you." We exchange banal pleasantries for another moment before his smile disappears. "So," he says, "what brings you here on a Sunday afternoon?"

"We were hoping you could provide a little information," I say. "We understand you used to work for Terrell Robinson."

"I did. He was my mentor. He gave me my first job when I was seventeen. He taught me everything I know about the construction business."

"How long did you work for him?"

"Thirteen years. I started as an apprentice carpenter. I had just been promoted to vice president when he was killed. It was a devastating loss."

It's a thoughtful sentiment, but his delivery is a tad melodramatic for my taste. "What kinds of projects are you working on nowadays?"

He slips effortlessly into sales mode. "Mostly design and build," he says. "We have relationships with several prominent architects. Most of our work involves commercial space. We also handle residential projects from time to time, which is nice because I can get the wife involved—if you see what I'm saying."

I do. He constructs and she remodels. "Would you be interested in helping us renovate our offices?" I ask. We aren't planning to remodel. I'm curious to see if he would work for a small-time operation like ours.

"It depends on the scale of the project."

"Sounds like you have more work than you can handle."

"We do. We're a qualified minority contractor. We've done several significant office projects for the city."

That's nice work if you can get it. Every major construction project for the city requires participation by one or more minority-owned firms. In theory, it's supposed to spread the work around. In practice, certain politically connected companies frequently get more than their share of the pie.

He adds, "We try to hire people from the Bayview. We think it's important to provide opportunities for the children in this corner of town."

Even though he's moved to a more upscale neighborhood like Noe Valley.

His eyes narrow, and the engaging tone disappears. "So," he says, "why did you really come all the way down to the Bayview today?"

Rosie is more than ready to get down to business. "We wanted to ask you a few question about the Fineman case," she says. "We were brought in to help with the final appeal. Unfortunately, our co-counsel had a heart attack on Friday. He's dead."

"I'm sorry to hear that."

Sure you are.

"When did you take over Mr. Robinson's operations?" Rosie asks.

"A few weeks after he passed away."

"It's very impressive that you were able to raise the financing to acquire his business so quickly."

Bryant tries for an offhand tone. "Mr. Robinson's bank gave me a loan. Most of his clients asked me to finish their projects. I was familiar with their needs. I appreciated their trust."

"Mr. Bryant," Rosie continues, "it's been documented that Mr. Robinson had other business interests besides his construction firm. In fact, he ran a lucrative heroin-distribution operation, didn't he?" She's looking for a reaction.

"All I know is what I've read in the papers. Those charges were never proven."

"He never mentioned it to you?"

The first hint of defensiveness creeps into his voice. "No, he didn't. I'm a legitimate businessman. I was not involved in any matters that extended beyond the scope of his construction business. My wife and I have funded several antidrug programs in this building. It's a huge problem. We're trying to do our part to stop the flow of illegal drugs into this community."

I didn't expect him to admit that he took over Robinson's drug cartel. Then again, his denial sounds a little too rehearsed for my taste—especially for a natural salesman like Bryant.

Rosie glances my way and I take the cue. "Have you ever met our client?" I ask Bryant.

"Once, when he visited Mr. Robinson's office."

"Weren't you concerned that your boss was meeting with a criminal-defense lawyer?"

"It isn't uncommon for people in the construction business to face civil litigation or even criminal charges from time to time. It's a cost of doing business. The fact that he was never convicted is a testament to his honesty and integrity."

Or that he hired a smart lawyer. "Some people think Mr. Fineman was involved in Mr. Robinson's heroin operation. In fact, it's been suggested that Mr. Fineman killed Mr. Robinson because he wanted to take over his business."

"I wouldn't know."

Rosie reenters the discussion. "Would you mind telling us where you were on the night Mr. Robinson was killed?"

His polished façade shows a hint of impatience. "I cooperated with the police ten years ago," he says. "Do we really have to go through this again?"

Rosie keeps her tone measured. "If you wouldn't mind," she says. "We're just trying to fill in some details."

"You can find them in the police reports."

"We were hoping you might be willing to give us the highlights."

He exhales melodramatically. "Yvonne and I were working late on a design project at the office." The corner of his mouth turns up slightly. "Then, well, if you must know, we ended up at her place. Those were our dating days, as she called them."

I might have used a slightly more colloquial term.

"Were you anywhere near the Golden Dragon that night?" she asks.

"Of course not."

Rosie ups the ante. "The police told us that a witness saw you in the alley behind the restaurant right after the shootings."

"It wasn't me," he says calmly. "People make mistakes."

"Do you really think he would have been mistaken about seeing an African American man in an otherwise empty alley in Chinatown at one o'clock in the morning?"

Still no discernable reaction. "It wasn't me," he repeats. "I was with Yvonne. You can ask her about it if you'd like."

She isn't going to change her story. I push him a little harder. "Mr. Bryant," I say, "it would make our lives—and yours—a lot easier if someone else could corroborate your whereabouts that night."

He pulls his whistle out of his pocket and walks toward his team. "This conversation is starting to sound a little too much like a cross-examination," he says. "I don't appreciate your tone or your implication, Mr. Daley." He blows his whistle and asks the children to line up on the end line. "We have to finish practice."

# # #

Rosie takes a deep breath of the heavy summer air. "You're smelling a bit raw, Mike," she says.

We're driving down Mariposa Street toward downtown at five-fifteen on Sunday afternoon. The good news is that the Giants won. The bad news is that we're sitting in an un-air-conditioned car in grid-locked ballpark traffic.

"Sorry," I say. You don't always get a lot of time to address some basic human needs when you're trying to stop an execution. I'll be making good use of the shaving kit that I keep in the trunk of the car for the next week or so. "I'll grab a shower back at the office."

She holds a finger to her nose. "A clean shirt and some deodorant might be nice, too."

"Duly noted."

Her eyes never leave the road as she says, "Bryant knows more than he told us."

"Yes, he does. So does Chin."

"I think Bryant is a better bet. Chin didn't seem like a guy who would have killed his father."

I pull out my cell and hit the speed dial. Pete picks up on the first ring. "Are you still in Chinatown?" I ask him.

"Yes. Did you get anything from Bryant?"

"A bunch of denials. I want you to have someone keep an eye on him."

"I will."

"Anything else?"

"Maybe. I found a retired cop named Carl Yee who was working undercover in Chinatown on the night of the shootings."

"Was he anywhere near the Golden Dragon that night?"

"We'll find out. I persuaded him to meet us for dinner tonight."

Sunday, July 12. 11:00 p.m.
6 days, 1 hour, and 1 minute until execution.

Pete's eyes move rapidly as he devours a plate of roast squid with salt and pepper, the house specialty at Yuet Lee, one of the city's finest and least pretentious seafood restaurants. As always, the squid arrived piping hot with a little dish of green peppers and two slices of lemon on top. The restaurant isn't big on atmosphere. It's located in a nondescript building at the corner of Stockton and Broadway, where Chinatown meets North Beach. The bright fluorescent lights and lime green interior make everyone look twenty years older, but once you start eating, you don't care. Open until 3:00 a.m., it's been a hangout for cops, writers, and night owls for years. The place is still packed at eleven o'clock on Sunday night.

You have to make certain accommodations when you have dinner with a couple of ex-cops. First, you have to let them sit at a table where they can see all of the entrances and exits. Second, you have to deal with the fact that they're watching everybody around them with unusual scrutiny. Third, you have to chow down quickly, because they eat fast.

My brother places a piece of his squid on a small plate and pushes it over to our dinner companion. "Try it," he offers.

Carl Yee demurs with a polite but firm "No thanks." The former undercover cop is a compact man in his mid-fifties with intense eyes, large hands, and a prominent scar that runs from the bridge of his nose across his forehead and under his closely cropped gray hair to his left ear. He picked up the souvenir three decades ago in a drug bust that went sideways. He adjusts the sleeves of his black leather bomber jacket and pushes the plate back to Pete. Then he continues to poke at a bland stir-fried vegetable concoction that the kitchen made up specially for him. "Bad stomach," he says.

"We appreciate the fact that you came tonight," I tell him.

"Roosevelt said you're okay," he replies.

Glad to hear it. "How long were you on the force?" I ask.

"Twenty-six years." He takes me through his curriculum vitae in clipped police dialect. Born in Chinatown; attended Galileo High; joined the SFPD when he turned twenty-one; spent much of his time undercover in Chinatown; lives in the Sunset; took early retirement eight years ago to start his own security firm. He and Pete could hold an entire conversation consisting of three-word sentences.

"Did you ever work with my dad?"

"Yep. Solid cop."

I'm not about to disagree with him. I ask him if he was working undercover on the night Nate was arrested.

"Yep." He says he was monitoring a delivery of amphetamines in an alley off Stockton Street. He found out about the events at the Golden Dragon the next day.

"Was anybody else working in the vicinity that night?"

"Yep."

"Who?"

He picks at his vegetables. "Don't know."

"You must have known about Alan Chin's organization," I say.

"Yep."

"Did you know Dave Low?"

"Yep." The admiration in his eyes is genuine. "Good cop. Huge loss."

"Any black marks on his record?"

There is an almost imperceptible pause. "Nope."

"Was he watching the Golden Dragon that night?"

"Don't know."

"There were some questions about the handling of the evidence."

"That was crap."

"The defense claimed the murder weapon was planted."

"More crap." He places his chopsticks on the table. "IA dealt with it."

"We've been told that Kevin Fitzgerald wasn't the most tenacious guy in IA."

"He did his job."

"Did you ever talk to him about the case?"

"Nope."

"The IA file is missing."

"I heard."

"Do you have any idea who may have taken it?"

"Nope."

Pete puts his chopsticks down. "You know that they found a witness who was in the alley that night, don't you?"

"Yep."

"You heard he got popped a couple of days later?"

"Yep. It was a robbery."

"Is that what really happened?"

"As far as I know."

It's a more equivocal answer than I expected.

Pete studies his former colleague's eyes. "Let me ask you something," he says. "Off the record, ex-cop to ex-cop. Why did you really come down here tonight?"

Yee tenses. "What do you mean?"

"You could have told us everything you've just said in a two-minute phone conversation. Why did you come all the way here to see us?"

He quaffs his ice water. "I was an old-fashioned cop."

"So?"

Yee's jaws tighten. "Look at it like this," he says. "Two drug bosses and a mob lawyer get popped in Chinatown. They find the accused in the alley with a gun in his hand. A potential witness goes down a couple of days later. Call it an old cop's intuition, but it didn't feel right."

That may be the most words that Carl Yee has strung together in years. Then again, we'll need more than an old cop's intuition if we're going to persuade the California Supreme Court and the Ninth Circuit to stop Nate Fineman's execution in the next six days.

Monday, July 13. 12:34 a.m.
5 days, 23 hours, and 27 minutes until execution.

"Nice shirt," Rosie says.

"Thanks," I say. "It isn't new."

"It's reasonably clean." She winks. "That's progress."

While Pete and I were eating squid with Carl Yee, Rosie was busy working on our habeas petition. I stopped at her house on my way home to read it. We're arguing two theories: first, that Lou Cohen's death will make it impossible for Nate to have adequate representation; second, that the missing IA file brings the integrity of the investigation —and Nate's conviction—into question.

I hold up the petition with admiration. "This is good," I tell her.

"Thanks. We'll get it on file when the courts open later today." Her expression doesn't change when she adds, "After it's rejected, we'll file another one tomorrow."

It's a realistic assessment. For the next five days, we will be fully engaged in a procedure known as successive petition litigation. It means we'll be filing a new habeas petition every day until the end. The process will continue until hours or even minutes before the execution. We'll challenge everything from the handling of the evidence to the inherently cruel nature of the death penalty. Since we are no longer allowed to dispute errors from the original trial record or matters previously raised on appeal, our best bet is to raise the possibility of new evidence. It would, of course, enhance our position considerably if we could actually find some new evidence. The rules now require us to go directly from the California Supremes to the Ninth Circuit without an intervening stop at the Federal District Court. If the Ninth Circuit buys our story, they may send us back to the district court for further proceedings. If they turn us down, we'll go directly to the U.S. Supreme Court, where our chances are almost nonexistent.

"Did you get anything from Yee?" she asks.

"He said there were undercover cops in the area."

"We already knew that, Mike. Any specifics?"

"Pete's looking."

"He needs to look fast. They've already asked Nate what he wants for his last meal."

# # #

At six-fifteen on Monday morning, I drag myself over to the Channel Two studios in Oakland for a live one-on-one with Jerry Edwards. I feign indignation at the suggestion that Nate was offered money to murder Robinson and Chin. I try not to come off as defensive or arrogant when Edwards tries to bait me. We volley back and forth as he tries to pin the blame for the missing file on my father. He mugs into the camera and cuts to a commercial just as I'm pleading for new information that might lead us toward identifying another suspect.

# # #

At the stroke of nine o'clock on Monday morning, our messenger files our papers with the California Supreme Court and the Ninth Circuit. At ten-thirty, we get a call from Ted Prodromou, who was the smartest guy in Rosie's law school class. Now he's the smartest staff lawyer at the California Supreme Court. He's also the designated death-penalty attorney for our case. It's always better to work with a bright lawyer—even if he's on the other side. The Ninth Circuit and the U.S. Supreme Court have each assigned a point person as well. They'll have the thankless task of coordinating the distribution of our papers to their respective bosses on short notice. By contemporary bureaucratic standards, the system is reasonably efficient.

"We received your papers," Prodromou tells us in his soft-spoken manner. "I already got a call from Irwin Grim."

We're required to provide Grim with a copy of everything we file with the courts. I can picture Dr. Death studying our papers in his windowless office. "What did the distinguished deputy attorney general have to say?" I ask.

I can hear the laid-back chuckle in Ted's voice. "He sighed."

True to form. "I take it this means he plans to respond?"

"He already has."

Impressive. He anticipated our filing and spent the weekend preparing a reply brief. "Did he have any other reaction after he finished exhaling?"

"Sure. He said your claim was without merit."

Big surprise. "Do you agree with him?"

"Hey, not my decision."

"Any hints from the folks in the black robes?" The big guys will make the final call. But they will rely heavily on the opinions of Ted and his cohorts to shape their views. Ninety-nine times out of a hundred, the staff attorneys get it right.

"I'll know more in a couple of hours," he says. "I understand the urgency."

Ted is astute enough not to show his cards.

"I was hoping you might be available to sit down with Irwin and me at one o'clock," he says. "I want to make sure everyone is on the same page."

It can't hurt to see what Dr. Death has to say. "We're in."

"I have to ask you for another favor."

"Which is?"

"You and Rosie have to promise not to sigh."

# # #

Deputy Attorney General Irwin Grim exhales with a melodramatic flourish at one o'clock on Monday afternoon. His thin tie is wound so tightly around his neck that it's hard to imagine any oxygen can reach his brain. As always, Dr. Death's nasal voice is flat. "I am duly sympathetic about Lou Cohen's death," he intones. "However, there is no legal authority to delay an execution just because the convicted murderer's attorney died shortly before it was scheduled. Furthermore, the missing IA file has no bearing on this case."

We're meeting in a workmanlike conference room on the third floor of the Earl Warren Building, a six-story masterpiece on the north side of Civic Center Plaza, where the California Supreme Court has conducted business since 1923. The classic granite edifice is a stylish mix of architectural elements inspired by the Italian Renaissance. Corinthian pilasters and cartouches embellish its southern facade, which is subtly bowed about eighteen inches at either end, thereby giving the optical illusion that the building is flat in elevation. Severely damaged in the Loma Prieta earthquake, the Warren Building underwent a two-hundred-million-dollar restoration that was completed almost ten years later, in 1998. The interior is still utilitarian, although the Supreme Courtroom, on the fourth floor, was restored to its original understated brilliance.

"You understand there's no way to correct a mistake if you execute an innocent man," I say to Grim.

"I do." He leans across the oak conference table. "That has no bearing on our interpretation of the law as long as your client is represented by competent counsel."

"This isn't a purely academic exercise," I say. "A man's life is at stake. You can choose to interpret the law to meet the needs of justice and fair play." He can't possibly argue with justice and fair play, right?

Wrong. "It is my policy to leave those decisions to the courts."

There's no convincing Dr. Death.

Ted Prodromou takes a sip of black coffee as he studies his notes. His unblemished features and trim, athletic build make him look younger than fifty. "The purpose of this meeting is to discuss the status of the pending habeas petition," he says to nobody in particular. "I am not in a position to comment on the substance of your arguments at this time. I want to be sure this case is handled in an orderly manner."

We nod in unison.

"When are you going to rule on the petition they filed this morning?" Grim asks.

"Soon."

"How soon?" I ask.

"Very soon," Prodromou says. "The standard is quite clear: we need to be sure that your client is adequately represented by competent counsel. I know for a fact that the attorneys in this room are all highly qualified."

As hard as I might try, it will be difficult to persuade him that I'm an idiot. He can't say it out loud, but he's telling us that our argument is a loser.

Prodromou consults his notes. "You've been through the drill," he continues. "We will make every effort to accommodate you. I can't stop you from pleading your case to the media. However, I would remind you that only the courts and the governor can rule upon this matter."

"What about the missing file?" I ask.

"As far as I can tell, there was no evidence of any irregularities in the investigation. Lieutenant Fitzgerald's agreement to provide a sworn summary of its contents mitigates the damage."

"It's going to be impossible for us to do anything meaningful in five days," I say.

"Legally, your client's position hasn't changed significantly since Mr. Cohen's death. Your petition is under submission. The fact that a new defense team will be handling the final stage is largely irrelevant to the legal ramifications of his case. Of course, our justices will take into account the seriousness of the charges and the finality of the consequences."

This time Grim doesn't sigh. In fact, a barely perceptible sideways grin crosses his face. He knows his cards are better than mine. He's perfectly content to run out the clock.

Monday, July 13. 3:30 p.m.
5 days, 8 hours, and 31 minutes until execution.

Mort the Sport is holding court from his wheelchair, which is perched on the front steps of Temple Beth Sholom, at Fourteenth and Clement. Despite more pressing matters, Nate insisted that Rosie and I attend Lou Cohen's funeral. The overflow crowd represented a multigenerational cross section of everybody who has ever been anybody in the San Francisco legal, political, and Jewish communities over the last half century. Rabbi Friedman delivered a heartfelt eulogy. Lou was the type of lawyer that I aspire to be. The rabbi is the type of clergyman that I never was.

Mort gestures to me with his unlit cigar. "Come over here, Mike," he says.

Despite the post-funeral setting, Mort pulls me down close to his face and starts firing questions. "Tell me quick—have you figured out a way to stop the execution?"

I don't want to have this conversation on the front steps of a synagogue fifteen minutes after the conclusion of a funeral service. "We're working on it."

"Work faster."

Thanks for the advice.

We watch in silence as Cohen's family walks past us. We have a full agenda, and I'm desperately looking for a polite way to make a fast exit. Cohen's son, Ben, looks like his father. He helps his mother into the limo, then moves toward us. He leans over Mort's wheelchair and extends his hand. "Thanks for coming," he says to him.

"You're welcome, Ben." Mort grips his hand more tightly. "I'm sorry about your father. He was a fine human being and a superb lawyer." The old warhorse never quite got around to burying the hatchet with Lou. This is the best that he can do.

Cohen's son is a noted attorney in his own right. He swallows hard. "Thanks, Mort. It would have meant a lot to him."

Rosie and I stand in silence as Mort and Ben exchange a quiet word. I can't help glancing at my watch. It's already three thirty-five. We still have a very full day ahead of us. A moment later, Ben turns and politely shakes Rosie's hand, then mine. "Thank you for coming today," he says. "I know you have a full plate."

"We're so sorry," I say.

"Thanks for stepping in to handle the Fineman appeal. My father always spoke very highly of you."

"He was an excellent lawyer." I mean it.

He nods. "I was going to call you tonight."

"Not necessary," I say.

"It may be." He pulls a scrap of paper from his pocket. "I found this phone number on a pad in my dad's study on the night he died. It's the number for the Shanghai Residential Hotel in Chinatown."

"And?"

Mort's eyes open wide. "Wendell Tsai used to live there," he says.

Monday, July 13. 4:35 p.m.
5 days, 7 hours, and 26 minutes until execution.

An hour later, Pete and I are standing at the door to Wendell Tsai's single-room apartment in a dilapidated tenement on Waverly Place, a lightless alley in the historical heart of Chinatown that runs parallel to Grant Avenue and extends two blocks from Sacramento to Washington. A century ago, Waverly was a commercial and residential hub. It was also the home of several bordellos, then known as parlor houses. The whorehouses are long gone, but the faded brick walk-ups with rusting ornamental grillwork are still crowded with low-income residents, most of whom speak only Chinese.

The aroma of sweet spices wafts through the dim hallway as Pete raps on Tsai's worn wooden door. "Mr. Tsai," he says gently, "could we talk to you for a minute?"

The door opens a crack. A slight man eyes us cautiously from behind large sunglasses. He's dressed in a black polo shirt and gray polyester pants. "Sorry," Tsai says in halting English. "I go to work."

Pete leans in front of the narrow opening. "This will just take a moment."

"Can't help."

"We have some information about your brother. We just wanted to ask you a few questions."

There is a hesitation before the door opens a little wider. Tsai quickly surmises that we'll never make the list of America's Most Intimidating People. "What you want?"

"We're sorry to trouble you," Pete says. "We're representing a man named Nathan Fineman. We've just taken over the case from Mr. Louis Cohen. I believe you may have spoken to Mr. Cohen."

Tsai freezes. "Eugene is dead," he whispers.

"We know. We're very sorry." Pete's voice is soothing. "I hope Mr. Cohen explained to you that our client had nothing to do with your brother's death."

Tsai nods.

Pete lowers his voice to a whisper. "Mr. Cohen died on Friday. We've been asked to help with the final appeals for his client."

Tsai's lips turn down, but he doesn't reply.

Pete tries again. "Would you mind telling us what you and Mr. Cohen talked about?"

Silence.

I invoke my priest voice. "Please, Mr. Tsai. This is a matter of life and death."

More silence.

Pete steps closer to the door and plays a hunch. "Did someone threaten you, Mr. Tsai?"

There's a pause. "Someone break into my room," he says.

"When?"

"Last Thursday."

Maybe it's the same person who smashed the windows of our cars. "Did they take anything?" Pete asks.

"Picture of Eugene."

My heart starts beating faster. "Mr. Tsai," I say, "we want you to be safe. I've been a lawyer for more than twenty years. I have excellent contacts with the police. We can get you protection."

This elicits a cynical eye roll. "Police promise to protect Eugene."

"Things are different now."

"Not true."

Pete tries to reassure him. "A man named Carl Yee used to be a police officer in the neighborhood. He now owns a security firm. We'll hire him to protect you."

"You pay?"

"Absolutely," I say.

Again, no response.

"Mr. Tsai," I say, "it is very disturbing to me that somebody broke into your room. I don't want anything to happen to you. Your brother was very brave. In his memory and in the interest of justice, I hope you'll be willing to help us. We would like to find out who was responsible for killing your brother just as much as you would."

He hesitates for what feels like a full minute. Then he decides to open the door.

# # #

"Eugene was seventeen when we come here," Tsai tells us. He's sitting on a worn sofa in the dark room. The furnishings include a small Formica table, two card chairs, and a three-drawer dresser. The walls were painted off-white long ago. Now they're dull gray. Across from the sofa are a noisy mini-refrigerator and a hot plate. The only hint of modern technology is a small TV with rabbit ears, which is tuned to a Chinese-language station. The bathroom is down the hall. The telephone is down the stairs. The laundry is down the street.

Tsai tells us that he and his younger brother came to San Francisco from Taiwan with their father after their mother died. Two years later, their father was killed in an accident in the clothing factory where he worked as a janitor. His death left the brothers to fend for themselves. They shared the rent for this single room. Wendell found a job as a bus-boy at Brandy Ho's restaurant. Eugene worked nights in the laundry at the Chinese Hospital.

"Eugene very smart," he says. He tells us that his brother took English classes during the day and worked at night. He used to walk home through the alley behind the Golden Dragon. He was only nineteen when he died.

"Did Eugene talk to you about what happened in the alley on the night of the shootings at the Golden Dragon?" I ask.

Tsai's eyes dart over my left shoulder. "Yeah."

"Did he hear any shots?"

"No."

"Did he see anyone?"

Tsai looks down. "He see black man."

The mere presence of an African American man in an alley in Chinatown in the middle of the night is suspicious. "What was the man doing?"

"Running."

"Where?"

"Out of alley."

"When did your brother tell you about this?"

"When he get home."

"Did he get a good look at the man?"

"No. The man stop for just a second."

"I understand that Eugene talked to the police."

Tsai nods. "I tell him not to. Eugene do it anyway."

Which may have gotten him killed. "Did you go with your brother to the police station?"

"No. Was working."

"Did the police show him any photos?"

"Yeah."

"Did he recognize anybody?"

He shakes his head vigorously. "No."

Hell. "And he was killed two days later?"

"Yeah." His tone turns adamant. "Stabbed."

"And the police never found the man who killed him?"

"No. Police said it was robbery. No witnesses."

"Do you think they were right?"

"No. I think it was man from alley."

"How did he know that your brother had talked to the police?"

His eyes narrow and his English becomes clearer. "No secrets in Chinatown."

I would give anything to prove that Tsai saw Marshawn Bryant in the alley. "Did your brother walk home by himself on the night of the shootings at the Golden Dragon?"

He's becoming more engaged—as if he's been waiting for the opportunity to tell his story. "No. He walk home with his friend. She live in apartment in the alley. She work at hospital, too."

"Do you know her name?"

"Jasmine Luk. Very pretty girl."

This could be huge. "Were they still together when Eugene saw the man in the alley?"

He nods. "Yeah."

"Did Jasmine see him, too?"

"Yeah."

"Did you ever talk to her about it?"

"No."

Pete and I exchange a glance. "Did she talk to the police?"

He scowls. "Don't know."

Roosevelt never mentioned any of this. "Do you know where we can find her?"

"No. She gone."

"Where?"

"Don't know."

"When did she leave?"

"Day after Eugene was killed. She got scared."

"Do you have any idea where she went?"

"No. Maybe back to China. Hard to find her now."

We're going to have to try.

# # #

"Did you get anything from Tsai?" Rosie asks.

"His brother saw an African American man in the alley," I tell her.

I'm standing on the corner of Waverly and Washington at six o'clock on Monday night. Pete, Tsai, and I just finished a meeting with Carl Yee, who agreed to watch Tsai for the next week at a slight premium over his standard rates.

"Any chance it might have been Bryant?" she asks.

"He couldn't make a positive ID."

"That isn't going to get us to freestanding innocence."

"Tsai walked home with a young woman named Jasmine Luk, who also worked at the hospital. They were together when Tsai saw the man in the alley. She must have seen him, too."

"Did she talk to the cops?"

"I don't know. I put in a call to Roosevelt."

"Can you find her?"

"Pete is already looking."

"So," she says, "we just need to find a phantom woman who may or may not exist, and who may or may not be able to identify a man she may or may not have seen for a second or two in a dark alley on a rainy night ten years ago."

That covers it. "It may be our best chance," I tell her.

"At the moment, it may be our only chance," she says.

"I take it this means the news isn't good on the appellate front?"

"Correct. The California Supremes and the Ninth Circuit ruled against us on the papers we filed this morning. We'll try the U.S. Supreme Court, but we aren't going to win."

"How are you doing on the next round of petitions?"

"They'll be ready to file first thing in the morning."

"What are we going to talk about this time?"

"I won't know until I start writing our papers, Mike."

We'll be having the same discussion every night for the next week. "When do we tell them about Jasmine Luk?" I ask.

"Not yet. Let's hold off until we see if we can find her." She clears her throat. "There's something else."

I can tell from her tone that something is wrong. I brace myself. "What now?"

"My mother just called. A man in a UPS uniform rang our door-bell and Grace answered. She thought he was delivering handles for our kitchen cabinets. He wasn't."

Uh-oh. "Is she okay?"

"Yeah."

"But?"

"Inside the package there was a photo of Grace and Jake that was taken in the last couple of days."

I can feel the back of my neck starting to burn. "Did she talk to him?"

"No. He left the package and ran."

"Did she call the cops?"

"Of course. They haven't found anyone in the area."

"Was there a note?"

"No, but the message is quite clear: somebody knows where we live."

Monday, July 13. 6:45 p.m.
5 days, 5 hours, and 16 minutes until execution.

"Everything is going to be fine," Roosevelt says to Grace. They're sitting on the sofa in Rosie's living room. The homicide inspector's melodious voice is calming. He's taken off his suit jacket and loosened his tie. His arm rests on her shoulder. He's the closest thing Grace has to a living grandfather.

Our daughter is visibly glum. Her hands are shaking as she tugs nervously at the sleeves of a black Giants sweatshirt. "I should have called you sooner," she tells him.

Roosevelt hasn't taken his eyes off her since he walked in the door. "You did everything you could, honey," he says.

"It wasn't enough. I should have followed him."

"No, you shouldn't have. There's nothing you could have done, Grace. He may have been very dangerous. You did exactly the right thing."

"He's still out there," she says.

"It's my job to find him. In the meantime, I want you to be extra careful."

"I will."

"Can you describe him?" he asks.

"I didn't get a good look at him. He rang the bell and left the package outside the door. Grandma was in the bedroom with Tommy. I saw him for just an instant. African American. Wearing a UPS shirt and hat. Didn't say anything. I'm sorry, Roosevelt."

"You have nothing to apologize for, Grace."

It is unusual for a San Francisco homicide inspector to take a police report in Marin County. But Roosevelt isn't a conventional cop. A Larkspur police officer is at his side. A sheriff's car sits in the driveway. I expect a battalion of San Francisco cops in riot gear to show up at any moment.

"How tall was he?" Roosevelt asks.

"About six-two. Probably about two hundred pounds."

"What time was he here?"

"A little over an hour ago." She says she called Rosie first, her boyfriend second, the Larkspur police third, and Roosevelt last. I feel left out of the loop. The Larkspur cops arrived within minutes. Their search of the area turned up empty.

"Do you think it was a real UPS driver?"

"I doubt it. I didn't see a truck and I didn't hear one pull away."

The intruder undoubtedly had a car, which means he has a good head start. We have no idea what type of vehicle he was driving.

Roosevelt strokes his chin and addresses all of us. "It is extremely important that each of you act with great caution," he says. "I don't have to tell you to be very careful. It's obvious. Call me right away on my private cell phone if you see anything unusual—no matter what time it is. Understood?"

We nod in unison.

"The Larkspur police will have a squad car in your driveway. We are doing the same for Jake and his family. Furthermore, I am assigning a San Francisco police officer to watch this house. You will have twenty-four-hour protection until this matter is resolved."

Rosie is demonstrably agitated. "Do you have any idea who did this?"

"I'm going to find out." He turns and gives Grace a grandfatherly hug. "I need to talk to your parents for a few minutes, Gracie. You don't mind, do you?"

"Is it okay if I call Jake?"

"Sure," Roosevelt says.

She heads toward her bedroom. I turn to Roosevelt and struggle to keep my tone even. "We're depending on you," I say, feeling helpless and guilty that my family is now a target.

"I've assigned my best people. They'll take care of you."

I can feel my throat constrict. "Is it okay for Grace to talk to Jake?"

"I've already talked to his parents. They understand the gravity of the situation. It's a bad idea *not* to let her talk to her boyfriend."

Probably true. "This isn't just a coincidence," I say.

"It's obvious that somebody is trying to distract you from the Fineman case."

"They're trying to do more than that."

He turns to Rosie. "Call me right away if Grace says anything else about the man who delivered that package."

"I will. I don't want our daughter to be caught in the middle of this exercise."

Roosevelt sighs. "I'm afraid she already is."

"Should we take her away until this case is over?" I ask.

It's Rosie who answers. "I'm not going to let somebody chase me out of my own house."

Roosevelt agrees. "We'll have plenty of cops outside. You'll be fine if you're careful."

I hope so.

He examines the grainy Polaroid taken of Grace and Jake as they were walking in front of Rosie's house. It's been carefully placed inside a clear plastic evidence baggie and tagged. "We won't find any prints on this photo," he says. "You may want to hire somebody for backup."

Pete is already on the phone with one of his best operatives.

Roosevelt addresses Rosie. "I'm going to arrange for an escort for you, too. Let me know if you need anything else."

"Thanks, Roosevelt."

# # #

Roosevelt and I are standing outside on Rosie's front porch a few minutes later. "I talked to Eugene Tsai's brother," I tell him. "I understand Eugene saw an African American man in the alley behind the Golden Dragon shortly after the shootings."

"He did, but he couldn't identify him."

"I take it this means you couldn't identify him, either?"

"Correct."

"It could have been Marshawn Bryant," I say.

"Bryant had an alibi."

"From his girlfriend."

"There was no way to refute it."

"You didn't try very hard."

"Yes, I did."

"Why are you being so defensive?"

"I did everything I could, Mike."

It wasn't enough. "Did you ever talk to a young woman named Jasmine Luk?"

"Yes."

"Why didn't you mention it?"

"It was irrelevant. She didn't provide any useful information."

"Tsai's brother said she walked home with Eugene and saw the same black man in the alley."

"Not according to her."

"What do you mean?"

"She said she didn't see anybody in the alley."

"How is that possible?"

"I don't know."

"She was so scared that she fled."

"I'm well aware of that, Mike."

I can feel my right hand squeezing into a tight fist. "You aren't telling me everything, Roosevelt."

"I've told you everything that I can."

"What *haven't* you told me?"

"Nothing."

My face is turning red. "There were two witnesses in the alley who saw the same black man. You didn't mention either of them to me."

"They provided no evidence that we could use."

"How can you withhold information less than a week before an execution?"

He folds his arms. "You can't expect me to do your job for you, Mike."

"Did the police plant the murder weapon?"

"Absolutely not."

We stare at each other in silence for a long moment. "Do you have any idea what happened to Jasmine Luk?" I ask.

"No."

"She just disappeared into thin air?"

"As far as we could tell."

I look into the eyes of my father's old partner. "Doesn't this bother you?"

"We did all that we could, Mike."

We haven't. "Any chance you could spare an unmarked car to keep an eye on *my* backside?"

"Probably. Are you going somewhere?"

"Yes. Just as soon as your people are in place to guard this house."

"Is Rosie okay with that?"

"She doesn't want me hovering around here. It makes everybody nervous."

"Where are you going?"

"Pete and I are having dinner at the Golden Dragon."

Monday, July 13. 7:38 p.m.
5 days, 4 hours, and 23 minutes until execution.

" **P**arty of two?" Vincent Hu asks in a modulated voice, looking at us over the top of a pair of thin Calvin Klein reading glasses. Jeff Chin's cousin is a meticulously dressed man of indeterminate middle age whose custom navy suit, powder blue shirt, and pressed kerchief exude understated professionalism. He's standing behind the ornate podium inside the entrance to the Golden Dragon.

"Yes, please," I say.

The glasses come off. "Right this way."

He escorts us through the inviting space that's decorated with intricate figurines of mythological winged beasts. Pete and I are enveloped in the aroma of spring rolls, broccoli beef, shrimp in lobster sauce, and Peking duck. The Golden Dragon is one of San Francisco's finest Cantonese restaurants. It's also its most notorious—a reputation that evolved long before the deaths of Terrell Robinson, Alan Chin, and Lester Fong. In 1977, a long-standing feud between two Chinatown gangs—Joe Boys and Wah Ching—boiled over into a botched assassination attempt in this very room. The dispute erupted after the Wah Ching had vandalized the graves of members of the Joe Boys. The surviving Joe Boys descended on the Golden Dragon—a Wah Ching stronghold—seeking vengeance. None of the Wah Ching were injured, but five innocent bystanders were killed and eleven others were hurt. The incident came to be known as the Golden Dragon Massacre. The attendant publicity took a significant toll on the restaurant's business and Chinatown's tourist trade. It led to the formation of the SFPD's Gang Task Force, which has been a model for similar units in other cities.

The dinner crowd is beginning to arrive as Pete and I take our seats in a red booth in the spacious dining room on the ground floor. "Your waiter will be with you momentarily," Hu tells us in unaccented English. He undoubtedly also speaks several dialects of Chinese. We accept his offer of tea. He quickly motions to a busboy to bring us water. "Would you care for forks?" he asks. The Golden Dragon's clientele is made up mostly of locals, but it also caters to the tourist crowd.

"No, thank you," I say. "Jeff Chin said you might be able to help us."

The mention of his cousin's name elicits a wary look followed by a rehearsed smile. "I am always happy to help friends of my cousin," he says.

Well, if you're offering. "My name is Mike Daley. This is my brother, Pete. We're handling the final appeal for Nathan Fineman."

The smile disappears. "It is my pleasure to meet you," he lies. "Welcome to the Golden Dragon."

Ever the consummate host. "We were hoping you would show us where Mr. Fineman met with Mr. Chin's father."

Hu purses his lips for an instant. "There is nothing of interest in that room. It has been used as a storage area for many years."

I'd still like to see it. "If it wouldn't be too much trouble, we'd appreciate it if you'd let us take a quick look." I can't imagine he's going to make us get a subpoena.

He glances at the line forming at the podium. "This is our busy time," he says. "I would be happy to show it to you a little later."

It seems unlikely that he'll run upstairs and rearrange the room. I opt for politeness. "Thank you, Mr. Hu. If you have just a moment, we'd like to ask you a couple of questions about what happened that night."

His eyes dart toward the line and then back to us. He's savvy enough to understand that it would be unwise to appear unhelpful. There is also the matter of seating his patrons. "It was a long time ago," he says.

It was also an event that he would prefer to forget. "Please, Mr. Hu?" I say.

He responds with a slight grimace. "Very well," he says.

"Were you here when the trouble started?"

"No. I left around midnight. Mr. Chin arrived a few minutes before I went home. I asked him to lock up for me after his meeting was concluded."

"Was anyone with him?"

"Just Mr. Fong."

I ask him if it was his policy to entrust his business to non-employees.

"Mr. Chin was my uncle and a cousin of the former owners. He dined here regularly. He used the room upstairs for meetings. We always obliged him when he requested access to the restaurant after hours. As family, he was afforded some special privileges. He brought us a substantial amount of business. So did Mr. Fong."

Sort of like the high rollers in Vegas. They also undoubtedly provided substantial gratuities to the owners and the staff for their service. On to the matters at hand. "Are you aware that your uncle was suspected of engaging in illegal activities?"

The first hint of defensiveness creeps into his voice. "I am not a lawyer, Mr. Daley. Those charges were never proven."

"Were you familiar with his operations?"

"He had banquets and family celebrations here."

Not the answer to my question. "Did you know that he was meeting another drug dealer that night?"

"I read about it in the papers."

It's another evasive answer. "Did you know about it beforehand?"

He shakes his head slowly from side to side. "My uncle valued his privacy. We respected his wishes. I really must take care of our customers. I will take you upstairs after you enjoy your dinner."

"Thank you," I say.

The corner of his mouth turns up. "It would be my pleasure to order for you. Our chef does an exquisite Peking duck."

It would be impolite to refuse. "Sounds great," I say, hoping he can put it together quickly. Despite the lovely surroundings, Pete and I have no time for a leisurely dinner.

I watch him closely as he returns to the podium. He ignores the line that now extends out the door. He picks up the phone, punches a number and glances in our direction as he speaks. He listens intently and nods several times. His expression turns somber. Then he hangs up the phone and begins to seat his patrons.

Pete and I wolf down our five-course feast in twenty minutes. Hu reappears as we're finishing our Peking duck. "I trust everything was to your satisfaction?" he says.

"Yes," I reply. "Thank you very much. We'll take the check, please."

"That will not be necessary. Your dinner is courtesy of Mr. Chin."

It's been a long time since the son of a man who was allegedly murdered by one of my clients bought me dinner. I protest to no avail. "Please express our deepest gratitude," I say.

"I will. He also asked me to extend his regrets for his abrupt behavior when you met him yesterday. He hopes he did not offend you."

We accosted him in a parking lot to question him about the man who was convicted of murdering his father. Now *he* wants to apologize to *us*? Interesting. "There are no hard feelings."

"I will inform him."

"Did you speak to the police officers who secured the scene?"

"Yes. We cooperated fully."

"Did you know any of them?"

"Yes. Many of the officers who work in the area are regular customers."

My dad used to say that you can always tell a good restaurant by the number of black-and-whites parked outside. "Do you recall seeing any of them in the restaurant earlier that night?"

"I am afraid not, Mr. Daley."

"Did you notice anything suspicious in the days leading up to the meeting?"

There's a hesitation. "No, Mr. Daley."

I probe for a few more minutes. He has precious little information to share. Finally, I say, "Would you mind showing us the room upstairs?"

He responds with another practiced smile. "Of course, Mr. Daley."

Way too easy. "Thank you, Mr. Hu."

# # #

"What was that all about?" Pete asks.

At nine-thirty on Monday night, we're standing beneath the fire escape from which Nate Fineman fell and broke his back. The only illumination in the alley comes from a single streetlamp that casts an eerie glaze on the heavy fog. If Nate had fallen today, he would have landed in a Dumpster emitting a putrid smell of leftovers from tonight's dinner.

"Hu was too accommodating," I say.

"I'm well aware of that," Pete says. "The question is why."

In addition to giving us a free dinner, he took us for a guided tour of a packed storage room on the third floor where three people—

including his uncle—met a violent end. It was jammed full of old kitchen equipment, tables and chairs, sacks of rice, and the remnants of a remodeling project that was finished years ago. He showed us the painted-over window through which Nate leapt to the fire escape. He pointed out the still-functional bathroom down the hall where Nate supposedly planted the gun. Finally, he took us down the narrow stairway that led from the meeting room to the alley. He said it was customary for Chin's guests to arrive through the back door.

"He wanted to appear cooperative," I say to Pete. "He knows we'll be back if we think he's trying to hide something."

"Why did Jeff Chin buy us dinner?"

I plant my tongue firmly in my cheek. "He's a generous soul who is trying to appear forthcoming."

"Yeah, right."

I ask Pete if he thinks Hu was working for Chin's organization.

"He didn't strike me as the type who would have been selling drugs on the street. He probably made the restaurant available to Chin whenever he asked. Drug lords have a lot of free time. I'm sure he was getting a nice gratuity for being discreet."

No doubt. "Did you notice anything about the meeting room?"

"The door opened directly into the hallway leading to the back stairway. It means the murderer—assuming it wasn't our client —probably came in the back door and left the same way. Presumably, the door would have been guarded unless somebody paid off the security people."

It's always helpful to get the impressions of a former cop. "What about the bathroom?"

"It had an old-fashioned toilet with a very small tank. There was no cabinet under the sink. It would have been very difficult for Fineman to have hidden a gun."

Antonio LaTona was born in Palermo more than six decades ago into a family that cooked on Italian ocean liners. At the age of seven, he was apprenticed to a master art restorer who specialized in churches. He moved to San Francisco as a young man and opened Caffé Sport in the heart of North Beach in 1969. Antonio furnished the two narrow rooms with his own artistic creations. He painted and carved every table and chair, tiled surface, and enameled pot. Majolica tiles and brightly colored paint cover the walls. He brings the same perfectionism to his cuisine. His seafood and handmade Sicilian pastas are covered with carefully selected Italian cheeses, shrimp, scallops, lobster, zucchini, and, most important, garlic.

Over the years, the curmudgeonly Antonio has become a Sicilian version of *Seinfeld*'s fabled Soup Nazi. His mercurial management style has filtered down to his waiters, who have developed their own reputation for surliness. In fairness to Antonio and his people, it's all a matter of understanding the context in which the restaurant operates. For more than thirty years, Antonio has created, selected, and prepared the entire menu. The waiters—fellow Sicilians and protective family members —know how much attention he gives to every dish. If Antonio can't find the ingredients or the time on a given evening to prepare a dish on the menu to his demanding standards, the waiters simply tell their patrons it isn't available. You can never go wrong if you listen to them.

Nick "the Dick" Hanson and I are sitting at his regular table in the corner of Caffé Sport at ten o'clock on Monday night. The diminutive octogenarian's rubbery face rearranges itself into a wide smile. He's chewing a prawn on the left side of his mouth as he speaks to me out of the right. "Nice to see you again, Mike," he croaks in a voice that is somewhere between Edward G. Robinson and Humphrey Bogart. He looks a little like Robinson, only he's considerably thinner. We had no reservation. We got in just the same because Nick isn't just a regular—he's an icon who has been patronizing Antonio's establishment since day one. He may be the only person outside Sicily who truly comprehends the proprietor's moods.

"Same here, Nick," I say. I tried to persuade him to meet me at his office over on Columbus Avenue. He wouldn't hear of it. I just finished my first dinner of the night at the Golden Dragon. If you want to meet with Nick, you have to eat with Nick. Pete got the better end of the deal. He went home to check on his wife and daughter and to make sure his operatives are keeping Rosie's house under guard. True to his word, Roosevelt arranged for a police officer to keep an eye on me. Antonio wasn't too happy about the black-and-white that's parked in the valet zone in front of his restaurant. It won't be there for long—this dinner will have to be short. It's late and there is still so much to do.

"You're looking a little ragged," Nick says. His meticulous attire is always perfect. I must look like a charity case.

"It's part of the drill when you're in the last week of a death-penalty appeal," I say.

"Indeed it is."

"How've you been?" I ask. It's an essential part of the rite. I have to give him an opportunity to expound upon his latest accomplishments, his medical report, and his children, grandchildren, and great-grandchildren, most of whom work for him.

"Just fine, Mike," he tells me. "I had a little surgery on my knee after I ran the Bay to Breakers. It's going to be okay. I just started working out at the Bay Club again."

I find it hard to picture the nattily dressed man sitting in front of me chugging away on a StairMaster at the upscale gym across the street from the Fog City Diner. My spies tell me he's there four days a week. Nick used to play ball with Joe DiMaggio on the North Beach Playground, and he's still a remarkable physical specimen. As always, he's sporting a custom-tailored Brioni business suit with a fresh boutonniere on his lapel. His new toupee is more serviceable than stylish, though still reasonably attractive. It's closer in hue to his black suit than to the few remaining strands of his natural hair. In traditional San Francisco style, he's pulled his large cloth napkin up over his chartreuse tie and starched white shirt.

He takes a long drink of the house red wine, then he powers down the remnants of his Scampi Prawns all'Antonio. He looks at the small plate piled high with prawns that he's just passed over to me. "Aren't you going to eat them?" he asks.

I glance at my watch. "I'm not that hungry," I understate.

He points a chubby finger at me. "Your body takes care of itself for the first fifty years. After that, you have to make an effort." He gulps down his wine and adds, "You need protein."

I shovel down a few of the prawns. Then he asks our waiter to bring out a platter of Calamari all'Antonio that's big enough for six. He castigates me until I eat my share. I'm about to explode from my second helping when Nick finally decides it's time to turn to business. "How's Nate?" he asks.

"Not so good. Putting aside the fact that he's scheduled to be executed in a week, he's in a wheelchair and his kidneys are failing."

"Why the hell are they so hot to execute a dying man?"

"It's the law."

"It's idiotic." He motions to the waiter to bring him an espresso and a piece of strawberry cheesecake. "I'm trying to get my strength back after my surgery," he explains.

"With cheesecake and coffee?"

"They're two of the major food groups."

"I understand that you were the PI on the Fineman case," I say.

"Indeed I was." His eyes light up. "Mort Goldberg hired me. He was still a real lawyer back then. That was before he decided to become a talking head on TV. What a waste of talent."

"I had a long talk with him yesterday. He thinks Nate is innocent."

"Maybe." He uses his fork as a prop to gesture. "It never made sense to me. Nate was a great lawyer. Not a popular guy, but somebody you'd call if you got in serious trouble. He didn't need the money. He didn't want to run a drug ring. The cops went after him because he made them look bad in the Posse case. There's no way that he killed those people. N-F-W. No fucking way."

I get the message. "He had some debts," I say.

"He owed some dough to the Garbage King of Oakland. B-F-D. Big fucking deal. His wife paid it. He didn't kill three people for the money."

"Jerry Edwards claims Aronis was going to forgive Nate's debt if he agreed to blow away his competition."

The piece of calamari that's been sticking to his right cheek for the last ten minutes finally falls harmlessly to his plate as his face transforms into a pronounced frown. "Edwards is full of shit. If Aronis really wanted to kill those guys, he would have hired a professional hit man. Lawyers are notoriously unreliable killers."

I'm not sure if that's a compliment or a dig. "Aronis's ex-wife has a different take."

"Patty Norman is a nutcase. It was all a setup."

I always feel like the straight man when I'm talking to him. "By whom?"

"If I knew the answer, Nate would be home playing with his grandchildren."

I got a similar response from Mort. "We're trying to prove the cops planted the gun."

"So did we, but we didn't get very far. They closed ranks."

"Do you think it's possible?"

"Over the years, I've learned that almost anything is possible." He takes a long drink of his wine. "Unfortunately for you, it will be almost impossible to prove."

"I hear Aronis isn't such a solid citizen, either."

"Indeed he is not. He supplemented his garbage business with real estate investments. Some of them went south, so he supplemented them with drug money. He was a small-time drug runner who wanted to break into the big time. He hated Robinson and Chin."

"Did he know about the meeting at the Golden Dragon?"

"Everybody who was anybody in the drug world knew about it. They were waiting to see how Robinson and Chin would split the pot."

"You're saying Aronis had motive?"

"Absolutely."

"Was he anywhere near Chinatown that night?"

"Absolutely not. He was in Vegas."

"He could have contracted it out."

"*Anybody* could have contracted it out. You have five days to prove it." My mind races. "Did Aronis ever use muscle in his trash business?"

"Indeed he did."

"Any chance he sent one of his enforcers to the Golden Dragon?"

"There's a chance."

"Any idea where we might start to look?"

"Take your pick: San Quentin, Folsom, Pelican Bay, Chino." He takes a sip of his espresso. "Lots of luck. First, you have no evidence that Aronis sent somebody over there. Second, even if he set it up, your chances of finding the triggerman are nonexistent. Third, the crime scene wasn't the work of some punk from East Oakland. Some idiot off the street would have killed Nate, too."

"Are you saying somebody was trying to frame Nate from the start?"

He shakes his head. "That seems unlikely. There's no way the killer could have known that Nate was going to jump out the window and go down the fire escape. A more likely scenario is that it was a crime of opportunity."

"By whom?"

"Somebody who knew how to stage a crime scene. They found a perfect set of prints on the gun that was carefully placed underneath his body to avoid contamination."

"Does that mean you think it was the cops?"

He arches a bushy gray eyebrow. "It means you'll never be able to prove it."

"Why didn't Aronis take over the San Francisco heroin business after Robinson and Chin were killed?"

"He got pushed out by a guy named Marshawn Bryant. He took over Robinson's business and muscled out Chin."

"Why haven't the cops busted him?"

"He's smart."

"We talked to him yesterday. He said he was an honest businessman who was nowhere near the Golden Dragon that night." I'm looking for a reaction.

"He's a liar who is one of the biggest heroin distributors in town."

"Do you think he's also a murderer?"

"I couldn't prove it."

"Did he know about the meeting at the Golden Dragon?"

"He must have. He was Robinson's right-hand man."

"Is there any way of placing him in Chinatown that night?"

"N-F-L, Mike. Not fucking likely."

"A man named Eugene Tsai told the cops that he saw an African American man in the alley behind the Golden Dragon. Did you ever talk to him?"

"No, but I talked to his brother after Eugene was killed. The brother told me that Eugene saw an African American man in the alley, but he couldn't identify him. The brother also told me that a woman named Jasmine Luk was in the alley with Eugene."

"Did you ever talk to her?"

"Nope. According to my sources, she told the cops that she didn't see anybody in the alley. She disappeared after Eugene was killed. We tried to find her, but she vaporized."

And Nate was convicted of capital murder. "Do you think Luk was killed, too?"

"Maybe. They never found a body."

I lay it on the line. "Do you think Bryant was involved in Tsai's death and Luk's disappearance?"

"Maybe. We couldn't prove it."

Which takes us back to square one. "Lou Cohen recently contacted Tsai's brother," I tell him.

"I know."

Huh? "How do you know?"

"Because Lou asked me to track him down."

"You were working for Lou?"

"Indeed I was."

Monday, July 13. 11:30 p.m.
5 days and 31 minutes until execution.

"How long were you working for Lou?" I ask Nick.

"It was a very brief assignment," he says. He's powering through his second piece of cheesecake. "He called me a few days before he died. He asked me to get him an address and phone number for Wendell Tsai."

It explains how Cohen got Wendell's address and phone number. "Did you talk to Tsai?"

"Nope."

"Did Lou also ask you to try to find Jasmine Luk?"

"We never got that far."

"Why didn't they call Wendell Tsai as a witness at the trial?" I ask.

"He had nothing to offer. His brother couldn't identify anybody in the alley."

"He could have talked about Luk."

"She was already long gone. Besides, she told the cops that she didn't see anybody in the alley."

Even if we track her down, there is no guarantee that she'll be willing or able to identify anybody in the alley ten years later. "Do you have any idea where we might find her?"

"Not a clue."

It may be another dead end. I ask him if he knew anything about the IA investigation.

"Everybody was cleared."

"Do you think there is any realistic possibility that the cops planted the murder weapon?"

He pulls off the napkin that's been hanging around his neck. "I don't know, Mike."

"Do you think the cops covered for each other?"

"I wouldn't know. I understand they investigated your father."

"They did."

"I read that he was also the last guy who had his hands on the IA file."

"He was. It doesn't mean he took it." I realize I sound too defensive as I say it.

"I didn't say he did. You have to admit, though, that it doesn't look so good."

"I know."

"For what it's worth, he had a reputation as a solid cop."

"That's true."

"The same can't be said about his partner at the time."

"So I've heard. Did you get anything on Little Joey?"

"He was a cowboy."

"Enough of a cowboy that he would have set up Nate?"

"I don't know. He didn't get to the Golden Dragon until after the shooting was over."

"He could have been involved in a cover-up."

"Be careful. If you make that accusation, it will also implicate your father."

We sit in silence for a long moment. Our waiter brings over the check. Nick reaches for it, but I pull it away from him. "Dinner is on me," I say.

"You're a good man," he says, wiping his chin.

Some people still think so. I take a sip of coffee and send up a final flare. "My brother is stretched a little thin. Any chance you might be willing to help us for a few days?"

"Standard rates?"

"Absolutely."

He smiles. "Indeed I am."

"Do you know anybody else who spoke to Jasmine Luk?"

"Just Carl Yee."

What? "The undercover cop?"

He corrects me. "The *retired* undercover cop. He went with Roosevelt when he interviewed Luk."

Neither Yee nor Roosevelt mentioned it.

25/ THAT'S WHY YOU CALLED AT THIS HOUR?

Roosevelt answers his cell phone on the first ring. "Is something wrong at home?" he asks.

"No," I reply.

"Is Grace okay?" The concern in his voice is genuine.

"Yes." I'm trying to juggle my cell phone, a bottle of water, and the steering wheel. I'm heading north on Doyle Drive toward the Golden Gate Bridge. "I just talked to Nick Hanson. He said Carl Yee was with you when you talked to Jasmine Luk."

"*That's* why you called at this hour?"

"I have a client who has an appointment with a needle in four days."

"I brought Carl along to interpret, but Luk spoke English."

"You didn't mention it."

"It was irrelevant."

"She saw an African American man in the alley, running away from the crime scene."

"No, she didn't."

"She couldn't have missed him. She was standing next to Eugene Tsai."

"Evidently she did."

"She lied to you because she was scared."

"I had to accept what she told me."

"How do you know that she wasn't killed like Tsai?"

There's a pause. "I don't," he says softly.

"What happened to her?"

"I don't know."

"I need more from you, Roosevelt. She may be the key to proving that an innocent man is going to be executed on Sunday."

I hear him take a deep breath. "She outran a full-blown police dragnet. We finally concluded that she was an illegal alien who was afraid she'd be deported if she came forward. Obviously, we were disappointed that we couldn't find her."

So are we.

# # #

"It's 1:00 a.m.," Yee snaps.

"I knew you'd be up," I reply. I'm *paying* you to be awake and guarding Wendell Tsai at this hour.

"Where are you?" he asks.

"The Golden Gate Bridge. Where are you?"

"Tsai's room."

Right where he's supposed to be. "All quiet on the western front?"

"Yep." He lowers his voice to a whisper. "Somebody was watching Tsai at Brandy Ho's tonight. Middle-aged Asian male. Dark hair. Medium build."

"That covers half of Chinatown."

"I know."

"I understand you talked to a witness named Jasmine Luk."

"I did."

"I'm told she was with Eugene Tsai on the night of the shootings."

"She was."

"And that she saw an African American man running through the alley."

"Nope."

"Tsai's brother said she saw him."

"That isn't what she told me."

Damn it. "Why didn't you mention it?"

"She said she didn't see anything."

"You told me you weren't involved in the Fineman case."

"I wasn't. Roosevelt asked me to come along to interpret. It turned out that Luk spoke English. She said she didn't see anybody in the alley. That's all I know."

It's consistent with Roosevelt's version. "Then why did she leave town?"

"She was friends with Eugene. She got scared."

"Didn't you offer her protection?"

"Yep. She bolted anyway. May have been here illegally."

"Did she have any relatives or friends in the area?"

"She had an aunt in Oakland. The aunt didn't know where she went."

Or the aunt was trying to protect her. "Did you consider the possibility that the aunt withheld information?"

"Yep." He doesn't elaborate.

"Do you recall the aunt's name?"

"Nope."

If she's out there, we'll find her.

# # #

A moment later, I hit the speed dial on my cell phone. I've already pissed off Roosevelt and Yee. I might as well add one more name to the list. My night can't possibly get any worse, and I can't worry about hurt feelings.

"Jerry Edwards," the tired voice answers.

"It's Mike Daley."

The *Chronicle*'s finest coughs ferociously. "Did you find the file?"

"No. Did you?"

"Of course not. Why the hell are you calling at this hour?"

You called me at the same time last night. "Does the name Jasmine Luk mean anything to you?"

"Supposedly, she was with Eugene Tsai in the alley behind the Golden Dragon."

"Why didn't you mention her when we talked?"

"She never testified."

"Did you talk to her?"

"Nope."

"Eugene Tsai saw an African American man in the alley just after the shooting stopped. So did she."

"That isn't what she told the cops."

"Nick Hanson thinks she lied."

"I wouldn't know."

I can do without the sarcastic tone. "Maybe we can get her to change her story."

"You'll have to find her first."

"I understand she may have been an illegal alien."

"I heard the same thing."

"Is that why she disappeared?"

"Could be. It may also have had something to do with the fact that her friend Eugene got stabbed a dozen times after word got out that he had talked to the cops."

True enough. "Evidently, she had an aunt in Oakland."

"She did."

"Did you ever try to track her down?"

"Maybe."

"Do you have a name?"

"What's in it for me?"

"The knowledge that you've fulfilled your duties of journalistic integrity."

"Not good enough."

"I'll give you an exclusive interview with my client." I'm not doing this out of the goodness of my heart. It may be the fastest way to find Luk's aunt. As a practical matter, I can always renege on the deal.

"The aunt's name was Amanda Wong," Edwards says. "She ran a print shop in Oakland."

If she's out there, we'll find her. "I'll make the arrangements for the interview," I tell him.

# # #

"This case is a nightmare," Rosie says. She's sitting on her sofa at one-thirty on Tuesday morning. The combination of stress and fatigue is starting to take its toll. She's eating a slice of leftover pizza as she proof-reads a draft of yet another habeas petition. In a conspicuous show of firepower, a Larkspur squad car is sitting in her driveway. An unmarked San Francisco police cruiser is in the alley. One of Pete's best operatives is in a car down the block, next to the plainclothes cop whom Roosevelt assigned to follow me. A smaller crew has assembled around the corner in front of Jake's house. "We're living on Domino's and working on a case we can't win in a house that's an armed fortress—without a kitchen. This is insane."

I'm sitting at the opposite end of her couch. A flip response will not play well. "It's the best we can do for now."

"I want to find the asshole who took that picture. We can't do it sitting here."

"We aren't going to play cops and robbers. Roosevelt will find him."

"He damn well better. I hate this."

"So do I."

Sylvia walks in from the kitchen, a heavy frying pan in her right hand. "How much longer are we going to be prisoners in this house?" she asks.

"Less than a week," I tell her.

"And if you actually manage to get a stay of the execution?"

"We'll figure it out when the time comes." Maybe we'll start digging a moat.

"What if I want to go to the store?"

"The cops will escort you."

"We're giving in to the bad guys."

"It's better to play it safe."

"And if Grace wants to see Jake?"

"We'll talk to the cops about it," Rosie says.

"She isn't going to like it."

"I know."

Sylvia swings the pan ominously. "If anybody tries anything, I'll nail him."

It isn't an entirely idle threat. Sylvia knocked a man unconscious when he tried to break into her house about ten years ago. It made the Mission District paper and got her a little airtime on Channel Seven. Nobody's tried it again.

"Hopefully," I say, "that won't be necessary."

My ex-mother-in-law gives me a defiant look. "Bring them on."

Rosie shakes her head in bemused disbelief. "We all feel much safer now, Mama."

"In that case," Sylvia says, "I'm going to bed." She makes a dramatic display of swinging the lethal pan as she walks down the hall toward Grace's bedroom.

I turn back to Rosie. "I wouldn't mess with her," I say.

"Neither would I."

"Are you all right?" I say.

The crow's-feet at the corners of her dark eyes become more pronounced as she frowns. "Somebody is taking pictures of our daughter and smashing the windows of our cars. I'm angry. I'm frustrated. I'm pissed off. I'm most definitely *not* all right."

"Is there anything I can do?"

Her eyes flash. "Remind me to rip your lungs out the next time you bring in a last-minute death-penalty appeal."

"Deal." I take her hand in mine. "Do you want to withdraw?"

She responds with the resolute expression that I've found intimidating and irresistible for the last twenty years. "No, I want to find out what really happened at the Golden Dragon. Somebody is going to a lot of trouble to try to keep us from doing that. I want to know why."

"Maybe we should pick another battle, Rosie."

"We're taking this one to the finish, Mike."

That's the end of the discussion.

She closes the brief. "We'll file with the California Supremes and the Ninth Circuit at nine o'clock," she says. "We'll have papers ready to go to the U.S. Supremes if we're rejected."

"What are we arguing this time?" I ask.

"That the Sodium Pentothal doesn't always work properly, which could lead to excruciating pain. Bottom line: death by lethal injection is cruel and unusual punishment."

"Is there any hope they'll buy it?"

"A little. There are some new studies that suggest that the Sodium Pentothal doesn't always make the defendant lose consciousness completely. We're also going to claim that it's illegal to kill a dying man. We'll argue that he's entitled to reasonable medical care."

"Our theory is that by killing him, they're depriving him of medical attention?"

"Essentially, yes. Unfortunately, there isn't any case law on point."

It's a creative, albeit somewhat circular, argument.

"Realistically," she says, "our appeals are going to be long shots unless we can find some new evidence or the courts decide they're in the mood to make some new law."

"N-F-L," I say.

She smiles knowingly. She's read all of Nick's books. "Did you and Nick have a good dinner?"

I would have appreciated it more if I hadn't stuffed myself at the Golden Dragon an hour beforehand. "Indeed we did."

"Knock it off." She listens attentively as I fill her in, then pronounces her judgment. "There's nothing that will get us a stay."

"What about Tsai's claim that his brother saw an African American man in the alley that night?"

"There was no positive ID. Besides, it's also uncorroborated hearsay."

"We'll have to try."

"We will. It doesn't prove freestanding innocence by itself."

"We'll also try to find Jasmine Luk."

She glances at her watch. "Where are you planning to start?"

I'm going to try to track down Luk's aunt. Then I'm going to meet with Alex Aronis and his ex-wife.

Rosie nods. "It would help if we could place Bryant in the alley that night."

The unyielding voice of reality. "There are only about a hundred thousand African American men who fit his description in the Bay Area." I look around her silent living room. "How is Grace?"

"She's more worried that she won't be able to spend time with Jake than she is about getting herself killed. I talked to Jake's parents. I suggested that their son may want to steer clear of our house for a few days.

Maybe you can explain the gravity of the situation to our daughter. I can't make her listen."

"She's fourteen, Rosie."

"Believe me, I know. Nowadays, I get a lot more out of Tommy than I do from her."

"That's what being the parent of a teenager is all about."

"I'm trying to keep things low-key. If all else fails, we could ground her—it's for her own good." She yawns. "She thought she heard somebody outside her window about an hour ago. The cops descended upon our backyard with everything they had."

"Did they find anything?"

"My neighbor's kitten."

"I trust they let her go with just a warning?"

"They did."

I lean over and take her hands in mine. "Are you going to be okay?"

"I'll be fine," she says. "Nobody is going to intimidate us." A sideways grin crosses her face. "Besides, if anybody tries something funny, they'll end up on the business end of my mother's frying pan."

Tuesday, July 14. 9:30 a.m.
4 days, 14 hours, and 31 minutes until execution.

It doesn't take long for Pete to track down Jasmine Luk's aunt. Sunshine Printing is a high-tech operation housed in an old building on Webster Street in Oakland's Chinatown. It publishes Chinese-language phone directories, menus, and coupons for the local businesses. A dozen employees are manning state-of-the-art computers and noisy, industrial-strength printers. The smell of photocopier ink hangs in the cold, dry air.

The petite woman with short gray hair eyes me suspiciously from behind the counter. She strikes me as the sort who hasn't missed a day of work or taken a vacation in forty years. She's wearing a tidy blue house dress. Her reading glasses hang from a simple gold chain. I'd guess she's in her sixties, from the depth of the crow's-feet at the corners of her eyes.

"How may I help you?" she shouts over the sound of the machines.

I extend a hand. "My name is Mike Daley," I say. "This is my brother, Pete. We're looking for the owner."

"I'm Amanda Wong."

I look around. "How long have you been in business?"

"My family started this business seventy-five years ago," she says proudly.

Oakland's crowded Chinatown is a modest stepcousin to its more famous counterpart across the bay. The working-class community is a combination of mom-and-pop businesses, restaurants, low-rise tenements, and modern apartment buildings, all within a few blocks of the 880 freeway. Except for the computers and a fresh coat of bright blue paint, Sunshine Printing probably hasn't changed much since World War II. It fends off competition from larger, national operations by focusing on the needs of the Chinese-speaking community.

"What can I do for you gentlemen?" she asks in perfect English. She was giving instructions to her staff in Chinese when we walked in.

"We'd like to ask you a few questions."

A burly young man appears from behind a row of printers. He surveys the situation and responds with protectiveness. "Is there a problem, Mother?"

She touches his arm. "Let me handle this, George."

The dutiful son takes the hint and returns to the printers. The fact that she spoke to him in English suggests she has nothing to hide. In all likelihood, it also means she has nothing useful to tell us.

I spot a collection jar packed with bills on the counter. A handwritten note in English and Chinese says that an effort is under way to raise money for medical treatment for the girl whose photo is taped to the jar. I pull a twenty from my wallet and stuff it inside. It's a good-faith gesture of concern and an attempt to curry favor.

I get the grateful nod from Amanda that I was hoping for. She reminds me of Sylvia. "That's very kind of you," she says. "Now, what can I do for you?"

"We represent Nathan Fineman," I say.

"I recognized you. I saw you on TV last night."

So much for the element of surprise. "We were hoping you might be able to help us locate a woman named Jasmine Luk. We understand she was your niece."

She eyes me suspiciously. "Actually, she was my great-niece."

I gingerly ask, "When was the last time you saw her?"

Her eyes dart toward Pete, and then back to me. "Why do you want to know?"

"We think she may have some information about the Fineman case."

Her lips form a small ball as she measures her words. "I can't help you."

"Could you tell us the last time you saw her?"

She absentmindedly fidgets with the ballpoint pen that she's been clutching since we arrived. "Almost ten years ago."

There's no way to ask the next question delicately. "Do you know if she's still alive?"

Her eyes fill with a pronounced sadness. "I'm not sure, Mr. Daley," she whispers.

"I'm sorry."

"So am I."

"What can you tell us about her?"

"Jasmine was a beautiful, intelligent girl who was born in China. She was only twelve when we brought her to America with her mother."

"And her father?"

"He never made it here." She doesn't elaborate. "Jasmine and her mother stayed with me for a short time when they first arrived. Then they moved to San Francisco, next door to my cousins. Jasmine's mother worked at my cousin's grocery store on Stockton Street. Jasmine picked up English quickly."

"Can we talk to her mother?"

"No. She took sick shortly after Jasmine graduated from high school. She passed away a few months later."

"How about your cousins?"

"I'm afraid they're gone, too, Mr. Daley."

"I'm so sorry. Did Jasmine move in with your cousins after her mother passed away?"

"No, she kept the apartment. We offered to help her with the rent, but she was very independent. She found a job at the Chinese Hospital and took classes at State. She wanted to be a nurse."

"We understand she knew a man named Eugene Tsai."

"They worked together at the hospital." She anticipates my next question and quickly adds, "They were just friends."

"Did she have a boyfriend?"

"No. Jasmine was more interested in school than boys. She spent most of her time working and studying."

I start fishing. "We've been told that her apartment was across the alley from the Golden Dragon Restaurant."

"It was."

"We understand she walked home with Eugene on the night that three people were killed at the restaurant."

"She did."

"We've also been told that they saw an African American man in the alley who may have been involved in the shootings at the restaurant."

Her tone turns more adamant. "She didn't."

"How do you know?"

"The police asked her about it. She told me that she didn't see anybody in the alley."

"We understand she left the area shortly after the events at the restaurant."

"Jasmine left after Eugene was killed," she says. "She was scared. I don't blame her. Somebody must have threatened her."

"Who?"

"She never told me."

Or you won't tell us. "Do you have any idea where she went?"

There is a hesitation. "I'm afraid not, Mr. Daley."

"Any guesses?"

"We had some distant cousins back in China."

"How would she have gotten there?"

"She was very resourceful."

It will be almost impossible to find her there. "Do you still keep in touch with the cousins?"

"I'm afraid not, Mr. Daley. I was terribly upset when she left. We hired a private investigator to try to find her. He couldn't."

"Would you mind giving us the name of the investigator?"

"He's dead, Mr. Daley."

I try another angle. "The police told us that there were problems with Jasmine's papers."

She tenses. "Jasmine came into this country legally. You can look up the records."

We will. "Was she a U.S. citizen?"

"No."

"Did she have any other relatives in the Bay Area?"

"Just my cousins in San Francisco."

"Our client is scheduled to be executed on Sunday," I say. "Do you have any idea where we might find her?"

There is a quiver in her voice. "I'm sorry, Mr. Daley."

"We can protect her."

"That's very generous of you."

Pete leans across the counter and plays a hunch. "Ms. Wong," he says, "has anybody else been asking about her lately?"

Her thin lips turn down. "No."

"Are you sure?"

"Yes."

He pushes a little harder. "Did somebody threaten you?"

"No."

"We can protect you, too."

She's now visibly agitated. "That won't be necessary."

He slides a business card toward her. "If anybody asks about her, would you mind giving me a call?"

She stares at the card for a long moment. "Yes."

# # #

"That didn't help," I say to Pete. We're standing in front of his rented white Ford Taurus, which is parked around the corner from Sunshine Printing.

"You weren't paying attention," he says.

"You think she knows where her great-niece is?"

"I think she knows more than she told us."

"Then why didn't she say something?"

"Somebody got to her, Mick. Or maybe she was trying to protect her great-niece."

"How do you know?"

"Just a hunch."

Rosie believes Pete is endowed with supernatural powers. In my opinion, he's just an astute observer of human nature. "How do we find out if you're right?"

"Let me watch her."

"We have only four days until the execution. I need you to watch Bryant."

"I'll have somebody else take care of him."

"You're supposed to be helping Nick Hanson look for witnesses in Chinatown."

"Nick can take care of it himself. Give me twenty-four hours."

"You aren't going to do anything illegal, are you?"

He responds with a crooked smile. "Of course not, Mick. That would be wrong."

Tuesday, July 14. 10:02 a.m.
4 days, 13 hours, and 59 minutes until execution.

"Nice place you have here," I say to Alex Aronis. I'm trying to sound reasonably genuine.

"Thanks, Mr. Daley," he replies. The garbage king of the East Bay is a big, gregarious man who once played offensive line at Cal. He now leads cheers on the sidelines at the football games. His wide face, flat nose, full head of gray hair, and enormous jowls evoke a grandfatherly air.

The world headquarters of East Bay Scavenger Service is on the twentieth floor of one of several nondescript steel-girder office towers that sprang up in downtown Oakland in the eighties and nineties. The new buildings obliterated much of the character of the once thriving shopping and business district adjacent to Lake Merritt, an urban oasis for over a century. Entire blocks have been bulldozed to make way for hermetically sealed office towers that are surrounded by asphalt parking lots.

"It's Mike," I tell him.

He extends an enormous paw. "Alex," he says. "Are you a Cal guy?"

"You bet." It couldn't hurt to soften him up with a little rah-rah.

"Good man, buddy."

I'm always leery of people who pepper their speech with words such as *buddy* and *pal.* "Go Bears," I say with as much enthusiasm as I can muster.

"Go Bears."

I'm as much of an Old Blue as the next guy, but I'm relieved when he doesn't break into a rousing rendition of "Sons of California." I sit back in my chair and admire his expansive office—a tribute to trash collection, sports, and himself. The walls are lined with photos of Aronis with Reggie Jackson, José Canseco, Mark McGwire, Tony La Russa, Al Davis, and Jeff Tedford. His immaculate mahogany desk is reserved for pictures of his two sons and six grandchildren. Conspicuously absent are shots of his ex-wife. Also missing are photos of his father and grandfather, who built the company he inherited.

"How long have you worked here?" I ask him. It won't take much to get him started. He's a talker.

"Since I was a kid, Mike." He looks like a basset hound trying to please. "My family is the living embodiment of the American Dream. My great-grandfather emigrated from Greece. He started this company in the early part of the last century. He ran it for fifty years, then my grandfather took over. My dad followed him. I'm an only child. It was a foregone conclusion that I would run the business. Both of my kids work here, too."

Putting aside the smarmy clichés and the jingoism, the essence of the message is probably true. "I take it you grew up around here?"

"In Piedmont. I still live there."

The leafy enclave on the north side of Lake Merritt became a separately incorporated municipality in 1907 when its wealthy residents decided they didn't want to fraternize with the common folk in Oakland and Berkeley. By the 1920s, it had more millionaires per capita than any other city in America. The affluent burg still maintains its own schools, firefighters, and police force. Though most of the original estates have been subdivided, it still boasts some of the most expensive homes in the Bay Area.

I resist the temptation to ask him if his company sells heroin to the students at Piedmont High. I look at the fully stocked wet bar and the polished conference table. I nod with feigned awe toward the life-size portrait of himself that he's had mounted on the wall opposite the flat-screen TV. "When did you move into this office?" I ask.

"Shortly after my father died, about fifteen years ago."

"So he ran the business from the garage?"

"Yeah. He always said it was important to keep an eye on things. Nowadays, we have too many employees to run the operation from there." He winks and adds, "Besides, my kids like to work in more pleas-ant surroundings—if you know what I mean."

I do. People who inherit their businesses frequently don't like to get their fingernails dirty.

He's still talking. "In order to remain competitive in the new mil-lennium, I try to focus on strategic goals and new markets. I think it's important to do some forward thinking. Since I took over management of the company, most of our growth has come from branching out into nonconventional areas."

I wonder if he's referring to the sale of heroin. He sure talks a good game. I'll bet he likes to quote pithy articles from airplane magazines.

"Have you ever thought about selling the company?" I ask.

He shakes his head vigorously. "I have no intention of retiring, Mike. I think it's important for my children to work hard and develop a sense of personal responsibility."

It's a refreshingly old-fashioned sentiment—even if it's bullshit. I sometimes wonder how my dad would have reacted if I'd told him I wanted to become a cop. It probably would have killed him on the spot. I don't have time to reminisce. "We're representing Nate Fineman," I say.

"I know." He pours himself a Perrier. "Nate was one helluva lawyer.

I still can't believe he killed those people."

His admiration seems genuine enough—for now. "How well did you know him?"

"Pretty well. We had him on retainer. He helped us with several cases."

"Criminal cases?" I ask.

"I prefer to think of them as unsubstantiated and baseless accusations."

So do all of my clients. "What were the charges?"

He dismisses me with the back of his huge hand. "People in the garbage business get hit with bogus claims all the time. Ninety-nine times out of a hundred, they're completely false."

And every once in a while, they turn out to be true. I try again. "What were the charges?"

His jowls quiver as he starts shaking his head again. "You name it, pal: money laundering; check kiting; financial fraud; tax evasion; pay-offs; kickbacks; intimidation. Once they tried to get me for trying to hire somebody to kill someone. That was a bunch of crap."

"How about drug dealing?"

"That's more recent and equally baseless."

Of course. "I take it nothing was ever proven?"

"None of the cases ever got to trial. The charges were bogus, and Nate was an excellent lawyer."

Clients judge defense attorneys by a single criterion: whether we get them off. "I understand you're currently under investigation by the Alameda County DA."

"More crap, bud. They're saying I tried to buy off a couple of members of the Oakland City Council. I make plenty of money without doing that kind of stuff. Besides, they'll never be able to prove it."

To guys like Aronis, you haven't done anything wrong until somebody proves it beyond a reasonable doubt in court, they lead you off to

San Quentin, and your appeals are denied. "I understand you're also a real estate entrepreneur."

"You bet." His chest pumps out as he glances at a large schematic drawing of a condo complex in Aspen. "It's like playing Monopoly with real money."

I wouldn't know. "Nate told us that he invested in one of your projects in Vail."

"He did." He's smart enough to know that he shouldn't volunteer any information.

"He almost defaulted, didn't he?"

"He paid his debt. That was the end of it."

Not quite. "We heard you had to lean on him."

"We had a couple of telephone conversations. Guys like Nate can't be intimidated."

"I understand Nate's wife wasn't happy about the deal."

The semipermanent frat-boy smile finally disappears. "She paid it just the same."

"Do you know anything about the events at the Golden Dragon?"

"Just what I've read in the papers." He quickly adds, "I was in Las Vegas that night."

"Did you know about the meeting beforehand?"

He laughs a little too hard. "Are you kidding? Guys like Terrell Robinson and Alan Chin didn't consult me about their business operations."

"There aren't a lot of secrets," I say.

"I'm not in the loop, I guess."

I ask him if he ever met Marshawn Bryant.

"I've known him for years. He managed the build-out of these offices. He's an excellent contractor."

It's a connection. I didn't realize they had a long-standing professional relationship. "Was he working for Robinson when you first met?"

"Yes. Terrell was one helluva contractor."

Evidently, he was also one helluva heroin dealer. "Did you know that he was also in the drug business?"

He tries to impress me with a solemn nod. "Not until it all came out during Nate's trial."

He's full of crap. "You know that Bryant took over Robinson's contracting business."

"Of course."

"Some people whose opinions I respect think he also took over Robinson's drug-distribution operation." They also think you tried.

He shakes his head emphatically. "Can't help you there, bud. I don't know anything about it."

On to the main event. "I understand you were married to a woman named Patty Norman."

"I was. We both grew up in Piedmont. Her family was in the cement business. Our parents were friends."

"How long were you married?"

His large face rearranges itself into a scowl. "Eighteen challenging years."

"I've been reading a lot about you in the papers the last couple of days. Your ex-wife has made some serious accusations."

The last vestiges of gregariousness disappear as his tone turns somber. "Patty is a frustrated, angry woman who needs to move on with her life."

"What caused the breakup?"

"We grew apart. It happens."

He doesn't want to talk about it. "Nate tells me you had her committed to rehab."

"I had no choice," he says emphatically. "Her drinking got out of control. It was very difficult for all of us—especially the kids."

"She claimed you hired somebody to take out Robinson and Chin."

He flashes an incredulous look. "Absolutely false. It's ridiculous. It's a last-ditch attempt to smear my name. I thought she had finally put the past behind her when she opened the bookstore—now she pulls this stunt. I'm thinking of bringing legal action against her for slander."

"And her insinuation that you're involved in the drug business, too?"

"Also absolutely false. I've helped set up several drug-education programs here in the East Bay. Our company has mandatory drug testing for our employees that's far more rigorous than the steroid-testing program in professional baseball. I've had offers to sell this company that run into nine figures. I don't need to do anything illegal to make big money."

Forgive me if I'm skeptical. "So you've never been convicted of a crime?"

"Not even a parking ticket."

"How about your employees?"

He pushes out a derisive sigh. "We're in the garbage-collection business, Mike. We can't afford to hire people with doctorates from Stanford. We have a firm policy that we terminate any employee who is convicted of a crime—no questions, no discussion."

"Have you ever been sued in a civil case?"

"Everybody gets sued. It's a cost of doing business."

That much is true. I'm fishing for somebody with a grudge who might be willing to talk to us. "Have you ever lost one?"

"What does that have to do with your case?"

"Nothing. I was just curious if Nate ever lost a civil case for you."

"Nope. That's why we hired him—he won."

Yes, he did. It also gives me an idea.

# # #

"I have a hunch about Aronis," I tell Rosie. My cell phone is plastered against my ear. The sun is hitting my face as I walk down Franklin Street in downtown Oakland, toward the lot where I left my rental car. "Let's see if we can find somebody who might be willing to give us some inside skinny about his organization."

"You're looking for a snitch?" Rosie asks, her mood uplifted.

I might have used a slightly more diplomatic term. "Yeah."

"That would rule out Aronis's children," she says. She loves this stuff.

"It doesn't rule out former employees. Aronis said his company has been sued a couple of times. Let's check the filings against East Bay Scavenger to see if any employees were named. Maybe somebody got fired and has a grudge. We should also cross-reference the names of the former employees against the inmate rosters at some of California's nastier prisons."

"Why would they talk to us?"

"Have you ever known an inmate who wouldn't talk to a defense lawyer?"

"We can't swap legal services for testimony."

"There's nothing that would prevent us from talking to a potential new witness."

"Right, Mike."

"Did you get our papers filed?" I ask.

"Yes. According to my sources at the California Supreme Court and the Ninth Circuit, the current betting is that the courts aren't crazy about the argument that death by legal injection is cruel and unusual punishment."

"We'll see. Did you hear anything from Dr. Death about the missing file?"

"He hasn't found it, but he sent over a sworn statement from Fitz describing its contents. Bottom line: Internal Affairs found no evidence of any wrongdoing. For the record, everybody was cleared."

Big surprise. "Did you hear anything from Nick Hanson?"

"He's scouring Chinatown for leads on Jasmine Luk."

The law-abiding citizens of Chinatown are being subjected to a full frontal attack by Nick the Dick and his offspring.

"Where are you going next?" Rosie asks.

"To find Patty Norman," I say. "I want to see how her story lines up with her ex-husband's."

Tuesday, July 14. 12:37 p.m.
4 days, 11 hours, and 24 minutes until execution.

I extend a hand to Aronis's ex-wife. "I'm Mike Daley," I say.

Patty Norman responds with a firm handshake and a feisty attitude.

"I know who you are," she says. "What took you so long? I thought you'd be here two days ago."

She's sitting behind the counter of her tiny bookstore in downtown Petaluma, a bucolic burg about thirty miles north of the Golden Gate Bridge. Its main drag, Kentucky Street, looks much the same as it did fifty years ago, except the feed stores have given way to boutiques, restaurants, and a popular multiplex movie house.

When I opened the door to Iron Woman Books, I expected to find a meek librarian type wearing a cable-knit sweater. Instead, I found a statuesque brunette who stands six-two and looks as if she could do laps around people half her age. Her long brown hair cascades down her back. Her skin is creamy. Her trim figure has the toned muscles of a professional athlete.

Iron Woman Books is squeezed inside a tight storefront where the floor-to-ceiling stacks are jammed with an eclectic assortment of new and used volumes emphasizing women's issues, physical fitness, and new age topics. Somehow, she's managed to fend off the chain stores that have sprung up in the vicinity. The walls are covered with photos of Patty as she's finishing various grueling triathlons all over the world. In a less than modest attempt at self-promotion, her window display has a poster of her recently released self-published memoir, the cover of which shows her arms upraised as she finished the Ironman Triathlon in Hawaii last year.

"I'd like to buy a copy of your book," I tell her.

She sits up taller. "You'd like to talk about the Fineman case."

"That too. Can I still buy a book?"

She flashes a charismatic smile. "Of course."

"Will you sign it for me?"

"Absolutely. How would you like it inscribed?"

It wouldn't be a good idea to ask her to write a note to Nate. "To Mike and Rosie," I tell her as I hand her the cash. She signs a copy and gives it to me. "What made you decide to write a memoir?"

Her expression turns thoughtful. "I had something to say to women in abusive relationships."

"What's that?"

"Don't take any shit from anybody."

"Good advice. I understand you went through some hard times with your ex-husband."

"I did. After what Alex and your client put me through, it's a miracle that I'm here. Doing triathlons is cathartic. Writing the book was therapeutic."

"Tell me about your ex-husband," I say.

"He's an asshole." Her long hair moves rhythmically as she talks. "It's a wonder our marriage lasted as long as it did. He treated me like living shit. I should have left him before things got out of hand."

She certainly seems willing to sling arrows at her ex. Hell, she wrote an entire book about it. My goal is to keep her talking long enough to see if she'll reveal anything that we can use. "What caused the breakup?" I ask.

"How much time do you have?"

"I'm not in any rush." Although I have a client who's scheduled to die in four days.

"He was possessive and jealous. You can add manipulative and mean-spirited to the list. He cheated. He lied. He was abusive to the kids. Do you want more?"

"I get the idea."

"I'm not sure you do. When my father lost his business, I lost my job and my mother had a nervous breakdown. Alex's idea of being supportive meant having an affair with his secretary. A divorce wasn't enough. He wasn't satisfied until he had me locked up like an animal. The truly sick part is that he seemed to enjoy it."

"I'm sorry."

"So am I." She points her pen toward me and adds, "Your client wasn't any better. He came up with the idea of having me put away. I was dealing with depression and alcoholism when he hired a couple of male hookers to flirt with me so they could get some compromising photos. How low can you get? Compared to Nate Fineman, Alex's divorce lawyer was Mother Teresa."

"You seem to be doing okay nowadays."

"I am. I'm proud of this store. It's helped me regain my dignity. It's a meeting place for people who are trying to work their way through destructive relationships. I'm donating the profits from my book to the Sonoma County Women's Shelter."

"That's very generous of you."

"There's more to life than money."

Tell me about it. "Do you have any contact with your children?"

"A little. Alex did everything he could to turn them against me. He convinced them that I was a drunk and an unfit mother. He took them into his business. He pays them a lot of money—in part to keep them away from me." She exhales heavily. "Despite his influence, they've turned out pretty well. I always see them on Mother's Day. I'm proud of them. I just wish I could have had a bigger part in their lives."

I genuinely feel for her. "I understand your ex was involved in the distribution of heroin in the East Bay."

There is no hesitation. "He still is. I've been waiting for the cops to nail him for years."

"I talked to him earlier today. He denied any involvement in the drug business."

"What did you expect? He's an exceptionally accomplished liar."

I need to push her. "He's never been convicted."

"He's always hired good lawyers—especially your client."

"How do you know that he's still involved in the drug business?"

"Money and the power are like drugs to him."

"Jerry Edwards claims you told him that your ex was looking to hire somebody to take out Terrell Robinson and Alan Chin at the Golden Dragon."

"That's true. It was before our marriage really went to hell. We were still on reasonably civil terms."

"Didn't it bother you?"

"Of course."

"Why didn't you do something about it?"

She gives me an incredulous look. "What was I supposed to do? Call the cops and tell them my husband was going to hire a killer to take out two competing drug dealers?" She pauses to regain her composure. "In that respect, maybe I was part of the problem, too. I could have done something to stop him. I'm not especially proud of it."

"Exactly what did he tell you?"

"He said he was looking for somebody to handle a 'delicate matter.'"

"I take it that was a euphemism for committing a crime?"

"A murder."

I stand corrected. "Are you saying he killed three people?"

"Absolutely not." She laughs derisively. "He never would have done it himself. Alex hates to get his hands dirty."

"But he was prepared to pay somebody else to do it?"

"You bet."

"That's a very serious accusation."

"It was a serious matter." Her voice fills with resignation. "You'll never be able to prove it. Alex was very good at covering his tracks."

"Why did he come to you for the name of a hit man?"

"His contacts in organized crime weren't interested. He was looking for someone in *dis*organized crime—punks, hoodlums, and thugs."

Not unlike most of the clientele of Fernandez and Daley.

"I worked for my father's cement business," she continues, "where I met some pretty marginal characters. I knew some people who were willing to do anything for the right price."

"But you didn't help him?"

"Of course not. I told Alex that I wasn't interested in getting involved in some half-baked murder-for-hire scheme."

"And that was that?"

"Not entirely. He told me that he was going to talk to your client about working out an arrangement."

"What sort?"

"He didn't say, but reading between the lines, it was clear to me that he intended to talk to him about killing Robinson and Chin."

"How much was he willing to pay for it?"

"A million dollars."

"Was he serious?"

"Alex never joked about two things: money and murder."

She's clearly prepared to implicate her ex-husband, but it's still a decidedly mixed bag for us. We could use her to show that Aronis had motive, money, and a propensity for murder. Unfortunately, she's also likely to further implicate Nate—unless we can show that Aronis hired somebody else. We'll also have to deal with significant credibility issues. Dr. Death will undoubtedly paint her as a bitter and alcoholic ex-wife who is out to get her ex-husband. Ultimately, it will be Alex's word against hers.

"Why are you bringing this up now?" I ask.

The pride in her eyes is evident as she looks around her store. "I finally thought it was time to clear the air."

"This isn't just some cheap publicity stunt to sell books?"

"I wrote a self-published memoir with a very limited audience. All the free publicity in the world isn't going to help."

"Would you be willing to testify about what you just told me?" I ask.

She cocks her head to one side. "How would that help you?"

It might not. "It raises the possibility that he paid somebody to kill Robinson and Chin."

"I will also have to testify that he was going to hire your client to do it."

It's a risk we may have to take. "We'll try to show that he paid somebody else."

"Lots of luck." Her eyes narrow. "More important, why in God's name would I *want* to help you?"

That's a more difficult question. "Because you strike me as someone who is interested in the truth."

This elicits a sarcastic glare. "You lawyers are completely full of shit, aren't you?"

For the most part. "You also seem more interested in justice than seeing an innocent man put to death—even if his behavior toward you was abhorrent."

She quickly corrects me. "I didn't say your client was innocent."

"Does that mean you think he did it?"

She answers me honestly. "I don't know."

I have only one arrow left in my quiver. "It may be a opportunity to nail your ex-husband."

She ponders the possibility for an interminable moment before the corners of her mouth turn up into a wicked smile. "I think we might be able to work something out."

Never underestimate the motivational value of revenge.

Tuesday, July 14. 2:27 p.m.
4 days, 9 hours, and 34 minutes until execution.

"Where are you?" Rosie asks.

"On my way to the office," I tell her. "Is everything calm at home?"

There's an edge to her voice. "My mother called and said Grace, Tommy, and Jake are watching DVDs."

"Anything out of the ordinary?"

I can hear the exasperation in her tone when she says, "My house is surrounded by cops. My kitchen is filled with contractors. Other than that, it's life as usual."

I'm driving south on the 101 freeway past the Marin Civic Center. We'll be going around the clock for the next four days. The struggle will only intensify as the hours wind down.

"Has anybody been following you?" she asks.

I glance in my rearview mirror at the unmarked San Francisco police car that's been following me all day. "Not as far as I can tell. What about you?"

"I don't think so."

My relief is tempered by weariness. It will take a while before my paranoia dissipates.

"How did it go with Aronis's ex-wife?" she asks.

"She's willing to testify that her ex-husband talked about taking out Robinson and Chin. She said he was prepared to pay for it."

"That helps."

"Maybe. She also said that he was going to approach Nate about hiring him to kill Robinson and Chin."

"That doesn't help. Did she have any proof that he cut a deal with Nate?"

"No."

"Can she provide any direct link between her husband and the killings?"

"No. And there are other issues. Her credibility is questionable and her motives are suspect. She may be doing this just to get back at her ex-husband."

"Or to get publicity for her book."

"It's a self-published memoir, Rosie. It's never going to sell a lot of copies."

"Sounds like a mixed bag. Besides, it doesn't get us any closer to freestanding innocence."

Rosie is the poster child for cold, hard reality. I ask if she's heard anything from the courts.

"The California Supremes and the Ninth Circuit are about to reject our latest petitions. Our papers are already on their way to Washington to the U.S. Supremes."

It is customary to make an anticipatory filing with the U.S. Supreme Court when you file your papers in the lower courts. The U.S. Supremes won't rule officially until the California Supreme Court and the Ninth Circuit have handed down their decisions.

"The odds are long at the U.S. Supreme Court," she says. "We have time to file a couple more habeas petitions. We need something new."

Swell. "Is there any *good* news?"

"Two things, actually," she says. "First, they finished my kitchen counter this morning. I have a faucet and a sink. I may have running water by tomorrow."

"That's great. What was the second thing?"

"I did a search of the civil cases brought against East Bay Scavenger. The company was sued by one of its former employees on a wrongful-termination claim. Aronis testified against him. The company ultimately prevailed."

Which means the former employee may be looking to get back at East Bay Scavenger or Aronis. "Can you find him?"

"I already did. His name is Floyd Washington. He's at San Quentin for selling heroin."

It's a potential connection to Aronis's drug-distribution business. We need to follow up right away. "What makes you think he'll talk to us?"

"I think he'll appreciate the company of a couple of defense attorneys who might be in a position to try to make his life a little easier."

"Didn't you remind me that we can't swap legal services for testimony?"

"We can still talk to him, Mike."

"When can we see him?"

"This afternoon. He isn't going anywhere."

"How much longer does he have?"

"The rest of his life."

30/ YOUR COOPERATION WILL NOT GO UNNOTICED

Tuesday, July 14. 4:32 p.m.
4 days, 7 hours, and 29 minutes until execution.

A dozen news vans are parked haphazardly in the driveways along the narrow road leading to San Quentin as I inch my way toward the east gate. The locals make a few extra bucks by selling their parking spots to the highest bidders. The most desirable locations are the driveways that are free from overhanging branches, which could interfere with satellite transmissions. The media mob has set up an encampment just outside the gate. The dearth of hard news has left most reporters with little to do except speculate and take turns filming background footage in front of the grimly photogenic San Quentin State Prison sign, which is conveniently placed directly in front of the building that houses the execution chamber.

Rosie and I meet in the parking lot. Despite the lack of sleep, she still looks great as we shove our way through the crowd of reporters and shout the usual platitudes about Nate's innocence, then go through the time-consuming procedures to gain entrance to the prison grounds. Inside the walls, the days leading up to an execution feel like the week before the Super Bowl. The air is filled with tense anticipation. In reality, little really happens unless you're one of the direct participants in the big event. The prisoners must endure lockdown conditions until the process plays its course. Rumors about final appeals and last-minute clemency deals become a form of entertainment. Certain inmates with a morbid streak and an entrepreneurial bent go so far as to make book on the possibility of a stay—with bets being paid in cigarettes. Such activities are strictly forbidden, of course. But the authorities have more important concerns and often turn a blind eye. One of my clients once collected a year's supply of Marlboros when an execution was called off at the final hour. It didn't do much for his health, but the win left him in good spirits.

We're escorted to the visitors' area for the general population, which is separate from the space reserved for the condemned. The guards express surprise when we tell them that we're here to see Floyd Washington instead of Nate. The dreary room with gray walls and a cracked linoleum floor has the same ambience as Little Joey's currency exchange. One of my clients once observed that the Plexiglas windows and mismatched chairs resemble the private viewing area in the adult theater that he frequented—until he was arrested, that is.

We have to communicate with Washington through the Plexiglas divider via a marginally functional wall phone. Our conversation will be conducted under the steady gaze of two armed guards and may be recorded.

Washington glares at us through the bulletproof shield. Aronis's former employee is an angry African American man whose rippled muscles and massive torso place a significant strain on his tattered jeans and tight-fitting cotton shirt. His head is shaved. His arms are covered with tattoos. It comes as no surprise that our reception is somewhat south of cordial.

"Who the *hell* are you?" he barks into the phone.

"My name is Michael Daley," I tell him. "This is my law partner, Rosita Fernandez."

"What the fuck are you doing here?"

Nice. "We need to ask you a few questions."

"I want to talk to my lawyer."

He probably hasn't spoken to an attorney in years. "What's his name?"

"Forget it. He won't return my calls."

"He might if we call him. We're representing Nate Fineman."

He grips the phone more tightly. Attorneys for the condemned have a slightly higher stature in the prison hierarchy in the weeks leading up to an execution. Such fame tends to be short-lived. Your stock can plummet precipitously if your client is executed.

He invokes a marginally more civil tone. "What do you want?"

"Information."

"I don't know anything about Fineman."

"We want to ask you a few questions about Alex Aronis."

He pauses. "What's in it for me?"

"We'll put in a good word with the warden. Your cooperation will not go unnoticed."

"What are you going to do if I don't talk? Throw me in jail?"

It's a legitimate observation. We have limited leverage. "You know we can't make any promises," I say.

"I'm stuck in this shithole for the rest of my life. You want something from me, but you can't make any promises?"

That's the gist of it. "We'll try to find somebody to help you."

"Not good enough."

"We have a client who is scheduled to be executed on Sunday morning."

"Then you'd better come up with something for me before then."

Rosie takes the phone from me—just the way we'd planned it. A man who has been incarcerated for a decade may be somewhat more likely to listen to reason when it's articulated by an attractive woman.

"We'll find someone to help you," she tells him calmly.

Washington becomes engaged. Rosie is pressing the phone to her ear and I can barely make out his words. "Why the hell should I trust you?" he asks.

"When was the last time you had a visitor?" she says.

"Six months ago."

"It'll be another six months unless you help us."

"Your partner said you can't make any promises."

"Let's cut the crap, Floyd. We have a client who has an appointment with a needle on Sunday morning. I looked at your case file. You may have some legitimate grounds for appeal. You can take a chance with us or you can wait for a lawyer who doesn't return your calls." She leans toward the glass. "We're the only game in town."

His eyes dart from her face down to her breasts and then back up. "Are you really going to talk to somebody?" he asks.

"Yes."

He considers his options for a long beat. "Not good enough," he finally decides.

Rosie nods to me and we stand; then she turns back to Washington. "We don't have time for bullshit, Floyd," she tells him. "The warden knows where to find us if you change your mind." With that, she places the phone into its cradle. She turns and walks toward the door.

Her hand is on the doorknob when we hear banging against the Plexiglas. I can't hear him through the divider, but I can read his lips. "Wait!" he shouts.

Rosie takes her own sweet time walking the three steps back to the Plexiglas. She picks up the phone and begins speaking quietly to him. They talk for a couple of minutes. Then the guard comes up from behind Floyd to cuff him and lead him away. I give Rosie an inquisitive look. Fully aware that the room and the phones are wired for sound, she leans forward and places her lips against my right ear. "I'll tell you about it outside," she whispers.

Tuesday, July 14. 5:15 p.m.
4 days, 6 hours, and 46 minutes until execution.

"All right," I whisper to Rosie. "Give."

We're standing in the neatly landscaped area just outside the oddly shaped little building that houses the execution chamber. It's hard to imagine that the nondescript structure made of locally hewn limestone can generate the level of anger, controversy, and division that it does.

Rosie glances at the armed guards who are awaiting authorization to let us enter the Row to see Nate. "We have to find Washington a lawyer," she whispers to me.

"Do you really think he has a chance on appeal?" I ask.

She arches an eyebrow. "I have no idea."

Huh? "You just told him you'd read his case file."

"Where would I have gotten it?"

"You lied?"

"I needed to get him to talk. I'll try to find somebody who can look into filing an appeal for him."

"And if you can't?"

"I'll deal with it myself."

This isn't an ideal time to reprimand her for taking on work for a client who can't afford to pay us. "What did he tell you?"

"He was a crew chief for Aronis."

"Trash or drugs?"

"Both."

"Who supplied them?"

"Terrell Robinson."

"Aronis wouldn't have arranged a hit on his own supplier," I observe.

"They had a falling out. Aronis had to find a new guy."

"Anybody whose name I would recognize?"

"Marshawn Bryant."

Hello again. It's another connection—if we can somehow fit the pieces together. "The guy who looked us straight in the eye and insisted he's never been involved in the drug business?"

"One and the same."

"You were able to get a lot from Washington."

She winks. "I can be very persuasive—especially when I'm talking to a desperate man."

I'm familiar with her powers. "Bryant worked for Robinson," I observe. "You're saying he went into competition with his boss?"

"Evidently, he was doing some freelancing on the side."

All's fair in love, war, politics, and drug dealing. "Is it possible that Aronis and Bryant got together to set up the killings?"

"They already knew each other, but they'll deny it. We have no hard evidence."

"What about Aronis's ex-wife?"

"She still thinks Aronis approached Nate. She can't finger Bryant. Besides, her motivation and credibility are questionable."

Terrific. I ask her if Washington is willing to testify.

"I think so. I would rather not base our final appeal on the testimony of a convicted felon who will be here for the rest of his life."

Neither would I. My mind races into overdrive. "Why didn't Washington cut a deal to testify against Aronis?"

"Because Aronis had already made his own deal to testify against Washington. Evidently, Washington was pocketing some of the drug money that he was supposed to pay over to Aronis. Guys like Aronis don't like to get ripped off by their own people, so he decided to teach Washington a lesson."

"Did it involve broken limbs?"

"He came up with something more creative. Aronis set up a bogus heroin sale. He made sure the cops were tipped off."

"He set up his own guy?"

"Yeah. It was brilliant. He turned Washington in and was the star witness at his trial. He made sure everybody knew that he'd crossed him. Washington got fired and went to jail. He still believes Aronis bought off the cops and the prosecutors."

"Did Aronis think of this scheme by himself?"

"Nope. According to Washington, our client did."

"Did you find anything?" Nate asks. His staccato delivery reflects a higher sense of urgency. His hair is disheveled and his face is red.

"We're looking into some new possibilities," I say. He listens attentively as I brief him on our plans for another round of habeas petitions. "We're going to try to prove the current procedures aren't administered uniformly." I purposefully leave out any use of the words *execution*, *death penalty*, and *capital punishment*. "We're also going to claim that Wendell Tsai has new and exculpatory information based on his discussions with his brother."

"It's inadmissible hearsay."

"We're still going to try."

"Do it faster," he says.

Duly noted. A somber Ilene Fineman is sitting next to her husband. Rabbi Friedman stands and gives us a pensive look. Rosie is next to the door. I'm sitting at the wooden table.

I address the rabbi. "I think it may be better if we speak to Nate in private."

Nate answers for him. "I keep no secrets from my rabbi."

"There are privilege issues," I tell him.

The rabbi removes his glasses and uses them to gesture. "I am not going to testify against Nate," he says.

"The prosecutors can send you a subpoena."

His large chin juts forward. "They can't make me testify."

"They can hold you in contempt."

"I already hold *them* in contempt. I'm prepared to deal with the consequences."

Nate can't pace, so he starts rocking in his wheelchair. He's been unfailingly upbeat every time I've spoken to him. Now the façade is showing a few cracks.

"I need to ask you some hard questions," I say.

Nate shoots a quick glance toward Ilene, then turns back to me. "Fire away."

"Aronis's ex-wife claims Aronis was going to offer to pay you a million bucks to kill Robinson and Chin."

"That's crazy."

"She pulled this whole story out of thin air?"

"I didn't say that, either."

"What exactly are you saying?"

"Alex never talked to me about it. He may have discussed it with *her*, but he never discussed it with *me*."

I don't have time for parsing. "Why, pray tell, did she come forward now?"

"It's a golden opportunity to nail her husband—and me."

"She may be willing to testify that her husband was trying to hire somebody to kill Robinson and Chin. That could help us."

"She'll also point a finger at me. I'll be left hanging out to dry."

"Unless we can prove he paid somebody else to do it."

"Like who?"

"Bryant."

"Do you have any evidence to that effect?"

"Not yet."

"Then you'd better find some."

"We were hoping you might be able to point us in the right direction."

"If I had the goods on Bryant, I wouldn't be here."

I take a deep breath. "We also talked to one of your neighbors."

"Somebody from St. Francis Wood?"

"Somebody from the West Cell Block. Does the name Floyd Washington ring a bell?"

He nods. "He worked for East Bay Scavenger. He was convicted of selling heroin from his truck."

"He told us he was dealing for Aronis, who got his inventory from Robinson and then Bryant."

His face twists into a frown. "Alex has never been convicted of dealing drugs," he says.

"Why are you defending him?"

"I'm not. I'm just stating the facts."

My hands start to shake in frustration. "Aronis is a bad guy. He wouldn't hesitate to throw you under a bus to save his own ass. I don't understand why you're covering for him. He sure as hell wouldn't do the same for you."

He lifts himself up to his full sitting height. "Alex was never convicted of selling drugs. I have no evidence that he had anything to do with the events at the Golden Dragon."

"Give us something to work with, Nate."

"I'm not going to make some wild accusations about a former client and friend. Besides, the courts aren't going to accept the word of a woman who has a grudge against her ex-husband and me, or a convicted felon who will say anything to get out of here."

"It's new information," I say.

"It isn't enough to prove freestanding innocence."

The room fills with intense silence. Ilene takes her husband's hand

and whispers softly to him. The resignation in his colorless face says more than any words.

#

Rosie and I regroup in my rented car in the San Quentin parking lot at six-thirty on Tuesday evening. The local TV stations have completed their early newscasts. The reporters and cameramen mill around a short distance from where we're sitting. I can see the fog rolling toward Berkeley. My mood matches the gray sky.

Rosie punches the End button on her cell phone. Her voice sounds fatigued. "My mother says everything is quiet over at the house."

"That's good."

"Yes, it is." She gets a serene look in her eyes as she watches the seagulls fly overhead. I'm always amazed by her ability to notice simple beauty during moments of great stress. She snaps back to reality. "I'm not going to be able to sleep until we find the person who delivered that picture of Grace and Jake to my house," she says.

"Neither will I." My cell phone rings and I answer it.

"It's Pete," the voice says. "How soon can you get across the bridge?"

"Twenty minutes," I say. "Why?"

"I just got a call from one of my operatives. Marshawn Bryant just walked into Little Joey's currency exchange."

Rosie and I drive separately from San Quentin to the nearby Larkspur ferry terminal, where I park my rental car and get into Rosie's Civic. Traffic is heavy as she weaves southbound on the 101 freeway through Corte Madera. An unmarked San Francisco police cruiser is keeping its distance behind us. I use the opportunity to eat an energy bar and gulp down a bottle of water. For the next few days, my diet will consist of products that you can purchase at your local gas station.

"Why is Bryant at Little Joey's office?" Rosie asks.

"He isn't there to cash a check," I say.

My cell phone rings again as we're heading down the Waldo Grade. "It's Tony Popovich," the husky voice says. The Mission District cop was an all-city offensive guard when I was a running back at St. Ignatius. He moonlights as a subcontractor for Pete. "Bryant and D'Amato left the currency exchange a few minutes ago. Bryant was heading toward his office. Joey went over to Shalimar for dinner."

I tell him that we'll be there as soon as we can, then hit the End button. I turn to Rosie and say, "Got a taste for Pakistani food?"

"Absolutely."

# # #

The traffic gods smile upon us, and our trip to the Tenderloin takes only twenty-five minutes. We find a parking space on Jones Street, two doors from Shalimar, a scruffy hole-in-the-wall with rock-bottom prices and the ambience of a truck stop. Rosie and I nod to Popovich, who is hunkered down in his dented Dodge van across the street. The unmarked police car that's been following us pulls in behind him.

We push open Shalimar's metal door and are met by the aroma of exotic spices. The floor is checkered linoleum, the tables are better suited for poker than for dining, and the chairs are secondhand Wal-Mart specials. Modern Pakistani music blares from the open kitchen. You place your order at the counter and carry your food to your table—if you're lucky enough to find one. The customers range from a Pakistani softball team to a group of button-down yuppies trying to appear hip by dining downscale on lamb chops, skewered chicken, and flatbreads stuffed with onion and potato. I order the *palak aloo methi*, a stew with spinach and herbs. Rosie opts for the chicken korma, a spicy curry with tender meat that falls off the bone.

Little Joey is leaning over a plate of skewered lamb at a table in the corner. "What now?" he snaps as we approach him.

"Nice to see you, Joe," I say.

"I thought you were trying to stop an execution."

"We still have to eat."

His rodentlike eyes gleam. "How long have you been watching me?"

"What makes you think we're watching you?" I say.

"I saw Tony Pop outside. I know he works for your brother."

Busted. Rosie and I pull up a couple of chairs. "Mind if we join you?" I ask.

"Do I have any choice?"

"No."

He sets down his fork. "Why are you harassing me?" he asks.

"You were one of the first officers at the scene," I say. "You're the only person who can give us firsthand information."

"Your father and I got there after the shooting stopped."

"Then give us the name of somebody else who got there before you did and we'll get off your back."

"Dave Low was already securing the scene."

"He's dead."

"I know." He wipes his lips with his napkin and tries to change the subject. "Did they find the IA file?"

"No."

"Did your father take it?"

"Of course not. The log said he checked it back in."

"It doesn't prove that he did."

"It doesn't prove that he didn't. Your name was on the log, too. What did the report say?"

He shoves another helping of lamb into his mouth. "The charges that somebody planted the gun were crap being spread by the defense lawyers. We were cleared."

Rosie takes a bite of bread and tries another direction. "How long have you known Marshawn Bryant?" she asks.

He looks up as he pauses to think about it. "About eight years."

"We understand you got together with him earlier this evening."

"I did." He looks down at his plate for an instant, then looks back up. He starts talking faster. "He handled the build-out of my business. I'm expanding my space. I asked him to submit a bid. He's a good contractor."

It's a convenient explanation. I decide to see if I can get a reaction from him. "Were you guys talking about our case?"

"Nope."

"Some people think Bryant is involved in drug dealing."

He's becoming more agitated as he sets his fork down. "That's ridiculous."

"Have you ever met a man named Alex Aronis?"

"Nope."

"His ex-wife claims he's running a big-time heroin-distribution operation in the East Bay. He was hot to break into the San Francisco market. She claims he was looking for somebody to take out Robinson and Chin. She said Aronis was going to talk to Nate about it."

"You really think Aronis paid Fineman to pop Robinson and Chin?"

"We think he paid somebody else to do it—like Bryant."

He takes a big bite out of a roll. "That's bullshit."

"Are you sure about that, Joe?"

His beady eyes form tiny slits. "Yes."

"Did you ever meet a guy named Floyd Washington?"

"Nope."

"He used to work for Aronis. He was convicted of selling heroin from the back of his garbage truck. He told us Aronis was trying to move into San Francisco. He also claimed Aronis was prepared to pay big money to take out Robinson and Chin."

"I don't know anything about it. You guys must be really desperate if you're trying to get an execution stopped with the testimony of a jail-house snitch."

We are.

Little Joey wipes his lips with a greasy paper napkin and starts to stand. "Anything else?" he snaps.

Rosie never loses her composure, but her balled fist indicates to me that she's as frustrated as I am. "Washington told us that Bryant was supplying Aronis with the heroin that was being distributed by the employees of East Bay Scavenger," she says. "He claimed Bryant was competing with Robinson."

"So you think Bryant was competing with his boss?"

"According to Washington, yes."

"Lots of luck proving it. If you ask me, that's nuts. At this point, you guys will say anything to try to stop the execution."

Rosie's eyes are locked on Joey's. "We think Aronis paid Bryant to set up the hit on Robinson and Chin," she says.

He responds with a patronizing smile as he shakes his head vigorously. "Marshawn isn't a drug dealer or a killer."

His heartfelt endorsement has a hollow ring. I try a measured bluff. "A witness saw Bryant in the alley behind the Golden Dragon right after the shootings."

He shakes his head. "Eugene Tsai said he saw a black man in the alley," he says. "That description fits thousands of people in the Bay Area."

"It was Bryant," I insist.

"There was no positive ID. You don't know what you're talking about. Marshawn is a legitimate businessman."

"Who deals heroin."

"Prove it."

"We will. Why are you defending him?"

"I'm not."

"Yes, you are."

"He's a reputable businessman. That's all."

Rosie pushes her tray toward Joey and points a long finger at him. "I want you to pass along a message to your friend Marshawn," she says. "We're going to be watching both of you. If we see any funny business, we're going straight to the DA. Understood?"

The left side of Joey's mouth turns up into a smug half grin. "Are you threatening me?" he asks.

"I'm making a promise."

He gives her a mocking smile, crumples his paper napkin in his fist, and slithers out of the restaurant without saying another word.

Tuesday, July 14. 8:05 p.m.
4 days, 3 hours, and 56 minutes until execution.

"Do you think it was a good idea to antagonize him?" I ask Rosie. We're sitting in her car down the street from Shalimar.

"We don't have time to be subtle," she says. "I want Pete to have his people watch Little Joey and Bryant. I want to know if they talk again."

"What if they do?"

"We'll know they're in on something. I want to make them nervous."

"You're making *me* nervous."

She glances in her rearview mirror at the unmarked police car. "That's why we have an army of cops watching us. It can't be a coincidence that one of the first cops at the Golden Dragon met with a drug dealer who may have been spotted near the restaurant that night. They had to be talking about more than blueprints."

# # #

I'm in my office at ten o'clock on Tuesday night, pacing. I just got off the phone with Rabbi Friedman, who left San Quentin a few minutes ago. He had spent a sobering evening with Nate going over the wrenching details associated with his impending death: updating his will and funeral plans. The rabbi said Nate was showing the first significant signs of accepting the inevitable. Even heavyweight fighters start to break down in the final rounds.

First Street is silent except for the tolling of the Ferry Building clock. I sit on the edge of my desk and punch in the number to Roosevelt's cell phone. He answers on the first ring. "Sorry to call you so late," I say. "Are you at the office?"

"Yes, I am. How is the family doing?"

"They're okay." I quickly reconsider. "Actually, they're doing amazingly well. Rosie comes from a strong gene pool."

"How are *you* holding up?"

"As well as can be expected."

"God, you need to get some rest," he says. "I can tell by your voice that you're running on empty."

"You're right."

"I'm always right. So, what is the purpose of your call?"

"Did you ever talk to Alex Aronis about Nate's case?"

"Yes. We talked to several of Fineman's clients. Aronis didn't provide any relevant information."

I play my cards faceup. "Did you seriously consider the possibility that he paid somebody to kill Robinson and Chin?"

"Yes. We had no evidence pointing in his direction."

"He admitted to me that he knew Marshawn Bryant."

"As far as we could tell, it was purely professional. I take it these questions aren't coming out of thin air?"

"We met a guy named Floyd Washington at San Quentin today. He used to work for Aronis. He was convicted of dealing heroin from his garbage truck. He said Bryant was supplying the heroin to Aronis. He also thought Aronis might have paid somebody to kill Robinson and Chin."

"You believed him?"

"I had no reason to disbelieve him."

"We found no evidence that would support your theory, Mike."

# # #

Rosie and I spend another long and sleepless night at the office, generating yet another set of papers. The pressure and fatigue finally overtake our better judgment as I'm sitting on the corner of Rosie's desk and reviewing a draft of the latest habeas petition at two-fifteen on Wednesday morning.

"They aren't going to let Wendell Tsai testify about what his brother told him," I say.

"He has new information," Rosie says. "He can talk about Jasmine Luk."

"It's hearsay."

"I'm well aware of that, Mike."

"You asked me what I thought."

Her dark eyes flash anger. "I asked you for constructive comments. That wasn't."

"I'm trying to be realistic."

"Then come up with something better."

"I'm trying."

"Try harder. What's *your* plan?"

"The plan," I say, "is to continue filing new petitions every day until 12:01 a.m. on Sunday. You know how it is with death-penalty cases. This isn't like a trial, where we have months to talk about strategy and prepare witnesses. We'll keep looking for anybody who might be able to cast some doubt on Nate's guilt. We'll take whatever we can find and throw it into a brief and hope we can persuade some overworked judge who has no incentive to help us to grant a stay."

Rosie takes off her reading glasses and slowly sets them down on her desk. Her tone is patronizing when she says, "Are you finished?"

I take a moment to regain my composure. "Yes."

"Do I really need to remind you that it will serve no useful purpose to snipe at each other?"

"No."

"Good. In that case, where does it leave us?"

I set the brief down in my lap. "We'll file this brief in the morning. In the meantime, Pete has people watching Aronis and Bryant. Our best bet is to try to foist the blame onto them. It would help if somebody can affirmatively place Bryant behind the Golden Dragon."

"How do we do that?"

"We need to find Jasmine Luk."

"She disappeared ten years ago."

"Pete is watching her great-aunt. Nick Hanson is still looking for people in Chinatown who may have seen her."

"It's beyond a long shot."

"Death-penalty appeals always are."

"It's time to get real, Mike."

"That isn't helpful," I snap.

Terrence the Terminator walks into the office and interrupts us with a peace offering in the form of some cold pizza. "You might find a way to channel your energy more productively," he observes. "Go home and get some rest. Things will look better in the morning."

# # #

My cell phone rings as Rosie and I are driving home through a thick blanket of fog at two-forty on Wednesday morning. "Where are you, Mick?" Pete asks.

"The bridge."

"Same old story, Mick—you're packing it up while I'm working."

Enough with the jokes. "What is it?" I ask.

"Something's going on at Amanda Wong's place."

"I'm not in the mood for twenty questions."

"A guy in a Ford Escort has driven around her apartment building a couple of times. The driver is staying low and wearing sunglasses."

"You think it's a cop?"

"I doubt it. He's too conspicuous. It isn't professional."

"What the hell is going on?"

"I'll call you back when I find out."

Wednesday, July 13. 3:04 a.m.
3 days, 20 hours, and 57 minutes until execution.

get the answer when my phone rings as I walk into my apartment. "False alarm," Pete says. "Edwards was in the Escort. I followed him back to the *Chronicle*."

Not exactly a smoking gun. "Why is he watching Wong?"

"For the same reasons we are, Mick—he must think she knows something about the whereabouts of Jasmine Luk."

"Maybe." I shift gears. "Can you pull the bank account records for Aronis and Bryant around the time of the shootings?"

"Sure, but it may take a little time. I take it this means you think Aronis paid Bryant to take out Robinson and Chin?"

"Maybe." I think about it for a moment and add, "While you're at it, why don't you pull up the financial records for Little Joey's business?"

"I'll see what I can find."

"Be discreet, Pete."

"I will." He waits a beat. "You got something, Mick?"

"I'm just playing hunches now. It's all that we have left."

# # #

I'm awakened from a brief and uneasy sleep by my ringing phone at five-thirty on Wednesday morning. I can tell that it's Edwards as soon as I hear the hacking smoker's cough. "Where the hell are you?" he barks.

"In bed." Don't you ever sleep? "Where the hell are you?"

"At the east gate to San Quentin. You promised me a live interview with your client this morning. I'm over here with a crew. Get your ass in gear."

# # #

"What were you doing at Wong's apartment last night?" I ask Edwards.

He tries to play it coy. "What makes you think I was there?"

"My brother saw you."

"You guys are so desperate that you're keeping reporters under surveillance?"

"He was watching Wong. Evidently, so were you."

It's a few minutes after eight o'clock on Wednesday morning. Edwards is gathering his belongings in the makeshift studio area where he just finished a live interview with Nate. Though Nate's hands were shaking uncontrollably throughout the session, he summoned every remaining ounce of strength to plead his innocence.

The wily reporter ponders for a moment. "I think Ms. Wong may know something," he says.

"Like what?"

"I'm not sure."

For the first time, I hope he's right. "I don't have time for this, Jerry. I had to pull a lot of strings to get you an interview with a man who is scheduled to be executed in three days. We know what that will do for your ratings."

"It isn't that I'm not appreciative. On the other hand, your client didn't say anything except that he was wrongly convicted. That isn't what I would call breaking news."

"What did you expect him to say?"

"He might have started by apologizing to the families of the victims."

"He has nothing to apologize for."

"Not according to the State of California."

"The State of California was wrong." I ask again. "Why were you really watching Wong?"

"Just a hunch. I think she knows what happened to her great-niece."

"Hunches are inadmissible in court. What haven't you told me?"

He pulls out a cigarette but doesn't light up. "Wong's business used to sell phony immigration papers for people who were trying to get out of China."

"How do you know?"

"One of my former colleagues did a series about it twenty years ago."

"You're suggesting she prepared false papers to help her great-niece disappear?"

"It's just a theory, Mike."

# # #

My cell phone rings again as I'm driving into San Francisco a short time later. "How did Nate's interview go?" Rosie asks.

"Fair. Edwards was hoping for a last-minute apology to the families, but Nate didn't accommodate him. Edwards also told me that he thinks something may be going on with Amanda Wong." I tell her about Edwards's claim that Wong's print shop used to produce phony immigration papers.

"Does he have any proof?" Rosie asks.

"Not yet. What's going on at home?"

"Things get tense when your house is surrounded by cops. My mother heard something outside last night. The cops came out in full force with their guns drawn. It looked like a scene out of *Kojak*. Fortunately, it was a false alarm."

"Is she okay?"

"She's a little shaken up, but she'll never admit it."

"What about Grace and Tommy?"

"About the same."

"And you?"

She waits a beat before she responds. "I'll be fine."

"I mean it, Rosie. Are you okay?"

I can hear her take a deep breath. "I'll be glad when this is over, Mike. Then we'll have a long talk about how we got ourselves into this mess and how we can avoid it in the future."

"Rosie, I agree. Anything from the courts?"

"Another day, another habeas petition. I filed first thing with the California Supremes and the Ninth Circuit. The Supremes have already said no to our request for a hearing to allow Wendell Tsai to testify. According to my sources, the Ninth Circuit will probably come to the same conclusion later this afternoon."

I'm glad somebody is doing the real legal work. "I'll be there with you as soon as I can," I tell her.

"Do what you have to do, Mike. Let's focus on moving ahead."

I hit the End button. My phone rings again a moment later.

"It's Pete. I should have the bank statements for Aronis and Bryant soon."

"Great. What about the financial information for Little Joey?"

"I'm hoping by the end of the day."

We're running out of time and options. "Are you still watching Wong?" I ask.

"Yeah. That's why I called you. At the moment, she's in San

Francisco."

"Doing what?"

"Meeting with Jeff Chin."

Huh? "Where?"

"The office of the Six Companies."

What's this? "Why is she meeting with the son of one of the victims?" I ask.

"Beats me."

"Don't take your eyes off her. I'll be there as soon as I can."

Wednesday, July 15. 10:04 a.m.
3 days, 13 hours, and 57 minutes until execution.

"Thanks for taking the time to see me on short notice," I say. Jeff Chin is sitting behind his cherrywood-inlaid desk. His understated office at the Six Companies has matching bookcases and a console. The walls are covered with subdued artwork from China. "Nice to see you again, Mr. Daley," he lies. "I only have a few minutes. What brings you here?"

"First, I wanted to thank you for dinner the other night."

He doesn't miss a beat. "It was my pleasure. I must apologize for my behavior the last time we met."

No, you mustn't. "There is nothing to apologize for."

"There is no excuse for rudeness."

Instead of debating whose manners were worse, we agree to call it a draw.

He rearranges a stack of papers and stands up, signaling that our conversation is coming to an end. "It was generous of you to come down to express your gratitude," he says. "It was also well beyond the call of duty. I know your schedule is very busy. If there is anything else that I can do for you, please feel free to call me."

He intended it as a token gesture, but it creates an opening. "Actually, there is."

He starts backpedaling. "I need to leave for a meeting."

"This will take just a moment. A young woman named Jasmine Luk lived behind the Golden Dragon. We've been told that she and a man name Eugene Tsai were walking in the alley around the time of the events at the restaurant. We think she saw somebody in the alley shortly after your father was killed. Unfortunately, she disappeared a few days later."

He holds his palms up. "I don't know anything about it. I'm sorry."

So are we. "Do you have any idea where we might find her?"

"I'm afraid not."

I raise the stakes. "Ms. Luk's great-aunt is Amanda Wong."

He looks down at the gold letter opener on his desk. Now he knows that we've been watching Wong—and perhaps him. He considers his response carefully. "That's quite a coincidence. I just met with Ms. Wong here in my office."

I decide to play it straight. "I know. We've been watching her."

"Why?"

"We think she might know more than she's told us about the whereabouts of her great-niece."

"You'll have to ask her about it."

"We already have."

"She's a very respected member of the community."

"I know."

"Are you suggesting that she had something to do with my father's death?"

I shake my head. "No. We were simply hoping to discover what happened to her great-niece."

His eyes narrow. "You're really quite desperate, aren't you?"

"Yes, we are. Would you mind telling me why Ms. Wong came to see you?"

"Certainly, but it had nothing to do with the events at the Golden

Dragon." He clears his throat. "She came to us for assistance in raising money for the treatment of a girl in Oakland who needs a heart and a lung transplant. The girl's parents are dead. She's living with her grand-parents. They have no medical insurance."

I feel like a jerk as I recall the contribution jar on the counter at Sunshine Printing. "What's her prognosis?"

"It depends on how soon they can find a donor. They're trying to raise a hundred thousand dollars."

Now I feel like a bigger jerk. I flash back to the three nights that Grace spent in the intensive care unit at Marin General after she got hit in the head by a batted softball during practice last summer. The doctors described it as a mild concussion with a slight bruise to her brain. I found it incomprehensible that anybody could have described *any* injury to the brain as slight. Thankfully, Grace recovered and our insurance took care of most of the costs.

"Will you be able to help them?" I ask.

"I believe so."

"Is there anything I can do?"

"It's kind of you to offer, but our community takes care of its own."

It's the answer I should have expected. "Do you know anything about Ms. Wong's great-niece?"

"No, Mr. Daley."

"Do you have any idea where she might have gone?"

"No, Mr. Daley."

It's another dead end. I'm still curious about one thing. "Why did you really buy us dinner the other night?"

Chin adjusts his tie. "You were just doing your job," he says. "I have no hard feelings toward you—even if you've chosen to represent Nathan Fineman." The corner of his mouth turns up slightly when he adds, "And perhaps to get you off my back." His expression turns serious. "My father and I had our differences, yet he was still my father. If your client murdered him, then I believe he deserves to die. If he didn't, it would only compound the injustice."

It is becoming clear to me that he had no involvement in his father's operations or the events at the Golden Dragon. Aronis and Bryant are more promising options. As I'm leaving the elegant offices of the Six Companies to try to find Bryant, I silently berate myself for wasting an entire morning drilling another empty well.

Wednesday, July 15. 12:03 p.m.
3 days, 11 hours, and 58 minutes until execution.

Marshawn Bryant greets me tersely: "I'm busy. You're going to have to make this quick."

"That's fine," I say.

I wasn't expecting a warm welcome. We're standing in a hard-hat zone just south of the Transbay bus terminal at the corner of First and Folsom, where the metal skeleton of a thirty-story office tower rises into the clear summer sky. Bayview Construction lost the "beauty contest" to become the general contractor on the project. However, it got a multimillion-dollar consolation prize when it was tapped to handle the build-out of the interiors.

The air smells of cement and debris. My khaki slacks and polo shirt are covered with dust. Somehow, Bryant's double-breasted pin-striped suit is spotless. The hard hats are working around-the-clock shifts to complete the exterior before the rains start in November.

After spending the morning fighting with Edwards at San Quentin and hitting a wall with Chin at the Six Companies, I'm anxious to get something—anything—from Bryant. At the moment, he appears to be our most promising alternate suspect—unless he can produce somebody other than his wife to verify his whereabouts on the night all hell broke loose at the Golden Dragon. I'm prepared to mount a full-blown frontal attack. As a practical matter, this probably means this will be my last chance to talk to him.

A huge crane revs its engine. I lean forward to shout into Bryant's right ear. "Is there someplace we can talk?"

He gestures toward a temporary structure near the street. I follow him past the warning signs that admonish us to wear our helmets at all times. The windowless trailer is filled with tools and blueprints. We sit down at a card table. My eyes water from the dust.

"We're behind schedule," he says. "What do you want now?"

I get right to the point. "We've found a witness who saw you in the alley behind the Golden Dragon shortly after the shootings." I'm stretching Wendell Tsai's description to suit my purposes. I'm also looking for a reaction.

This elicits an eye roll. "We've covered that issue. It wasn't me."

"What would you say if I told you there was another witness?" It's another bluff.

He dismisses me with a wave of the back of his hand. "It wasn't me."

"Then who was it?"

His tone turns acerbic. "Beats the hell out of me. Go ahead and bring out your witness. Either they're mistaken or they're flat-out lying."

"We talked to a man named Floyd Washington. He says you've met."

"Doesn't ring a bell. Is he in the construction business?"

"No, he's in the incarceration business. He's at San Quentin."

He takes a deep breath of the heavy air. "You pulled me away from a busy work site to ask about some low-level hoodlum with an ax to grind?"

"He mentioned you by name. He used to work for Alex Aronis. Now do you remember him?"

"Nope."

"Do you know Aronis?"

"I've known Alex for years," he says with feigned nonchalance. His eyes drift over my shoulder. "I was the construction manager on the build-out of his company's office space in Oakland."

"When was that?"

"I don't remember exactly. I was still working for Terrell Robinson. It was probably about fifteen years ago."

It lines up with Aronis's story. "Do you keep in touch?"

"Sure." His eyes are still dancing. "A couple of years ago I did some work on his house. What does this have to do with the guy at San Quentin?"

"Washington said your old boss used to supply heroin to Aronis, which was then distributed from the garbage trucks operated by Aronis's company. He also told us that Aronis got into a fight with Robinson and needed to find a new supplier." My eyes bore into his. "That's when he turned to you."

"That's crap."

"So you're saying he's lying?"

He stretches to his full, intimidating height and folds his arms. "Damn right."

I'm just starting. "Washington also said you and Aronis were trying to get a piece of the heroin trade in San Francisco."

The volume of his voice goes up as he becomes more agitated. "That's bullshit. It's obvious that he'll say anything to get out of jail." He points a finger at me. "If you're going to make these wild accusations, I'll have my lawyers call you."

I've always found it effective to respond to bullies with an even tone. "Are you threatening to sue me now?"

"Nope." He shifts to the dialect of the hood. "I'm talkin' straight."

"Have you been smashing the windows of our cars?"

"Nope. You should be more careful where you park."

I move in closer to him. "Did you have a package delivered to my ex-wife's house with a photo of our daughter and her boyfriend?"

"Of course not."

"You and Aronis are partners in the drug-distribution business, aren't you?"

"You're crazy."

"Why have you been spending so much time with a former cop who was one of the first officers at the Golden Dragon?"

"What the hell are you talking about?"

"We know that you and Joey D'Amato are pals."

"He's a customer."

"I hear he's more than a customer."

He shakes his head with authority. "That's insane."

"Are you paying him off to keep his mouth shut about seeing you in the alley behind the Golden Dragon?"

"Of course not. I'm helping him remodel his business."

It's my turn to jab a finger in his face. "Look, Marshawn, everybody in town knows you and Aronis are dealing heroin. You're living on borrowed time. The cops are going to put it together and you're going to be in a world of trouble."

"You're full of shit. You're in way over your head."

"You're in deeper."

"Get the hell out of here."

"We'll see you in court."

My heart races. Next time, I'll be back with Terrence the Terminator to serve a subpoena.

#

"Did you get anything from Bryant?" Rosie asks.

"Deny, deny, deny."

"That's helpful. Are you coming back to the office?"

I press my cell phone against my right ear as I walk up First Street toward Market. My head throbs. "Not yet," I tell her. "I'm going over to Oakland to take another run at Aronis."

38/ WE FOUND FIFTY THOUSAND DOLLARS
WORTH OF HEROIN IN HIS TRUCK

A ronis is unrepentant. "Floyd Washington was a small-time thug," he insists. "The experience made us realize the importance of doing background checks on new hires."

We're sitting in a rarely used office in a barracks-style structure adjacent to the maintenance yard of East Bay Scavenger. The walls are a faded oatmeal color. The metal desk is government issue. The dented furniture looks as if it came straight from a Salvation Army thrift store. A small black-and-white photo of the company's founder is mounted on the wall next to a tiny window, soiled by decades of exhaust fumes. Aronis's great-grandfather ran a multimillion-dollar operation from this dingy headquarters that resembles the back room of your average gas station. I can understand why Alex prefers to work in his hermetically sealed office tower in downtown Oakland.

"How long did Washington work for you?" I ask.

"About ten years. He was never any trouble until he decided to run a pharmaceutical business from his truck."

"He's made some pretty significant accusations about you."

"Doesn't surprise me. We turned him over to the police after we found fifty thousand dollars worth of heroin in his truck." His right eyebrow darts up for emphasis. "We had no choice. I testified at his trial."

It begs the question of where Washington got his hands on the stockpile in the first place. "He claimed it was a setup," I tell Aronis.

He can't conceal a phony smile. "What did you expect him to say, bud?"

I lean forward and place my hands on the dented desk. "He also told us you were supplying the heroin."

He shakes his head. "That's not true."

I push harder. "He told us that you were getting your inventory from Marshawn Bryant."

His large mouth transforms into an emphatic scowl. "That's not true, either."

"And that you were planning to take over Terrell Robinson's operations in San Francisco."

He sits up as tall as he can and gestures with two stubby fingers. "Washington is full of shit," he says.

# # #

"Where are you?" Rosie asks.

"Sitting in traffic at the Bay Bridge toll plaza," I reply. The sun is high in the summer sky over Treasure Island as I drum my fingers on my steering wheel. I tell her about my conversation with Aronis. "I'd rip him to shreds if I could get him in court under oath," I say.

She's less sanguine. "That isn't going to happen unless we come up with some new evidence. The California Supremes and the Ninth Circuit have rejected our petitions. I expect the U.S. Supremes to follow suit any minute now."

Damn it. "Have you heard anything from Sacramento?"

"The governor is down in L.A. shooting a public service announcement to encourage businesses to stay in California. He'll be back tomorrow."

A photo op trumps a death-penalty appeal. "Did you get any hints from his people?"

"They said not to get our hopes up."

Big surprise. It's bad politics for the governor to interject himself into the middle of a death-penalty appeal. "Any other news?"

"Nick Hanson left a message on our machine. He wants you to call him right away."

# # #

"How the hell are you?" the ever-cheerful Nick Hanson chirps.

"Just great." I'm inching forward through the tunnel on Yerba Buena Island in the middle of the Bay Bridge. The upper deck of the two-level structure once carried three lanes of auto traffic in each direction. The lower deck was reserved for trucks and electric trains. The trains were dismantled in the fifties. Five lanes of westbound traffic are grinding at a snail's pace. I wish the trains were still rolling.

"You got news?" I ask.

"Indeed I do." The master storyteller pauses for effect. "Do you believe in ghosts, Mike?"

I'm in no mood for banter. "What are you talking about, Nick?"

"I talked to one of Jasmine Luk's former coworkers at the Chinese Hospital. He said he thought he saw her in Chinatown about a month ago. She disappeared into a crowd."

"Was he sure it was Luk?"

"Pretty sure."

Not good enough. "Absolutely sure would be better."

"We aren't there yet."

"What was Luk doing there?"

"Beats me."

"Did he have any idea where we might find her?"

"Your guess is as good as mine. Chinatown is a place where some-body like Luk could hide in plain view."

# # #

My next call goes to Pete. "Where are you?" I ask.

"My car."

He loves to give me that answer. "You already got your windows fixed?"

"Yeah. I have people who take care of that kind of stuff for me."

I wish I had people. "And where is your car?"

"Oakland. I'm still following Amanda Wong."

I tell him about my conversation with Jeff Chin. "He probably called Wong," I say. "She must know that we're watching her."

"Doesn't matter, Mick. I'll be discreet."

He will. "Is anybody behind you?"

"Probably." He listens intently as I describe my conversation with Nick the Dick. "Do you think Luk is still somewhere in the area?" he asks.

"Don't know."

"She disappeared ten years ago, Mick."

"I'm well aware of that."

"I'll stay with Wong."

I put the cell phone into the drink holder and drive to the city in silence.

Wednesday, July 15. 7:07 p.m.
3 days, 4 hours, and 54 minutes until execution.

N ate's puffy red eyes are locked intently on mine. He isn't getting any sleep. Ilene is sitting next to him as he leans forward
in his wheelchair in the cold, silent visitors' area. Rosie is
standing by the door. San Quentin's thick stone walls provide a back-
drop of eerie calm. Nate's mood is decidedly somber. The tired voice of
the trial lawyer reappears for what may be his final appeal. "Did they
find the IA file?" he asks.

He's starting to forget things. We talked about this yesterday. "No,"
I say. "They refused to grant a stay just because it's missing." As a practical matter, the cops have no incentive to keep looking. We've sent a
team of investigators to search through the massive storage warehouse.
Not surprisingly, they've come up empty.

He grimaces. "Was Pete able to pull the bank records for Aronis and
Bryant?"

"Yes." The news isn't good. "We couldn't identify any pattern of
cash transfers around the time of the shootings. Pete's trying to get his
hands on some recent financial records for Little Joey D'Amato."

"What are you looking for?"

I answer him honestly. "I'm not sure. Anything we might be able to
use."

"Damn it." The old warrior heaves a resigned sigh. "It's over."

"Not until 12:01 on Sunday morning."

He reaches across the small table to grasp his wife's hand. "We have to finish making arrangements," he says to her.

"It isn't going to happen, Nate," she tells him.

"It's going to happen sooner or later. It looks like it's going to be sooner."

"We're going to file another round of petitions in the morning," I tell him.

His frustration manifests itself in the form of sarcasm. "What brilliant legal theory have you concocted this time?"

"That it's impossible to tell whether somebody is completely unconscious after they administer the Sodium Pentothal."

His rubbery face vibrates as he shakes his head vigorously. "It isn't going to work," he says. "They've already turned down our argument that the death penalty is cruel and unusual punishment. I appreciate your efforts, but we need to start turning our attention to concluding these proceedings with a shred of dignity. It's time to be realistic. The deck has been stacked against me from day one."

"We still have time for more appeals," I say.

"The courts aren't going to listen."

"Then we'll have to make them listen."

There is a mawkish silence. "What's it really like?" he whispers.

"What do you mean?"

"You know what I mean—when they do it."

I dart a glance to Rosie, whose lips form a tight line across her face. "You don't want to go there," I tell him.

"Yes, I do."

I've been dreading this moment. I had to sit through the excruciating experience of watching the execution of a client named Lonnie Felton a dozen years ago. It was the only time I ever lost a death-penalty case. It's also something that I wouldn't want to repeat. Though I am generally opposed to capital punishment, I would be hard pressed to suggest justice was not served in that case. Lonnie was a remorseless gangbanger from Hunters Point who broke into the house of a young couple in search of drug money. He shot the husband at point-blank range, then tied up the wife and two young daughters and systematically raped and tortured them for the next eight hours. He then shot the children in full view of the mother before turning the gun on her. Lonnie was still sitting triumphantly in the bedroom of the house, surrounded by death, when the police arrived. I was the last in a series of lawyers who fended off his execution for eighteen years.

I take a deep breath. "The guards will be very polite," I tell him. "They'll escort you inside the chamber. They'll help you lie down on the table. They'll strap you in and insert some needles."

"Will you be there?"

I swallow hard. "Yes."

"Can the witnesses see everything?"

"Yes."

He cringes. "How long does it take?"

"Just a few minutes." I don't mention that it took the guards fifteen minutes to find a usable vein in Lonnie's arm.

"Does it hurt?"

"They tell me it's no worse than drawing blood." Except you die.

"Then what?"

"You'll go right to sleep as soon as they start the Sodium Pentothal. You won't feel anything after that." At least that's the idea. Lonnie flailed around for a couple of minutes before he finally succumbed.

"Will I vomit?"

"Probably not." Maybe.

"Will I...soil myself?"

"Probably not." Lonnie did.

"Will I twitch?"

"That's unlikely." Lonnie looked like a two-hundred-pound vibrator.

An exasperated Ilene finally stops him. "Why are you talking about this?"

Nate pushes out a heavy sigh. "I want to know what happens." He holds up a hand to his wife. "I don't want you and the children to see me die."

"We're allowed to be there," she says. "I want you to see the face of someone who loves you."

"I want you to remember me the way I am today—not the way I'm going to look after they've injected me with poison."

She grasps his hand tightly. "We'll talk about it again later, Nate."

"No, we won't."

I try to find a more positive subject. "We're still going to file the new petitions in the morning," I say.

"They'll be rejected by noon," he replies.

"Then we'll file another set on Friday."

"They'll reject those even faster. Judges hate to work weekends."

"I'm not that cynical."

"I am."

I look for a hint of hope. "Nick Hanson talked to somebody in Chinatown who may have seen Jasmine Luk a few weeks ago."

His eyes perk up. "Were they sure it was Luk?"

"Pretty sure."

"Pretty sure isn't good enough."

"Pete is still watching Amanda Wong. Maybe she'll try to contact her great-niece."

"It would be helpful if she did before 12:01 a.m. on Sunday," he says.

Yes, it would. "We're working on an alternate version of our next habeas petition. It will say that we've located a key new witness."

The damp room fills with another cool silence. "Let me give you some advice," Nate says. "When your client is three days from an execution, you'd better come up with something more than a phantom witness whose name will be inserted into a generic brief. Death-penalty cases are a zero-sum game. Your success or failure will be measured by whether I'm still breathing at 12:02 on Sunday morning."

He's right.

"Keep the papers short," he says. "Judges like you to get straight to the point."

We have no other choice.

# # #

Rosie and I meet with Ilene outside the visitors' area at eight-fifteen on Wednesday night. Ilene's voice is filled with a grim resignation. "Mr. Daley," she says, "I want to thank you and Ms. Fernandez for everything." We've told her repeatedly that she can call us by our first names. She isn't a first-name person. Nate is inside with Rabbi Friedman for a few moments of the sort of spiritual counseling that I was never very adept at providing when I was a priest.

"Everything is going to be all right," Rosie tells her.

Ilene hands me an envelope. "This is a check for another fifty thousand," she says. "I know you and your team have been working around the clock. I want to be sure that everybody is paid."

It's the last thing on my mind. "Thank you," I whisper.

Her eyes are red. "I take some comfort knowing that Nate won't be suffering much longer."

"This fight isn't over," Rosie insists.

"I want my husband to die in peace."

"We don't want him to die at all."

Ilene takes out a tissue and wipes her eyes. The former society matron repeats her mantra in a tone that reflects a dignified inner strength. "My husband is not a murderer," she says simply. "Now he's going to pay the price for keeping murderers out of jail for all those years. I don't know how I'm going to live with it." Then she summons the guard to take her back to her husband and her rabbi.

# # #

"They're giving up," Rosie says.

I'm sitting in front of the fireplace in her living room at quarter to twelve on Wednesday night. I'm trying to focus on proofreading our latest petitions. The quiet setting is a stark contrast to my churning stomach. You can't afford to question yourself in the final stages of a death-penalty appeal. "We can't let them lose hope," I tell her.

"Easy for you to say."

I feel my cell phone vibrating. I hit the Talk button. Mort Goldberg apologizes for not returning my call sooner. He says he had a little kidney problem. "Why did you call?" he asks.

"I wanted to ask you something about the trial. Did you ever raise the possibility that Aronis and Bryant somehow got together to take out Robinson and Chin?"

I can hear him wheezing. "We looked," he said. "We never found anything we could use."

"Aronis is clearly a player. Bryant took over Robinson and Chin's operations."

"It wasn't that easy, Mike. Aronis has never been convicted of anything. Bryant has never even been arrested."

"We think our best bet—and maybe our only hope—is showing a connection between them," I say.

"If you can do it, you're a better lawyer than I am."

"Is there anybody else we can talk to?"

The line goes silent. I can envision him rolling his unlit cigar between his fingers. I'm about to say goodbye when I hear his voice again. "I'm sorry, Mike."

"How much longer?" Grace asks impatiently.

"Until 12:01 on Sunday morning," I tell her.

My response is not well received. I think back to the times my father came home from a long shift bone-tired. I always resented the fact that he gave more time to his job than to us. I've come to understand him a little better as I've gotten older.

My daughter and I are sitting at opposite ends of Rosie's sofa. Grace's legs are crossed. She's wearing a gold Cal sweatshirt that once belonged to me. When I was her age, I was focused on making the freshman football team at St. Ignatius. By the end of my sophomore year, it was apparent that I was going to have to get by on brains. I got straight A's my junior and senior years and a ticket to Cal. Grace is compulsive about her grades. She wants to get into the supercompetitive UC system. I never would have gotten into Cal today. She's a little young to be obsessing about it. That's the way she's drawn—just like her mom.

She tosses her long black hair away from her face. Her full lips form an exaggerated pout. "Does that mean I'm grounded until Sunday?" she asks.

"More or less." I take a sip of Diet Dr Pepper. "I'm sorry, honey."

"Sure you are."

Rosie is sitting at her desk, reworking our latest brief. She looks up over her laptop. "We've talked about this a couple of times, Grace," she says.

"Jake has tickets for the Giants game on Saturday."

"You can go later in the season."

"It's fireworks night."

"I'm sorry."

"What if the cops come with us?"

Everything is a negotiation. "I don't think so."

"How about a movie?"

Rosie's patience is not unlimited. "Next week," she says.

Grace isn't going down easy. "Nobody has bothered us for a few days. There are a zillion cops outside."

"We don't want to take any chances."

"You should have thought of that before you took this case."

It's a classic standoff between two strong-willed people who are used to having the last word. It's difficult to argue with someone who can mimic your entire repertoire of facial expressions.

"We'll consult you next time," Rosie tells her.

"I sure as hell hope so."

Our daughter's language tends to turn a bit salty when she's angry. Rosie doesn't react. It's a bad idea to wallow in the mud with an angry teenager.

Grace's anger bubbles to the surface. She heaves a melodramatic sigh that would make Irwin Grim proud. "This case is ruining my life!" she says.

Rosie tries a patient tone that Grace will almost certainly interpret as patronizing. "It's almost over. We'll take a break after it's done."

"Sure you will." Grace drops her chin and her nostrils flare in a dead-perfect imitation of the annoyed expression that Rosie has honed over forty-seven years. She makes a point of saying goodnight to her grandmother, but not to Rosie or me. In some respects, I will be greatly relieved when she leaves for college.

###

"She isn't happy," Sylvia says with characteristic understatement.

"She'll be okay," Rosie says.

"Take it easy on her."

"We will, Mama."

Sylvia isn't quite finished. "I mean it, Rosita. It isn't her fault."

Her implication is more than clear: it's ours.

"Is there something else?" Rosie asks her mother.

Sylvia touches her daughter's cheek. "Nothing," she says.

"Come on, Mama."

The Fernandez family matriarch arches an eyebrow. "She reminds me of you."

"Is that a good thing?"

"For the most part."

###

"Are we crappy parents?" Rosie asks me. Her question is not merely a rhetorical one. We're sitting a few feet from each other at opposite ends of her sofa at one-ten on Thursday morning.

"At times," I whisper. I try to avoid asking myself those types of questions, because I rarely like the answers. I pull a couple of pages from the printer that's perched on a card table next to Rosie's couch. Her house is silent. We've been editing for the last hour. Sleepless nights are not conducive to writing pithy briefs. We have to keep our voices down because Tommy is sleeping soundly on a blanket on the floor. He came out for his nightly visit about a half hour ago, and he promptly fell asleep in front of the TV.

"What percentage of our parental time falls into the 'crappy' category?" she asks.

I glance at Tommy. "The last few days have been pretty bad for our approval ratings. Generally, I'd say just a couple of hours a week. We make it into the 'exceptional' category for about the same amount of time."

"I'm serious, Mike."

"So am I."

"And the rest of the time?"

"I'd say we're about average."

"That's all?"

"Maybe a little above. I didn't want to brag."

"Do you ever stop making wisecracks?"

"Not if I can help it. It keeps me going."

Her tired eyes show the hint of a twinkle. "Do you think we have much to brag about?"

I lean over and peck her on the cheek. "Given our inherent limitations and the fact that we manage to eke out a living representing criminals, I think we're doing okay."

"But we could do better."

"You can always do better. Grace and Tommy are pretty well-adjusted in spite of us."

"How do we take it to the next level?"

"It might help if we stopped taking on last-minute death-penalty appeals. In the meantime, we shouldn't dwell on our shortcomings—at least until this case is over."

She acknowledges that it isn't a great idea to reevaluate your major life decisions two days before an execution.

I tap the completed petition. "I think we're finished," I say.

"Then we're set to file at nine o'clock this morning." She yawns.

"We need more time."

Time is not on our side. Nick Hanson called a little while ago and said he hadn't been able to locate anybody else who may have seen Jasmine Luk. He correctly noted it seemed unlikely that he'd find her walking the empty streets of Chinatown at this hour. Pete is parked across the street from Amanda Wong's apartment. Her doors were locked and her lights were out. I'm starting to measure time in hours and minutes instead of days.

# # #

I'm about to turn out the light in my musty bedroom at two-thirty on Thursday morning when Pete calls from Oakland. "Something's up," he says. "Amanda Wong just drove over to a building beneath the 880 freeway. The lights are off."

"What the hell is she doing there at this hour?"

"Beats me."

"Is anybody else there?"

"I can't tell." The reception from his cell phone starts to break up. I can hear the unmistakable sound of tension in his voice when he says, "Somebody's coming, Mick. I gotta go." He quickly gives me an address. I can barely make out his voice when he says, "How soon can you get here?"

Something bad is happening. The line is dead by the time I say, "I'm on my way."

Thursday, July 16. 2:35 a.m.
2 days, 21 hours, and 26 minutes until execution.

The first call is always to Rosie, who answers immediately.

"Something's wrong," I say. I tell her about the call from Pete.

There is no hesitation. "I'll pick you up in five minutes," she says. There is also no discussion about who is going to drive us. Rosie could race at Daytona.

My second call is to Nick Hanson. "How the hell are you?" he chirps.

I'm not sure. "Pete may have found something. Can you meet us in Oakland?"

"Indeed I could."

The final call goes to Roosevelt. "I'll meet you there," he says.

# # #

Rosie and I are speeding across the Richmond Bridge when my cell rings. "Any word from Pete?" Roosevelt asks.

"Not yet."

"He'll call."

I hope so.

"Is there a black Dodge van behind you?" he asks.

I turn around and look. "Yes."

"It's one of our guys."

Doesn't surprise me. "Thanks for the escort."

"You're welcome. Could you ask Rosie to slow down to seventy-five? If my guy gets stopped, you'll have no cover."

"Sure." I ask him if he's found out anything about the building where Pete saw Wong.

"Title is held in the name of Sunshine Printing. We think it's used as a storage facility for Wong's business."

I don't ask him how he managed to obtain this information in the middle of the night.

# # #

My mind is playing tricks on me as we're heading south on the elevated 880 freeway near downtown Oakland. This stretch replaced the infamous two-level Cypress Structure that collapsed during the 1989 Loma Prieta earthquake and crushed dozens of people. The new single-level roadway is wider and easier to navigate—especially when there is no traffic, at three o'clock in the morning. I'm concerned about Pete, who still hasn't checked in. I'm trying to play out the ramifications if he's found some new information about Jasmine Luk. I keep thinking we need to find a connection between Aronis and Bryant. I'm still wondering what happened to the IA file, and whether Little Joey is somehow involved with its disappearance.

Finally, and perhaps inevitably, I keep flashing back to my dad. The memories are like old snapshots now. I think of all the late-night calls that used to send my mom into a state of abject fear. The time he got rolled by a car while he was making an arrest in the Mission. The trips to Las Vegas, the football games at St. Ignatius, and the wild celebration after Cal beat Stanford in my older brother Tommy's last game. The look on his face when the two marines came to our house to inform us that Tommy was missing in action. Pop was never the same. I think of how hard he pushed us—not so much because he could, but because he wanted us to have more than he did. With the benefit of age and parenthood, I've started to appreciate the fact that my father, Officer Thomas Daley Sr., was a complex man who saw the world in black and white. I'm a simple man who sees the world in shades of gray. There was plenty of room for both of us. Time has made me more forgiving of his real and perceived shortcomings. For sure, it would have been great to have had more time together. Little Tommy is sleeping back at Rosie's house. I wonder how he'll remember me in another forty years.

I call Pete's cell number again, but I get his voice mail. "Why doesn't he answer?" I ask, frustrated.

Rosie tries to reassure me. "He will."

We drive in silence to the Broadway off-ramp. We make our way to Sixth Street, which runs adjacent to the freeway at the edge of Chinatown. It's poorly illuminated. Homeless people sleep in abandoned vehicles. The once thriving residential neighborhood near the Alameda Tube was bifurcated when the freeway was built forty years ago. We drive past a dilapidated playground called Railroad Square Park, where children must avoid broken bottles on rusted equipment.

Rosie drives slowly down the empty street toward the only remaining structure on the block, a boarded-up two-story building. A single streetlight throws off a spooky glow through the heavy fog.

"Something's definitely wrong," I tell her.

"Try Pete again," she says.

I punch in his cell number. Once again, the computer-generated voice asks me to leave a message. Roosevelt doesn't answer. Neither does Nick.

We inch toward the entrance to an alley, where I spot Pete's gray Chrysler. The lights are off. There is no sign of my brother.

"Do you want to wait for Roosevelt?" Rosie asks.

"No." I motion toward the two plainclothes cops who are getting out of the Dodge behind us. "We have reinforcements."

She parks next to Pete's car and kills her engine. We get out of the car. The street is eerily silent. There is no sign of Wong or Pete. "Where the hell did he go?" she asks.

I walk past the passenger side of Pete's car toward the building, when I hear Rosie's voice from behind me. "Oh shit," she hisses.

I spin around and see her standing next to the driver's side door of Pete's car. "Call 911!" she screams. "Pete's in the car. He's been shot!"

Thursday, July 16. 3:30 a.m.
2 days, 20 hours, and 31 minutes until execution.

Roosevelt's expression is grim as he kneels down on the rutted sidewalk next to the bullet-riddled door to Pete's car. "The ambulance will be here in a minute," he says.

"Tell them to hurry," I snap.

I'm sitting in the passenger's seat, trying to keep my baby brother warm. His face is pale. He's fading in and out of consciousness. I'm pressing a blood-soaked blanket against his left hip to try to control the bleeding. I'm trying to stay calm as my heart races. Pete could bleed out before the ambulance arrives. Rosie stands a few steps away. She's on her cell, talking to Pete's wife. Nick Hanson arrived a few minutes ago. He's helping the cops search for the shooter. The blinking lights of the four Oakland squad cars that Roosevelt summoned create a surreal strobe-light feel as they reflect off the façade of the freeway through the fog.

Pete labors to take a breath. "Are you going to give me the last rites?" he whispers.

"No. I got out of that line of work. You're going to be fine."

"When did you become a doctor?"

"I watch *ER* reruns on cable every night."

"Son of a bitch hurts more than when I broke my collarbone."

He ended up on the wrong side of a Pontiac when he and his part-ner were chasing down a pimp. This one's much worse.

"Is it only the leg?" I ask.

His face contorts into a grimace as the pain shoots through him. He struggles to catch his breath. "Yeah," he finally manages to say.

All things considered, this may be reasonably good news if I can keep him from bleeding to death. Then again, a shattered hip isn't a walk in the park, either.

Roosevelt leans inside the car and squeezes Pete's hand. "What hap-pened?" he asks.

Pete struggles to find his voice. "Wong had just gone into the build-ing across the street," he whispers. He gasps for air. "A black panel van pulled around the corner. The guy in the passenger's seat started shoot-ing. African American. Left-handed."

Always a cop.

"He shot low," Roosevelt observes. "Maybe he was just trying to scare you."

"He succeeded. Didn't get a good look at him. Didn't see license plates."

"Had you seen the van before?"

Pete coughs. "No."

"Why didn't you answer your cell?" I ask.

"Couldn't reach it. I fucked up."

"It's okay, Pete."

"Good cops never let their guard down."

"It happens."

"Not to me."

Most cops aren't put in life-threatening situations by their idiot brothers.

"Did you call Donna?" he asks.

"Yes. She's going to meet us at the hospital."

"How did she take it?"

"She's okay," I lie. "She said she's going to kick your ass as soon as you're healthy."

He forces a chuckle that quickly transforms into a cough. Then his expression turns into one of abject panic. "What about Margaret?" he asks. "I don't want her to see me like this."

"Donna's sister is going to stay with her."

There is a hint of relief in his eyes. His breathing is coming in short spurts. "You can't let me die, Mick."

"I won't. I still have a pipeline to God. I use it only on special occasions—like now."

He squeezes my hand. "I'm going to take a little rest, Mick."

"I need you to stay awake with me."

"I'll try." His eyelids flutter. He summons his remaining strength to point a finger at Roosevelt. "Somebody has been breaking our windows," Pete says to him. "Somebody has been taking pictures of my niece." Pete fights to catch his breath. "I must have been getting close to something. You need to find out what really happened before somebody else gets hurt."

Roosevelt swallows hard. "I will," he says. "You need to take care of yourself."

Pete doesn't respond. The ambulance pulls up. Paramedics leap out. It takes them only a moment to pull Pete out of the car and lift him onto a stretcher. The IVs go in. His eyes close.

"Where are you taking him?" I ask.

"Highland."

The hospital in North Oakland is the nearest trauma center. "I'm coming with you," I say.

"Are you family?"

"I'm his brother." And I'm not going to let him die.

Thursday, July 16. 5:00 a.m.
2 days, 19 hours, and 1 minute until execution.

"You look like hell," Rosie says.

At five in the morning, after a sleepless night from hell, I look as good as anybody can. We're sitting in the worn plastic chairs in the dreary waiting room of Highland Hospital, which makes the visitors' area at the Row look cheerful. Pete has been in surgery for the last hour. They're trying to stop the bleeding and piece together his hip.

"I got my brother shot," I say, "trying to save a guy who has spent his life defending people who sold drugs to kids. What the hell was I thinking?"

"It wasn't your fault."

"Yes, it was. Our daughter has been threatened. Your house is a prison. We never should have taken the case."

Her dark eyes narrow. "Don't beat yourself up. We made the decision together."

"It was my call."

"There's plenty of blame to go around."

I'm ready to accept most of it.

My sister-in-law walks in from the hallway. Donna Andrews is an energetic woman in her early forties with shoulder-length blond hair, striking blue eyes, and an unwaveringly calm demeanor. She runs the accounting department of a big law firm. She manages to keep a reasonably positive outlook even though she spends most of her time providing adult supervision to a group of pit bulls whose reputation for winning cases is exceeded only by their penchant for boorish behavior. I've known her for more than a decade. This is the first time I've seen her come close to losing her composure. Given the circumstances, it's entirely understandable.

She pulls at her hair nervously. "He's going to be okay," she says. She's trying to convince herself as much as she's trying to assure us. "He has to be."

"If there's anything we can do—" I say.

"I'll let you know. I'm glad Margaret is too young to understand what's going on."

Me too. Grace isn't, of course. Rosie spoke to her a few minutes ago. The children of criminal-defense lawyers learn that phone calls in the middle of the night are part of the program. She took the news with stoic concern. It will give her additional ammunition in our ongoing war of disapproval.

Donna tugs at the strings of her gray sweatshirt. "I just want Pete to be able to watch Margaret grow up," she says.

"He will," I assure her.

The minutes turn into an hour. An hour turns into two. Donna keeps glancing at her watch. Rosie and I try to help her pass the time by keeping her engaged in strained small talk. In an effort to do something productive, I donate a pint of blood for Pete. It makes me woozy, but I can't possibly sleep now. I try to reach Roosevelt and Nick several times. Neither of them answers. I still don't know if they talked to Amanda Wong, or why she drove over to a dark building under the freeway.

I close my eyes and my mind starts to wander. I think back to the days when Pete and I used to throw a football at the foggy Sunset Playground, a few blocks from our house; his graduation from St. Ignatius; and his first day in uniform. I think of his strained relationship with our father—a man he couldn't please, though he never stopped trying. There was something in their wiring that wouldn't allow them to breathe. Maybe they were too much alike. I fast-forward past his dismissal from the SFPD and the subsequent opening of his PI agency. Past the cases we've worked on together. I chastise myself for asking him to help me for free on countless occasions. My mind flashes to his smiling face in the wedding photo on my living room wall, next to Margaret's baby picture. Like all brothers, we've had our differences. Pete's fundamentally a good man who deserves another opportunity. I have my own selfish interests, too—I don't want to lose my only living brother.

At seven-thirty in the morning, a young surgeon wearing a light green gown enters the waiting area, accompanied by an officious-looking nurse. My heart is pounding. They always come with a nurse when the news is bad. I take Donna's hand in mine.

The doctor removes his mask. He looks at us through wire-framed glasses. "I'm Dr. Nguyen," he says.

"How is he?" Donna whispers.

I'm holding my breath.

"Stable, but not out of the woods," the doctor says. "If we can keep the bleeding under control and avoid infection, he should be okay."

Donna lets out a deep breath. She hugs the doctor, the nurse, Rosie, and me. Then she bursts into tears. I hold her gently as her emotions pour out.

I squeeze Rosie's hand as we try to focus on Dr. Nguyen's quiet voice. He explains that Pete has a broken leg and a shattered hip socket. He's lost a substantial amount of blood. The leg will heal. The hip will require replacement. The blood loss may create complications, so the doctor has ordered him into intensive care. If all goes well, he'll start light physical therapy in a few weeks. "All things considered," Nguyen says, "he's very lucky."

So are we.

"Can we see him?" Donna asks.

"He's going to be in recovery for a while. He'll be under heavy pain medication when he wakes up. We'll let you know when you can go in for a few minutes."

I fight back tears and offer a silent thanks to the Almighty. It's the closest I've come to praying in a long time. Life is too short, and frequently unfair. We just caught an enormous break.

# # #

"Hey, Mick." My brother's whisper is barely audible.

"How are you feeling, Pete?"

"I've been better." His left leg is immobilized in layers of bandages, and an IV is attached to his arm. He's wearing an oxygen mask. "I'm thirsty," he says.

I pour him a cup of water from the hospital-issue plastic pitcher. He drinks it slowly through a straw.

"Thanks for donating the blood," he says. "They told me I may need it."

"There's plenty more where that came from. You would have done the same for me."

This gets the hint of a smile. He glances down at his leg. "Look at that mess."

"You're going to be fine."

"Damn right. I told the doctor that my brother is a hotshot lawyer who will shut this place down if I'm not up and running in a couple of weeks."

That very same brother almost got him killed. "It may take a little longer," I say.

"I'm patient."

No, you're not.

"What time is it?" he asks.

"Ten after ten."

"Where's Donna?"

"Rosie took her down to the cafeteria to get some breakfast. They'll be back in a few minutes. Do you need anything?"

"A new hip."

"The doctor is working on it."

"How about a corned beef sandwich?"

"I'll talk to the nurse."

"Get your ass over to Saul's."

"I'll get right on it, Pete."

This elicits a weak smile. "I can still guilt-trip you into doing anything."

"You can work me all you want."

He grimaces. "Remember the time Pop took that bullet?"

"Yeah." I was twelve when our dad took one in his foot while he and Roosevelt were trying to stop a liquor store robbery. It wasn't life threatening, but it was certainly more than a flesh wound. "Remember when he insisted on going to work the next day?"

"The next day? Hell, he refused to let them take him to the hospital."

"And then he passed out. Remember how he wouldn't use the cane that they gave him? He was as stubborn as they come—just like you."

"Stubborn guys make good cops," Pete says. He points to his leg. "What do you think he would have said about this?"

"That you're a hero."

"Come on, Mick."

"No shit, Pete. In Pop's book, anybody who got hurt in the line of duty was a hero—no questions asked." I touch his shoulder. "He was proud of you. He thought you were a good cop."

"He never mentioned it to me."

"He mentioned it to me—a lot."

My brother's tired eyes open wide. "Really?" he says.

After all these years, he's still looking for that elusive fatherly affirmation. "Really."

He thinks about it for a long moment. "What are you going to do about the case?" he says.

"We'll ask for a continuance."

"Do you think they'll agree to it?"

"Maybe. Maybe not." It doesn't seem quite as important at the moment.

"Did you talk to Roosevelt?"

"I left a message."

"Did he talk to Amanda Wong?"

"I don't know. By the way, he's posted a uniform outside your door just in case."

"In case of what?"

Somebody decides to finish what he started earlier this morning. "Just in case," I say.

"Did he find the shooter?"

"Not yet."

"So I got myself blasted for nothing."

"He'll find the shooter. Besides, you were trying to save somebody's life."

"It would have been pretty ironic if I'd gotten myself killed trying to save a dying man who is set to be executed in two days."

True enough.

Pete's frown becomes more pronounced. "This was no random shooting, Mick. Somebody was following Wong—or me. I must have been getting close to something."

"Who?"

He shakes his head. "It's got to be Aronis or Bryant," he says. "Maybe both of them."

"How can we prove it?"

He glances down at his bandaged leg. "That's up to you now, Mick." Pete's eyes close and I think he's drifting off to sleep. Then they reopen suddenly and he tries to sit up. "Mick?" he says.

"Yeah?"

"Be sure to go down to the impound lot and get my car."

"Don't worry about it, Pete. The insurance will pay for the repairs."

"I'm not worried about the damage. There was an envelope in the trunk."

"What was in it?"

"Bank account information for Aronis and Bryant." He quickly adds, "And Little Joey's currency exchange."

"Anything we can use?"

"I don't know. I didn't have a chance to look at it."

Pete's eyes light up when Donna and Rosie return a few minutes later. He points toward Donna's coffee. "Is that for me?" he asks.

"Maybe a little later, honey."

"Is Margaret okay?"

"She's fine. She's going to stay with my sister so I can be here with you."

"Are the people at your office going to be okay with that?"

God forbid she should miss a day of work.

"They understand, Pete."

They talk quietly for a few minutes. Then the nurse shoos us out. Pete's spirits are reasonably good, but his stamina is not. He's drifting to sleep as we make our way to the waiting area, where Donna excuses herself to use the phone.

Rosie and I sit next to each other in silence. The TV is on, but neither of us is watching. "I'm glad you're here," I tell her.

"I wouldn't be anywhere else." She means it.

"What do we do about Nate's habeas petitions?"

"They're already filed."

What? "How?"

"I emailed them to the office last night. Terrence filed them this morning."

I don't know how we practiced law without the former prizefighter with a criminal record a mile long. "They weren't signed," I say.

"He signed them for us. He's very adept at forging our signatures."

"Technically that's illegal."

"Feel free to turn yourself in. I don't think Nate is going to sue us for malpractice."

I turn to more disturbing matters. "We could be next on somebody's hit list."

She remains resolute. "Roosevelt is still providing us with round-the-clock police protection."

"He couldn't protect Pete."

"Pete was flying without a net."

I ask if she talked to Grace again.

Her chin juts forward. "Yes. She now has a greater appreciation of the gravity of our situation. She's planning to spend the day at home."

"Swell." My head is throbbing. "I don't want to leave Pete."

"There isn't much that we can do. Donna's parents are here, too. They'll call if anything changes."

The ICU's volunteer comes in a moment later. "You've had two more messages from Inspector Roosevelt Johnson," she says. "He said you should call him right away."

# # #

"How's Pete?" Roosevelt asks me.

"It looks like he's going to be okay." I'm standing just outside the main entrance to Highland. I'm holding my cell phone against my right ear.

"That's good."

"Yes, it is. Have you figured out who shot him?"

"We're working on it."

"It wasn't an accident, Roosevelt. Somebody involved in the Fineman case went after him."

There is an interminable pause before he says, "I'm beginning to think you may be right."

I was hoping for more. "You need to help us fix this, Roosevelt."

"I will."

"Did you find Amanda Wong?"

"Yes. Can you come down to the Hall of Justice?"

"I'll be there as soon as I can. What's up?"

"We'll talk about it when you get here."

Thursday, July 16. 12:02 p.m.
2 days, 11 hours, and 59 minutes until execution.

"How's Pete?" The concern in Ted Prodromou's voice is genuine.

I press my cell phone tightly to my ear. "It looks like he's going to be okay," I tell him. The wheels of justice are still spinning rapidly as Rosie and I drive across the Bay Bridge. Donna promised to call us immediately if there is any change in Pete's condition. "Did you get the petition we filed this morning?"

"I did." He clears his throat. "It may be my imagination, but your signatures looked a little different than in your last filing."

It would be a bad idea to lie to a staff attorney for the California Supreme Court. "We had our secretary sign for us," I tell him.

"I wasn't planning to report you. I would suggest that you not make it a habit."

"Thanks, Ted."

"You're welcome." There is a pause. "I was impressed by your argument about the reliability of the Sodium Pentothal. The new study that you cited was prepared by a well-respected doctor at Stanford."

All of which is well and good. "But?"

"The decision isn't going your way."

It's been that kind of day. "We're going to file another one as soon as we can."

"On what grounds?"

"Change of circumstance. Our defense has been irreparably impaired because our investigator has been incapacitated."

"I don't know if there's any authority on point. I'll look at it as soon as it comes in."

It's his polite way of saying it's another loser.

"Have you talked to Ken Conroy?" he asks.

Conroy is the respected staff attorney at the Ninth Circuit who is assigned to our case.

"He's my next call."

# # #

The response from Conroy is essentially the same. He expresses polite concern about Pete. Then he assures me in no uncertain terms that the Feds were unimpressed by our filing.

"We're going to file another habeas petition," I tell him. "Pete's situation substantially impairs our capacity to handle this matter."

"I'm sympathetic. On the other hand, I don't know if that's per se grounds to delay an execution."

"You can do better, Ken."

"I'm sorry, Mike. You know the death warrant is good for just one day—Sunday. If the execution doesn't happen then, it could be months."

It's true. This isn't a question of trying to sway public opinion in order to halt an execution. Legally, a death warrant has a twenty-four-hour shelf life. "You can't fix the mistake if you execute an innocent man," I say.

"I'll present your arguments to the judges."

# # #

"Glad to hear Pete's going to be okay," Roosevelt says. I find him sitting behind his cluttered metal desk in the bull-pen area that houses the SFPD's homicide division. Except for the wanted posters on the walls and the guns worn by each of the plainclothes inspectors, it looks like the back office of an insurance company. "It reminded me of the time your father got shot. I had to carry the old cuss to the car after he passed out. He couldn't believe it when he woke up at San Francisco General with a cast on his foot."

"Pete's the same way."

"The apple didn't fall far from the tree." His eyes narrow. "He *is* going to be all right, isn't he?"

"Yes."

"I'm going to hold you to that."

"That's fair. Do you have any idea who shot him?"

"Not yet. Oakland PD found a stolen panel van near Jack London Square. The plates were missing. No identifiable prints."

"Who's the owner?"

"A contractor in East Oakland. He's very happy to have his truck back."

"Does he have a criminal record?"

"No. He's clean."

"What about gunpowder residue?" Rosie asks.

"They found traces. They can't do anything unless Pete can identify the shooter."

Which he can't.

"The investigation is ongoing," Roosevelt says. "I intend to exert as much pressure as I can on Oakland PD."

It's his way of saying that he isn't going to rest until he finds the shooter. "Did you have a chance to inventory everything in Pete's car?" I ask.

Roosevelt nods. He opens his top drawer and hands me a manila folder. "We found this in the trunk of his car. I made you a copy of everything."

"Thanks." I open the file and glance at the contents. "What is it?" I ask.

"Bank account information for East Bay Scavenger and Bayview Construction." He quickly adds, "There's also some stuff for Little Joey's currency exchange."

"Anything that might be helpful to our appeal?" I ask.

"I don't know, Mike. It just came in. I haven't had a chance to go through it."

I will. "Did you talk to Amanda Wong?"

"Yes."

"What was she doing at a building under the freeway in the middle of the night?"

He looks around to make sure that nobody is within earshot. "Have you talked to Nick Hanson?" he asks.

"He hasn't been answering his phone."

"That's because he's sitting down the hall."

What the hell? "Is he under arrest?"

"Of course not. He helped our guys canvass the area. They found Amanda Wong down the block from where Pete was shot. She wasn't alone."

45/ THIS COULD GET A LITTLE CHIPPY

Thursday, July 16. 12:30 p.m.
2 days, 11 hours, and 31 minutes until execution.

We find Nick the Dick chatting amiably with a uniformed officer outside an interrogation room down the hall. "I've been trying to reach you all morning," he says to me. "Is Pete going to be okay?"

"I think so."

"Good." He points toward the door. "There's a couple of people you'll want to meet in there." He arches an eyebrow. "This could get a little chippy."

Roosevelt opens the door and leads Rosie and me inside. When Nick tries to follow us, Roosevelt stops him. "Official police business," he says.

Nick tugs at the rose on his lapel and smiles broadly. "Come on, Roosevelt. We go back a long way."

Roosevelt is in no mood for banter with the talkative PI. "Outside," he says.

"Whatever you say."

The claustrophobic room is furnished with a table and four chairs and smells of a rank combination of stale coffee and cigarette smoke. Rosie and I take the two open seats. Roosevelt stands guard by the door.

I nod politely to Amanda Wong. "Nice to see you again," I say.

She responds with a guarded nod. She turns to Roosevelt. "Can we leave now?" she asks.

"Not yet," he tells her.

A petite young woman is sitting in the other chair. She's staring intently at the wall. Her black hair is cut short. Her eyes have a soulful sadness.

"I'm Mike Daley," I tell her.

"Heather Tan," she whispers.

Roosevelt interrupts her. "With Nick's help, our people found Ms. Wong and Ms. Tan while I was with you and Pete," he explains. "Ms. Tan lives in an illegal residential unit on the second floor of the building. Ms. Wong went to see her last night."

I say to Tan, "Are you in the habit of receiving visitors in the middle of the night?"

She looks straight down. "It was an emergency." She doesn't elaborate.

Roosevelt picks up again. "Ms. Tan used to be known by another name."

"Would that be Jasmine Luk?" I ask.

There's a pause. "Yes," she says.

My heart beats faster. Pete was right after all. It may be the break we've been hoping for. I turn to Wong. "I take it that you went to warn your great-niece that we were looking for her?"

"Yes, I did."

It's a little cloak-and-dagger for my taste. "Why didn't you just call her?"

"Telephones can be bugged, Mr. Daley."

# # #

It takes the former Jasmine Luk just a few minutes to give us an abbreviated version of her autobiography. She did in fact assume a new identity after the events at the Golden Dragon, using counterfeit papers provided by her aunt. She's been living under her new name in the apartment on the second floor of the Sunshine Printing warehouse ever since. She says she's paid her bills by working as a bookkeeper for her great-aunt's company.

Rosie summons a maternal tone. "Why did you run?"

"They killed my friend Eugene."

"Who killed him?"

"I don't know. I was scared. I couldn't stay in the city." She shoots a glance at her great-aunt. "There were other issues."

"What kind?" Rosie asks.

No response.

I turn to Wong. "What's going on?" I ask.

"We can't talk about it."

Rosie summons a sympathetic voice. "You're only going to make it worse if you don't cooperate," she says.

"It's complicated," Wong says.

"We're prepared to represent you and Ms. Tan. Everything you tell us is covered by the attorney-client privilege."

The stuffy room is completely silent for a long moment as Amanda Wong ponders her options. She looks at Roosevelt and says, "I'm not comfortable talking about this in front of Inspector Johnson."

"Everything we say here is off the record," Roosevelt replies.

"No, it isn't," I snap. "Could you excuse us for a minute? We'd like to talk to our client."

Roosevelt scowls. "I'll be right outside the door."

"Thank you."

As soon as the door is closed, Wong speaks for her great-niece. "There were some issues with Heather's immigration papers when she came over from China."

"What kind of issues?" Rosie asks.

"They were phony. We got quite adept at putting together counterfeit paperwork. I want to assure you that we only did it to help our family. We never made a profit from selling counterfeit papers."

Of course not.

Wong nervously fingers the small pendant hanging from a gold chain around her neck. "Heather and her mother came to this country illegally," she says. "We were afraid Heather would be deported if she talked to the police. It was too dangerous for her to stay in San Francisco. That's when we brought her over to Oakland."

"Why weren't the police able to figure this out?"

Wong gives us a knowing look. "We gave her a new identity." She shoots a loving glance at her niece. "Heather was also very careful."

Or the cops didn't try very hard. Or maybe they didn't try at all.

Rosie offers a practical way out. "We've handled a number of immigration cases. We'll make sure Heather isn't forced to leave the country, but there's something we'll need from you."

"Which is?"

"Full cooperation—including her testimony—in the Fineman case."

Wong raises her hands in a defensive posture. "That's out of the question. We aren't going to put Heather in danger again."

Rosie addresses Tan in a softer tone. "You have to trust us."

"Why?"

"Because you have no choice. There are some very bad people out there who know where you live. They've been following us and they've already shot our investigator. We've been threatened and we're living with police protection. We can protect you if you cooperate. No one can protect you if you try to run now."

The former Jasmine Luk looks to her great-aunt for guidance. The street-smart Wong realizes the game is over. "We have no choice, honey," she says. "You'll have to tell them everything."

The former Jasmine Luk–turned–Heather Tan swallows hard.

Rosie doesn't miss a beat. "You walked home with Eugene Tsai on the night that three people were killed at the Golden Dragon, didn't you?"

Luk's eyes are looking straight down at the table. "Yes."

"Did you hear any shots?"

"No."

"Did you see anyone in the alley that night?"

She doesn't respond.

Rosie mentally counts to three before she tries again. "You and Eugene saw a man in the alley, didn't you?"

Tan pauses. "Yes," she whispers.

Yes!

"Where were you when you saw him?"

"Standing in the doorway of my apartment building."

"Was Eugene with you?"

"Yes."

"Did you get a good look at the man in the alley?"

She closes her eyes and nods.

"Did he say anything to you?"

"No." Her hands are shaking. "He stopped right in front of me and pointed his finger. He made a threatening gesture."

"What type?"

"He pretended to slit my throat."

"Then what did he do?"

"He ran out of the alley."

That's memorable. I reach into my jacket pocket and pull out a dog-eared photo of Bryant that I've been carrying with me for the last couple of days. "Was this the man?" I ask.

She studies it for a moment. "It could have been," she finally decides.

I was hoping for something more definitive. "Are you sure?"

"Pretty sure. It was a long time ago."

It's the best we can do. "You talked to the police, didn't you?"

"Yes."

"What did you tell them?"

She takes a deep breath. "That I didn't see anyone."

"You lied?"

"I was scared," Tan says.

I can understand why.

Rosie touches Tan's shaking hand. "We need you to testify."

There are tears in Tan's eyes. "I can't."

"Yes, you can. Our client has been on death row for ten years. He's going to be executed in two days. You can change the outcome."

"The man who killed Eugene is still out there."

"Give me just a moment," I say. I open the door and find Roosevelt standing in the hallway. I shut the door behind me. "We'll need protection for Ms. Tan," I tell him.

"I'll see what I can do."

"You'll have to do more. She's prepared to ID Bryant in the alley behind the Golden Dragon. I need to be sure that she lives long enough to do it."

He eyes me steadily. "Do you believe her?"

"Yes."

His worn face transforms into a pronounced frown. "I want to talk to her," he says.

He starts to walk around me and I stop him. "No," I say. "She's my client. I will instruct her not to say anything to you unless you agree to protect her."

"I can't provide protection until I evaluate her credibility."

"I'm not going to let her talk to you or anybody else until you provide protection. I need you to fix this right now."

"I'm doing everything I can, Mike."

"No, you're not. You've been dragging your feet from the day we were hired. I don't know who you're protecting, or if you're just trying to cover your ass. Either way, I've had more than enough."

"Calm down, Mike."

"I'm not going to calm down, Roosevelt. My brother has been shot. My family has been threatened. I've been working around the clock and I've just found a witness who can place Bryant at the scene." I point to my watch. "You need to decide if you're going to do the right thing. If somebody else gets hurt, it's going to be on your conscience."

The old warhorse inhales the stale air. His eyes turn to steel. "We're going to fix this right now," he says.

I open the door and follow him inside.

"Ms. Tan," Roosevelt says, "I understand that you have some important information concerning the events at the Golden Dragon ten years ago."

Tan looks toward her great-aunt, who nods. "Yes," Tan says softly.

"Is this information different from the statement you gave me when we last spoke?"

"Yes."

"So you lied to me?"

Tan looks down. "I'm sorry, Inspector."

"Are you prepared to testify?"

Wong responds for her. "Only if you're prepared to provide protection."

"I am."

Tan isn't convinced. "You promised the same thing to Eugene."

"As long as you promise to testify truthfully," Roosevelt says, "you will remain under my protection. I will personally guarantee your safety."

Most homicide inspectors don't double as bodyguards.

Tan's eyes show tentative signs of interest. "Where?" she asks.

"We can find you a place to stay here at the Hall of Justice."

"No way."

Roosevelt considers his options. "You can stay in the spare bed-room at my house. There will be at least two officers with you at all times, and a police car in front of the house twenty-four hours a day. You'll have a police escort to court." He nods toward Wong. "You can keep your great-niece company."

"I will."

Tan asks another practical question. "What happens after this is all done?"

Rosie answers. "We'll work out your issues with the immigration authorities."

"Then what?"

It's Roosevelt who responds. "Your great-aunt and I will arrange for you to disappear again. This time, not even Nick Hanson will be able to find you."

# # #

A small convoy of squad cars escorts Tan and Wong to Roosevelt's house in the Sunset. Rosie and I head back to Oakland to visit Pete and Donna at the hospital. His spirits rise noticeably when I tell him that he found Jasmine Luk.

Rosie and I return to the office late Thursday night to put the fin-ishing touches on a new set of habeas petitions that will reflect the discovery of a new witness. We alert Ted Prodromou and Ken Conroy to be on the lookout for our filings on Friday morning. We hint that we have big news, but we provide no details. They promise to begin their reviews as quickly as possible. We're down to the final forty-eight hours.

It's almost midnight when Rosie walks into my office. Her hair is disheveled and her eyes are tired, but she still looks beautiful to me.

"Are you finished with the petitions?" she asks.

"I want to go through them once more."

"You're going to be up all night, aren't you?"

"Probably."

Her lower lip juts out. "It's been quite a day."

"Yes, it has. At least it looks like Pete is going to be okay."

"Thank goodness."

"And we now have a witness who can place Bryant at the scene—if she's telling the truth and if she can maintain her composure on the stand."

Rosie allows herself a hint of cautious optimism. "We might have a chance after all."

"Maybe. Her ID is still pretty tentative. It was a long time ago on a rainy night in a dark alley. It's awfully hard to prove freestanding innocence."

"Yes, it is. Do we have anything else?"

I point to a large manila folder on my desk. "Those are some bank statements for East Bay Scavenger and Bayview Construction around the time of the shootings," I say. "There's also some financial information from Little Joey's business. They were in the trunk of Pete's car."

"Anything we can use?"

"I'm going to look at them tonight."

Friday, July 17. 8:00 a.m.
1 day, 16 hours, and 1 minute until execution.

"Long time no talk," Edwards wheezes.

Not long enough. "I've been busy," I tell him.

I'm standing outside the main entrance of Highland Hospital. I stayed up all night reworking our habeas petition, then came over to see Pete. He's improving. I took the opportunity to use his bathroom for a shower and shave. The cup of bitter hospital coffee in my hand won't stop the ringing in my ears or cure my sore throat.

He starts with sugar. "I'm glad your brother is going to be okay," he says.

As if you really care. "I got a message that you were trying to reach me."

"I hear you're filing a new petition this morning."

"That isn't a news flash. We've filed papers every day this week."

"Is this about the missing file?"

"It's still missing." At this point, nobody is looking for it. Realistically, it isn't going to be a factor in our investigation.

"I heard you found a new witness in Oakland on Wednesday night."

"We did."

The phony engaging voice disappears. "What's going on?"

I want to pique his interest, but I don't want to identify Jasmine Luk. It was hard enough to persuade her to testify. She may change her mind if a horde of reporters starts hounding her. "We're filing new habeas petitions at nine o'clock," I tell him.

"On what grounds?"

"We have compelling new evidence that was not revealed at the trial."

"What evidence is that?"

"We've found a witness who is going to place Bryant in the alley behind the Golden Dragon."

"Does this witness have a name?"

"Yes."

"Are you going to tell me what it is?"

"No."

"You found Jasmine Luk, didn't you?"

"In due course, Jerry."

# # #

"How's your houseguest?" I ask Roosevelt.

He isn't amused. He's sitting at his desk in homicide at ten-fifteen on Friday morning. He takes a sip of cold coffee and responds with a terse "Fine."

I take a seat in the beat-up swivel chair opposite his desk. "Did Jasmine have a good night?"

"Yes. I now live in the safest house in the Bay Area."

"I need to talk to her again."

"If it's absolutely necessary."

"It is. I have a client who is set to receive a needle in less than two days."

"Understood." His voice fills with frustration when I ask him if he has anything about the guy who shot Pete. "I just got off the phone with Oakland PD. No leads yet, but they tell me that they're looking hard."

I open my briefcase and hand him a peace offering in the form of a grainy old photo that I brought from home, in which Roosevelt is standing next to my father on the steps of the Hall of Justice. Roosevelt was wearing a business suit. Pop was in uniform. "It was taken during the Fineman trial," I tell him. "You were good-looking guys."

His expression turns melancholy as he looks at the picture. "Your father was a fine cop," he says.

Pop always said Roosevelt was the best cop he ever knew. "So are you."

"I just work behind a desk."

"You know that isn't true, Roosevelt." I point to the photo. "Do you remember what you were talking about?"

He's still staring intently at the old black-and-white—almost as if he's trying to get his old friend to talk to him. "It was a long time ago, Mike. I don't recall."

He tries to hand it back to me, but I stop him. "Keep it," I say.

"Thanks."

I pull out a manila file folder. "These are copies of the bank statements that were in Pete's car."

"Anything useful?" he asks.

"I couldn't find any direct financial link between Aronis and Bryant around the time of the shootings," I say. "It's possible that they were smart enough not to leave a trail." I hand him a small stack of computer-generated printouts that I've tabbed with yellow Post-its. "These are from Little Joey's currency exchange."

He studies the paperwork with the tiny numbers. "So?"

"I spent half the night going through this stuff." I point to an entry on the first page. "There's a recurring monthly deposit of ten grand that comes in by wire transfer from an unidentified source. The payments started right after Joey opened his business."

"It's probably from one of Joey's customers."

"Maybe. Ten grand a month seems like a lot of money in a nickel-

and-dime business like Joey's."

"You think somebody is bankrolling Joey?"

"Maybe."

"What does this have to do with your case?"

I answer him honestly. "Maybe nothing. I'd like you to find out where the money was coming from. Can you do it?"

"Probably." He waits a beat. "You're grasping."

Yes, I am. "Please, Roosevelt."

He looks down at the file again. "Let me see what I can find out."

# # #

"Now you think Little Joey was involved?" Rosie asks.

"I'm not sure," I tell her. "All I know is that he's been getting ten grand a month from somebody."

"It doesn't mean it had anything to do with Nate's case."

"True enough."

It's two-fifteen on Friday afternoon. Rosie's office is stuffy as we wait for a response from the California Supreme Court and the Ninth Circuit on the petitions we filed this morning.

Rosie looks intently at the bank statements from Little Joey's currency exchange. Finally, she takes off her glasses and sets them down. "Joey didn't open his business until a couple of years after Nate was convicted. How could this be relevant now?"

"I don't know, Rosie."

"What did Roosevelt think?"

"He didn't know either."

"Maybe he knows something, but wouldn't tell you."

"He wouldn't have been that coy—especially so close to an execution."

"Or maybe the cops really planted the murder weapon. Maybe

Roosevelt doesn't want to point the finger at another cop," she says.

"He wouldn't hesitate to point the finger at Little Joey."

"Unless it also meant pointing a finger at your father."

# # #

"Where are we?" Nate asks me.

We've regrouped in the airless visitors' area at San Quentin at four o'clock on Friday afternoon. Rosie is sitting next to me. Ilene is waiting outside.

"We'll call the governor again," I tell him. "Then we wait."

Nate is agitated. "For how long?" he asks.

We've been hounding the death-penalty clerks at the California Supreme Court and the Ninth Circuit every half hour since ten o'clock this morning. The fact that they've waited this long may suggest they're considering our petitions seriously. Then again, it could mean somebody decided to take a long lunch.

I look at the ancient analog watch that my father wore for forty years while he walked the beat in some of San Francisco's toughest neighborhoods. He gave it to my older brother when he was accepted at Cal. Tommy gave it to me for safekeeping when he left for Vietnam. He never had a chance to reclaim it. "They promised to respond by the end of business," I say. "We'll try again at four-thirty."

"What's your gut?" he asks.

"Somebody is going to bite."

"What makes you think so?"

Because I'm an incurable optimist. "Jasmine Luk is a legitimate new witness."

"We still have to demonstrate that her testimony would have caused the trial court to have reached a different conclusion. Freestanding innocence is a lot harder to prove than reasonable doubt.

We need to show that somebody else did it."

"We laid it out in our petition. She can place Bryant at the scene. That refutes his alibi. It also proves that the man who took over Robinson's operations was at the Golden Dragon that night. The courts will be able to put the pieces together."

At least I sure as hell hope so.

# # #

We're summoned to the guard station at 4:20 p.m. to take an emergency call from Ted Prodromou. I can tell immediately from his tone that the news is bad. "They were very impressed that you found Ms. Luk," he says, "but they didn't think her testimony would provide sufficient evidence to have caused a different result at trial."

In plain English, it means the California Supreme Court has rejected our habeas petition.

"For what my two cents are worth," he adds, "I think you made a legitimate argument."

In this instance, his two cents aren't worth much. The color drains from Nate's face when I return to the visitors' area and break the news to him. We've been living on adrenaline and hope for the last week. I remind him that the Ninth Circuit is still considering our latest petition. We sit in silence as we wait.

The call from the Ninth Circuit finally comes in an hour later. I hold my breath as Ken Conroy speaks in a somber monotone. "I am calling to inform you that a three-judge panel of the Ninth Circuit Court of Appeals has ordered an emergency evidentiary hearing at ten o'clock tomorrow morning in the Federal District Court before Judge Robert Stumpf. The purpose is to hear the testimony of a woman named Jasmine Luk. You may call other witnesses to corroborate her testimony. We will expect you to submit a witness list by nine o'clock tonight."

"We will." My mind races as my heart beats faster. "Any chance we can do it a little sooner?"

"No. I would encourage you to use your time wisely. Judge Stumpf expects you to finish by noon."

It's good news. It also means that we're going to get only one chance to convince Judge Stumpf to grant a stay.

# # #

For the first time since we were hired, we allow ourselves a brief moment of guarded optimism. There are hugs and high fives when we regroup in the visitors' area.

There is a newfound sense of purpose in Nate's voice as he reverts to lawyer mode. "Where do we start?" he asks.

"Nick Hanson is going to muster his army of relatives to serve subpoenas to a laundry list of potential witnesses," I tell him. "Roosevelt has agreed to testify if we need him. So has Patty Norman. It may take a little more persuasion for Floyd Washington. We'll serve subpoenas on Aronis and Bryant. We're going to spend the evening trying to prep Tsai and Luk."

Nate the Great leans back in his wheelchair. The old trial lawyer's mind kicks into gear. "We have to plan this out carefully," he says. "We don't have much time."

It's a diplomatic way of saying that we'll have two hours in court tomorrow morning to save his life. There will be no second chances.

"What's our strategy?" he asks.

"We need to deal with the fact that this hearing will be different from a full-blown trial. It'll be short, so we'll have to watch our time. We'll be making our presentation before Judge Stumpf, so we won't need to dumb things down. He's very bright, and he doesn't have to worry about a jury. He may give us a little more leeway in our questioning."

"On the other hand," Rosie says, "he has a reputation for being a stickler on procedure. He isn't going to give us carte blanche."

"Neither will Irwin Grim," I add.

Nate watches intently as Rosie and I finish each other's sentences. Finally, he holds up a hand and asks, "Are you going to put Jasmine Luk on first?"

I look around at the drab walls and consider our options. "No," I say. "I think we should start with Fitz."

Nate responds with a puzzled look. "Why?"

"I want to establish that the investigation was so hopelessly botched up that they called in IA to investigate."

"But everybody was cleared."

"It doesn't matter. This is theater. I want the judge to understand that the cops were accused of planting the murder weapon. After we hammer Fitz, we'll put up Nick Hanson. He'll testify that Wendell Tsai told him that his brother saw an African American man in the alley. Now he can also say that Luk identified Bryant as the man in the alley."

"That's inadmissible hearsay."

"That doesn't matter either. Everybody loves Nick. He's a strong witness. I'll get him to ID Bryant."

"That's still inadmissible."

"The judge will pretend to ignore it, but he won't be able to purge it from his mind."

"Judge Stumpf is too smart to fall for a cheap trick like that."

"Judge Stumpf is as human as the rest of us. He can't totally disregard the fact that the newspapers will report that the legendary Nick the Dick testified that Bryant was in the alley. He doesn't want to be second-guessed by Jerry Edwards on *Mornings on Two*."

Nate isn't entirely convinced. "Then what?"

"We'll put up Tsai's brother to confirm what Nick said."

"That'll be hearsay, too."

"We'll argue that the judge should make an exception to the hearsay rule because of the compelling nature of the testimony. Even if he decides it's inadmissible, the more times he hears it, the more likely he'll be to believe it."

"And after Tsai?"

"We'll put up Luk to close the deal. I want her to ID Bryant and get off the stand as fast as possible."

Nate does a brief calculus. "You need more than reasonable doubt to prove freestanding innocence. You need to show that somebody else did it."

"Then we'll try to push the blame over to Aronis and Bryant. They're our best options."

"How?"

"Floyd Washington and Patty Norman will testify that Aronis was trying to move into the San Francisco heroin market. We'll put Aronis on the stand and lean on him."

"He'll deny everything. Besides, we can't place him at the Golden Dragon."

"But now we can place Bryant there. We'll put Bryant up after Aronis."

"He'll deny everything, too."

"Then I'll hammer him."

"And if that doesn't work?"

I'll have to wing it. "We'll throw everything we can think of at the judge and see if anything sticks." I don't say it out loud, but in reality this is going to be two hours of high-stakes improvisational theater.

Saturday, July 18. 1:07 a.m.
22 hours and 54 minutes until execution.

"**A**re you ready?" Rosie asks. Her voice is tired. Her eyes are red as she looks at me through the reading glasses that replaced her contacts a couple of hours ago.

"Ready as I'm going to be," I tell her.

It's the calm before the storm. We're sitting at opposite ends of her sofa. Sylvia is in the kitchen, preparing a fruit salad. Grace is in her bedroom, talking on the phone with Jake. We're pretending not to hear her. Tommy is asleep down the hall. He'll reappear for his nightly visit in a couple of hours.

We've had a frantic night of serving subpoenas and preparing Jasmine Luk and Wendell Tsai for their testimony. The degree of difficulty of our task was compounded by the fact that Luk is terrified and Tsai speaks limited English. Rosie and I won't say it aloud, but we know that their direct exams tomorrow will be a crapshoot. Their ability to withstand Grim's cross is an even bigger question. All things considered, we're still in better shape than Nate, who is spending what may be his last night in a holding cell next to the execution chamber.

Rosie is wearing a sweatshirt and no makeup—and she still looks beautiful to me. She studies the handwritten list of witnesses. "You're absolutely sure that you want to start with Fitz?" she asks.

"Yes." I'm not absolutely sure about anything. If I can't persuade Judge Stumpf to grant a stay, I'll be second-guessing myself for the next twenty years. "I want to establish that the cops were accused of planting the murder weapon."

She responds with a skeptical look. "There's nothing new about that claim. Besides, Fitz isn't going to roll over. He'll testify that he conducted a full investigation and everybody was cleared."

"I'll go after him."

She bites down hard on her lower lip. "And tell me again how that will prove freestanding innocence?"

"It won't. It will give the judge a little more ammunition to grant a stay."

"He's going to follow the law."

"He's also human. At the end of the day, he's going to have to decide whether Nate lives or dies. I want him to think about how it will play in the papers if he sentences Nate to death after we've shown that the cops botched the investigation."

Rosie shakes her head. "It's nowhere near enough."

"It isn't intended to win the case. It's just setting the table."

The dark circles below her eyes become more visible as she scowls. "You'll need to cut it short if you can't get to him in a hurry."

"I will."

She looks down at her list again. "Then you want to put up Nick?"

"Yes."

"He has nothing new to add."

"He's a strong witness who is credible and engaging."

"He wasn't there."

"That doesn't matter. I want him to prime the pump. I'll get him to testify that Wendell told him that his brother saw an African American man in the alley. Then he'll testify that Jasmine recently confirmed it was Bryant."

"That's all hearsay. The judge won't allow it."

"We went through this with Nate. We'll argue that the interests of justice trump the technical provisions of the hearsay rules."

"There's no assurance that Judge Stumpf will agree with us."

"All we can do is try. In any event, I want the judge to hear from three different people that Bryant was in the alley: first from Nick, then from Wendell, then from Jasmine. By third time, he might actually start believing it."

"It doesn't get us to freestanding innocence."

"Floyd Washington and Patty Norman will smear Aronis. We'll put Aronis on the stand and pound on him. Then we'll ask Bryant what he was doing in the alley on the night of the shootings."

"They'll deny everything. Besides, it doesn't place Bryant inside the Golden Dragon."

I look down at my watch. "We're going into court in less than nine hours. I'm well aware of all of the potential holes in our case."

She doesn't respond. Neither of us will verbalize the cold, harsh reality: the odds of proving freestanding innocence are still very long.

I reach across and take her hand. "I'm going home to try to get some sleep," I tell her, knowing that I'll be up all night again.

"That's a good idea," she whispers, knowing that she won't be sleeping, either.

We're still looking at each other when Grace walks in and takes a seat on the floor. She's wearing a pink sweatshirt and matching sweatpants. Her voice is melancholy. "So," she says, "it will all be over by this time tomorrow."

"Yes, it will," Rosie replies.

Our daughter tugs at her hair as her voice fills with genuine concern. "Are you ready?"

Rosie's voice is barely audible. "Yes."

Grace turns to me. "What about you?"

"As ready as I'm going to be, honey."

Her eyes narrow. "Are you going to be able to stop the execution?"

I answer her honestly. "I don't know, Grace."

"They said on the news that you found a witness who might be able to place somebody else at the scene."

She's been following this case more closely than she's let on. "That's true."

"Does that mean you know who the real murderer is?"

"We aren't sure."

She eyes me closely. "You have no idea how this is going to go down, do you?"

I hold my palms up. "Nope."

She responds with a shrug, then stands and heads toward her room. As she's about to disappear from sight, she turns around and says, "Good luck."

"Thanks, honey." We're going to need it.

Saturday, July 18. 10:00 a.m.
14 hours and 1 minute until execution.

"All rise," the bailiff intones.

The Honorable Robert J. Stumpf Jr. walks purposefully to the bench in his workmanlike courtroom on the nineteenth floor of the Federal Building at precisely ten o'clock on Saturday morning. The native of southern Indiana is a lanky man in his mid-fifties who played high school basketball against Larry Bird. A consummate professional with boyish good looks, a businesslike tone, impeccable academic credentials, and a nearly perfect judicial temperament, he takes his responsibilities seriously. He also injects healthy doses of self-deprecating humor into his courtroom. Because he is widely regarded as one of the finest wordsmiths on the federal bench, his name comes up every time there is an opening on the Ninth Circuit. He takes his seat in a tall leather swivel chair between the Stars and Stripes and the California state flag, taps his gavel, and motions us to sit down. With only fourteen hours until Nate's execution, the final chapter in this story is going to be written this morning.

Unlike the artfully restored California Supreme Court and the majestic Ninth Circuit Court of Appeals, the unremarkable building that houses the Federal District Court typifies the mundane architecture of the fifties and sixties that gave our city such uninspired landmarks as Candlestick Park and the Bank of America tower. Judge Stumpf and his colleagues dispense justice in a drab, boxy structure that resembles a steroid-laden PG&E substation. The building's appearance became even more Stalinesque when the Feds erected unsightly concrete barriers on the entrance plaza to reduce the threat of terrorist attacks.

It's a slow news day in the middle of a slow news summer, but the stuffy courtroom is packed. There's nothing like a two-hour hearing to decide whether a man will live or die to get people up early on a Saturday morning. The fourth estate is well represented by reporters from the usual local and national TV and radio outlets. Jerry Edwards is sulking in the first row. The strident woman from Court TV is sitting next to the bellicose lawyer who represented Scott Peterson's mistress. They're competing for seating space with the beautiful former ADA who used to be married to our mayor. She now works for Fox News.

The legal establishment is here in force, too. The attorney general came down from Sacramento to garner some sound-bite time. Ted Prodromou and Ken Conroy are sitting together in the third row. The ADA who lost the Bayview Posse case is sitting stoically near the door. His colleague who put Nate away in the first place is sitting in front of Mort Goldberg, whose wheelchair is parked behind the back row. They haven't said a word to each other.

Jasmine Luk is sequestered in an office down the hall, under Roosevelt's watch. Our other witnesses are lined up outside, away from the prying eyes of the media. They won't be allowed inside the courtroom until it's their turn to testify.

Nate sits at the defense table between Rosie and me. He has a legal right to be here and he's hardly a flight risk. He looks like a retired law professor, in a subdued charcoal suit, but his demeanor is closer to that of a caged tiger. Ilene sits behind him, flanked by her children and

Rabbi Friedman. Pete is, of course, conspicuously absent. I talked to him again this morning. His recovery is progressing.

Irwin Grim stands at the prosecution table. It seems appropriate that he's dressed in a black business suit. Dr. Death will try to poke holes in our presentation. Then he'll drop back into a prevent defense and try to run out the clock.

Judge Stumpf glances at his watch, flips on his computer, and asks the bailiff to call our case. After that ceremonial task is completed, the judge looks out over his wire-rimmed bifocals at the silent courtroom. "We're on the record," he says. "This is a hearing to consider petitioner's request for a writ of habeas corpus. Unlike a full trial, our sole charge is to determine whether there is sufficient new evidence to prove petitioner's 'freestanding innocence.' In other words, petitioner must demonstrate this evidence clearly proves he did not commit the crime for which he was convicted. Are counsel ready to proceed?"

Grim and I respond in unison. "Yes, Your Honor."

"Mr. Daley," the judge says to me, "I take it you will be addressing the court on behalf of Mr. Fineman?"

"Yes, Your Honor."

Dr. Death adjusts his gold cuff links and addresses the judge without an invitation. "Irwin Grim on behalf of the attorney general," he announces. "We will be speaking for the people of the State of California."

All forty million of them. Judge Stumpf is unmoved by Grim's inflated self-importance. "This hearing is the only matter on my docket today," he says. "Everyone here understands its magnitude. I have read counsel's papers and I won't need a rehash in the form of opening statements. We must conclude by noon. Please call your first witness, Mr. Daley."

Showtime. "We call Lieutenant Kevin Fitzgerald."

The deputy at the rear of the courtroom opens the door. Fitz walks forcefully down the center aisle, is sworn in, and takes his place in the witness box. He's testified in hundreds of trials. He's in his element. Having ditched his upscale outdoor wear for a stylish Italian suit, he could pass for an investment banker or the president of a Fortune 500 company.

Fitz responds in an even tone when I ask him about his occupation. "I worked for the SFPD in various capacities for thirty-four years." Everybody *wants* to believe the distinguished veteran with the ruddy good looks and the commanding voice. "I taught at the police academy for five years after my retirement from active duty."

"Lieutenant," I say respectfully, "you spent much of your career investigating cases of alleged misconduct by other police officers, didn't you?"

"Yes."

I'll try to control the pace and direction of his testimony by eliciting short answers. "You were asked to conduct an official inquiry into police misconduct in the Fineman case, weren't you?"

He corrects me. "Alleged misconduct, Mr. Daley."

Fine. "You were asked to conduct such an investigation, right?"

"Yes."

Okay. "Would you agree that Internal Affairs is called in only in the most serious of circumstances?"

"Generally."

"So the allegations in the Fineman case were serious, right?"

Grim tries to break up my rhythm. "Objection," he says. "Asked and answered."

"Sustained."

"I'll rephrase," I say. I haven't taken my eyes off Fitz. "Lieutenant, were there allegations of serious police misconduct in the Fineman case?"

"Yes."

"In fact, Mr. Fineman's attorneys alleged that the police planted the murder weapon, correct?"

Fitz calmly adjusts the microphone. "That allegation was never substantiated."

"Please answer my question, Lieutenant. Isn't it true that you were asked to investigate allegations that the police had planted the murder weapon?"

He doesn't fluster. "That allegation was never substantiated."

Like a good politician, he's going to stay on message. "Yes or no, Lieutenant. Did you investigate allegations that the murder weapon had been planted?"

"Yes." He repeats his mantra: "That allegation was never substantiated." The experienced pro continues deliberately. "Mr. Fineman's attorneys made some wild accusations. There was no evidence of any misconduct by our officers."

He's good. I shift gears. "Did the police find any evidence of gunpowder residue on Mr. Fineman's hands or clothing?"

"Objection," Grim says. "This was covered at trial."

"Your Honor," I say, "Lieutenant Fitzgerald's testimony on this subject is directly related to the information that our new witness will provide shortly." It's a bald-faced lie. I'm simply trying to plant another seed with the judge that the cops screwed up.

"I'm going to give you a little leeway," the judge says, "but I want to hear something new very soon."

"Thank you, Your Honor." I turn back to Fitz and say, "Did the police find any gunpowder residue on Mr. Fineman's hands or clothing?"

He eyes me warily. "No."

I move in closer to Fitz. "The weapon found underneath Mr. Fineman was shown to be the one that fired the fatal shots at the Golden Dragon, right?"

"Yes."

"Wouldn't you have expected to find gunpowder residue on the hands and the clothing of an individual who had just fired that gun?"

"Objection," Grim says. "Again, this was covered at trial. In addition, Lieutenant Fitzgerald is being asked to testify as to matters for which his expertise has not been established."

"Your Honor," I say, "Lieutenant Fitzgerald spent thirty-four years in high-ranking positions with the SFPD. He spent several years thereafter teaching at the academy. Surely he is qualified to provide an expert opinion with respect to a basic issue about the residue left by an expended firearm."

"Overruled."

Fitz invokes a clinical tone. "Ordinarily, one would expect to find such residue."

Was that so hard? "Thank you, Lieutenant," I say.

"I'm not quite finished," he says.

"You've answered my question."

This time the judge interjects. "Let him finish, Mr. Daley."

Fitz can't hold back a smile. "It is likely that any identifiable traces of gunpowder residue were washed away by the rain."

"But you don't know that for sure."

"No, I don't. However, my investigation revealed no wrongdoing on the part of our highly professional officers."

"It is also possible that no gunpowder residue was found because Mr. Fineman never fired the weapon, isn't it?"

"Objection," Grim says. "Speculative. Argumentative."

"Sustained."

"Which officers did you talk to?" I ask.

"Everyone who helped secure the scene."

"That would have included David Low, Joseph D'Amato, and Thomas Daley?"

"And several others."

"Did you consider the possibility that they covered for each other?"

"Objection," Grim says. "Speculation."

I'm trying to plant the idea that the cops invoked the Code of Silence. "Your Honor," I say, "I'm not asking the lieutenant to speculate as to whether they actually did cover for each other. I'm merely asking if he considered the possibility."

"Nice try, Mr. Daley. The objection is sustained."

It's the right call. Time to move on. "When did you conduct your investigation?"

"After the conclusion of the trial."

"How long did that take?"

"About a week."

I invoke a skeptical tone. "You were able to get statements from all of the relevant witnesses and complete a full investigation in just a week?"

"Yes."

"You're very efficient."

He responds with a patronizing half smile. "I like to think so."

"You prepared a report on your findings, didn't you?"

"Yes, I did."

"That report was placed in a permanent confidential file within the Internal Affairs Division, wasn't it?"

"Yes, it was."

"We subpoenaed a copy of that report, didn't we?"

"Yes, you did."

"But you were unable to provide it to us."

"That's correct. The file is missing."

"The file is missing," I repeat. "So we'll never have an opportunity to review its contents, will we?"

"It appears that way." He can't contain a smirk. "According to the records, the last person who checked out the file was Officer Thomas Daley."

"You're referring to my father?"

"Yes."

"The record also indicated that he checked in the file, didn't it?"

"I believe so."

"Are you suggesting he had something to do with its disappearance?"

"I'm not suggesting anything." His smirk broadens. "I'm simply noting that he was the last person who checked out the file."

Bullshit. "And neither you nor the records division have been able to locate it?"

"No, but I was asked to provide a written summary of its contents."

"Which means you're asking us to take your word for it."

He nods with authority. "Yes."

"Which also means my client's life rests on whether you did your job back then and whether you're telling us the truth now."

Grim stands. "Objection, Your Honor. Argumentative. I must also object to this line of questioning. Lieutenant Fitzgerald has provided a written statement under oath as to the contents of the file. Courts at the state and federal level have already concluded that Lieutenant Fitzgerald's written statement is an adequate substitute for the file."

"Your Honor," I say, "the information in that file has direct bearing on the issue of whether my client is going to be executed in less than fourteen hours."

Grim sucks up to the judge. "Your Honor," he says, "we're prepared to waive any objections if Mr. Daley wishes to call additional witnesses who have knowledge of the contents of that file."

It's a hollow gesture. "Your Honor," I say, "we can't possibly know who to call, because we can't examine the file."

Grim fires back. "Your Honor," he says, "we've made every possible effort to locate that file. Lieutenant Fitzgerald has provided a comprehensive list of every person that he interviewed."

"We'll never know if that list is complete," I say. "If we find a new witness tomorrow, it will be too late."

"Lieutenant Fitzgerald submitted the statement under oath," Grim snaps. "If Mr. Daley believes he's committed perjury, he can bring charges. In the meantime, we are offering the testimony of the man who prepared it—Lieutenant Fitzgerald."

Who is going to repeat himself until he's blue in the face: everybody was exonerated; everybody was exonerated. "Your Honor," I say, "it is an egregious miscarriage of justice to proceed with my client's execution without giving us an opportunity to review the investigative file concerning this case. We will never be able to know all of the facts unless we obtain that file."

Judge Stumpf has been taking in our sniping contest with his chin resting in the palm of his right hand. "The objection is sustained," he finally decides. "The best evidence that we have with respect to the contents of that file now comes in the form of Lieutenant Fitzgerald's sworn statement, which I have already admitted into evidence."

"Your Honor—"

"I've ruled, Mr. Daley. Anything else for this witness?"

"Yes, Your Honor." I turn back to Fitz and bore in. "Lieutenant, isn't it true that several of the officers who secured the scene at the Golden Dragon had been involved in an investigation of a group of drug dealers known as the Bayview Posse?"

"Objection," Grim says. "That investigation has nothing to do with this case."

"Your Honor," I say, "I will show a direct connection in just a moment."

"Overruled."

"Yes," Fitz says. "Several of the officers who secured the scene at the Golden Dragon were also involved in the Bayview Posse investigation."

"That would have included an undercover officer named David Low?"

"Yes."

"And Officers Joseph D'Amato and Thomas Daley?"

"I believe so."

"The investigation of the Bayview Posse led to the arrest of several individuals in connection with the deaths of three students at Galileo High School from heroin overdoses, didn't it?"

"Yes."

"Were those defendants ever convicted?"

"No." Fitz takes a deep breath. "The charges were dropped."

"Why?"

His voice fills with contempt. "Legal technicalities," he mutters.

"The Posse hired Mr. Fineman to represent them, didn't they?"

"Yes."

"Mr. Fineman got the charges dropped when he convinced the court that the police had conducted an illegal search of a house owned by the Posse's leader, didn't he?"

Fitz's nostrils flare. "The judge made a mistake," he says through clenched teeth. "He set a group of killers free."

Grim stands again. "I fail to see the relevance, Your Honor."

"Please, Your Honor," I say, "I was just getting to the most important part."

"Proceed, Mr. Daley."

"Lieutenant Fitzgerald, isn't it a fact that the officers involved in the Posse investigation were extremely upset that their efforts did not result in a conviction?"

"That investigation had nothing to do with this case."

"Answer the question, please."

"Everybody involved in the investigation was disappointed."

"In fact, they blamed Mr. Fineman for the disaster, didn't they?"

Grim is up again. "Objection. Lieutenant Fitzgerald isn't a mind reader."

"Sustained."

I keep pushing. "Isn't it true that the police who investigated the Posse held a grudge against Mr. Fineman?"

"Objection. Speculation."

"Sustained."

I'm just starting to ask speculative questions. "Isn't it also possible that the police framed Mr. Fineman for murder and closed ranks as a payback for the botched investigation several years earlier?"

Grim is still standing. "Objection," he shouts. "This line of questioning is pure speculation."

Yes, it is.

"Sustained."

I make one more blatant play to the gallery. "It's possible, isn't it, Lieutenant?"

"Objection. Speculation."

"Sustained."

I've done everything that I could to plant the seed of police misconduct. "No further questions, Your Honor."

"Cross-exam, Mr. Grim?"

"Just one question, Your Honor." Grim addresses Fitz from his seat. "Just so we're absolutely clear about this, did you find any evidence of any wrongdoing of any kind on the part of the hardworking officers who helped secure the scene at the Golden Dragon, and who helped put a vicious murderer in prison?"

It's my turn to stand. "Objection to Mr. Grim's characterization of my client as 'vicious,'" I say.

"Sustained."

A smug Grim rephrases the question. "Lieutenant, did you find any wrongdoing on the part of any of the officers involved in securing the scene?"

"No."

"No further questions, Your Honor."

"Please call your next witness, Mr. Daley."

The table is set. It's time to go on the offensive. "We call Nicholas Hanson, Your Honor."

Nick the Dick stretches to his full height in the back of the courtroom. He tugs at the lapels of his navy suit and begins a slow saunter down the center aisle in a dead-on imitation of Edward G. Robinson in *Little Caesar*. Any lingering effects of his recent knee surgery are not discernable. He sports a broad grin as he works the room like a seasoned politician, pausing to shake hands with people seated along the aisle. I gesture to him to speed up. Evidentiary hearings aren't like soccer games, where extra time is added at the end to compensate for minutes lost during stoppages of play.

When he reaches the front of the courtroom, he greets the bailiff by name and raises his right hand. The bailiff recites the words that every devotee of *Law and Order* can repeat by heart: "Do you solemnly swear to tell the truth, the whole truth, and nothing but the truth, so help you God?"

"Indeed I do." Nick climbs into the heavy wooden chair in the witness box. He pours himself a glass of water. He leans forward in anticipation as I button my jacket.

"May we approach the witness?" I ask the judge.

"Yes, Mr. Daley."

I'm halfway to the witness box when I hear Grim's voice from behind me. "A word, Your Honor?"

"Yes, Mr. Grim?"

I haven't started and he's already whining. In fairness, it isn't a bad strategic move. The clock is running in his favor.

Grim takes a deep breath. "As I mentioned during Lieutenant Fitzgerald's testimony, the sole legal purpose of this hearing is to bring forth new evidence that was not introduced at trial or during prior appeals. There is nothing in Mr. Daley's papers to suggest Mr. Hanson has anything new to add. His testimony therefore has no place in this proceeding."

The only way to respond to this sort of bellyaching is with a tone of unquestionable reason. "Your Honor," I say, "Mr. Hanson is here to offer brief testimony as to new information that was not addressed at the trial."

"Mr. Hanson's testimony is never brief," Grim grumbles.

Now *that's* gratuitous. "It will be today," I shoot back. It *has* to be.

The judge silences the smattering of chuckles in the back of the courtroom with an upraised hand. "I will hear Mr. Hanson's testimony," he says. "I will also expect you to show some new information immediately."

"Yes, Your Honor." I resist the temptation to give Grim a sarcastic glare for being a niggling ass. I place my right hand on the edge of the witness box. "You've been a private investigator for many years, haven't you, Mr. Hanson?"

A jumpy Grim is up again. "Objection, Your Honor. Leading."

"Sustained."

I don't have time for a sniping contest. "I'll rephrase the question." I ask Nick how long he's been a PI.

"Seventy years."

"Did Mr. Fineman's attorney hire you to assist his defense team?"

"Objection," Grim says. "This material was covered at trial."

Come on. "I'm simply allowing Mr. Hanson to explain his role in this case," I say.

"Overruled."

I repeat the question. Nick nods respectfully toward Mort. "Indeed he did."

"When did he hire you?"

"The day Mr. Fineman was arrested."

"What was your assignment?"

"I was asked to locate witnesses who had information about the case."

"Did the witnesses include a man named Eugene Tsai and a woman named Jasmine Luk?"

"Yes."

I need to phrase the next question in a manner that will give Nick a chance to place Bryant in the alley before Grim can lodge a hearsay objection. "Mr. Hanson," I say in an offhand tone, "what can you tell us about them?"

The corner of Nick's mouth turns up and he delivers the goods. "Mr. Tsai and Ms. Luk were employed at the Chinese Hospital. They were walking home together in the alley behind the Golden Dragon Restaurant immediately after the shootings occurred, when they were accosted by an African American man named Marshawn Bryant."

Perfect.

As expected, Grim is up on his feet immediately. "Move to strike," he says. "The trial record indicates that Mr. Hanson never spoke to Eugene Tsai or Jasmine Luk. That means he must have obtained this information from a third party. As a result, this testimony is inadmissible hearsay that should be stricken from the record and disregarded."

"Your Honor," I say, "Mr. Hanson obtained the information with respect to Eugene Tsai from Mr. Tsai's brother. In addition, while Mr. Hanson didn't speak to Ms. Luk at the time of the original investigation, he did in fact speak to her on Thursday."

Grim is still standing. "It's still hearsay," he says.

He's right. The purpose of this charade is to plant the idea with the judge and the gallery that Eugene and Jasmine saw Bryant in the alley. Even if Judge Stumpf decides to strike Nick's testimony—which he probably will—I'm hoping that he won't be able to strike it completely from his memory. I will have Wendell and Jasmine repeat the same story in a few minutes.

Judge Stumpf addresses Nick directly. "Mr. Hanson," he says, "did you interview Eugene Tsai?"

"No, Your Honor."

"Where did you obtain the information about what he saw?"

Nick answers him honestly. "From Mr. Tsai's brother."

"Did you interview Ms. Luk?"

"Yes, Your Honor. Two days ago."

Grim interjects, "Classic hearsay in both cases, Your Honor."

Indeed it is. We'll have the same issue when Wendell takes the stand and I ask him what his brother told him, unless I can persuade the judge that an exception to the hearsay rule should apply. Here goes. "Your Honor," I say, "as we delineated in our papers, among other things, Mr. Hanson's testimony is admissible under Rule 807 of the Federal Rules of Evidence."

Rule 807 is sometimes called the "catchall" or "residual" exception to the hearsay rule. It allows the admission of statements by an unavailable witness if the information goes to a material fact and has substantial evidentiary value, and there is no other reasonable way to present it. Rule 807 also makes reference to the "interests of justice," a wonderfully vague notion that allows lawyers to serve up high-sounding platitudes without offering any real substance. Judges are generally reluctant to invoke Rule 807 because nobody really knows what it means.

"Your Honor," I continue, "Mr. Fineman's execution is less than fourteen hours from now. We have no time to engage in a lengthy appellate process. Rule 807 is intended to ensure that a rote reading of the hearsay rule does not lead to a gross miscarriage of justice. In this case, that would result in the ultimate penalty—Mr. Fineman's death."

Grim fires back. "Your Honor," he says, "with all due respect to Mr. Daley and the interests of justice, it is well established that the residual exemption should be used sparingly because its parameters are not well defined. A jury weighed the evidence. The appellate process has played its course. It would be an even greater miscarriage of justice to overturn the will of a jury by admitting unreliable hearsay ten years later."

Judges are loath to overturn jury decisions. "Your Honor," I say, "just because Rule 807 is invoked infrequently doesn't mean it shouldn't be invoked at all—especially in circumstances where the stakes are high and the ramifications are irreversible."

"That doesn't address the inherent unreliability of this testimony," Grim says.

Nick leaps back into the fight. "Who are you calling unreliable?" he snaps.

The judge reminds him that this is an issue for the attorneys to resolve.

We volley for five more precious minutes before Judge Stumpf finally makes the call. "I'm generally reluctant to invoke Rule 807," he says. "However, there appears to be no realistic alternative. Given the graveness of the penalty and the lateness of the hour, I am prepared to admit some limited hearsay testimony."

I turn and catch Rosie's eye for an instant. This is a victory for our side.

The judge is still talking. "I want to set some ground rules. It is settled that such testimony should be proffered by a person who has the greatest credibility with respect to the unavailable witness. Mr. Hanson never spoke to Eugene Tsai and only recently spoke to Jasmine Luk. I am therefore ruling that Wendell Tsai should testify as to what his brother told him, and Jasmine Luk should testify as to what she saw."

It isn't ideal, but I can get what I need from them. "That's fine with us, Your Honor."

It isn't fine with Grim. "Your Honor," he whines, "the circumstances surrounding this case do not change the inherently unreliable nature of this testimony. It is still inadmissible hearsay that may be highly prejudicial. It should be disregarded."

"I've ruled, Mr. Grim."

He slumps back into his chair. "Yes, Your Honor."

The judge looks over the top of his glasses at me. "Do you have any further non-hearsay questions for Mr. Hanson?"

"Just one, Your Honor." I turn back to Nick. "Mr. Hanson," I say, "did Mr. Eugene Tsai and Ms. Jasmine Luk testify at Mr. Fineman's trial?"

"No."

"Why not?"

He turns and speaks directly to the judge. "Mr. Tsai was killed a few days after the shootings at the Golden Dragon. Ms. Luk disappeared shortly thereafter."

Saturday, July 18. 10:32 a.m.
13 hours and 29 minutes until execution.

Wendell Tsai's body language makes it clear that he'd rather be having a root canal than sitting in the witness box. He tugs at the sleeves of an ill-fitting black suit that he must have borrowed for the occasion. He gulps down his second glass of water. It is difficult to elicit convincing testimony from a terrified witness. It's even trickier when he speaks halting English. I'll have to keep the questions simple and lead him one step at a time.

I start slowly. "Your brother was only seventeen when you came to America, wasn't he?"

I've told him to look at me, but he's staring straight down. "Yes."

"He found a job at the Chinese Hospital?"

"Yes."

"He went to school to study English during the day?"

"Yes."

"Eugene was a bright young man, wasn't he?"

Grim starts to stand, then reconsiders. It's another blatantly leading question, and Tsai hardly qualifies as an expert on Eugene's IQ. Nevertheless, he correctly surmises that he'll look petty if he objects.

Tsai takes a drink of water and gives me a confused look. "Repeat question."

"Your brother was a bright young man, wasn't he?"

"Yes."

"And ambitious?"

"Yes."

"He picked up English quickly, didn't he?"

"Yes."

"He wanted to be a doctor?"

"Yes."

I play for a little emotion. "He never had a chance, did he?"

He swallows hard. "No."

The courtroom is stone-cold silent.

"He was killed ten years ago, wasn't he?"

Tsai folds his arms as if he's trying to find a place to hide. "Yes."

"How old was he at the time?"

"Nineteen."

"Nineteen." I pause to let it sink in. "Did the police ever find the person who killed him?"

He shakes his head vigorously. "No."

The warm-ups are over. "Your brother used to walk home from work through an alley behind the Golden Dragon Restaurant, didn't he?"

Grim finally decides to stop the flow. "Objection, Your Honor. Leading."

"Sustained."

I rephrase. Tsai confirms that his brother used to cut through the alley. I ask him if Eugene took that route on the night three people were killed at the Golden Dragon.

"Yes."

"How do you know?"

"He tell me."

Grim tries again. "Objection, Your Honor. Hearsay."

"Overruled." The judge sternly reminds Grim that he's already ruled on the admissibility of Wendell's testimony.

I hold up a hand to reassure my bewildered witness. "Mr. Tsai, did Eugene see anyone on his walk home through the alley that night?"

Grim is still standing. "Objection, Your Honor. Foundation. There is nothing in the record to establish that the witness knows if his brother saw anyone on his walk home that night."

"Overruled." The judge addresses Tsai in a soft tone. "Please take your time and answer Mr. Daley's question."

His eyes dart around the courtroom. "He see black man in alley."

Good. "Did the man say anything to him?" I ask.

"No."

"Did your brother talk to the police?"

"Yes."

"Was he able to identify the man?"

He shakes his head from side to side. "No."

"Is it possible that the man's name was Marshawn Bryant?"

"Objection. Speculation."

"Sustained."

I knew that was coming. I'm still trying to burn Bryant's name into the judge's mind. "Your brother was quite sure that it was an African American man?"

Grim is back up. "Objection, Your Honor. Asked and answered."

"Sustained."

Grim isn't satisfied. "Your Honor, I must protest this line of questioning. Not only is Mr. Daley leading this witness, there isn't a shred of evidence that a man named Marshawn Bryant was in the alley behind the Golden Dragon on the night in question."

He's overreacting. He's also doing me a favor by repeating Bryant's name. I decide to tweak him. "Your Honor," I say, "we will be calling another witness in a moment to provide further proof that Marshawn Bryant was in the alley. At this time, we are simply pointing out that

Eugene Tsai also saw him."

Grim's voice rises. "There was no such evidence," he says. "Mr. Tsai did not make a positive ID. Moreover, Mr. Bryant was questioned by the police and his alibi was verified. Mr. Daley is attempting a last-ditch effort to save his client by introducing uncorroborated hearsay testimony from an unreliable witness at the eleventh hour."

That's the whole idea of a habeas petition. "Your Honor," I say, "Mr. Grim is now calling Mr. Tsai a liar."

"No, I'm not," Grim says.

"Yes, he is." It's my turn to make a speech. "Mr. Grim's behavior is inappropriate and disrespectful. Mr. Tsai's brother was tragically killed after he had the courage to come forward with information about the events at the Golden Dragon. Mr. Tsai should be commended for showing the same type of bravery by testifying today. If Mr. Grim wishes to question his credibility, he will have an opportunity to do so on cross. In the meantime, he should limit his comments to legally recognized objections."

"Your Honor," Grim whines, "Mr. Daley is testifying."

Judge Stumpf goes my way. "The objection is overruled."

So there. I'm scoring points, but I haven't hit one out of the park and the clock is running. I turn back to Tsai. "Did your brother walk home by himself that night?"

An emboldened Tsai sits up a little taller. "No."

"Who was with him?"

"Pretty girl live in alley in back of restaurant. Name Jasmine Luk. She work at hospital with Eugene." He nods and adds, "They walk home together a lot."

"Eugene told you that they walked home together that night?"

Grim starts to stand, then changes his mind.

"Yes," Tsai says.

"Was Ms. Luk with your brother when he saw the man in the alley?"

"Yes."

"Did she see the man, too?"

"Yes."

"How do you know?"

"Eugene told me."

"Did she talk to the police?"

"Yes."

"Did Ms. Luk testify at the trial?"

"No."

"Why not?"

"Got scared after Eugene was killed. Left town."

I take a step back and lower my voice. "Mr. Tsai," I continue, "why didn't your brother testify at the trial?"

His eyes turn downward. "Was killed."

"When?"

"After he talk to police. Somebody find out."

"Do you know who killed him?"

"No."

"Was his murder ever solved?"

"No."

"Why didn't the police provide protection?"

"They try." He purses his lips with contempt. "Do bad job."

So it would seem. I move directly in front of the witness box. "Do you believe his death was an accident?"

"Objection," Grim shouts. "Speculative."

"Sustained."

My eyes are still locked on Tsai's. "Do you have any information regarding the circumstances surrounding your brother's death?"

He starts to shake and his voice cracks as it gets louder. "Not an accident," he says. "Not an accident."

"No further questions, Your Honor."

"Cross-exam, Mr. Grim?"

"Just one question, Your Honor." Grim addresses Tsai from his seat. "Mr. Tsai," he says, "did your brother positively identify the man that he supposedly saw in the alley?"

Tsai shakes his head. "No," he says softly.

"No further questions, Your Honor."

"Please call your next witness, Mr. Daley."

On to the main event. "We call Ms. Jasmine Luk, Your Honor."

The conventional wisdom says a trial lawyer should never ask a question unless he already knows the answer. That rule isn't going to apply to our direct exam of Jasmine Luk. The good news is that she speaks fluent English. The bad news is that we have little idea what she's about to say—or how convincingly she'll say it. Our goal is modest: to place Bryant in the alley behind the Golden Dragon. Then we want to get her off the stand as fast as we can.

Rosie has a softer touch, so we've agreed that she'll handle Luk's direct exam. She stands a respectful distance from the witness box and starts with an easy one. "Would you please state your name for the record?"

"Jasmine Luk." Amanda Wong's great-niece is uncomfortable using her given name. It's been a while. She stares straight down as she tugs at a silk scarf that she borrowed from her great-aunt. If she were wound any tighter, she'd explode.

Rosie shoots a reassuring glance at Wong, who is seated behind me. Rosie asks the judge for permission to approach Luk, then she moves in cautiously. "Jasmine, you were born in China, weren't you?"

"Yes."

"You came to this country when you were just twelve, didn't you?"

"Yes."

"And you lived in an apartment in Chinatown?"

"Yes."

"And your mother passed away shortly after you graduated from high school?"

Grim finally offers a halfhearted objection. "She's leading the witness, Your Honor."

Yes, she is. Luk isn't exactly a hostile witness, but she isn't going to be wildly helpful, either. "Your Honor," Rosie says, "Ms. Luk is a reluctant witness who is here at great personal sacrifice. I would appreciate some latitude to make this easier for her."

In other words, she wants permission to lead her shamelessly.

"I'll give you a little leeway, Ms. Fernandez. However, the objection is sustained."

There are no surprises as Rosie takes Luk through the highlights of her life story, which Luk delivers in a detached monotone with her eyes trained on her toes. She came here from China with her mother, with assistance from her great-aunt. She found a job at the Chinese Hospital after she finished high school. That's where she met Eugene Tsai. She stayed in the apartment in the alley behind the Golden Dragon after her mother died.

"You were still living in that apartment when three people were killed at the Golden Dragon, weren't you?" Rosie asks.

"Yes."

"You walked home from your job at the hospital that morning?"

"Yes."

"What time did you leave work?"

"A few minutes before one."

"Were you alone?"

She glances at her great-aunt. "I was with Eugene Tsai. He also worked at the hospital."

"What time did you get to the alley?"

"About ten minutes after one."

"Were you with Eugene the entire time?"

She nods a little too forcefully. "Yes."

"Did he walk with you all the way to your apartment?"

"Yes."

Rosie gives her a reassuring nod. "Did you hear any gunshots?"

Luk's delicate features contort into a pronounced grimace. "No."

"Did you see anyone in the alley?"

"Police and paramedics."

I can see a hint of frustration in Rosie's eyes. "Did you see anyone *before* the police and the emergency personnel arrived?"

My heart starts beating faster when Luk hesitates. "A black man," she finally says.

"Was Eugene still with you when you saw this black man?"

Luk clamps her mouth shut tightly as she nods. "Yes," she whispers.

"Did Eugene see him, too?"

"Yes."

"Where were you standing when you saw him?"

"In front of the door to my apartment building."

Rosie moves in closer and cuts off Luk's view of Grim. "What was this man doing in the alley?" Rosie asks.

"Running," Luk says.

"Did he see you?"

"Yes."

"What did he do when he saw you?"

"He stopped."

"How far away from you was he when he stopped?"

"I'd say about five feet."

"Did you get a good look at him?"

Luk shoots another look at her aunt. Her voice is barely audible. "Yes."

"Did you see his face clearly?"

"Yes."

"Did he say anything to you?"

"No."

"Did he gesture at you?"

Her eyes close as she nods. "Yes."

"Can you show us what type of gesture he made?"

Luk swallows hard and then painstakingly pantomimes the act of slitting her throat.

Rosie turns to the court reporter. "The record will reflect the fact that the man threatened to slit Ms. Luk's throat." While Luk regains her bearings, Rosie approaches the bench and introduces into evidence an enlarged photo of Bryant. Grim has already seen it and doesn't object. Rosie then holds the picture up in front of Luk and says, "Was this the man?"

Luk's petite body tenses. Her voice cracks when she whispers, "I think so."

Rosie turns to the court reporter and says, "Let the record reflect that Ms. Luk has identified a photo of a man named Marshawn Bryant."

There are a few scattered whispers in the gallery. Out of the corner of my eye, I can see Jerry Edwards writing furiously in his notebook. We've done what we've set out to do: placed Bryant in the alley—albeit tenuously.

Rosie tries to neutralize Grim's cross by providing a reason why Luk didn't come forward ten years ago. "Ms. Luk," Rosie says, "I understand you talked to the police a couple of days after you saw the man in the alley."

Luk's eyes turn downward. "I did."

"But you told them that you didn't see anyone in the alley that night."

Luk forces out a heavy sigh. "That's true."

"I guess that means you didn't exactly tell the truth."

Her voice cracks. "No, I didn't."

"Could you please explain to Judge Stumpf why you chose to do that?"

Luk dabs her eyes. "They killed Eugene. I was afraid."

"Is that when you decided to leave town and change your identity?"

"Yes. My great-aunt helped me. I moved to Oakland." She shoots a helpless look at Wong. "I wanted to be safe."

"Why did you decide to come forward now?" Rosie asks.

Luk closes her eyes for a moment, then reopens them. "I wanted to tell the truth. I don't want to hide anymore."

"No further questions, Your Honor." Rosie takes her seat at the defense table, but her eyes remain locked on Luk's. Her testimony lasted less than three minutes.

Grim jumps up and looks like a tiger on the prowl as he heads for the witness box. "Ms. Luk," he says, "had you ever seen the man in the alley before?"

"No."

"Was it dark outside?"

"Yes, but—"

"And raining?"

"Yes, but—"

"Objection," Rosie says. "Mr. Grim is not allowing the witness to answer."

"Sustained." The judge instructs Grim to let her have her say.

An emboldened Luk juts her delicate chin forward. "As I explained to Ms. Fernandez, the man stopped right in front of me and threatened to kill me. I could see him very clearly. I will *never* forget that face."

Grim pushes forward. "Do you remember what he was wearing?"

"A black jacket."

"Do you remember the color of his eyes?"

"Brown."

"How long was his hair?"

"He had an Afro."

"How tall was he?"

"Over six feet."

"Are you pretty sure about that?"

"Objection," Rosie says. "Asked and answered."

"Sustained."

"Ms. Luk," Grim continues, "exactly how long was he standing in front of you?"

Luks shrugs. "A couple of seconds."

"Two seconds? Five seconds? Ten seconds?"

"Objection," Rosie says. "Asked and answered. The witness has already said a couple of seconds."

"Overruled."

Luk shoots a helpless glance our way, but we can't help her now. Her features rearrange themselves into a scowl. "A couple of seconds," she finally whispers.

"You mean two seconds?"

She shrugs. "Probably."

Grim spreads his arms and invokes a sarcastic tone. "So," he says, "you're absolutely sure it was the same man, even though you saw him for two seconds on a dark and rainy night ten years ago?"

I nudge Rosie, but she holds up a hand. It will undercut Luk's credibility if we try to protect her. Rosie's instincts are rewarded when Luk doesn't fluster.

"I know what I saw, Mr. Grim," she says.

A frustrated Grim takes her in another direction. "Ms. Luk," he says, "you said you were born in China."

"Yes."

"And you came to this country when you were a child, didn't you?"

"Yes."

"There were some problems with your immigration papers, weren't there?"

"Objection," Rosie says. "Relevance. This has absolutely nothing to do with the subject of this hearing."

"Your Honor," Grim says, "this has direct bearing on Ms. Luk's credibility."

Judge Stumpf's raised eyebrow signifies his skepticism. "How's that, Mr. Grim?"

"Ms. Luk is in this country illegally. We think she intentionally misled the police in order to avoid drawing attention to herself. We believe that Mr. Daley and Ms. Fernandez have offered her legal assistance in order to elicit testimony that will help their client."

"Your Honor," Rosie says, "Ms. Luk's immigration status is irrelevant to this case. She did, in fact, talk to the police shortly after the events at the Golden Dragon. She's already acknowledged that she misled the police about what happened that night because she was afraid that she would have been killed like her friend Eugene."

"Your Honor—" Grim says.

A visibly annoyed Judge Stumpf interrupts him. "Ms. Luk's immigration status has nothing to do with the matters at hand. The objection is sustained."

Grim moves within two feet of the front of the witness box. "Ms. Luk," he says, "did Mr. Daley and Ms. Fernandez agree to help you with your immigration problems in exchange for your testimony today?"

Rosie jumps up again. "Objection," she says. "Your Honor has already determined that Ms. Luk's immigration status has no bearing on this hearing."

"Sustained. Anything else for this witness, Mr. Grim?"

"Yes, Your Honor." Grim turns back to Luk and asks, "Did you see the African American man *inside* the Golden Dragon Restaurant that night?"

She shakes her head. "No."

"Do you have any personal knowledge as to whether he was inside that establishment that night?"

There's a hesitation before she whispers, "No."

"No further questions, Your Honor."

"Redirect, Ms. Fernandez?"

"No, Your Honor." It will only open the door to more abuse from Grim.

Nate leans over and whispers to me, "Is it enough?"

"Not yet." Luk's ID might have been enough to establish reasonable doubt at the trial. It isn't enough to prove freestanding innocence.

"What next?"

"We're going to start slinging mud at Aronis and Bryant."

The corner of Nate's mouth turns up. The old warrior suddenly seems to be enjoying the battle. "Lou said you were a fighter."

"I'm just warming up."

Saturday, July 18. 11:05 a.m.
12 hours and 56 minutes until execution.

Floyd Washington beams as he struts to the stand. He's pleased to be out of San Quentin for a few hours. Dressed in khaki pants and one of my light blue dress shirts, he now contains the anger that he displayed at San Quentin. He seems to view this as an opportunity for some form of vindication. I've told him to keep his expectations low and his answers short.

"How long have you been incarcerated?" I ask.

His left eye twitches nervously. "Twelve years."

"For what?"

His shoulders hunch forward slightly. "Selling heroin."

"Did you sell the drugs from your house?"

"No, I sold them from my garbage truck. I used to work for a company called East Bay Scavenger."

So far, so good. "Would you please tell us the name of the person who provided the heroin that you were selling?"

His gold teeth gleam as he smiles triumphantly. "Alexander Aronis."

Perfect. "The chairman of the board of East Bay Scavenger?"

The grin broadens. "Yeah."

"He actually furnished the heroin directly to you?"

"No, but his people instructed us where to pick it up and where to drop it off."

The whispering in the gallery stops when Judge Stumpf taps his gavel.

I move up in front of Washington. "When you were arrested, did you tell the police about Mr. Aronis?"

"Yeah." He wiggles his head like a football player getting loose during pregame warm-ups. "He hired a sleazy lawyer who cut him a deal with the prosecutors."

"Move to strike," Grim says. "Mr. Washington couldn't possibly have any personal information about such matters."

"Sustained."

"Who was Mr. Aronis's lawyer?" I ask.

He looks over my shoulder toward Nate. "Your client."

The whispers in the gallery turn to murmurs as I let his answer hang. "Did Mr. Aronis testify at your trial?"

"Yeah."

"Was he asked if he supplied the drugs that you sold?"

"Yeah. He lied." His upper body starts shaking in anger. "Money talks, Mr. Daley."

"Move to strike," Grim says. "Foundation."

"Sustained."

"Mr. Washington," I say, "are you suggesting Mr. Aronis bribed the prosecutors to drop any charges against him?"

"Objection," Grim says. "Foundation."

"Sustained. Move on, Mr. Daley."

"Yes, Your Honor." I turn back to Washington. "Do you know where Mr. Aronis obtained the heroin that you were selling?"

"Objection," Grim says. "Mr. Washington has no firsthand knowledge of such alleged distribution channels."

"Yes, he does," I say. "He worked for Mr. Aronis for many years. He was very familiar with all aspects of Mr. Aronis's operations."

"Overruled."

Grim sits down in frustration.

Washington is starting to enjoy the attention. He shoots a conde-scending look at Grim. Then his voice turns forceful. "Aronis got the heroin from a man named Terrell Robinson. Then they got into a fight, so he started getting the stuff from a guy named Marshawn Bryant."

"Mr. Bryant used to work for Mr. Robinson's construction com-pany, didn't he?"

He nods emphatically. "Yeah."

Hang with me, Floyd. We're almost done. "So Mr. Bryant and Mr. Robinson were running competing drug-distribution businesses?"

"Yeah."

"In other words, Mr. Bryant was in competition with his own boss?"

"Objection," Grim says. "Asked and answered. Furthermore, there isn't a shred of evidence in support of these wild accusations."

"Your Honor," I say, "we have already established that Mr. Washington was familiar with Mr. Aronis's operations."

Grim isn't backing down. "There is no evidence that he was famil-iar with Mr. Robinson's operations."

"Overruled."

"Yeah," Washington says triumphantly. "That's exactly what I'm saying: Bryant was competing against his boss."

"And then his boss was killed at the Golden Dragon?"

"Right."

"Are Mr. Aronis and Mr. Bryant still involved in the distribution of heroin?"

Grim tries again. "Objection. Mr. Washington has been incarcer-ated for many years. He has no personal knowledge of what's currently going on in the drug world outside San Quentin."

He probably knows more about the drug world than the SFPD does.

"Sustained."

I've gotten everything I can from him. "No further questions, Your Honor."

"Cross-exam, Mr. Grim?"

Grim can't wait. "Yes, Your Honor."

Here it comes.

Grim moves to a spot within three feet of Washington's face. His voice fills with unvarnished contempt. "You currently reside at San Quentin State Prison, don't you?"

Washington's bravado disappears. "Yeah."

"You'll be there for the rest of your life, won't you?"

He slinks back into his chair. "Yeah."

"You were promised special treatment by Mr. Daley and Ms. Fernandez if you agreed to testify here today, weren't you?"

Enough. "Objection," I say. "Argumentative."

"Sustained."

Grim rephrases. "Did Mr. Daley and Ms. Fernandez promise to help you with your legal problems if you testified today?"

Washington darts a concerned look my way, then locks eyes with Grim. "They said they would look into it."

"In other words, they've offered you legal help if you testify a certain way today, right?"

I need to stop the bleeding. "Objection," I say. "We would never exchange legal services for testimony."

The judge eyes me suspiciously. "Sustained."

Grim tugs at his lapels and continues in a condescending tone. "Let me put it this way," he says to Washington. "You have a substantial vested interest in testifying in a manner that will assist Mr. Daley's client, don't you?"

"Objection. Argumentative."

"Overruled."

Washington gives Dr. Death his own version of a Death Stare and summons his best prison-yard voice. "I'm telling the truth," he says. "Alex Aronis is a liar and a criminal."

Sometimes you get help from unexpected sources.

Grim astutely realizes that he isn't going to like the answers if he asks any more questions. "Nothing more for this witness," he says.

"Redirect, Mr. Daley?"

"No, Your Honor." We need to pile on Aronis a little more, and I have just the person to do it. "We call Patty Norman."

Saturday, July 18. 11:10 a.m.
12 hours and 51 minutes until execution.

atty Norman is wearing a beige cardigan sweater when she takes her place in the witness box. Her hair is pulled back into a French twist. A pair of reading glasses hangs from a silver chain around her neck. It's a subdued look for a mudslinging party.

I'm standing at the lectern, pretending to study my notes while Patty gets her bearings. The purpose of this exercise is to have her confirm Washington's testimony that Aronis and Bryant were involved in the drug business. I will also have her testify that her ex-husband wanted to hire somebody to take out Robinson and Chin. Any additional editorial comments that she might like to offer about her ex-husband's upstanding character will also be gratefully accepted.

I start with an easy one. "What do you do for a living?" I ask her.

"I own a bookstore in Petaluma. I do triathlons in my spare time."

Here we go. "Ms. Norman, were you married to a man named Alexander Aronis?"

"Yes."

"For how long?"

"Eighteen long years."

"He runs a trash-collection company in Oakland, doesn't he?"

"Yes." Her right eyebrow darts up. "He is also one of the most successful heroin distributors in the Bay Area."

Just the venomous tone I was looking for. It also gets Grim's attention. "Move to strike," he says. "There is no evidence that Ms. Norman has any expert knowledge of her husband's business."

Oh yes she does. "Your Honor," I say, "Ms. Norman just testified that she was married to Mr. Aronis for eighteen years. She knew everything about her husband's operations." And it's payback time.

"Overruled."

"Ms. Norman," I continue, "did your ex-husband's drug-related activities adversely impact your marriage?"

Her long brown hair bounces as she nods vigorously. "Yes. It was very difficult being married to a heroin dealer. It was even worse being married to a serial adulterer."

We may not get a stay, but we're going to settle some scores. "Why did you decide to come forward now?"

"I thought it was time that somebody told the truth."

Few people have an opportunity to slaughter their ex-spouse in front of a live audience. She's clearly going to enjoy it. "Was your husband ever arrested for selling drugs?"

"He was arrested, but never convicted. The police were never able to gather enough evidence." She turns and glares at Nate. "He hired a smart lawyer named Nathan Fineman, who was prepared to do anything to keep my ex-husband out of jail."

I don't want to give her a chance to take any more shots at Nate. "Did your ex-husband ever mention the names of some of the other prominent Bay Area drug dealers?"

"Yes. They all know each other."

How cozy. "Did those names include Terrell Robinson and Alan Chin?"

"Yes."

She's fearless. My only regret is that she won't have a chance to stare down her ex-husband in court. He has to wait outside until it's his turn to testify. "Did your ex-husband ever express an interest in expanding his operations into San Francisco?"

She smiles broadly. "Many times. He made several inquiries to Mr. Robinson and Mr. Chin to see if they were interested in combining their organizations. They weren't."

"When was that?"

"Shortly before he had them killed at the Golden Dragon."

"Move to strike!" Grim shouts. "There isn't a shred of evidence for these wild accusations."

"Sustained."

The courtroom is intensely quiet as I soldier on. "Ms. Norman," I continue, "do you know why Mr. Robinson and Mr. Chin didn't want to join forces with your ex-husband?"

She responds with a wicked grin. "They thought Alex was a small-time thug."

Sounds about right. "How did he feel after they rebuffed his advances?"

Grim is up. "Objection," he says. "Speculative. Mr. Daley is asking Ms. Norman to read her ex-husband's mind."

No, I'm not. "Your Honor," I say, "I'm simply asking Ms. Norman to describe his reaction."

"Overruled."

"He was upset," Norman says.

That would be an understatement. "How did he react when he was upset?"

"Badly."

"Did he get angry?"

"Yes. He also got even."

"Was he ever violent?"

"Yes."

"Toward you?"

"No." Her eyes gleam. "He knew better."

I like it. I shoot a glance toward Aronis's two lawyers, in the back row, who are writing furiously on their legal pads. It's their job to brief their client about Patty's testimony. "Did he ever talk about putting together a plan to move into the San Francisco market?"

"On several occasions. At one point, he asked me for assistance, but he was looking for something that I couldn't give him."

The same could be said of their marriage. "Which was?"

"The name of a professional killer."

Grim has been on his feet throughout Norman's testimony. "Move to strike," he says. "This testimony lacks foundation."

Judge Stumpf is listening intently. "Overruled."

"Ms. Norman," I say, "did he mention why he wanted to procure the services of a hit man?"

"He wanted to take out Terrell Robinson and Alan Chin."

I wonder what Dr. Phil would have to say about this. I still have a little more business. "Ms. Norman," I continue, "did your ex-husband ever mention a man named Marshawn Bryant?"

"Oh, yes. He was a flunky for Robinson."

"Did they know each other?"

"For years. They met when Robinson's firm handled the build-out of my ex-husband's offices. Bryant took over Robinson's construction business after he was killed."

"Was Mr. Bryant also involved in the drug business?"

Grim is up again. "Objection," he says. "While Ms. Norman may be familiar with her husband's business, we have no reason to believe that she has any familiarity with Mr. Bryant's operations."

Judge Stumpf stares him down. "Overruled."

"Yes," Norman says. "Bryant also took over Robinson's heroin-distribution business after Robinson was killed."

"Do you know if your ex-husband and Mr. Bryant had any involvement in the deaths of Terrell Robinson and Alan Chin?"

Norman responds with a grimace. "I don't know for sure."

I go for broke. "Did he hire Mr. Bryant to kill Mr. Robinson and Mr. Chin?"

"I don't know."

I was hoping for a little more. "Is it possible that your husband and Mr. Bryant pooled their resources to kill Mr. Robinson and Mr. Chin?"

"Objection," Grim says. "Speculation."

"Sustained."

I shoot a glance at Rosie, who closes her eyes—the signal to wrap up. If I push Patty, she might turn on Nate. "No further questions, Your Honor."

"Cross-exam, Mr. Grim?"

"Yes, Your Honor." He barrels through the well of the courtroom toward the witness box. "Ms. Norman," he says, "you and your ex-husband had a very acrimonious separation, didn't you?"

She leans forward to meet him head-on. "Yes."

"In fact, he had you committed to a mental institution, didn't he?"
"Yes."

"And he got full custody of your children, didn't he?"
"Yes."

Rosie and I exchange a helpless glance. We can't stop the onslaught.

"You contacted the newspapers recently and made some very serious accusations about your ex-husband, didn't you?"

"They weren't accusations, Mr. Grim. They're the truth."

"So you say."

"Objection," I say. "Argumentative."

"Sustained."

Grim is parked right in front of her. "You're still angry at your ex-husband for taking away your children, aren't you?"

"Yes."

"In fact, you would do or say anything to get back at him, wouldn't you?"

"Objection," I say. "Argumentative."

"Sustained."

Grim has made his point. "Ms. Norman," he says, "do you know for certain that your ex-husband hired someone to kill Terrell Robinson and Alan Chin?"

"No."

"Isn't it true that your ex-husband told you that he was going to hire Nathan Fineman to kill Terrell Robinson and Alan Chin at the Golden Dragon Restaurant?"

"Yes."

"No further questions."

The judge scowls. "Redirect, Mr. Daley?"

I have to try to undo the damage. "Just one question, Your Honor." I address Norman from my chair. "Do you have any evidence that your ex-husband did in fact contact Mr. Fineman about killing Mr. Robinson and Mr. Chin?"

"No."

"No further questions."

"Please call your next witness, Mr. Daley."

Patty's ex-husband is entitled to equal time. "We call Alexander Aronis, Your Honor."

A supremely self-assured Alex Aronis takes the stand and immediately tries to portray himself as a titan of industry. "I am the chief executive officer and majority shareholder of one of the largest waste-management companies in the country," he says.

I didn't think he'd say that he inherited a trash-collection operation from his father. I also don't expect to hear the words *pal* or *buddy* during his testimony. Dressed in a tailored Armani suit, a monogrammed white shirt, and a pink tie, he takes his fashion cues from Donald Trump. His blue eyes are locked intently on mine. A well-rehearsed sneer crosses his wide face. Aronis may be an overgrown frat boy, but he's a smart one.

I'm working against the clock and an individual who has no reason to help me. Washington testified that Aronis was in the drug business with Bryant, but he will be perceived as a jailhouse snitch who would say anything to shorten his prison term. Norman said that Aronis knew Bryant and was trying to hire somebody to take out Robinson and Chin, but her credibility is tainted by her disdain for her ex. All of which isn't likely to get us to freestanding innocence unless I can somehow find a way to connect the dots from Aronis to Bryant to the Golden Dragon.

Unlike with some of the earlier witnesses, where I started with a few easy ones, there will be no grace period for the garbage czar of Lake Merritt. "Mr. Aronis," I say, "do you know a man named Floyd Washington?"

"Yes."

Experienced witnesses never volunteer anything. "Where did you meet him?"

His tone is patronizing. "He drove a truck for our company. We fired him for selling drugs. We have a zero-tolerance policy for employees who engage in criminal activities."

I look away from him and mutter, "Except for you."

"Excuse me?"

"Nothing." I turn back and look squarely into his condescending eyes. "You testified at his trial, didn't you?"

"Yes."

"You cut a deal to testify against him in exchange for immunity, didn't you?"

Aronis darts a glance over toward Grim, who could object on the grounds that it's a leading question, but doesn't move. Grim is in an awkward position—it's his job to defend a man who he undoubtedly believes is a drug dealer. He also probably figures Aronis can take care of himself. There's a hesitation before Aronis finally says, "No."

"Did you hear my question?"

"Yes." The vestiges of the gregarious man who leads cheers behind the Cal bench at home football games are gone. "We cooperated fully with the police and the district attorney. No charges were filed against us."

I hate it when people use the "royal we." I want to see if I can get a rise out of him. "But they originally planned to file charges against you, too, didn't they?"

"We had discussions about certain ancillary claims in connection with the Washington case. Those charges were dropped."

Nice try. "That's because you agreed to roll over on Mr. Washington, right?"

His jowls wiggle as he shakes his head. "No, Mr. Daley. It was because they didn't have any evidence."

He parses better than most politicians. "Just because they didn't bring charges against you doesn't mean there wasn't any criminal behavior on your part," I say.

He smirks. "I can't prove a negative, Mr. Daley. I'm not going to play semantic games with you."

It's a good answer. He's more polished in court than he was at the garage. "Where did Mr. Washington obtain the heroin that he was selling from his truck?"

"I don't know."

Sure you do. "Are you aware that Mr. Washington testified at this hearing?"

"I was told that he was on your witness list."

And his two flunkies in the gallery undoubtedly gave him a blow-by-blow of Washington's testimony while his ex-wife was on the stand. I point an accusatory finger at him. "He said you supplied the heroin that he sold from his garbage truck."

He dismisses me with an upraised hand. "Mr. Washington is a convicted felon. He would say anything to cut a deal to get out of jail sooner."

"Perhaps the same could be said about you."

Grim stands up. "Objection, Your Honor. There wasn't a question there."

No, there wasn't. "Withdrawn."

Grim is still on his feet. "Your Honor," he whines, "we're spending an inordinate amount of time discussing unsubstantiated accusations about Mr. Aronis. This is completely irrelevant to the subject matter at hand."

"Your Honor," I say, "we've already shown a direct connection between Mr. Aronis and Mr. Bryant, who has now been placed at the Golden Dragon on the night of the shootings."

"Allegedly placed there," says Grim.

"You had a chance to question Ms. Luk," I say. "Her testimony speaks for itself."

"She wasn't credible," Grim says.

Judge Stumpf cuts in. "I'll be the judge of that, Mr. Grim." He points to his watch. "We're wasting time, Mr. Daley."

"Yes, Your Honor." I turn back to Aronis. "Do you know a man named Marshawn Bryant?"

He nods with confidence. "Yes. I've known him for years."

"How did you meet him?"

"He used to work for a man named Terrell Robinson, whose construction firm handled the build-out of our offices. Mr. Bryant took over Mr. Robinson's operations after Mr. Robinson was killed. He's handled several other projects for us. He's an excellent contractor."

"Is he also an excellent drug dealer?"

"Objection," Grim says. "Argumentative."

"Sustained."

"Mr. Aronis," I say, "Mr. Washington testified that Mr. Bryant was supplying heroin to you, which you provided to your drivers for resale."

"That's absolutely false."

"Mr. Washington also testified that you were anxious to expand your operations into San Francisco."

His voice fills with contempt. "That's also absolutely false."

"You're under oath, Mr. Aronis."

"I'm well aware of that, Mr. Daley. It's still false."

He isn't going to budge, so I move on to some postmarital counseling. "You were once married to a woman named Patty Norman, weren't you?"

"Yes."

"She recently made some serious public accusations about your participation in the events at the Golden Dragon, didn't she?"

He places an elbow on the edge of the witness box and uses his hand to punctuate his response. "My ex-wife is an angry, bitter woman," he says slowly. "There isn't a shred of truth in what she said."

"She also testified that you were involved in the distribution of heroin in the East Bay."

He flashes anger. "How many times do I have to say this? That's false."

"And she said you were interested in moving into the San Francisco heroin market."

This time he jabs his finger toward me. "That's false, too."

Deny, deny, deny. "Your ex-wife also testified that you asked for her assistance in finding someone to kill Terrell Robinson and Alan Chin."

He makes no attempt to mask his disdain for me. "That's ludicrous."

"A lot of people seem to be telling lies about you, Mr. Aronis."

He responds with a smirk. "I can't control what other people say about me."

"In fact, she suggested that you and Mr. Bryant may have pooled your resources to take out Mr. Robinson and Mr. Chin."

"False."

I bore in and fire away. "You paid Mr. Bryant to take out Mr. Robinson and Mr. Chin, didn't you?"

"No."

"You wanted to take over their operations, didn't you?"

"No."

"You're saying it was just happenstance Mr. Bryant was in the alley behind the Golden Dragon immediately after three people were shot to death?"

He takes a deep breath as he sits up straight. "I don't know what you're talking about, Mr. Daley. I am not involved in the drug business in any way, shape, or form. Neither is Mr. Bryant. I can assure you that

Mr. Robinson and Mr. Chin were not my competitors. I know absolutely nothing about what happened at the Golden Dragon ten years ago."

I fire away for five more minutes, but he doesn't budge. Grim correctly surmises that there is nothing to be gained by engaging in cross.

"Please call your next witness," the judge says.

Our last chance is to tee it up against Bryant. "We call Marshawn Bryant," I say.

Saturday, July 18. 11:47 a.m.
12 hours and 14 minutes until execution.

ryant exudes an understated self-confidence as he sits with his arms folded in the witness box. Sporting a gray suit and a dignified rep tie, he could pass for a partner at a downtown law firm. His two equally well-dressed lawyers are sitting in the gallery and preparing to take copious notes. For the next few minutes, we'll be going toe-to-toe. In the best-case scenario, I will get him to confess to murder—an unlikely prospect, except on *Perry Mason* reruns. At a minimum, I need to paint him as a lying drug dealer who will say anything to save his ass—no small task, either.

When I ask him to state his name for the record, he invokes a forceful tone. "My name is Marshawn Bryant. I want to make it absolutely clear that I wasn't at the Golden Dragon Restaurant on the night that your client murdered Terrell Robinson, Alan Chin, and Lester Fong."

I expect him to head straight for the door. I address the judge. "Your Honor," I say, "would you please instruct the witness to answer my questions without embellishment?"

"Please limit your responses to the questions asked."

Bryant feigns contrition. "Yes, Your Honor."

I move in closer. "Mr. Bryant," I say, "a short time ago, we heard

testimony from a witness who said you were in the alley behind the
Golden Dragon immediately after three people were shot and killed at
the restaurant."

His eyes are locked on mine. His demeanor is ice-cold. "That's
false."

"You're saying that witness was lying?"

He carefully enunciates each word. "They were mistaken."

"Have you ever heard of a man named Eugene Tsai?"

He closes his eyes and reopens them as he shakes his head slowly.
"No."

He's lying. "He saw you in the alley behind the Golden Dragon."

"No, he didn't."

"Yes, he did. In fact, he was prepared to testify that he saw you."

His voice remains perfectly even. "He was mistaken."

I move in a step closer. "Are you aware that Mr. Tsai was unable to
testify because he was stabbed to death shortly after he spoke to the
police?"

The right side of his mouth turns up slightly. "That was quite
unfortunate, but he was still mistaken."

I try to rattle him. "You found out that he was going to testify,
didn't you?"

"I didn't know anything about it."

"And you killed him, didn't you?"

His tone is indignant. "Absolutely not."

"Did you know that Mr. Fineman's attorneys attempted to introduce testimony from Mr. Tsai's brother about your presence in the alley
that night?" It's a bluff. Wendell was deemed too unreliable to put on
the stand. Any testimony about what Eugene may have told him would
have been hearsay.

"No, I didn't."

"Did you know that the trial judge didn't allow his testimony because of some technical evidentiary rules?" This isn't true, either. I'm looking for a reaction.

He doesn't fluster. "I wouldn't know. I'm not a lawyer, Mr. Daley."

"Well, I am, Mr. Bryant." I glare straight into his condescending eyes until he blinks. "I was able to persuade Judge Stumpf to allow Mr. Tsai's brother to testify. He told us that his brother saw you in the alley behind the Golden Dragon." It's a bluff—in reality, Tsai testified that Eugene saw a man who may have resembled Bryant in the alley. "Would that information cause you to reconsider your story?"

He doesn't move. "No, Mr. Daley."

I get right into his face. "Eugene Tsai saw you, Mr. Bryant."

His smugly confident expression never changes. "He was mistaken."

"I'll bet you figured you were off the hook after you killed him."

"That's ridiculous, Mr. Daley."

"You'll feel a lot better if you finally get this off your chest and tell the truth."

"That's absurd, Mr. Daley."

Grim gets to his feet and invokes a respectful tone. "Your Honor," he says, "Mr. Daley is intentionally mischaracterizing prior testimony and badgering the witness. Mr. Bryant has answered his questions. There is nothing to be gained by repeating these baseless accusations. We therefore respectfully request that you instruct Mr. Daley to move on."

The judge nods. "Please, Mr. Daley."

I come back swinging. "Mr. Bryant," I say, "does the name Jasmine Luk mean anything to you?"

He makes no attempt to mask another condescending smirk. "I'm afraid not."

"She lived in an apartment behind the Golden Dragon. She walked home with Eugene Tsai on the night that three people were killed. She testified that she and Mr. Tsai saw you in the alley behind the restaurant immediately after the shootings. Ring any bells?"

He doesn't move. "She was mistaken, too, Mr. Daley."

"A lot of people seem to be mistaken about you, Mr. Bryant." I turn my back to him and take a couple of steps toward the defense table, then stop and spin around and face him. "Let me fill you in on some of the details," I say. "Ms. Luk and Mr. Tsai saw you running down the alley. You stopped right in front of them and threatened them. In fact, you showed Ms. Luk precisely how you planned to slash her throat. Is any of this coming back to you, Mr. Bryant?"

"She was mistaken, Mr. Daley."

I can feel the back of my neck starting to burn. "It turns out that you caught another break. After Mr. Tsai was killed, Ms. Luk got scared and left town. Conveniently for you, she never had a chance to testify in this case—until today."

Bryant repeats his mantra: "She was mistaken, too."

"We have a witness, Mr. Bryant."

"She was mistaken or she was lying."

"She was not mistaken, Mr. Bryant. And she had no incentive to lie. In fact, she was so terrified of you that she left town and changed her identity."

Judge Stumpf's courtroom is deathly silent as Bryant wags a menacing finger at me and gets up on his soapbox. "You defense lawyers will say anything to get your clients off. I'm the biggest employer in the Bayview. I've built a community center and baseball fields in a place where people like you never come. I am not about to let you or anyone else take shots at my reputation." He takes a deep breath. "Your accusations are completely false. I wasn't at the Golden Dragon that night. In fact, I was home with my wife. She would be happy to testify on my behalf. Are we done with this blatant attempt at character assassination?"

He might as well stand up and scream, "Catch me if you can!" I glare into his arrogant eyes. "You understand that perjury carries serious penalties?"

"Yes, Mr. Daley."

"Last chance. Do you wish to reconsider your prior testimony?"

His right fist is clenched in a tight ball. "No, Mr. Daley. I told the truth back then. I'm telling the truth today."

"You were lying back then, and you're lying today."

"Objection," Grim shouts.

"Sustained." Judge Stumpf is glaring at me. "You've made your point, Mr. Daley. Move on."

I walk back to the defense table to take a moment to gather my thoughts. I look down at a note that Rosie has written on a pad that she's placed where I can see it. It simply says, "Nail him."

I wheel around and walk forcefully across the well of the courtroom until I'm standing inches from the witness box. I start asking questions in rapid succession. "You used to work for a contractor named Terrell Robinson, didn't you?"

"Yes."

"He was one of the victims at the Golden Dragon, wasn't he?"

"Yes."

"You were a vice president in his business, weren't you?"

"Yes."

"He was also involved in drug trafficking, wasn't he?"

He doesn't move. "No."

My tone is incredulous. "You didn't know that he was one of the biggest heroin distributors in San Francisco?"

"Correct."

"You took over Mr. Robinson's business after his death, didn't you?"

"Yes."

"Where did you get the money to buy out a successful contracting business?"

"Our bank gave me a loan."

"Which you supplemented with money that you earned when you

took over his heroin operation, didn't you?"

"No."

I keep pushing. "You've benefited quite handsomely from Mr. Robinson's death, haven't you?"

"I never intended things to happen the way that they did."

"Of course not. Do you know a man named Alexander Aronis?"

"I've known him for years."

"You know that he's also a heroin dealer, don't you?"

"That's not true."

"You knew that he wanted to take out Terrell Robinson and Alan Chin and move into the San Francisco heroin market, didn't you?"

He doesn't flinch. "I don't know what you're talking about, Mr. Daley."

"I think you do."

"Objection," Grim shouts. "Argumentative. Asked and answered."

"Sustained."

His icy demeanor never cracks. He's going to deny everything until they walk Nate into the execution chamber. I have nothing left to lose. "You and Mr. Aronis pooled your resources and killed Terrell Robinson and Alan Chin, didn't you?"

"No."

"Or maybe Aronis paid you to set up the hit so he wouldn't get his hands dirty."

"No."

"And you and Mr. Aronis planned to split the San Francisco market, didn't you?"

"No."

"And that's precisely how everything worked out, isn't it, Mr. Bryant?"

"Objection," Grim shouts. "Asked and answered. Argumentative. Foundation."

All of the above.

"Sustained," the judge says.

I haven't moved from my spot in front of the witness box. As far as I'm concerned, Bryant and I are the only two people left on the face of the earth. "What were you doing at the Golden Dragon that night, Mr. Bryant?"

"I wasn't there."

"Yes, you were."

"No, I wasn't. You can't prove it."

"We already have. You aren't going to be able to talk your way out of it this time."

Bryant is now sitting ramrod straight with his fists clenched. He shakes his head slowly from side to side. "This is obviously nothing more than a last-ditch attempt to save your client's life."

I level a final desperate blast. "This is nothing more than a last-ditch attempt to deny the truth. You were at the Golden Dragon that night. You killed three people. You set up Nate Fineman. You killed Eugene Tsai. You threatened Jasmine Luk. You may have gotten away with it ten years ago, but you aren't going to get away with it now."

"Objection!" Grim shouts. "Argumentative. Asked and answered."

"Sustained."

My hands are shaking as I glare at Bryant. "No further questions," I say.

"Cross-exam, Mr. Grim?"

"No, Your Honor."

As I trudge back to the defense table, I'm already starting the post-mortem on what else we could have done. Deep down, I knew I wasn't going to be able to extract a confession from Aronis or Bryant. As a practical matter, all they had to do was sit back and deny everything—which they did. Because we had little hard evidence against them and almost no time to prepare, the deck was stacked against us from the start. This awareness still provides little solace as I take my seat next to

Nate, who is staring straight ahead with his arms crossed.

Judge Stumpf is looking at me. "Any other witnesses, Mr. Daley?"

"One moment, Your Honor." I huddle with Rosie and Nate at the defense table.

"You got anything else?" Nate asks.

I don't say it out loud, but we're down to Hail Mary passes. I look at Rosie and say, "What's left?"

Rosie glances around the courtroom for an instant. Then she hands me a note that's written on a yellow Post-it. "A uniform handed this to me a few minutes ago," she says. "It's from Roosevelt."

I look down at it and recognize Roosevelt's meticulous handwriting. It says that the ten-thousand-dollar monthly payments to Little Joey's currency exchange came from an account controlled by Bayview Construction. I reach for the folder that contains the bank statements from Joey's business that we found in the trunk of Pete's car.

"What does it mean?" Rosie asks.

"I'm not entirely sure, but I'm going to find out." I look toward the prosecution table, where Roosevelt has taken a seat next to Grim. He gives me a subtle nod, then he turns away. The next thing I hear is Judge Stumpf's voice from behind me.

"Any other witnesses, Mr. Daley?"

I can feel my palms sweating as I turn around and face him. "Just one, Your Honor. The defense calls Joseph D'Amato."

Saturday, July 18. 12:09 p.m.
11 hours and 52 minutes until execution.

M y adrenaline is pumping as I carry the file containing Little Joey's bank account information to the front of the court- room. Judge Stumpf has already informed me in no uncertain terms that Little Joey will be my last witness. I look down at the file for an instant when I reach the witness box; then I look up at Little Joey. "Mr. D'Amato," I begin, "what do you do for a living?"

Little Joey is dressed in an ill-fitting black suit with a gaudy poly- ester tie. He's sitting back in the chair. "I run a currency exchange in the Tenderloin."

"How long have you operated that business?"

"About eight years."

"What did you do prior to that time?"

His tone fills with pride. "I was a San Francisco police officer for twenty-four years."

"Why did you leave?"

"I took early retirement to open my business."

It will serve no useful purpose to delve into the circumstances of his departure from the force. "Mr. D'Amato," I continue, "you were one of the first officers at the scene on the night that three people were killed at the Golden Dragon Restaurant almost ten years ago, weren't you?"

"Yes."

"There was an investigation into your actions that night, wasn't there?"

Joey's eyes narrow. "The charges were dropped."

"Those allegations included planting the murder weapon, didn't they?"

A sneer crosses his face. "The charges were dropped," he repeats.

I glance down at the bank statements for an instant, then move in another direction. "Mr. D'Amato," I say, "are you acquainted with a man named Marshawn Bryant?"

"Yes."

"How do you know him?"

"He's done some work for my business."

"When did you meet him?"

"About eight years ago. He handled the build-out work on my business."

"That was after the events at the Golden Dragon?"

"Yes."

I shoot a quick glance toward Roosevelt. I turn back to Joey and ask, "Did you happen to see Mr. Bryant anywhere near the Golden Dragon on the night of the shootings?"

"No, Mr. Daley."

"You're sure about that, too?"

"Quite sure."

"You didn't see him in the vicinity when you were on your way to the restaurant?"

"Objection," Grim says. "Asked and answered."

"Sustained."

"Mr. Bryant," I continue, "would your testimony change if I told you that another witness testified earlier today that she saw Mr. Bryant in the alley behind the Golden Dragon on the night of the shootings?"

Daley."

him?"

an ongoing relation-

ank statements. "Your

bank statements from

e. We have already pro-

g into Grim's ear. "No

ys.

a pair of cheap reading

here did you get these?"

got his hands on them

confirm that these are

ount of your currency

I think so."

ail to see the relevance,

thing more exhilarating

ts in open court. I move

the first bank statement.

386

I realize that I'm speaking faster

to be a recurring monthly deposi

ments."

Joey nods grudgingly. "Yeah."

"They seem to have started

Joey curls his lip. "Yeah."

"Would you mind telling us

He swallows his words when

"Ten thousand dollars," I repe

been paying you ten grand a mo

No answer.

My voice is filled with sugar.

Still no answer. Joey is now s

"Your Honor," I say, "would

answer?"

"Mr. D'Amato," the judge say

question."

Joey responds by pouring him

"Mr. D'Amato?" the judge says

Joey's narrow eyes are now sta

"Mr. D'Amato," I say, "you've

an offshore account controlle

Construction, haven't you?"

He clamps his mouth shut.

"Mr. D'Amato," I say, "we've

mation. You can save us a lot of tim

Little Joey bites down hard on

icy to reveal confidential informati

"It's also against the law to co

"I can't help you, Mr. Daley."

"Your Honor?" I say.

Little Joey's tone turns patronizing. "No, Mr. Daley."

I push him harder. "Why are you protecting him?"

"I'm not."

"But you would acknowledge that you have an ongoing relationship."

He scowls. "He's a reputable contractor."

"Is he also a reputable drug dealer?"

"Objection," Grim says. "Argumentative."

"Sustained."

I turn to the judge and hand him the bank statements. "Your Honor," I say, "we would like to introduce these bank statements from Mr. D'Amato's business into evidence at this time. We have already provided copies to Mr. Grim."

I turn around and see Roosevelt whispering into Grim's ear. "No objection, Your Honor," Grim says.

"You may proceed, Mr. Daley," the judge says.

I hand the papers over to Joey, who puts on a pair of cheap reading glasses and pretends to study them intently. "Where did you get these?" he asks.

"From your bank," I say. Precisely how Pete got his hands on them is a topic for another forum. "Would you please confirm that these are copies of the statements for the checking account of your currency exchange for the last eight years?"

He's trying to speed-read the documents. "I think so."

Grim offers a halfhearted objection. "I fail to see the relevance, Your Honor."

"I was just getting to that, Your Honor."

"Proceed, Mr. Daley."

Trial lawyers will tell you that there is nothing more exhilarating and terrifying than following your gut instincts in open court. I move in closer to Little Joey and point to an entry on the first bank statement.

I realize that I'm speaking faster than usual when I say, "There appears to be a recurring monthly deposit reflected on each of these bank statements."

Joey nods grudgingly. "Yeah."

"They seem to have started eight years ago."

Joey curls his lip. "Yeah."

"Would you mind telling us how much it is?"

He swallows his words when he says, "Ten thousand dollars."

"Ten thousand dollars," I repeat. "Would you please tell us who has been paying you ten grand a month?"

No answer.

My voice is filled with sugar. "Mr. D'Amato?"

Still no answer. Joey is now squeezing the rail tightly.

"Your Honor," I say, "would you please instruct the witness to answer?"

"Mr. D'Amato," the judge says, "you'll have to answer Mr. Daley's question."

Joey responds by pouring himself a cup of water.

"Mr. D'Amato?" the judge says.

Joey's narrow eyes are now staring straight ahead.

"Mr. D'Amato," I say, "you've been receiving these payments from an offshore account controlled by a company called Bayview Construction, haven't you?"

He clamps his mouth shut.

"Mr. D'Amato," I say, "we've subpoenaed the wire-transfer information. You can save us a lot of time if you simply answer my question."

Little Joey bites down hard on his lower lip. "It is against our policy to reveal confidential information concerning our clients," he says.

"It's also against the law to commit perjury," I say.

"I can't help you, Mr. Daley."

"Your Honor?" I say.

"Answer the question, Mr. D'Amato."

"But Your Honor—"

"Answer the question or I'll hold you in contempt."

"Yes," Joey grunts. "It's from Bayview."

"That would be the firm owned by your good friend Marshawn Bryant?"

He hunkers down in his chair. "Yeah."

"A moment ago, you testified that Mr. Bryant's firm had performed construction contracting services for you."

"Yeah."

I arch an eyebrow. "If he was doing work for *you*, wouldn't it follow that you should have been paying *him*?"

The courtroom is silent as Joey tugs at his garish tie.

"Mr. D'Amato," I say, "why has Mr. Bryant been paying you ten thousand dollars a month for the last eight years?"

Little Joey pulls at his ear. "For financial services," he finally says.

Please. "Multimillion-dollar contracting businesses like Bayview don't use small-time currency exchanges like yours to handle their banking needs. They certainly don't pay them over a hundred grand a year for the privilege."

Joey doesn't respond.

"Mr. D'Amato, I'm going to ask you once again. Why has Mr. Bryant been paying you ten grand a month for the last eight years?"

Every eye in the courtroom is fixed on Little Joey. He makes the tactical error of trying to stonewall again. "For financial services," he repeats.

"You know that isn't true, Mr. D'Amato."

No answer.

"And as a former police officer, you are undoubtedly well aware of the penalties for perjury, aren't you, Mr. D'Amato?"

Little Joey is no longer smirking.

My mind flies into overdrive. "Mr. D'Amato," I say, "you saw Mr. Bryant in the alley behind the Golden Dragon on the night of the shootings, didn't you?"

No answer.

"And you didn't report it, did you?"

Still no answer. Grim could object, but he's choosing to sit on his hands. Clearly, he's prepared to let the chips fall where they may—perhaps after a discussion with Roosevelt.

I move within two feet of Joey's face. "Bryant killed Terrell Robinson, Alan Chin, and Lester Fong, didn't he?"

Joey shakes his head. "No."

"He's paying you to keep your mouth shut, isn't he?"

"No."

"You helped him plant the gun and frame my client for murder, didn't you?"

"No."

"That makes you an accessory after the fact."

"No."

Grim finally stands and tries to slow me down. "Objection," he says. "This is pure speculation on Mr. Daley's part."

"Overruled."

I haven't moved from the front of the witness box. "Mr. D'Amato," I say, "you decided to blackmail Mr. Bryant about the events at the Golden Dragon, didn't you?"

His eyes are now darting. "No."

"And you've been taking ten grand a month from him ever since, haven't you?"

"No. You have no evidence."

"How about a million dollars of payments over the last eight years?"

His voice turns defensive. "You can't prove anything."

"I already have. You're already in for obstruction of justice, extortion, and maybe even murder, Mr. D'Amato. If you come clean now, you might be able to avoid adding a perjury charge."

Little Joey slinks back in his chair. "I want to talk to my lawyer," he says.

I shoot a look at Roosevelt, who closes his eyes. I turn back to the judge and say, "No further questions, Your Honor."

"Cross-exam, Mr. Grim?"

"Just a few questions, Your Honor." He walks up to the witness box and says, "Mr. D'Amato, do you have any evidence placing Marshawn Bryant inside the Golden Dragon Restaurant on the night that three people were killed ten years ago?"

"No."

"Do you have any information suggesting Mr. Bryant was involved in a scheme to kill three people?"

"No."

"Do you have any proof that Mr. Bryant was involved in payoffs in connection with the killing of three people?"

"No."

"Were you involved in planting evidence or any sort of cover-up in connection with the events at the Golden Dragon Restaurant?"

"No."

"No further questions, Your Honor."

"Redirect, Mr. Daley?"

"No, Your Honor."

Judge Stumpf strokes his chin as he looks at the clock on the wall in the back of his courtroom. "We've already gone over our allotted time," he says, "but I'm willing to give each of you a moment to make a very brief closing statement. You're first, Mr. Grim."

Grim keeps it succinct. "Your Honor," he says, "in order to grant a stay, the law requires the appellant to prove freestanding innocence.

While we have heard some interesting testimony and raised some new possibilities, the fact remains that the appellant has not met that threshold. In such circumstances, the law requires that the petition for a writ of habeas corpus be denied."

The judge's stoic expression hasn't changed. "Mr. Daley?"

"Your Honor," I say, "we have placed Marshawn Bryant at the Golden Dragon Restaurant on the night in question. We have heard testimony that Mr. Bryant has paid Officer D'Amato over a million dollars to buy his silence." I look over at Nate, whose eyes are fixed on mine. I turn back and face the judge. My voice starts to crack as I offer a final plea. "You get to play God today, Your Honor. You get to decide whether Nate Fineman will live or die." I swallow hard and fight to regain my composure. "I don't know for sure if we've succeeded in proving freestanding innocence precisely in accordance with the letter of the law. I do know for sure that the testimony we've heard this morning would make it a tragic and unconscionable and…immoral miscarriage of justice if you permit this execution to proceed."

The judge takes off his glasses and folds his hands. His tone is solemn when he says, "I understand the gravity of the situation. I am going to take this matter under advisement. I will rule later today."

Saturday, July 18. 5:15 p.m.
6 hours and 46 minutes until execution.

It takes us more than an hour to get back to San Quentin, where the narrow road outside the east gate is jammed with news vans, placard-waving advocates, and idealistic clergy. The turnout is overwhelmingly anti–death penalty. The surreal, carnival-like atmosphere also includes the group of gawkers and hangers-on who seem to materialize at every significant public event, as well as a few mercenaries who are peddling anti–capital punishment T-shirts and bumper stickers. It's sometimes difficult to discern where the protests end and the parties begin. The crowds will get larger as midnight approaches.

Nate is in a philosophical mood when we finally get back to the Row. He, Ilene, Rosie, Rabbi Friedman, and I regroup in the somber holding cell adjacent to the execution chamber. "It was nice to get out for a while," Nate says. "It's been a long time."

Almost ten years. We can hear the solemn chants of the demonstrators outside through the thick prison walls. "We aren't done yet," I say.

He takes a deep breath. "Before all hell breaks loose, I want to thank you. We knew the odds were long when we brought you in. Free-standing innocence is a lot tougher to prove than reasonable doubt. It's damn near impossible unless somebody confesses."

"We gave the judge a lot to work with," I say. "We placed Bryant at the Golden Dragon. The payments to Little Joey showed the cops knew something—or that they were in on it."

"Don't get your hopes up," he says.

"We still have more than six hours," I say. "We aren't giving up yet."

"You did everything you could. How did you figure out that Bryant was paying Little Joey?"

"Roosevelt."

His tired eyes open wide. "Really?"

"Really."

"Let's see if Judge Stumpf buys it."

"I think he will." In reality, I'm not sure.

Nate gives me a thoughtful look. "You got us a lot closer than I ever imagined. I never figured we'd get a hearing."

"Judge Stumpf has enough to grant a stay," I say. "We still have a chance with the governor, too."

"At least we're going down swinging."

"We haven't gone down yet."

"We'll see. You guys reminded me of my favorite lawyer today."

"Perry Mason?"

"Nathan Fineman." He chuckles heartily. "For a moment, I thought you were going to accuse everybody in the courtroom of murder."

I can feel a lump in my throat as I return his smile. "I didn't accuse the judge."

"Maybe you should have. We had nothing to lose."

He has six hours to live and he's trying to make *us* feel better. The banter stops and the cramped cell goes silent. I look straight at my client. "Can you tell us anything else about what happened at the Golden Dragon that night?"

"Jews don't do confessions," he says.

"I'm not looking for that. I want to know if there's anything else we can use before we call the governor again."

"You never give up, do you?"

"Not when I know I'm right."

"It's a fair question," he says. "I guess Judgment Day is here."

"So it would seem."

He holds up a tired hand. "I didn't kill those people, Mike. With God as my witness, I'm telling you the truth."

#

A clean-cut young guard knocks on the door at seven o'clock. "You had a call from Judge Stumpf's clerk," he says.

"Good news or bad news?" I ask.

"He didn't say."

"What *did* he say?"

"The judge wants to meet with you in his chambers as soon as possible."

Saturday, July 18. 7:45 p.m.
4 hours and 16 minutes until execution.

"I'm sorry for the short notice," Judge Stumpf says to us. Rosie and I are sitting on a leather sofa in his cramped chambers in the Federal Building. Irwin Grim scowls at his notes as he sits in an antique armchair. Roosevelt stands near the door. It is impossible to discern whether the news is good or bad from the impassive expressions on the faces of everybody in the stuffy room.

My heart pounds as Judge Stumpf studies a legal pad on which he's scripted notes in an elegant cursive. He chooses his words with judicial care. "Based upon today's testimony and additional information provided by Inspector Johnson," he says, "I am issuing a stay of Mr. Fineman's execution. I am ordering him released immediately."

I can feel Rosie squeezing my hand. My breaths come faster. It's a complete victory.

The judge is still speaking. "Mr. Grim and I just got off the phone with the San Francisco district attorney. At my request, she has just concluded confidential negotiations with Mr. D'Amato and his attorney. In exchange for the DA's agreement not to press charges against him, Mr. D'Amato will testify that he saw Mr. Bryant walking down Broadway when he and your father were driving to the Golden Dragon. Neither Mr. D'Amato nor Officer Thomas Daley reported it." He looks over at Grim, who nods. "While it may not constitute freestanding innocence precisely within the letter of the law, it certainly complies with the spirit of the statute. Mr. Grim and I have therefore concluded that it would be unconscionable to proceed with Mr. Fineman's execution under these circumstances."

I'm not inclined to quibble about the fact that it merely places Bryant at the scene. Nor does it prove that he pulled the trigger. What matters is that Nate Fineman is going to live. In fact, he's going to be released from jail. "Did my father see Bryant?" I ask.

"Mr. D'Amato said he did. We'll never know for sure."

"It didn't appear in the IA report."

"We now believe that the IA investigation was flawed."

And the file is gone. "Does that mean Bryant killed three people?" I ask.

"No." The judge takes off his glasses. "Inspector Johnson and I went over the timeline again. We now believe that Mr. Tsai and Ms. Luk saw Mr. Bryant in the alley immediately prior to the moment the first shots were fired. We further believe that Mr. Bryant could not have killed three people, planted the gun under Mr. Fineman's body, and gotten to the corner of Columbus and Broadway in time for Mr. D'Amato—and perhaps your father—to have seen him as they were making their way to the Golden Dragon. There simply wasn't enough time. We therefore have concluded that he could not have fired the fatal shots."

"Then it had to be Officer David Low," I say.

Judge Stumpf nods. "Based upon the information now available to us, I think it is very likely that you are right. Inspector Johnson has provided us with Officer Low's bank account records. In addition to paying a monthly stipend to Mr. D'Amato, Mr. Bryant also paid Officer Low a lump sum of fifty thousand dollars in cash shortly before the shootings. Though we have no hard and fast evidence, we believe it is likely that Mr. Bryant obtained the funds from Mr. Aronis."

"Was Low that desperate for money?" I ask.

It's Roosevelt who responds. "It was an open secret within the SFPD that he had a gambling problem. There were rumors that he was on the payrolls of the drug lords he was investigating—including Robinson and Chin."

It means that Nate walked into a setup. "If Aronis and Bryant were working together," I say, "how did Bryant end up with control of the San Francisco heroin market?"

"Aronis got everything else," Roosevelt says. "He controls everything from Daly City south to San Jose, as well as the entire East Bay. All's fair in love, war, and drug dealing. Bryant is still his primary source of heroin."

Washington was telling the truth. "Why didn't Bryant do it himself?"

"Maybe he couldn't get a gun inside the Golden Dragon. Maybe he didn't want to get his hands dirty. Low was also smart enough to spread the risk. We think he made Bryant clear out the bodyguards himself. That left him with an unobstructed path to Robinson and Chin. We think Low went upstairs and blew everybody away, except for Fineman, who dove out the window onto the fire escape."

"Why didn't he kill Nate, too?"

Roosevelt gives me a knowing look. "It may have been a crime of opportunity. Low was an experienced undercover cop with an aptitude for improvisation. When he found Fineman unconscious in the alley, he realized he had another option. He planted the gun in Fineman's hand. He told everybody—including Joey and your father—that he got there right after the shooting had stopped. He was a decorated hero. Nobody wanted to question him about it. There was a lot of history between the SFPD and your client after the Bayview Posse case went south. Low was able to pin the murder of two drug dealers on the most infamous mob lawyer in the Bay Area and collect a pile of cash—not a bad result for him. Bryant got control of the San

Francisco heroin market and Robinson's best construction contracts. Aronis got the rest of the Bay Area heroin market. Low knew that Bryant and Aronis couldn't rat him out without implicating themselves."

It was the proverbial win-win situation. "And Eugene Tsai and Jasmine Luk?"

"They were in the wrong place at the wrong time. It's likely that Bryant killed Tsai or had him killed. I may never be able to prove it."

"Why didn't he kill Luk, too?"

"She left town before Bryant could get to her."

"Which means the only loose ends were Joey and my father."

"Bryant didn't know that until later. Now we know that D'Amato—and perhaps your father—withheld evidence. It now appears that Joey and perhaps some of the other officers who secured the scene at the Golden Dragon also took the opportunity to settle some old scores from the Bayview Posse case."

"Was Little Joey really blackmailing Bryant?"

"That's the only logical explanation. When Joey was forced to take early retirement, he needed money to open his currency exchange. He had the goods on Bryant. He took advantage of the situation."

"Was my father involved in the blackmail scheme?"

"It seems unlikely. Bryant started making payments to D'Amato after your father died." He waits a beat. "If you must know, I checked your father's bank records, too. There was no evidence of any payments to him."

My relief is tempered by the knowledge that he may have withheld crucial evidence in a murder trial. "It still means he and Joey let Nate take the rap," I say.

"I'm sorry, Mike," Roosevelt says. "Your client may not be a murderer, but he was no Boy Scout, either."

"Did Bryant shoot Pete?"

"If I were a betting man—which I'm not—I would say the chances are pretty good that he ordered the hit."

"Why?"

"He probably thought Pete was getting close to something."

He was.

Rosie asks, "What about the photo of Grace and her boyfriend that was delivered to my house?"

"We're going to lean on Bryant's people to trace it back to him."

And hopefully our lives will now return to some semblance of normal.

Roosevelt takes a deep breath. "I have to give you credit," he says. "You put the pieces together to stop an execution in less than two weeks."

"We had a lot of help," I say. I've also probably ruined my father's reputation along the way.

"For what it's worth," he adds, "please tell Nate that I'm sorry."

"I will." I turn back to Judge Stumpf. "Where does this leave us?"

"At this point, it's up to the DA to decide whether she's going to file new charges against your client. I intend to discourage it."

We will also be bringing a civil action on Nate's behalf for wrongful imprisonment.

"What about Bryant and Aronis?" I ask.

"They've been detained for questioning. The investigation will be headed by Inspector Johnson." Judge Stumpf holds up an authoritative hand. "The system got the wrong result ten years ago. We were less than five hours away from executing an innocent man. We can't possibly make up for the losses suffered by Mr. Fineman and his family, but I want to be sure that we get it right this time."

"Will charges be brought against anybody else?" I ask.

"Probably not. The DA would have brought murder charges against Mr. Low, but he's dead."

"What about Joey D'Amato?"

"The DA has agreed to grant him limited immunity from extortion, obstruction of justice, and perjury charges in exchange for his testimony against Mr. Bryant and his agreement to shut down his business."

"And my father?"

"We are unsure of his precise role in the cover-up—if any. The fact that he is deceased means that no charges will be brought against him."

For the first time in a week, a sense of calm envelops me. We may never be able to demonstrate for certain that Dave Low pulled the trigger. It will take years of legal maneuvering to make any charges stick against Aronis and Bryant. Nevertheless, after ten long years, there finally may be some modest degree of justice for Nate Fineman.

“It's your deal,” Nate says.

I lean back in my card chair. “You cleaned me out,” I tell him.

“I can spot you a few extra bucks.”

“I'd have to put up my Corolla as collateral.”

“Suit yourself.”

A week ago, it was inconceivable to me that I'd be playing five-card stud with Nate the Great, Mort the Sport, and Nick the Dick in the sunny courtyard of the Jewish Home under the smiling gaze of Ilene Fineman. Nate was released from San Quentin late last night. There was a celebration up at St. Francis Wood. This morning, there was a brunch at Temple Beth Sholom. Rabbi Friedman led the community in prayers of thanksgiving. Then we drove Nate to the Jewish Home, where he moved into a room not far from Mort. After all these years, they'll be down the hall from each other once again.

Nate holds up his cigar. “You got a light?” he asks.

“Afraid not,” I say. “Since when do they let you smoke here?”

“I cut a deal with the board of directors. I get one cigar a week.”

I look over at Mort. “Aren't you on the board?”

“Yes, I am. I have the same deal.”

I might have known. The raucous poker game continues for a few minutes; then Nate looks around at his old compatriots. “A toast to all of us,” he says. “We're finally back together. We're going to start making up for lost time right now." He raises a glass. "*L'Chaim.*"

Ilene beams. Nate will spend much of his time over here. He will also have regular visits to St. Francis Wood.

Nate pulls me aside a few minutes later. "I'm sorry Rosie couldn't make it."

"She wanted time with Grace and Tommy." She's also trying to negotiate a final schedule with her contractor to finish the work on her kitchen.

"You'll bring her over here so that I can properly express my gratitude?"

"Of course."

"When is Pete coming home?"

"Hopefully soon. I'll bring him over as soon as he's able."

He winks. "Do you think you guys could have cut it any closer?"

"We had four hours to spare."

The old lawyer's eyes turn melancholy. "I owe you big-time," he says.

"I knew you weren't a killer, Nate."

"I'm glad somebody thought so. You'll send me a final bill?"

"You're all paid up."

He takes a deep breath of the warm breeze. "I'm an old man. I'm not in a position to offer much. If there is anything I can do for you, just name it."

"It isn't necessary, Nate. We did our job. You paid our bill."

"You saved my life."

I'm not the type to call on favors, but I'm prepared to make an exception in this case. "First," I say, "there's a girl in Oakland who needs a heart and lung transplant. Her parents are gone and she's living with her grandparents. They have no insurance."

"How much?"

"A hundred grand. Jeff Chin and Amanda Wong are raising the money."

"I'll take care of it."

"Second," I say, "I'd like you to hire our firm to handle your civil case for wrongful imprisonment."

"I wouldn't think of hiring anybody else. I want you to take them for every penny."

"I have a condition."

"Name it."

"I want you to donate a portion of the judgment to the California Appellate Project."

"Done."

"Third, I was wondering if your son still has seats next to the Giants' dugout."

His eyes light up. "When do you want them?"

"The Dodgers are in town in a couple of weeks."

"How many do you need?"

\# \# \#

"The usual?" Big John asks.

"Thanks," I say. Two weeks later, Pete and I are sitting at one of the worn wooden tables along the wall at Dunleavy's.

My uncle hands me two pints of Guinness. "When did you get home?" he asks Pete.

"This afternoon."

"You came over here on your first night home?"

"This is home, too. Donna needed a little break, so I made my big brother take me out for a beer."

"I'm honored," Big John says. Our genial host gives him a bartender's smile. "How long are you going to be in that wheelchair?"

"A couple more weeks."

"Are you supposed to be drinking beer?"

"Nope."

"You want another one?"

"Absolutely."

Big John heads back to the bar. I turn to Pete, who is wearing a Giants jacket and cap. "How's it feel?" I ask.

"Better than it did two weeks ago." His doctors want him to heal a little before they start talking about hip-replacement surgery. "If it's all the same to you, I'd like to stay out of hospitals for a while."

"Is there anything I can do?"

"You can keep an eye on Donna and Margaret. You can take me out for a beer every once in a while."

"Deal."

His eyes brighten when I offer him a field-level seat to the Giants/Dodgers game next week, but then his expression turns serious. "I may have to close the agency," he says. "In case you haven't noticed, I'm not quite as mobile as I used to be. I would also like to do something where the hours are a little more regular."

"You don't have to make any decisions for a while," I say. "Give it some time. See how you're feeling."

"I already have another offer."

"From whom?"

"Nick Hanson."

"Are you serious?"

"Indeed I am."

Dear God. "Are you going to work for Nick?"

"I haven't decided yet."

"Does that mean you're going to talk like Nick?"

He smiles. "I haven't decided that either."

We watch the Giants game on TV for a few minutes. Pete downs his beer and wipes his lips with a brown paper napkin. His tone is somber when he asks the question that I've been expecting for the last two weeks.

"Why didn't Pop say something?"

It's the first time we've talked about it. "Maybe he was trying to protect Low and D'Amato," I say. Or himself.

"Do you really think Pop bought into the Code of Silence crap?"

"He was a pretty old-fashioned guy."

"He wasn't old-fashioned enough to let Nate rot in jail for ten years."

"Maybe he really didn't see anything. Maybe he really was trying to settle an old score with Nate after the Posse fiasco. We'll never know for sure. Frankly, it doesn't matter anymore." As I say it, I realize that I'm trying to convince myself as much as I'm trying to convince him.

"You're in an awfully forgiving mood."

"He's gone, Pete. There's nothing we can do about it. Rosie says I should let it go."

"Doesn't it bug you?"

"Yeah."

"But?"

"I guess sometimes you discover that your heroes have feet of clay."

He gives me a thoughtful look. "Was Pop really one of your heroes?"

"In a way, yes."

"You guys were at each other's throats for forty years."

"I still respected him as a cop."

"How about as a father?"

"I thought he needed a little work there."

"So did I." He arches an eyebrow. "Do you think Margaret will be saying the same thing about me in twenty years?"

"Not a chance."

"You don't seem to have big problems with Grace."

"She reserves most of her venom for Rosie." I tap my brother's arm. "Are you going to be able to deal with this?"

"Eventually." His scowl becomes more pronounced. "Donna and I have been talking about making some changes."

Uh-oh. "What kind?"

"We're thinking about selling the house and moving out to the burbs. It's probably a good time to cash in our chips. We saw a little place in San Anselmo that we liked." He hesitates. "Are you going to be okay with that?"

"Of course. Why now?"

"I've been living in the same house for more than forty years. I'm tired of the fog. Besides, it will be better for Margaret. The schools are better in Marin."

We'll also be neighbors. "Are you sure about this?" I ask.

"I think it's time to move on."

It's a big change for Pete. If you ask me, it's also the right one. There are too many memories in our parents' house—good and bad. He's overdue for a fresh start. I point toward the bar. "Have you cleared this with Big John?" I ask.

"Not yet."

"He isn't going to be happy about it."

"I'll break the news to him gently."

Big John returns with another round of beers, including one for himself. The bar is empty and he's a talker. He pulls up a chair. "These are on the house," he says.

"I'd feel better if you'd let me pay for them," I say.

He waves his huge paw. "Your family kept us in business in the lean times. The least I can do is spot you a couple of beers."

"Thanks, Big John."

He gives me a sideways look. "Are you lads okay?"

"We're fine," I say.

"You don't look so fine. Bartender's intuition."

His is finely tuned. "It's been a couple of long weeks," I tell him.

"You got a good result for Nate Fineman." He turns to Pete. "You're out of the hospital."

"That's true," Pete says.

"So what's the big deal?"

I take a long drink of my beer. "We discovered that our father may have withheld information during the original trial that could have changed the result. It's possible that he did it to try to settle some old business with Nate."

"You mean the Bayview Posse case?"

"Yeah."

He responds with a bartender's knowing half smile. "Does that have anything to do with the arrest of Marshawn Bryant and Alex Aronis?"

"It does."

"So what?"

"We're having a little trouble dealing with the fact that some things we thought about our father may have been untrue. Did he ever say anything to you about seeing Bryant on the night of the shootings?"

"Afraid not, lad."

I take another sip of my Guinness. I look my uncle straight in the eye. "So," I say to him, "now that everything's said and done, maybe you can tell us what really happened to that IA file."

"What makes you think I know something, Mikey?"

"Lawyer's intuition."

The corner of his mouth turns up. "Is this conversation covered by the attorney-client privilege?"

"It's also covered by the bartender-customer privilege and the uncle-nephew privilege."

"Good enough." There's a long pause. "He took it, Mikey."

"He stole it?"

"You might say that he borrowed it."

"Why?"

"He said he didn't intend to keep it. He didn't trust Fitz and the guys in IA. He wanted to make a copy in case somebody started asking questions down the road. He never quite got around to returning it. After a while, I guess he figured nobody was going to ask about it."

Until now. "Did you see it?"

"Nope."

"Do you know where it is?"

"I'm sure it's long gone, lad."

He's undoubtedly right.

"Don't look so sad, Mikey. Fitz told you the truth about what was in the report—everybody was cleared."

"Which was completely wrong."

"It was a fitting testament to Fitz's investigative prowess."

Amen.

Big John straightens out a faded black-and-white photo of Juan Marichal that hangs on the wall above our table. He puts a heavy hand on my shoulder. "Did you know that my father went to the seminary?" he says.

Pete and I exchange a glance. Big John's dad was a world-class carouser. "He never mentioned it," I say.

"Do you know how close he came to being ordained?"

"Nope."

"One day."

"Are you serious?"

"Yep. If he hadn't changed his mind at the last minute, I never would have been born." He winks and adds, "Your aunt used to say that sometimes she wished he'd decided to go ahead and become a priest."

It sounds like her. "The priesthood isn't all that it's cracked up to be," I say.

"You were a good priest, Mikey."

"You may be the only person who thinks so. What does that have to do with us?"

Big John glances up at the Dunleavy crest. "My dad and I didn't always get along real well," he says, "but I always figured I owed him something for giving up the priesthood. Whenever I got really mad at him, I tried to give him the benefit of the doubt."

"So?"

Big John sets his mug on the table. "I don't know for sure what your daddy knew about the Fineman case. I don't know anything about a grudge against Nate Fineman. I sure as hell don't know what possessed him to lift that file. I will grant you that it wasn't the smartest thing he ever did. What I *do* know for sure is that Tommy Daley was my brother-in-law, my best friend, and the most stand-up guy that I ever knew. You lads can choose to remember him any way you'd like. If I were in your shoes, I'd give him the benefit of the doubt."

# # #

"What time is Grace coming home?" I ask Rosie. Our daughter went to a movie with Jake.

"I told her that she could stay out until midnight. She's had a couple of tough weeks."

So have we. We're sitting in front of Rosie's fireplace, both of us relieved that we're no longer living in an armed camp. I just put Tommy to bed for the third time tonight. We're enjoying a glass of merlot and a quiet moment.

"How's Pete?" she asks.

"All things considered, not bad."

"Donna called and said she appreciated that you took him out tonight."

"They've had a couple of tough weeks, too."

"Yes, they have." The fire reflects off her eyes. "Are you going to be all right?"

"I'm fine, Rosie."

She leans over and kisses me. "You're a lousy liar. You've been in a different world for the last two weeks."

"Death-penalty appeals are exhausting."

"Maybe we should go away."

"I'd like that."

"Where do you go with a teenager and a toddler?"

"Disneyland." It isn't my first choice, but our options and finances are limited.

"I'll check it out," she says. Her tone turns serious. "What's bugging you, Mike?"

"The case."

"I think everything turned out pretty well. Nate was released. Bryant and Aronis were arrested. Roosevelt may have enough to prove that Low was the triggerman. If everything works out, we'll collect a pile of fees in Nate's civil case. That isn't bad for less than two weeks of work, Mike."

"That's great," I say. "You might even finish the remodeling job on your kitchen before Grace goes to college."

"Then what's the problem?" she asks.

"Pete got shot."

"He's going to be fine."

"We destroyed the reputations of some good cops."

"Dave Low was a murderer. Joey D'Amato was a blackmailer."

"I was talking about my dad, too."

"I know." She takes a sip of her merlot. "He wasn't perfect, Mike."

"I thought he was a perfect cop."

"It turns out that he wasn't." She cups my face in her hand. "It's a tough job. Maybe he had a problem with Nate. He was getting close to retirement. He made some bad decisions. Give him a break."

"Tell that to Nate."

"He was no saint, either. Think about the parents of the kids who died from the drugs they bought from the Bayview Posse. You're always looking for perfect justice. You need to accept the fact that we live in an imperfect world. There are things that lawyers just can't fix." She pulls me toward her and kisses me.

"What's that for?" I ask.

"For never changing. If I take you to Disneyland, will you promise to let it go?"

"Yes, Rosie."

"If you don't behave, I'll make you ride the flying Dumbos until you puke."

"I get the message."

Her eyes twinkle. "I need to show you something." She hands me a large manila envelope. "This came in the mail from Ilene Fineman. It's addressed to both of us."

"What is it?"

"I don't know. I was waiting for you to get here before I opened it."

"Go ahead."

She tears open the envelope and looks at the first of two stacks of neatly bundled papers. She studies the first pile for a moment. I can see her blinking back tears.

"What?" I ask.

She hands the papers to me. "Look," she says.

They are the divorce papers that Ilene mentioned when we first met. The handwritten note expresses her gratitude and indicates that she won't be needing them. I can feel a tear in the corner of my eye. "That's very nice," I say.

"Very nice indeed." She pulls out the second stack. Her eyes get wider. "Oh my God," she says.

"What is it?"

She stares at the papers in disbelief. "The deed to this house."

"What are you talking about?"

She swallows hard. "Nate and Ilene bought it for us. We're now the proud joint owners of a 950-square-foot palace with no kitchen and a leaky roof."

"Are you serious?"

"Yes."

"We can't possibly accept it," I say.

"Why not?"

"It isn't right."

"They've insisted. Besides, it's already a done deal."

"Come on, Rosie."

"*You* come on, Mike. Get off your high horse. How much is Nate's life worth? We busted our butts for them. We stopped an execution. We've been harassed and threatened. We just took a hundred grand in legal fees from them. If they want to give us a gratuity, we shouldn't deprive them of the pleasure."

"It still isn't right."

"For once in your life, swallow your pride. Accept a gift graciously."

"And if I say no?"

"Then I'm going to accept it myself. If you want to be pigheaded about it, that's your business. If Ilene Fineman wants to share part of her trust fund with me, I'm prepared to accept it—woman to woman."

"Are you sure you really want to do this?"

"I've never been surer about anything in my life."

I glance down at the papers. "Did you notice that they put the deed in both of our names?"

"I did."

"Do you think they're suggesting something?"

"Like what?"

"That we should move in together?"

"I think they're giving us the option."

Here we go again. "How do you feel about it?"

She gives me the knowing smile that I've found irresistible for almost two decades. "We seem to do better when we have a little separate space."

"I agree."

"I still think we should accept their gracious gift. I can continue to live here, and you can keep your half as an investment."

I look around at our new estate. "Why not?" I say. "It isn't St. Francis Wood, but it isn't bad."

ACKNOWLEDGMENTS

I am very grateful to the many people who have been so generous with their time and expertise in contributing to this story.

Many thanks to my publisher, David Poindexter, for your insight, wisdom, and support. Thanks to my tireless and patient editor, Dave Adams, for your perceptive comments, thoughtful suggestions, and unfailing good humor. Thanks also to Scott Allen, Julie Burton, Melanie Mitchell, Elizabeth Poindexter, Dorothy Carico Smith, Megan Murphy, and the entire team at MacAdam/Cage. You make my life a lot easier, and I'm very appreciative.

Thanks to my agent, Margret McBride, and to the team at the Margret McBride Literary Agency: Donna DeGutis, Anne Bomke, and Faye Atchinson. You're the best!

Thanks to criminal-defense attorney David Nickerson, and to John Donhoff and Mark Howell of the California Attorney General's Office, who provided insights into the Byzantine world of death-penalty litigation. You are extraordinary professionals who embody everything that is admirable about the legal profession. Keep fighting the good fight.

Thanks to Bonnie DeClark, Meg Stiefvater, Anne Maczulak, Liz Hartka, Janet Wallace, and Priscilla Royal for looking at the early drafts of this book and providing insightful comments. Thanks to Bill and Elaine Petrocelli for your ongoing support.

Thanks to my friends and colleagues at Sheppard, Mullin, Richter & Hampton for your continuing support and encouragement.

Thanks always to Charlotte, Ben, Michelle, Margaret, and Andy Siegel; Ilene Garber; Joe, Jan, and Julia Garber; Roger and Sharon Fineberg; Jan Harris Sandler and Matz Sandler; Scott, Michelle, Stephanie, Kim, and Sophie Harris; Cathy, Richard, and Matthew Falco; and Julie Harris and Mathew, Aiden, and Ari Stewart.

Finally, thanks to my wonderful wife, Linda, and our twin sons, Alan and Stephen, for your unending support and understanding—especially when I'm on deadline. I can't do this without you!